Reader's Comments

"Move over, J. K. Rowling, there's a new fantasy novelist in town—and her name is Jenny Cote. She takes the reader on a year-long journey of mystery, danger, and intrigue aboard Noah's ark. It's a wild adventure that deserves to be on the big screen."
—**Vonda Skelton,** author of The Bitsy Burroughs Mysteries and
Seeing Through the Lies: Unmasking the Myths Women Believe

"The Amazing Tales of Max and Liz series is a delight. I applaud Jenny Cote for her masterful job. The depth of her characters and powerful story line will propel readers to want more."
—**Bernard Kearse,** American Children's Authors Guild,
Radio Show Host and Author of The Bethany Adventures

"I loved following Max, Liz, Al, Kate, and the gang on one rollicking adventure after another as they make their way to the ark. The characters come to life with laugh-out-loud humor, all the while providing engaging biblical and historical lessons that are fun, fun, fun. Readers get a great glimpse of 'how it might have happened.' "
—**Claire Roberts Foltz,** American Children's Authors Guild,
Author of The Mutt Tales

"*The Ark, The Reed & The Fire Cloud* is nothing short of magical!"
—**Lisa,** age 45

"*The Ark, The Reed & The Fire Cloud* has a good story line, with lots of great morals and lessons. It's really heartwarming."
—**Alex,** age 12

"I loved it! I couldn't stop reading. I loved all of the imagery, the characters, and, the lessons. God has big plans for Jenny's book."
—**Rob,** age 29

"*The Ark, The Reed & The Fire Cloud* is a book that will surely capture the hearts and minds of readers. Its lovable characters tell of an adventure that is perfect for any age."
—**Becky,** age 17

"*The Ark, The Reed & The Fire Cloud* is truly God inspired."
—**Paul,** age 69

"I loved this book! I found myself actually reading extra fast to see what was going to happen next."
—**Katherine,** age 16

To Caroline!
Enjoy the
adventure!

The ARK, the REED, & the FIRE CLOUD

Jerry L Cote

JENNY L. COTE

Living Ink Books
An Imprint of AMG Publishers, Inc.
Chattanooga, Tennessee

Library of Congress Cataloging-in-Publication Data

Cote, Jenny L., 1964-
    The ark, the reed, and the fire cloud / Jenny L. Cote.
        p. cm. -- (The amazing tales of Max and Liz)
    Summary: Max the dog and Liz the cat become the brave leaders for a group of animals
called to journey to the Ark.
    ISBN 978-0-89957-198-0 (pbk. : alk. paper)
    [1. Dogs--Fiction. 2. Cats--Fiction. 3. Animals--Fiction. 4. Adventure and adventurers--Fic-
tion. 5. Noah's ark--Fiction. 6. Christian life--Fiction.] I. Title.
    PZ7.C8245Ar 2008
    [Fic]--dc22
                                          2008031570

Alex ~

Little did you realize how special Max and Liz would become when you chose them to join our family. And little did I realize how incredibly special *you* would become when God chose you to start our family.

Thank you for how you have inspired The Amazing Tales of Max and Liz, but thank you most for being the amazing son that you are.

Love ye,
Mom

This is a work of fiction based on truth.
For the true story, read Genesis 6–9.

Contents

PART FOUR
THE HERO AND THE FLOOD

PART FIVE
THE TRUTH AND THE PROMISE

Acknowledgments

Behind The Amazing Tales of Max and Liz™ are some truly amazing people who have made this new book series possible.

To the Maker, I stand amazed at what You've done for me on this life journey. I can only say, Thank You, God. I give You the total the credit for the words that fill these pages. May You be glorified and pleased.

To Casey, my wonderful husband. Thank you for encouraging me to pursue my dreams with this book and the many books to come. I'm glad "yer me forever love!"

To Alex, my awesome son. See the dedication page. (I want to make sure you read it.)

To my parents, Paul and Janice Mims, my in-laws, Jerry and Carol Demery, my immediate and extended families, thank you all for your constant love, support, and encouragement.

To Lori Marett, my incredibly talented screenwriter and "twin" sister—thank you for the amazing work you've done on the screenplay for *The Ark,* and in turn, the book. Because your ideas and creativity are woven throughout this book, it's a far better read.

Thank you for enduring all the "tipped buckets" along the way. I look forward to what God has in store for us next.

To Mary Busha, my wise, sweet, never-ending, encouragement-giving literary agent—how can I thank you for all you've done for me? You led Max and Liz to the perfect publishing home and have never stopped pointing me in the right direction as well.

To Dan Penwell—what an amazing editor, friend, and cheerleader you are! Thank you for immediately capturing the vision for Max and Liz, and rallying the troops at AMG. I am honored and grateful for your oversight in making the manuscript the best it can be with your editorial TLC. Many thanks to you and the AMG team: Dale Anderson, Joe Suter, Trevor Overcash, Rick Steele, Warren Baker, Mike Oldham, Gin Chasteen, Amanda Donnahoe, Donna Coker, and all the support staff in Chattanooga.

To Rich Cairnes whose proofreading abilities far exceeded any expectations. Great job, Rich.

To Rob Moffitt, my beyond-talented illustrator, photographer, friend, and fellow Scot. You have brought Max, Liz, and the characters in this book alive with your sketchpad. I'm so proud of you and will be forever grateful for that day you sketched out a front cover . . . just for fun.

To Daryle Beam, designer and logo developer extraordinaire! Thank you for giving Max and Liz such an awesome identity and making the visual part of this project so much fun.

To Lisa Hockman, my sweet sister in Christ. Thank you for "giving" me your beloved Albert to be the lovable one that he is on these pages. And thank you for being my first reader, encourager, and friend.

I'm blessed to be part of the Student Ministry at Dunwoody Baptist Church. My students rock and have given me crazy inspiration and support. A special thanks to Katelyn Wisenbaker and Emily Craddock for your "names" and fun ideas.

This book has been sharpened with the feedback iron of my children's author colleagues, Claire Roberts Foltz (The Mutt Tales) and Bernard Kearse (The Bethany Adventures series). Thank you for the meetings, emails, readings, and discussions—you guys are the best.

Thank you especially to my early test readers: Jenny Keeton and her fourth-grade class at Mount Pisgah Christian School, and Sherrill Weihe and her third-grade classes at Montgomery Elementary School. Yes, kids, you're my very best critics.

I'm forever indebted to the many who have given of their time to read and endorse this book.

See what I mean? Amazingly, I could go on with many more names of dear friends and church family for their love and prayers. Thank you, everyone.

Last but certainly not least—to the REAL Max and Liz: Thank you for filling our home with fun and love. And thank you for completing the mission you were given to inspire me. Much love, me wee ones.

PART ONE

MAX AND
THE REED

CHAPTER 1

A Dark Night

The roar of thunder was deafening. The ground itself seemed to shake from the angry skies lashing out above. Nothing was beyond the reach of the storm. The lightning cracked in all directions, looking like the skeleton of a dead tree in the sky. The shadows of the unknown appeared for brief moments at a time, taunting him, serving only to make the dark night more terrifying. Why did dark shadows grow larger than their otherwise normal objects, turning them into grotesque beasts? He was breathless as he bolted out from under a tree after lightning struck nearby. The lightning was after him, or so he thought.

He ran until his lungs ached from the effort. Where was he running? He knew of no safe place out here, but he reasoned that if he kept running, he was at least doing something to preserve his life. The rain blew sideways, stinging his eyes in a blinding fury. The thunder continued to jeer at him, laughing at his perilous condition. He tripped on an unseen rock and landed face first in a bog of slimy mud that covered the right side of his head. He tried desperately to shake the mud off as his feet sank into the dark, thick muck. He panicked as he struggled to free himself of its cold clutches. Finally, he broke loose and ran into the night.

The storm had an ally in its terrorizing pursuit. In the distance he heard the unmistakable howls of a pack of wolves on the chase. His heart was now thumping overtime in his chest. The blood-curdling growls of the wolves came closer. He could hear them panting as the gap narrowed between them. He felt immense fear, knowing he was surrounded. There was no way out; they were closing in.

Suddenly the ground beneath him disappeared, and he was in midair for a split second as he fell off the rock face. Violently he rolled along the rocky slope, hitting every outcropping on the way down. He felt a searing pain in his left leg before he landed with a breath-stealing thud on the hard ground below. He could feel the warm blood oozing from his leg that was now serving to arouse the wolves. They smelled his blood, and sensed his fear.

A jagged bolt of lightning lit up the dark sky followed by a violent boom of thunder. The instant flash illuminated three scowling wolves looking down at him. They growled, teeth snarling and pungent breath stinking up the air around them. Their yellow eyes stared menacingly at him. There was nowhere else to run, even if he could have run away. He was cut off; he knew it, and they knew it. The leader of the pack lifted his head high, nose turned toward the sky. He howled at the storm to declare victory, and the end.

"MAX! WAKE UP, LAD! DID YE HEAR ME THEN? WAKE UP! WAKE UP! WAKE UP!"

Where was he? Wait . . . his leg . . . the wolves . . . the storm. What was happening? His heart was still racing. He was wet but not from the rain—he was sweating. He looked around and listened.

All he heard was the sound of crickets with an occasional frog answering back. Everything else was still. Not even a breath of wind blew. The dark night wasn't over but at least all was calm, and he was exactly where he was supposed to be. He breathed a sigh of relief and rolled over.

Morning couldn't come soon enough.

CHAPTER 2

A Mysterious Wind

The morning mist was unusually thick as Max stepped out of his cozy burrow and walked down to the loch. The wetness settled lightly on his wiry black fur but made Max feel soggy as he walked through mist that he liked to call "land clouds." He imagined he was walking on air, high above the ground. He liked that feeling for he was a small animal. His short, stocky build made him quick and strong but kept him low to the ground, the heights out of reach. Max trotted along the dewy moss, smiling as he wondered if clouds were as soft as the lush, green turf of Scotland.

Beads of mist ran down his large, square head. *Aye, if only I could sip enough of this mist off me head, I could skip the long walk ta the loch. Ah, well enough. It's always good ta tr-r-rot the Glen.*

The forest was buzzing with the dawn of a new day. Max breathed in the woodsy air as he trotted down the well-worn path his scruffy paws had made. His daydream of cloud walking was interrupted as he looked up. He couldn't help but notice how incredibly small he was under the towering hardwood trees. He wondered what the view must be like from up there.

Birds must have the life, thought Max. *Aye, but the Maker gave me plenty. Ta be a Scottish terrier is a gr-r-rand thing.*

Sometimes it bothered Max that he was so small. But he was brave enough, he reasoned. Max was rarely frightened. Indeed, there were only two things that scared Max, but they were guarded secrets known by only one other animal.

What spooked most creatures didn't faze Max. In fact, he looked forward to a challenge. His characteristic deep-throated growl let others know when something was amiss. Max's pointy, bushy ears would perk up attentively. His fur would rise along the back of his spine to the tip of his short tail. Max was the eyes and ears of the forest, definitely the finest watchdog in all of Scotland. The Glen was his territory, and he saw to it that no invader brought harm to those who trusted him. He came from a long line of protectors—the Bruce Clan were good stock.

Max could pick up the faintest scent with his long nose. He would chase, corner, and capture the swiftest of pesky small creatures, but often he wondered what would happen if he came face to face again with a mighty beast. Would he be up for the challenge? Max's recurring dream made him ponder many things.

There was no denying his braveness, but even more so, there was no denying his heart. Max had an undying sense of loyalty to his fellow creatures and a remarkable tenderness as well. So although he could be gruff as protector, he was gentle as friend. It was often said that Max wore the joy in his heart on the outside. The warmth in his deep brown eyes let others know he could be trusted. One could not help but be happy around Max as he smiled—his white teeth showing in a continually open grin.

Because of his bravery around the forest and his big heart, Max became known as Maximillian Braveheart the Bruce.

He would always help the lost baby rabbit who wandered away from its mother. If a turtle rolled down the hill, Max would push it back up the hill again. Sometimes the young calves would chase butterflies across the hillside and become disoriented, and Max would guide them back to their herd. His strong jaws frequently pulled frightened sheep out of the bogs. And, of course, there was special help for the old goat that grazed the lush green hillsides just outside the forest up above the loch. Gillamon was his name—a ripe old mountain goat who had wandered this countryside for many years.

Sometimes Gillamon's age showed because of his poor eyesight. At times he would mistake one cave for another, thinking it was his own, only to find an upset mother fox telling Gillamon to find his own cave. Max regularly guided Gillamon back home. And Gillamon guided Max in the ways of life.

Max was deeply indebted to Gillamon. When Max was a puppy, Gillamon was the one who found him one night when he roamed to the edge of the Glen. Perhaps this is why Max felt the tug on his heart to help other lost creatures. He knew how bad it felt to be lost. And he knew how wonderful it felt to be found. This encounter long ago started a friendship that became stronger with the passing seasons in the Glen.

The mist lifted as Max left the forest. Today the sun was up over the horizon and beams of light burned the moisture out of the air.

"Ah, well enough, I'll enjoy the sun while it chooses ta warm the Glen. It will hide soon," said Max.

At the edge of the forest was a wide opening onto the fields of the Glen. The hillsides looked like waves of green, dappled with rocks. Max smiled and paused to appreciate the vast expanse in front of him before he took off running across the fields to the loch. The wide-open valley made him feel free as his short legs took him lightning fast across the meadow, the brisk breeze blowing in his face.

As Max approached the loch, he noticed the reeds at the waterline vigorously blowing in the wind. They seemed to be bowing down to touch the surface of the water. It was a strange sight because the flowers and grass next to the reeds barely moved. Only

7

the reeds appeared to be caught in the path of the wind. Curious, Max slowed his trot to a cautious walk. The rising sun was now shining brilliantly on the water like diamonds, blinding Max. He squinted as he walked over to the bank for a closer inspection. The reeds then began to hum.

"'Tis a strange sight, this is," said Max out loud to no one. "Now wha' could be causin' such a thing? The wind's got the r-r-reeds ta blow an' even hum."

The reeds grew along the spot of the loch where Max usually got a drink of water. He walked to the waterline and his paws sunk slightly in the cool mud. He lapped the cold, fresh water that soon soaked his chin. The reeds began to blow harder and hum even more loudly, this time in varied tones. Some sounded high, some sounded low, but they hummed in harmony.

Suddenly the reeds bent over Max's large ears and hummed what seemed to be a single word:

"Come. "

Max's head snapped up at attention as his spine stiffened and a growl rumbled in his throat. "Who said that?"

The only reply came from the humming reeds,

"Come. Come. Come."

Max darted his gaze from right to left, shaking the water from his chin onto the clan tartan, plaid collar tied around his neck. He wondered if one of the young lake rats was hiding in the reeds, teasing him. "Aye! I know yer in ther-r-re! Come out wee r-r-rat!"

No answer. No creature to be found. Just the reeds blowing in the wind, continuing to hum,

"Come. Come. Come."

Max stared quizzically at them, water still dripping from the black fur on his chin. "Aye, I dunnot know how this is happenin' but I like the sound of the r-r-reeds. Wha' a thing ta hear the music they make! Hummmmm . . . Windpipes, I think I be a callin' them.

Wha' a gr-r-rand Scottish instrument," said Max. He resumed lapping the water, enjoying the sound swirling around him.

Suddenly there came three unmistakable words emanating from the reeds:

"COME TO ME."

The harmonious hum of the reeds had become one Voice, speaking with authority.

Max was not easily frightened, so although this was curious, he remained brave as he answered the Voice. "Who are ye an' wher-r-re is it ye want me ta come?"

The Voice simply replied,

"COME TO ME."

"Aye! I hear-r-rd ye the fir-r-rst time! But WHO ar-r-re ye an' wher-r-re exactly do ye want me ta come?" said Max, feeling flustered with the Voice.

The nearby birds scattered as the reeds slapped the water and the Voice replied,

"FOLLOW THE FIRE CLOUD."

Max blinked and looked in the sky, yet saw nothing but clear, blue skies. Not a cloud in sight, which was unusual in Scotland. "There's no 'fir-r-re cloud,' not even a white cloud in the sky! An' why would I follow it even if it were ther-r-re?" replied Max.

"COME TO ME,"

was the only reply as the wind suddenly died down to a soft breeze, causing the reeds to stand up tall, straight, and silent once more.

Max looked around. He was the only creature in sight. *I got ta find Gillamon,* Max thought as he took off running from the loch to the hillside above. He trotted through the swaying wild flowers that tickled his nose with their sweet fragrance. Higher and higher Max climbed until he reached the uppermost ridge of the Glen.

CHAPTER 3

Gillamon

From up here the view was amazing. To the east, he could see the green valley stretching over rolling hills down to the loch and on to the forest. To the west, Max could see the deep blue ocean crashing into jagged cliffs far beneath him. He gulped slightly and stepped back from the edge a bit. Max breathed in the salty air and felt his body relax as the sea tonic cleared his confused mind. Somehow, up here where he could see everything, Max didn't feel so small and uncertain. He liked feeling this way. He liked it up here.

Aye, seems things are clearer up here where I kin see the whole Glen an' the sea. Maybe I jest had a day dr-r-ream down by the loch. Still, the windpipes hum in me head, Max thought to himself. He sat down a moment to catch his breath, gazing out to sea.

"Good morning, Max," came a deep voice from behind.

Max grinned and turned around to see his old friend Gillamon, standing majestically on a boulder. Gillamon was rather tall for a mountain goat. His long white hair blew in the wind, making him appear even larger. His slightly curved brown horns and double-bearded goatee gave him a distinguished appearance. Quite the elegant animal, he was a giant in Max's eyes for more reasons than others could appreciate. Gillamon had come to Scotland years ago, choosing the rugged northern land as his home. He had a wealth of wisdom accumulated from his travels abroad, and Max was ever eager to learn from him. Gillamon had kind eyes and a gentle, strong voice. Max always felt safe in his presence.

"Gillamon, I were comin' ta see ye," said Max as he jumped up to greet his friend.

"Well, and so you have," said Gillamon. "What brings you to the heights this sunny day?"

Max started pacing back and forth in front of Gillamon as he revealed what had happened. "Ah, Gillamon, me wise fr-r-riend. Today has been filled with oddities like I've never seen! The mist were extra heavy early this mor-r-rn but then bur-r-rned off ta a br-r-right, sunny day. Then, as I got ta the loch as I do each mor-r-rn, a mysterious wind were blowin'. The r-r-reeds on the bank were blowin' so har-r-rd they almost touched the water. Not only that, they were hummin' an' makin' this str-r-rangely beautiful music."

"That is odd, indeed," Gillamon replied.

"That's not the full of it yet! The r-r-reeds then actually *talked* ta me, Gillamon."

Gillamon raised one eyebrow in curiosity as Max stopped pacing. And as if hearing the words for the first time himself, Max slowly exclaimed, "The r-r-reeeds said, 'Come ta me.'"

"Come to me?" asked Gillamon, his interest growing.

"Aye, aye, 'Come, come, come ta me,'" Max eagerly replied, once again pacing quickly, his voice fast and thick with his Scottish brogue. "I thought I were goin' mad, like some cr-r-reature were teasin' me in the r-r-rushes, but not a one were ther-r-re."

"I see. Go on, Max," encouraged Gillamon.

"I asked the Voice who it were, an' where it wanted me ta come."

11

"What did it say?" asked Gillamon.

"This gets even str-r-ranger, me friend! The Voice said ta follow the fir-r-re cloud," Max replied, looking for some sign of understanding from his wise mentor.

"Hmmmm, the fire cloud, you say?"

"Aye, fir-r-re cloud."

"I see," said Gillamon calmly as he walked over toward the cliff.

"Wha' do ye see, Gillamon? All I see is clear-r-r blue skies! Not a cloud in sight! An' Gillamon . . . wha' exactly is a fir-r-re cloud?" asked Max, his brown eyes pleading for an answer.

Gillamon didn't reply immediately, as was his habit. He looked out to sea, closed his eyes, and took a deep breath. Max was used to Gillamon's "thinking ways." He learned long ago not to interfere but to give Gillamon time. He would respond.

Max lay down, putting his feet behind him, back paws facing the sky, chin resting on his front paws. The cool grass felt good. Max didn't realize how heavily he was breathing. He needed to calm down from the morning's excitement. He had learned to do this by watching Gillamon over the years. Whenever Max came running into Gillamon's presence, flustered and talking with his Scottish brogue thick as this morning's mist, Gillamon made him stop and collect his thoughts before he spoke another word.

A pair of seagulls flew overhead, crying out their hellos to Max and Gillamon. Gillamon remained still, eyes closed, thinking. Max rolled over onto his back to wave hello to the gulls. They said something but Max couldn't quite make it out as they disappeared into the distance. After a while, Gillamon finally spoke.

"Max, lad, this is quite the puzzle. Never in all my years or in all my travels have I heard of such a strange spectacle. But there is always a reason for things. There is always a purpose behind everything, even when there is not an explanation. We must begin by not explaining what happened, but by trying to find the purpose behind it."

12

He listened with rapt attention as Gillamon continued. Max's pointy ears were up and his eyes were solidly fixed on the old mountain goat.

"It appears that the natural order of things was altered today. I was considering the things I saw early today as you were describing the events in the Glen. From where you were in the forest, you could not see the red sky on the horizon over the ocean. The sun rose like a red ball of fire and a mighty wind blew so hard that even I, surefooted as I am, had to brace myself. I watched as the wind blew past me and cut a path in the tall grass down to the loch. It was as if the wind were traveling on a path to an intended spot," Gillamon said. He paused before driving home his most important observation. "Or to an intended creature."

Max sat up and cocked his head to one side. "Ye mean that ye felt this mysterious wind, too? An' it came from the red sun across the sea down ta *me*?"

"It appears so, my young friend," said Gillamon. "And this would lead me to think that you were the intended one the wind was after, since it, indeed, spoke to you."

"But wha' does it mean, Gillamon?" questioned Max.

Gillamon looked at Max, thinking how special his small friend had become to him in his old age. Max had faith in Gillamon's explanations, trusting him for answers to the many questions he had. Gillamon knew that this mysterious wind was bigger than the sea below them. He knew he needed divine wisdom to give the guidance Max needed.

Gillamon spoke with affirmation and confidence. "I do not know where you are being called to go, but I do know that wherever it is must be significant. The Voice gave you two guiding words. It said, 'Come' and it told you how to get there, by following the fire cloud. If this Voice truly is one of authority, it will do as it said. The fire cloud will come. Max, you have been chosen. I believe you are being called because of your character. The Voice knows you're brave and trustworthy, and that your heart is good. The Voice has something important for you to do."

"But how do ye know this, Gillamon?" pleaded Max. "An' how could I ever leave the Glen? Wha' if I leave an' harm comes here? Who will watch over ye an' the creatures? An' how could I ever make it without ye ta guide me, Gillamon?"

"Sometimes a question grows into more questions rather than a single answer. 'Tis the way of life, Max. If there is a purpose for you beyond what you know, the all-powerful One—the Maker—always has a way of making it known. He will give you a revelation and show you what to do. You may not understand it. You may fight it. You may be afraid of it. But if it comes from the Maker, you can always trust it." Gillamon paused and leaned in close to look Max right in the eye. "The true question is: Will you follow it, Max?"

Max looked back at Gillamon, then shifted his gaze down to the ground. "This is too uncertain, Gillamon. Aye, aye, I trust the Maker. But wha' if, ye know, *it* happens an' I need ye? How could I make it alone?"

"Max, I have long guided you whenever your secret fears made you cower. I was glad to be the one to help you on that hard night long ago, and other times since then, but here is what you must know. You have always run to me, but it is the Maker who holds the true answers. He allowed me to help you with your weakness until the time came for you to lean on Him alone," said Gillamon.

Gillamon paused and then continued. "Although He made all of creation perfect, something happened and it became marred. Now, not one creature is perfect. Every creature has some weakness that can make it think it doesn't need the Maker. Ah, but that is a sad way to live. Dependence on the Maker—who made everything and knows everything— is the best way. The secrets and questions of life are His alone to reveal, and in His own time."

"Are ye sayin' then that it were the Maker who called ta me?" Max softly questioned.

"Yes, Max. That is what I believe," answered Gillamon. "And if He is calling you, you have got to trust that He will guide you exactly as He said."

"Aye, I see wha' yer sayin' ta me. I jest don't understand why . . . an' how . . . an' when . . . an' where," said Max, turning his gaze up to the skies. "I have never left the Glen, Gillamon. I dunnot know wha's out ther-r-re. Aye, but ye do. Ye have been over many lands an' seen many things."

"Yes, I've traveled far and wide and there is much to see beyond the borders of the Glen. Many things I know you will be excited to see, Max. You are a creature who lives for adventure and challenge, and that is what you will have. But in order to embrace the adventure, it has to begin with that first step out of the Glen."

"Aye, I do love a challenge, 'tis true," said Max with a grin. "Do ye think I will see one of those . . . wha' do ye call them— *bodies*?"

"Hmmmm. Very possible, Max. What troubled creatures these humans are," Gillamon replied, a wrinkle in his brow. "My grandfather once told me the story of how the Maker created them to live in paradise in a beautiful garden, without a care in the world. They lived in harmony with the Maker and all of creation."

"Sounds heavenly. Wha' happened?" questioned Max.

"The humans became greedy for knowledge and power. And the Evil One tricked them into believing that they could be as great as the Maker. Of course, the Maker knew all about it and banished them from the Garden. And that was when creation first knew sadness. What was perfect became broken." Gillamon shook his head.

"Ah, wha' a ter-r-rible thing," Max said. "Why in the world would ye mess up such a good thing with the Maker? I jest dunnot understand it."

"The Maker gave His creation a choice. He loved them enough to allow them to choose between loving and obeying Him, and having their own way. He created humans to love them. But

15

He wanted them to love Him with their hearts of free will, not because they could feel no other way. So, the humans chose poorly. But the story gets even worse," continued Gillamon.

Max's eyes widened, "Worse?! How? Wha' happened next?"

"The Maker told the humans to leave the Garden and never return to it. They would now have to work hard to get their food, and they would know pain. And the humans have been sad ever since. They ruined their chance with the Maker because of the choice they made. The Maker still loves them, but the humans' actions have consequences. And they have been a troubled race ever since. They hurt one another, kill one another, steal from one another—ah, it's a terrible thing," Gillamon explained sadly.

"It sounds like they need help if ye ask me," replied Max.

"Yes, Max, they do. And I'm sure they could have it if only they asked the Maker. But they continue to do things their own way, not the Maker's way. If you ever see humans, be kind to them. For it's their lost, broken hearts that make them act so badly," Gillamon explained. "Know this secret—humans do respond to love over time. And with your large heart, I'm sure you could bring them joy.

"A word of caution," Gillamon continued, but with a serious tone. "The Evil One who started the trouble in the Garden remains, causing problems for humans and for all of creation. Always be on your guard when you're around humans. Wherever there are humans, you can be sure that the Evil One will be near as well. And he is a deceiver, Max. If he so easily deceived them, you can be sure he can easily deceive animals as well."

"Aye, I will, I will. An' I'll be br-r-rave enough," said Max with head held high.

Gillamon coughed a deep, wet cough, startling Max. "Gillamon, are ye alright? Ye have been coughin' harder lately. It worries me greatly."

Gillamon smiled and said, "I have lived many years now. I am tired. I am old and sick. It is the natural way of things. The Maker has blessed me with many years and with many friends, especially you, Max. An old goat could not want more."

"But Gillamon, how could the Maker ask me ta leave ye if yer sick?" pleaded Max.

"Only the Maker knows, Max. He will bring me to meet Him when the time is right and take care of me until that time. I am not afraid. If He is calling you away from me and from the Glen, I know that it is time for you to go. I will miss you, lad. But I get a thrill in my heart when I think of the adventure that lies ahead of you," Gillamon said, a twinkle in his wise, old eyes.

Max lowered his head, his heart heavy at all that Gillamon was saying. "Aye. I don't like it, but I have ta trust wha' ye be tellin' me."

Suddenly Max lifted his head, his ears perked up with hope. He had an idea. "Gillamon! Ye could go with me."

Gillamon struggled to lower himself to the rocks. He needed to rest. He turned his gentle gaze to Max, "You will not be alone, my friend. Take one of the reeds with you. It will remind you of the Voice."

17

"But, I dunnot know how I kin do this, Gillamon," Max objected.

Gillamon closed his eyes for a moment and said, "Remember my words, Max. Remember what I have taught you."

"Gillamon, please come with me!" Max pleaded.

The old mountain goat opened his eyes and looked lovingly at his uncertain little friend. "The reeds did not call me."

Max stayed with Gillamon as he rested, not wanting to leave his side all day. Later in the evening as the sun was setting they sat together on the cliff overlooking the sea outside Gillamon's cave. The two rested next to a boulder that still radiated warmth from the sun's rays. Ribbons of red, yellow, and orange streaked the sky as the sun dipped below the horizon, turning the sea into a mirror of the sky. They drifted off to sleep as the soft sea breeze lulled them into slumber.

"Max, wake up," whispered Gillamon.

Max was in a deep sleep, dreaming of trotting long distances in strange lands as he faintly heard a voice calling him. Slowly he realized it was Gillamon.

"Max, wake up. It's time," said Gillamon softly, reverently.

Max opened his eyes to see the warm gray eyes of his friend, looking knowingly back at him. Then he noticed that Gillamon had the most beautiful colors washing over his long white hair. Max blinked hard as he looked at Gillamon, wondering if he was dreaming.

Gillamon paused, looked toward the horizon, and then said, "It's here, Max. The fire cloud is in the southern sky."

Max looked to where Gillamon directed his gaze, and there in the sky was the most unusual, beautiful cloud he had ever seen. In between two billowy rows of white clouds was a single cloud of red, yellow, and orange flames bursting from the center. Max and Gillamon sat there in silence, watching this amazing spectacle surely never before seen in all of Scotland.

Gillamon finally spoke. "I've been watching it for an hour. It has moved slightly to the southeast. It waits now for you, Max."

Max looked at Gillamon, his heart sinking with what Gillamon was saying. He was telling Max it was time for him to go. It was time for him to leave the Glen and all that was familiar to him. It was time to trust the Maker and not himself. And it was time to tell Gillamon goodbye.

Max turned to Gillamon with eyes full of sadness. "Gillamon, I don't want ta go, but I know I must. Will I ever see ye again?"

Gillamon returned Max's anguished plea with the calm, comforting voice that Max had come to love and trust. "If we do not see each other again, it is well enough that we have seen each other before now. You're in my heart, but you're also in the Maker's hands. And there is no better place to be."

Max had to know something before he left to follow the fire cloud out of the Glen. "Gillamon, since I won't be able ta ask ye for advice no longer, kin ye tell me wha' ye do when ye close yer eyes an' think?" said Max.

Gillamon smiled, "Why, I talk to the Maker, Max. That's all. It will serve you well to do the same."

Max grinned back, "I thought as much. Yer wise for a reason, me friend."

With that Max and Gillamon put their heads together for a last embrace.

"Farewell, Maximillian Braveheart the Bruce. You will go far. Know that you are loved and that you are able."

"Goodbye, Gillamon. I kin't ever thank ye enough for all ye meant ta me. I will make ye p-r-r-roud, I pr-r-romise."

Max looked around the Glen below one last time. The wind began to pick up and blow hard. He smiled and said, "Ah, well enough, here I come."

As Max trotted down the valley and on to the border of the Glen, Gillamon stood with eyes brimming but with a heart full of pride for his friend, wondering at the coming adventure that awaited him. He watched Max until he could no longer see the little black speck on the hillside. He smiled to himself and closed his tired eyes, thanking the Maker for his friend, and praying for his protection on the journey.

19

CHAPTER 4

The Reed

"Come her-r-re, ye cr-r-razy piece of gr-r-rass!" Max fussed as he desperately tried to catch a reed blowing back and forth in the brisk wind.

He finally grabbed the reed with his strong teeth and tightly clamped it between his jaws. Tug . . . tug . . . tug, he went as he put his full weight on his hind legs low to the ground. His front feet dug into the soft muck surrounding the reed. Max pulled and pulled, then jerked his head side to side as he growled through clenched teeth, "Come he-r-r-re! Come he-r-r-re! Come her-r-re!"

Snap! The reed broke off and Max went tumbling backward, landing on the marshy bank. "Aye! I knew ye'd come ta me, ye stubborn stick." Max jumped up, gave a good shake from tip to tail, flicking mud everywhere. He picked up the reed and took off running through the meadow.

It took Max several hours to reach the edge of the Glen. As he came to the big creek that separated the Glen from the unknown place, Max stopped and sat down. He had been running for miles on end with the exhilaration of his grand adventure. Although sad to leave Gillamon, he was tingling from the tip of his ears to the tip of his tail with excitement. But now was the moment of truth as he reached the border of all he knew and loved. Max sat and looked across the big creek to the land that lies beyond, tongue hanging out as he panted to cool down.

This is it, lad, Max said to himself. *No turnin' back once ye cr-r-ross the big cr-r-reek. Wait, wha' am I sayin' then? After I cr-r-ross . . . Aye! Water. Why'd it have ta be water of all things?*

Walking by the water wasn't a problem for Max. Neither was splashing and playing at the water's edge. But crossing it was a different matter entirely.

For a moment Max hesitated, looking back toward the Glen. Maybe he should go back and not leave the Glen, Gillamon, and all his friends. But he knew in his heart that that was not the right choice. He looked up and saw the fire cloud, feeling it beckoning him to take the next step. If only Gillamon were here.

"I need ye, Gillamon," said Max. But there he sat, alone, not a sound but the rushing water in front of him and the rhythm of his panting breath.

It looked totally impossible. There was no way he could jump across the creek. It was way too far for Max's short legs to carry him. And swimming was out of the question.

I don't see a way across. This looks impossible ta me, sighed Max.

He closed his eyes. He could almost hear Gillamon whispering to him, *"He will give you a revelation and show you what to do. Max, know that you are loved and that you are able."* Max's heart grew warm. He was loved, indeed, and love can empower even the smallest of creatures to do great things. He was able, indeed, he knew. But sometimes there remains a big gap between the knowing and the doing.

Max decided to do as Gillamon had taught him. He got very still and, looking up at the fire cloud burning brilliantly in the southern sky, began to talk to the Maker.

21

"Ah . . . halloo, Maker? Um . . . Max here. I'm not very good at water, ye see? If ye have, indeed, called me ta come ta ye, well . . . tell me, how is it I'm ta cross this big cr-r-reek?"

There was no reply. Max forgot to ask Gillamon what a reply sounded like or even looked like. He guessed he would just have to figure this one out on his own. So he sat awhile.

He sat awhile longer.

And he sat a little while after that.

He heard nothing. He saw nothing. Perhaps this was because his eyes were still closed.

Max felt the words come in his heart,

"OPEN YOUR EYES. LOOK TO THE LEFT."

Max opened his eyes and looked at the rushing water of the big creek in front of him. He looked to his left and noticed a large tree log floating toward him, bobbing up and down. Max was amazed that the water could carry something so large so easily.

"TAKE YOUR REED AND HOLD IT OUT OVER THE WATER," whispered the Voice.

"Wha' ?! How's that goin' ta help me then?" replied Max.

"TRUST ME," answered the Voice.

Max looked up at the fire cloud, not sure he was hearing correctly. But he did as he was told. He took his reed and held it out over the water. The bobbing log suddenly floated closer to him, and slowly turned until it was wedged between the banks of the big creek.

"Aye, a br-r-ridge. I'm gr-r-rateful ta ye, Maker. Ah, well enough. Now I have no excuse ta keep me from cr-r-rossin'."

Max jumped onto the log. It rolled slightly under his weight. He started to walk slowly across the big creek, trying not to look down, but it was too late. He gulped as he saw the water rushing under him, swirling and making white foam as it carried leaves along to an unknown destination. The log was covered with slime, and Max began to slip. Max took the reed in his mouth and steadied himself by wedging it in a knothole in the log.

Whew! That were close! he said to himself. *Gillamon were right for me ta br-r-ring along this r-r-reed.*

Max's strong legs regained a good footing on the log, and he continued across. As he jumped off, he felt the log give way and slide into the rushing currents of the creek. "Aye! I dunnot know me own strength." Max landed on the soft grassy bank with a thump and a harrumph.

The Maker had provided a way across when it looked impossible. Max remembered another "Gillamonism": *"The Maker will never ask you to do something without giving you the ability to do it."*

Aye, Gillamon. Ye were right. Giddy right, me friend, Max thought to himself with a smile.

He looked back toward the Glen. It was as if a door closed behind him now that he stood on the other side of the creek.

"No turnin' back," Max said. "I best be on me way."

Off he trotted into uncharted territory. No longer was he in a land he knew inside and out. Now he would see if the courage he had in the Glen would remain in this new land.

The sun was setting, and Max was tired. He looked up at the fire cloud and saw that it had stopped. Max decided it was time to rest for the night. Realizing he was quite hungry, he used his large nose to find a blackberry bush and ate until he was full to bursting. Then he plopped down next to a big boulder just inside a small cave and lay down. He was tired and sore . . . and alone.

"Aye, I would like ta have a friend with me," Max said with a long yawn. "'Tis a lonely thing ta travel so far with nothin' but a stick an' a cloud for company."

The sky was going black but the cloud was white against it, the fire lighting up the night sky. It comforted Max to know the fire cloud remained lit above him. He fell asleep quickly after a long day of trotting across Scotland, and he dreamed of home.

23

CHAPTER 5

Adam, Lamech, and Noah

dam's eyes fluttered as he awakened. Slowly pulling himself to sit up, he stretched his arms around his legs and listened to the sounds of morning. The lush foliage around him was covered with dew, and the smell of blooming flowers was exquisite. He looked up to see a pair of birds fly overhead, chirping their morning hellos. Adam rubbed his side. Something felt oddly wonderful although nothing appeared to be out of the ordinary on this beautiful morning. Finally pushing himself off the ground from where he had been sleeping, Adam saw the most beautiful creature standing in front of him.

"IT IS NOT GOOD FOR MAN TO BE ALONE. I WILL MAKE A HELPER FOR HIM."

Adam heard the Voice echo in his spirit as he gazed in wonder and awe at the most beautiful living thing to ever enter the Garden.

Adam's hand again rubbed his side as he looked at this living human smiling back at him. "Bone of my bones. Flesh of my flesh. You shall be called *wo-man* because you were taken from man," he said, walking over to her. Tracing his finger across her cheek he softly smiled and said, "I shall name you *Eve*, because you will be the mother of all men."

She smiled and placed her hand atop Adam's as he cupped her face. They shared a deep gaze of excitement and awe that was suddenly broken by the sound of animals. The Garden was teeming with them.

"Have you named everything here?" Eve asked, looking around and reaching out to touch a beautiful white flower next to her.

Adam extended his hand and smiled, saying, "Come . . ."

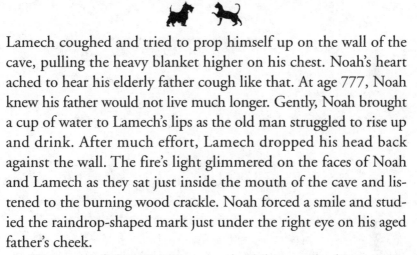

Lamech coughed and tried to prop himself up on the wall of the cave, pulling the heavy blanket higher on his chest. Noah's heart ached to hear his elderly father cough like that. At age 777, Noah knew his father would not live much longer. Gently, Noah brought a cup of water to Lamech's lips as the old man struggled to rise up and drink. After much effort, Lamech dropped his head back against the wall. The fire's light glimmered on the faces of Noah and Lamech as they sat just inside the mouth of the cave and listened to the burning wood crackle. Noah forced a smile and studied the raindrop-shaped mark just under the right eye on his aged father's cheek.

"I'm sorry, father. Bringing you back here and asking you to tell these stories over and over only tires you," Noah said as he patted the blankets around Lamech.

The wise old man shrugged and said, "It's important! These are things you must know."

"I wish I had known our great father," Noah said.

A smile came to Lamech's lips. "He was a kind, humble man. I spent much time with him in my youth." Lamech's breathing grew labored. He was too tired to continue.

"Rest, father. I'll come back later and hear how he named some of the flowers," Noah said as Lamech nodded and closed his eyes. Noah knew time was precious, but he knew that for now, his father needed to sleep. He quietly stepped out of the cave into the sunlight.

25

CHAPTER 6

Something Big

I t was early when Max felt a soft breeze blowing across his face. He opened his eyes and looked out from the inside of the cave to see the fire cloud greet him with a presence that seemed to tell Max to get going again. He stood up, stretching long and hard, shaking from nosetip to tail before picking up his reed. He was still full from last night's supper, so he decided to trot awhile before stopping to eat.

As the morning wore on, Max entered new terrain. He began to see types of trees he had never seen. And the yellow flowers he ran through in the meadow made him smile.

Wha' a bonnie sight! Gillamon would love these buttercups—love ta eat them, that is, Max chuckled to himself.

He followed the pretty flowers along the meadow, his gaze off the fire cloud as he trotted along. Max didn't notice that the dwindling flowers were leading him to the entrance of a great forest. The trees were tall, and he felt as if he were back in the Glen that housed his burrow. Fearlessly, Max proceeded into the unfamiliar wooded area, trotting at the same spunky speed as he had across the meadow.

He heard the usual sounds of the forest as he heard at home. He looked up and wondered the same thoughts he did there. It felt good to have a taste of something familiar in an unfamiliar place. As he got further into the woods, however, the trees grew dense and began to block out his view of the sky above. He could no longer see the fire cloud. Max became concerned. He didn't want to go in the wrong direction.

He came to a small clearing that had three trails leading off the far side. Max sat down to consider his choices, laying his reed on the ground.

Hmmmm. Her-r-re's a puzzle. Which path do I take, I wonder?

The left path was the widest of the three and it bore the footprints of many woodland creatures. The center path was not as wide, but was clearly a route also used by the forest dwellers. It could be a good choice. The right path was much narrower and dense. It was the least appealing of the three paths. Max thought it made the most sense to go on the widest path, where obviously most creatures traveled.

His decision made, Max picked up his reed and began to walk toward the left path.

Suddenly a voice said, "I wouldn't go doon that path if I were ye."

Max dropped his reed and looked at it suspiciously. "Aye! Are ye talkin' again ta me?"

His reed just sat there and said nothing. Max spun around but saw no creature around who could have uttered the warning. He was getting used to hearing voices telling him what to do, so he decided to heed the voice's advice. He picked up his reed and started down the center path.

He heard it again. "No, no, that path won't do either."

Max stopped and looked around to see if he could find the source of the voice. How did he know if what he was hearing was right? The first two paths were the obvious choices out of the three. He looked at the third path but it was not very inviting. It was dark, and the entrance had sticker bushes that Max knew would grab his wiry fur. So he sat a minute, puzzled as to what to do.

"Did ye not hear me, lad?" said the voice.

Max stood up and took one step toward the right path. "Sure, that'll do," said the voice.

Max couldn't stand it any longer. He had to know where in the world this voice was coming from. After all, he wasn't praying to the Maker, nor was a mysterious wind blowing. How could he trust this voice to guide him?

"Who is tellin' me where ta go?" said Max.

"Me, o' course," replied the voice.

"Well, 'me', who are ye an' wher-r-re are ye?" said Max.

Max heard a rustle in the tree above the entrance to the right path. "Up here, lad."

Max looked and didn't see anyone. All he saw was a tall tree with colored leaves of red, orange, and gold, and glimpses of sunlight dancing among them.

"I don't see ye. Jest a bunch of leaves. Aye, gr-r-reat. First talkin' r-r-reeds, now talkin' leaves," said Max.

"What kind o' nonsense is that?! Look harder, lad. I'm here sure as yer standin' there below," said the voice.

Max squinted and this time saw something move among the leaves. It was a tail. A long, bushy, orange striped tail. He looked harder and saw that attached to the tail was a huge, fluffy ball of orange fur. And attached to the fluffy ball of orange fur was a pair of big green eyes staring at him. It was a large, orange cat.

"Aye, I see ye now. Who are ye an' how do ye know where I should go anyway?" said Max.

"Top o' the mornin' to ye, lad. Name's Albert Aloysius for long, but Al for short. Me friends sometimes call me Big Al. I've got good reason to know where ye should go, because I climbed up here to figure out the path I should take meself," said Al.

"Aye, aye, I see. Me name's Maximillian Braveheart the Bruce for long, but everyone calls me Max ta make talkin' shorter. Kin ye come down an' chat with me then?" asked Max.

"Well, that's the problem. I'm hidin' and I'm afraid to move," said Al.

"Hidin' from wha' ?" asked Max.

"Enormous flyin' beasts!" answered Al.

"Wha' kind of cr-r-razy thing are ye sayin'?!" said Max.

"I'll tell ye the story, lad. I'd been travelin' a long while, and I were really hungry. It had been at least two whole hours since I had eatten. As I climbed up a tree to see if I could see a way out o' the forest, I spotted an unusual brown pouch hangin' from the tree. It smelled sweet, like food! I thought I would jest help meself to some o' whatever it were, so I stuck me paw inside a hole in the bag. Ah, Max. It were the sweetest, yummiest stuff I ever tasted! It did make quite the mess with me fur since it were sticky, though.

"As I were purrin' with delight, these enormous flyin' beasts came after me! They had big black eyes and fangs that bit me over and over again! It were terrible! I jumped down branch by branch while the cloud o' enormous flyin' beasts followed close behind. I landed on the ground and began runnin' around in circles through the forest. I must have lost them 'cause I made me way back to the clearin' again. I ran up this tree as fast as I could and I saw this branch o' red and orange leaves where I could hide. It worked 'cause the enormous flyin' beasts flew right by me and on into the forest. 'Twas quite the terrible experience, Max! Sure, and I never been so scared in all me life!" exclaimed Al.

"I guess it were scary . . . for a cat. Me, I'm not scared of anythin'," said Max. *Well, almost anythin',* Max thought to himself.

"Ye had to see it, Max! I know it would have scared ye, too!" argued Al.

"Well, there doesn't seem ta be any 'enormous flyin' beasts' around now. Why don't ye come on down? I'm here an' will keep an eye out ta protect ye," said Max.

Al gratefully smiled and slowly made his way from branch to branch, looking cautiously around him as he hit the ground with a thud.

"Much obliged to ye, lad. And pleased to make ye friendship," said Al.

Max grinned. Al was, indeed, big. He had never seen such a large, orange cat. Al's pink nose was framed by white fluffy fur, as was the underside of his big belly. His whiskers reached far out to either side of his face, sitting on top of the wide collar of fur around his neck. Al bent down to nudge Max with his nose in appreciation, accidentally smearing some honey on Max's face.

"So, tell me, Big Al, wha' exactly did ye see up there?" asked Max, using his tongue to lick away the honey. He smiled when he tasted the sweet goo.

"Oh, I seen the cloud I been followin' for a few days," replied Al as he began licking the sticky honey off his paw.

"Cloud? Wha' does it look like an' wher-r-re is it now?" eagerly asked Max, still licking his chops.

"It's white and puffy but has a strange fire comin' from it. It's along the path I were tellin' ye to take," said Al.

"Aye, well enough. I been followin' the same fire cloud meself! Do ye know anythin' aboot it? How did ye come ta follow it?" asked Max.

"Well, lad, I hail from fair Ireland on the west coast—aye, the most beautiful coast the Maker ever did create. One day I were baskin' in the sun after a big breakfast and I fell asleep. I were up high on the cliff overlookin' the sea when this huge wind started to blow. It blew me to rollin' over, it did! Sure, and I thought it were goin' to blow me off the cliff."

Max sat eagerly listening to Al's story, a growing excitement stirring inside. He was licking his chops, but now mainly from what he heard this cat say.

"All o' a sudden I heard this Voice echoin' in the cave nearby tellin' me to 'Come.' Now what in the world were I to do with such a thing, I ask ye? I never heard such! So I crept over to the cave and it spoke again and said, 'Come to Me.' I thought it were me friend playin' a joke on me in the cave so I walked inside, but there were no one in it. The Voice then said to 'Follow . . .'"

"The fire cloud!" interrupted Max.

"Aye, lad! It did sure as yer standin' there low to the ground," replied Al, drawing a stern look from Max, who didn't take "short comments" very well.

"Well, I'll be, Al! I kin't believe we were called the same way! I heard the Voice, too, blowin' in the r-r-reeds. Aye, I been on a journey from Scotland," replied Max.

"Where do ye suppose it be leadin' us, Max?" asked Al.

"I don't know. But me wise friend Gillamon told me it must be the Maker callin' me ta do somethin' important," Max said, fondly thinking of his wise old friend.

"Ye don't say! The Maker Hisself? Aye, must be somethin' big if He done called the two o' us. What do ye suppose it is?" asked Al.

"I really have no idea, Al. I only know that the fire cloud is leadin' me an' when it stops, I stop. When it goes, I go. 'Tis a gr-r-rand adventure. I were jest thinkin' last night how it would be good ta have a fr-r-riend on the journey. An' look if I didn't r-r-run into ye," said Max.

"Aye, lad. I were a bit lonely and a bit scared. I'm glad to have yer company, too," replied Al.

Max and Al were grinning with the joy of having found a friend, feeling a weight of burden off their shoulders simply of not being alone any longer. Just then, a bee came buzzing around Al.

"Ahhhhhhhhhhh! Help! Help me, Max! The beast has returned to get me!" cried Al.

Max looked at the bee and at his newfound friend and thought to himself, *Wha' a scaredy cat, this!* He took his reed and shooed the bee away into the forest.

He came back and said, "Bumbees? Yer 'enormous flyin' beasts' are bumbees? I see why yer friends call ye 'Big Al.' It certainly isn't jest for yer gr-r-rand size from yer gr-r-rand appetite, lad. It must be from yer gr-r-rand imagination, too."

"Aye! But they sure seemed like enormous flyin' beasts when they were chasin' me," explained Al.

Max just looked at Big Al, not saying a word. Al looked down at his sticky paws. "Aye, ye did tell the truth, Max. I do have this way o' makin' things bigger than they sometimes are," said Al.

"Ye need always be true, Al. Yer friends will tr-r-rust ye if yer tr-r-rue in wha' ye say," replied Max.

"Aye, I know. I will try harder, Max. If ye see me doin' it again, ye have permission to set me right, okay?" said Al.

"Ah, well enough. That's wha' friends are for, ta shoot ye straight, I always say. No worries, lad. Let's get on with our journey an' see where this fire cloud is tellin' us ta come," suggested Max.

The two new friends started down the right path that led in the direction of the fire cloud. As they entered the dark, dense path, a canopy of trees and sticky bushes enveloped them.

Al stuck close to Max, nervous at the sounds coming at them from every angle. There were frogs ribitting, insects buzzing, birds squawking, and unknown creatures making noises that continually made Al jump and ask, "What were that?!" Max felt somewhat annoyed that this big animal breathing down his neck was such a big baby. *Ah, well enough, I'll learn patience in leadin' me new friend,* thought Max. *I'm grateful for his company, close as it is ta me.*

Max and Al walked for a long while, getting to know each other and talking about their respective homes and friends. Max told Al all about the Glen, Gillamon, and how the reeds blew and spoke to him. Al asked why he carried the reed and Max told him of how Gillamon suggested he bring it as a reminder. But more importantly, it was the reed that had helped him cross the big creek.

Al had never left the coastal area of Ireland. Like Max, he felt many of the same feelings about leaving home. Al told Max all about Ireland, a wonderful green island full of beauty surrounded by the deep blue sea. But Max was curious—how did Al get across the sea to Scotland?

"Well, I'll tell ye how I crossed the great sea. I walked on the water, sure as yer standin' there, lad," exclaimed Al. Max looked at his friend with fresh doubt, wondering as to the truthfulness of Al's story.

"Walked on water? Jest how did ye manage ta do it there, laddie?" asked Max sarcastically, a stern look on his face.

"Ye don't believe me, do ye?" said Al sadly.

"Nooo, I don't!" replied Max. "I told ye ta tell the tr-r-ruth ta yer friends. How do ye expect me ta believe such a cr-r-razy thing?"

"Aye, I know it appears I be tellin' a big story but it's true. Here's the full o' it. I were walkin' by the sea and lookin' at the fair shore o' Scotland, wonderin' how I could get across. For ye see, the fire cloud were sittin' right on top o' yer fair land, it were. I followed the beach as it curved around and soon came to a skinny part that just kept goin'. I were on the bottom of the sea, but it were sittin' on top o' the water," explained Al.

Max was curious, but not convinced Al was telling the truth. Still, he remembered how the Maker had provided a way across the big creek for him. If Al was also called to follow the fire cloud, surely the Maker would do the impossible for him as well.

"An' jest how is the bottom of the sea supposed ta sit on top of the water?" questioned Max.

"I'm not sure—it jest did. It were as if a tiny stretch o' beach kept reachin' across the sea. I jest walked on top o' it. There were

33

water splashin' on either side for it were a skinny piece o' beach. But it were there sure as yer standin' there low . . ." Al caught himself before he made another "short comment" about Max.

"Hmmmm. Well, I guess it could happen that there were land under yer feet out into the sea. At least ye made it ta Scotland," said Max.

Al smiled with relief to see his new friend dare to believe him, for it was an unusual story. He didn't like the feeling of not being trusted. It hurt his spirit, for Al truly had a good heart. Max and Al kept making their way through the thick shrubs of heather that lined their scrubby path.

The woodsy smells of the forest were a sweet aroma to Max. It felt as if he could bite the air and chew the tasty fragrance. It dawned on him that he was hungry, thinking such daft thoughts. "How aboot we find some food ta eat?" asked Max.

"Aye, me feelin's exactly!" replied Al excitedly.

"We're in luck, Al. Up ahead methinks I see strawberry plants. An' even a chestnut tree as well," said Max. The two friends stopped and ate their fill, glad to have a time to rest.

They traveled on after their meal, eager to reach the end of the forest and see the fire cloud once more. But they would not reach the end of the forest before nightfall. And Al was about to become far more scared than he had been in his entire life.

CHAPTER 7

The Forest

Exhausted, Al finally plopped down and told Max he couldn't walk another step. "Aye, I think we kin stop now," agreed Max. "'Tis dark an' we need ta rest."

They happened to stop right under a big tree covered with grape vines. Max knew Al was tired when he didn't bother to climb up and get some grapes for a bedtime snack. Al's head was no sooner placed on top of his paws than he was asleep and snoring.

Max was thirsty. He decided to go find a drink of water and left Al sleeping by the tree. He could hear the faint sound of running water, and made his way through the darkness to a small stream. The water was cool and fresh, and felt good on Max's tongue. He sat down, thanking the Maker for the day when suddenly he heard Al's cry: "AHHHHHHH! MAX! . . . HELP! . . . HELP!"

Max sighed and thought, *Wha' now?!* He went running back to the tree and saw black creatures flying all around Al.

"Now *these* are DEFINITELY enormous flyin' beasts, Max. Help! They're out to get me," cried Al.

"I wouldn't say 'enormous' but they are, indeed, flyin' beasts," replied Max.

He moved in closer to see exactly what they were and why they were swooping down on poor Al. A low growl came from his throat as he barked at the unknown black beasts. "Get away from me fr-r-riend, ye wee beasts!" growled Max. "Wha' do ye mean givin' this kitty such a scare?!"

"Evenin', sir. We're jest pickin' after wha' we dropped, tha's all. No harm meant by it. We don't ate cats," replied one of the beasts with a thick accent.

Max got closer and saw that the beasts were actually bats. Al was stiff and mute with fear as their wings fluttered around his fur, now twice its size from fright. Max noticed Al was covered in grapes, his eyes bulging wide.

"Wha' in the name of Pete are ye doin'?" Max asked the bats.

"Oh, well, we were up in th' tree and th' vine fell that we were feedin' from," explained one of the bats. "Muscadine grapes is our favorite food. Bu' it landed on this cat so we decided ta jest keep eatin'. Blimey! I never seen such a fraidy cat before," answered the bat as he leaned in to whisper to Max.

"Well, if ye don't mind, I'll pull the grape vine off me friend so ye kin eat without the clumps of fur in yer grapes," said Max.

The bats obliged and hovered in the air. Max walked over to Al, whose orange face now looked completely white, and pulled the vine over to the side of the tree. The bats resumed eating and Max nudged Al to see if he was okay.

Al hoarsely whispered to Max, "I thought for sure those enormous flyin' beasts had followed me from the beehive—and had grown."

"Sorry there, little kitty. We 'ope yer alright," said the bat.

Max laughed, "Oh, Al, bats are part of the forest life here in Scotland, an' kin smell fr-r-ruit from far away. The beasties' ears are gr-r-rand at hearin' the faintest of noises. They are harmless."

"Es'cuse me, Sir, but yer not in Scotland," remarked the bat.

"Wher-r-re are we, then?" asked Max, surprised.

"In England, of course. Can't ye tell by me lovely accent?" asked the bat.

"I had no idea we'd left Scotland," said Max, amazed to know he was in a whole new country.

"Yeah, well, yer in central England, righ' in th' heart of our fair land. Where ye headed?" asked the bat.

"We aren't sure where we're headed, jest that we're followin' the fire cloud ta get there," answered Max.

"Fire cloud? Never 'eard of it," remarked the bat, not really listening but talking over Max. "It must be a bloody good gamin' event or somethin', ay? Fire cloud followin', ye say?"

"But it's not a game, it's . . ." Max tried to explain while being interrupted.

"We don't get out much, ye see. Everythin' we need is righ' 'ere in th' forest, so we're not up on th' latest things," continued the bat.

"I'm tryin' ta tell ye that it's—," Max attempted to continue.

"Well, we must be movin' along. I smell a lovely bunch of currants 'alf a mile from 'ere. Best o' luck on yer fire cloud game," bid the bat.

The cloud of bats took off into the black night of the forest. Max and Al were once again alone by the tree.

"Wha' a buffoon," declared Max. "Aye, bats may be good at hearin' but they sure aren't good at listenin'. They're jest . . . batty. Al, try ta get back ta sleep now. Ye had a hard day an' even lost some fur from the fr-r-right," said Max.

"I'll try, Max. Me heart is still thumpin' in me chest," replied Al.

Al lay down and looked all around him, especially up, to see if there was anything else out to get him. All seemed quiet so he once again rested his head and closed his tired green eyes. Max thought he'd better stay near his friend, just in case another forest creature happened to pay them a visit.

37

A cool mist settled in on the forest floor. Max and Al were sleeping soundly. An owl perched above the two tired travelers, golden eyes glowing in the darkness. He softly hooted as he sat there eyeing the forest nightlife. Something moved behind the owl in the distance, cracking a twig with a snap. The owl turned its head full around to see if it could make out the source of the noise. The forest floor was too dense from his vantage point to make out much of anything. More twig snaps. There was clearly more than one creature. And the noise was moving closer.

Then the owl heard the distinct call of the creature and knew exactly what it was.

"AH-OOOOOOO. AH-OOOOOOO."

Wolves. Max woke up immediately, as did Al. It was that hard kind of waking up when you've been in a deep sleep. Al couldn't quite remember where he was. Was he still in Ireland, by his cave? No, wait—green hills, sea, Scotland, honey, flyin' beasts, Max, bats! "Aye, now I remember where I be! Max! Wolves! Do ye hear them beasties howlin'?! What should we do?" cried Al.

"Steady, Big Al. Jest keep yerself still an' quiet," calmly whispered Max.

Al put his paws up over his mouth so he wouldn't yell out. He closed his eyes and tried to make himself smaller, but it did little to help his fear. Hearing more twigs snapping and the sound coming closer, Al was up the tree, clawing his way to safety when he ran headlong into a big pair of round, glowing eyes.

"AHHHHH, there's no escape!" cried Al as he ran right into the owl.

The owl flapped his wings and screeched, "HOOOOT-HOOOOT." Al went clawing his way back down the tree and landed on top of Max. Max quickly got up and shook off his companion.

"Ye jest couldn't wait, could ye? Now hush."

Al cowered so closely behind Max that his now doubled, fluffy, orange fur blended into Max's small form, giving Max the appearance of a lion. They both sat quietly yet couldn't hear a thing. Silence. The noises had stopped. Were the wolves gone? Or were they closer still, watching them in the darkness?

Al, trying to be quiet, held his breath to the point of almost passing out. Max held a firm stance, tail up sharply, fur raised, and body poised for defense. His eyes were set in defiance to this new threat. But there was nothing.

"Al, kin ye see anythin'?" whispered Max.

"Not with me eyes closed," answered Al.

"Well, seein' how ye have eyes that kin see in the blackness, maybe it would be a gr-r-rand idea if ye opened them ta see if the wolves are comin'," replied Max gruffly.

Al opened one eye slowly, afraid to see anything. He quickly closed his eye and said, "I don't see anythin'."

Just then they heard a distant howl. It sent chills up their spines. But the wolves had moved on. Even so, Al dove into a pile of leaves.

Max chuckled and remarked, "There, ye see? No wolves dar-r-red tangle with me! They moved r-r-right along, they did."

Al hid in the leaves, terrified and causing them to shake as he whined, "Max, I jest can't handle anymore o' this. Fire cloud or no fire cloud, I think we should head back. What's so great about followin' the fire cloud anyway? We can't even see it now. How do ye know it's still there? It's probably jest a dream we both had, and here we are out in this black forest surrounded by scary creatures, not knowin' what's comin' next. Aye, 'tis daft for the two o' us, I say, to continue on. Let's turn back."

Max stood there with his ears up and stern gaze directed at the pile of leaves. "Are ye quite thr-r-rough there, laddie? I have never quit anythin' in me entir-r-re life an' I don't plan on startin' now! Sure, ye been fr-r-rightened, but when were bein' frightened ever a good enough reason ta quit? Gillamon told me that the

39

Maker Hisself called me, an' He has somethin' important for me ta do."

Max picked up his reed and threw it in front of the leaves. "Look at this, kitty. Look at this."

Two green eyes emerged from the leaves.

"This were not a dr-r-ream. This r-r-reed spoke ta me, sure as yer layin' there cower-r-rin' in those leaves. An' when sticks start speakin' ta me, I listen," exclaimed Max with his thick Scottish brogue.

Max looked at Al and noticed that his big friend was about to cry. His heart softened as he considered that Al was not very brave. Max remembered Gillamon's gentle ways with him, so he calmed down.

"Look, me friend. I'm here ta protect ye. Has anythin' been able ta harm ye yet?" asked Max.

Al sniffed and said, "Well . . . no. I been scared but nothin' has really hurt me."

"Aye, an' nothin' will as long as I'm with ye," encouraged Max. He paused before he started to speak again, allowing a moment of comfortable silence as his words sunk in to Al's frightened heart.

"But how do ye know, Max?" asked Al. "How do ye know ye can protect me?"

"Because Gillamon said that if the Maker calls me ta do somethin', then He'll help me ta do it. If He's called us ta follow the fire cloud, it's goin' ta lead us somewhere. An' if the fire cloud is leadin' somewhere, then it wouldn't make sense that we couldn't reach it, wherever it may be," explained Max.

"Gillamon also said when the Maker asks ye ta do somethin', it isn't always goin' ta be easy," Max continued. "The right path through the forest were the hardest of the three, but it will lead us ta the other side where we'll see the fire cloud again. Sometimes the least appealin' path ta take is the only right one ta take. An' I'd rather have a harder path that puts me in the best place than an easy one that leads me no where I want ta be."

"But, why? Doesn't the Maker know we're jest two wee creatures? Why wouldn't He make it easy for us?" questioned Al.

Max remembered another Gillamonism. "All creatures need ta grow. An' ye kin't gr-r-row without str-r-ruggle."

Al thought a minute but didn't quite understand. The sun was beginning to rise, bringing light to the forest once more.

Max took a deep breath and added, "An' no dar-r-rk night ever lasts forever, me friend."

"AH-OOOOOOO. AH-OOOOOOO."

"Aye! What's the stick sayin' now?!" asked Al, jumping out of the leaves.

Max snatched up his reed and they once again started running through the forest. Max could smell the scent of the wolves, and wondered if they would see them again. If so, he would be ready.

CHAPTER 8

A Bonnie Lass

The sea spray from the cresting waves exhilarated the two seagulls as they skimmed the surface of the water.

"Woo-hoo!" yelled Crinan as his wings grazed the salty water before turning to fly up straight into the sky.

"Wait for me!" called Bethoo, flying up, up, up to meet Crinan in the air.

What fun these two lovebirds were having, twirling around each other with sheer delight, enjoying the amazing world in which they lived. The sun sparkled on the dark blue sea below. As they flew higher, the large waves appeared as white specks on the surface.

"Do ye suppose we kin get closer this time?" asked Bethoo.

"I don't see why not, me love. Let's try!" said Crinan with a grin.

Off the two flew into the mysterious region of the cloud they had followed for days. The cloud radiated power. It surged with energy and curious sovereignty. They flew in and out of the white puffy clouds but dared not go near the flame coming from the center. The fire held an irresistible attraction for them, almost pulling the two gulls into itself. Yet they could not bear the awesome brightness and heat that it produced. So they air danced all around it, reveling in the mystery and the beauty of this incredible spectacle. Sometimes they would coast for hours on the wind currents formed from the heat of the cloud.

When the cloud stopped moving, Crinan and Bethoo made their way to solid ground to wait. They didn't know exactly where they were going, just that they heard the whisper of the fire cloud on the air current one day telling them to follow along. Their hearts were pure and trusting, and the love they had for each other grew as they traveled together.

They were making loops in the air when Bethoo noticed a white speck on the beach below. It was running back and forth along the shoreline.

"Wha' do ye suppose it could be, dear?" asked Bethoo.

"I'm not quite sure, me love. Let's go see," answered Crinan.

Crinan led the way as they swooped down to the cresting waves. They landed on a large rock at the water's edge and shook the sea spray from their wings. The little white speck came running up to them and stopped. It was a white dog—a West Highland Terrier. She was panting and had a pained look on her face.

"Halloo, miss," greeted Crinan. "We saw ye runnin' back an' forth on the beach here below. Is everythin' okay?"

"Good day ta ye. Thanks ever so much for comin' ta see me. I jest don't know wha' ta do," answered the little Westie.

Bethoo nudged Crinan. "Oh, of course, where are me manners? Let us make yer acquaintance, miss. I'm Crinan an' this is me wife, Bethoo. We're from the upper west highland area of Scotland. Pleased ta meet ye."

"Nice ta meet ye both. Me name is Bonnie Katelyn Maitland, but most friends call me Kate. I'm from Scotland, too! An' I'm so happy ta see ye!" answered Kate.

"Ah, 'tis always grand ta meet another Scot, lass. Now wha' seems ta be troublin' ye?" asked Crinan.

"Well, I've been followin' that strange cloud in the sky up there. A Voice back in Scotland told me ta follow it. I know that sounds odd, but 'tis true. Now I've reached the end of the land an' I'm not sure wha' ta do," explained Kate.

Crinan and Bethoo looked at each other, thinking the same thing. They weren't the only two creatures that had been called to follow the fire cloud. There was a twinkle in their eyes as they smiled and turned to Kate.

"Lass, we been followin' the fire cloud, also. We don't really know where we're goin' ta end up. We jest follow the cloud when it moves, an' stop when it stops. Ye mean ta tell us ye been doin' the same?" asked Crinan.

"Aye! I were in me burrow back in Scotland when I heard the Voice say, 'Come ta Me. Follow the fire cloud.' So I left an' been travelin' for days now. I feel so much better that I'm not the only one. Wha' do you suppose this is all aboot?" asked Kate, relief pouring into her eyes as she realized she wasn't alone in this mysterious journey.

"Well, we kin tell ye that there is somethin' powerful comin' from the fire cloud. We been up flyin' all around it, an' it is nothin' like we ever seen. It's not natural if ye know wha' I mean," replied Crinan.

Bethoo spoke up, "Do ye suppose it's the Maker Hisself in that cloud?"

"I've wondered the same thing, Bethoo," replied Kate. "Wha' other bein' could make such a spectacle in the sky? An' wha' other bein' could call us like this? I never before felt such a pull at me heart. I feel drawn ta go, an' scared ta go, but filled with a feelin' of rightness aboot followin' all at the same time. I thought I were daft at first, but I come ta believe it's the right thing. It's got ta be the Maker."

"I think ye fine lasses are right. Yer hearts are so close ta yer feelin's an' the Maker that I trust wha' yer sayin'. It makes sense that it is Hisself callin'. Me question is . . . why?" said Crinan.

"I don't know. I been tryin' ta figure it out, but I get nowhere. An' now I really will get nowhere if I kin't follow the fire cloud over this water," replied Kate sadly.

Bethoo flapped her wings, leaving the rock and landing on the ground next to Kate. "There, there, dearie," replied Bethoo. "We kin figure somethin' out. There's always a way, especially with the Maker's help."

Kate and Bethoo shared a smile. "Aye, but I wish He'd show it ta me," replied Kate.

Crinan and Bethoo looked at each other, feeling helpless to assist their newfound friend. They, of course, could keep flying and following the fire cloud. But how could they leave Kate behind?

The fire cloud burned brilliantly in the sky, pulling their hearts onward. The trio sat on the beach staring at the cloud and then out to sea, wondering what they could possibly do.

45

Al continued to run and jump up on the rocks at a fast pace while Max trotted steadily on the ground below. The smell of sea breeze was getting stronger.

"Max, I think we're gettin' close to the sea," yelled Al, bounding from rock to rock.

"Aye. I kin smell it, lad. Do ye see anythin' from up there on those r-r-rocks?" asked Max.

"Jest a green hill up ahead. Maybe when we get up there we'll be able to see the water," replied Al.

Max already wondered about that water. What if this land they were on was a big island? If they reached the sea, that would surely mean they would be at the end of their destination with the fire cloud . . . or would it? Max picked up his trotting pace and started to run. He had to know. He went blazing past Al, who had stopped up on a rock to play with a patch of swaying green grass, chewing on the ends of the tallest blades.

"Hey, wait for me!" yelled Al, spitting grass and running after Max.

Max ran ahead of Al and reached the rocky ledge that overlooked the wide expanse of ocean below. The coastline spread as far as the eye could see in either direction. The sea breeze blew into Max's face, and he closed his eyes, drinking in the salty aroma. Below was a steep incline leading down to the water's edge.

Max sat a moment and thought to himself, *Well, this must be the end of the journey. It weren't as far as I thought it would be, an' we didn't go ta as many different lands as I thought we would, but it were still a gr-r-rand adventure. Now wha' was this all aboot, I wonder?*

Al broke Max's train of thought as he belly-crawled up next to him and exclaimed, "Look, Max! The fire cloud is there in the southern sky. Sure, and it's still movin'. Where are we supposed to go?"

Max looked at the fire cloud, and, indeed, onward it moved. This was a puzzle. Suddenly his eyes drifted to movement on the beach below.

"There's someone down ther-r-re," Max said, keeping his gaze on the beach.

Al didn't look down at the beach but rolled over on his back against the rock ledge. "Jest tell me they're friendly. Tell me they're not wolves, or things that howl. Or flyin' things, or creatures that bite or beasties with fangs or creatures that come out in the night . . ."

"Shhhh!" Max said.

"What is it? What do ye see, Max?" Al said nervously.

"It's a Westie. A white Westie," Max replied.

Al squeezed his eyes shut, "No, no, not a Westie! How big is this beast? Does it have fangs? Does it eat cats? Is it enormous and fly and have—"

"I'm goin' down," Max said, leaving Al rambling on about his fear of the Westie while he bounded down the rocky ledge toward the beach.

"No, Max. Ye can't leave me!" Al cried.

Suddenly Al heard a howl in the distance. Out popped his claws and down he scooted, bottom first all the way down the cliff's edge, scratching the rocks and screaming at the top of his lungs.

CHAPTER 9

Questions and More Questions

Crinan, Bethoo, and Kate turned from the fire cloud to locate the source of the noise behind them on the beach. A black dog was running toward them, followed by a big, screaming, orange cat.

"As I live an' breathe! Look, me love! It's Max from the Glen!" said Crinan excitedly to Bethoo.

"Are ye sure?" asked Bethoo, squinting to make out the animal running toward them.

"I could spot him a mountain away," Crinan grinned.

"Well, goodness me, it sure is! Maximillian Braveheart the Bruce!" Bethoo exclaimed.

Kate looked up to see Max trotting toward them. Her heart caught in her chest. A black Scottie. Oh, and wasn't he handsome?

"I believe Max has a cat chasin' him," Bethoo said with concern on her face.

"Yes, love, I believe ye are correct. Kate, would ye excuse us for the moment?"

Crinan and Bethoo took off flying past Max. They started dive-bombing an out-of-breath Al. Max didn't notice the gulls fly overhead or the commotion behind him. His gaze was focused on the beautiful white dog rushing up to him.

Max smiled, "Halloo, miss—"

Kate returned the smile. "Me name is Bonnie Katelyn Maitland, but please call me Kate."

"Me name is Max. Maximillian Braveheart the Bruce. But ye kin call me whatever ye want," Max said, gazing into Kate's beautiful eyes.

Max and Kate stood gazing at one another. They didn't hear anything but the sound of the crashing waves . . . and the beating of their hearts in their ears. Chemistry! The moment was interrupted when the ruckus between the seagulls and Al escalated. Kate looked over, growled, and rushed over to aid Crinan and Bethoo. Max turned to follow her, and it was only then he recognized the gulls.

"Hold it right there, kitty! Ye dun scared me friends! An' wha' do ye mean chasin' such a fine dog?! Who are ye, an' wha' do ye want?!" scolded Kate.

Al covered his head with his paws, looking frantically at Kate and at the two gulls, then back at Kate. This was clearly a strong-willed female dog. She must be the ringleader of these new, violent creatures.

"I beg yer pardon, miss. Me name's Al. I didn't mean to frighten yer friends. Believe me, I know how they feel, and that's the last thing I want any creature to feel on account o' me," explained Al. "I'm not chasin' the dog, I'm with him. MAX! Tell them. Tell them I'm with ye."

Max was grinning from ear to ear. What a fiery lass this Westie was. She was trying to defend him—from Al! He chuckled and then trotted over to the confused bunch of animals.

"Crinan! Bethoo! How in the world is it that yer here in England? We're all a wee bit away from home, aren't we, now?" said

49

Max excitedly, his tail wagging in the sea breeze. "No need ta worry aboot the big, orange kitty. Al, here, is me friend. He's on this journey followin' the fire cloud with me."

Al's face flooded with relief as the gulls stopped pecking, and the Westie stopped scolding. Their attention was now on Max, who defended him.

Crinan answered, "We've been followin' that fire cloud for days. In fact, we called ta ye an' Gillamon that we were headed out when ye were up on his cliff. Ye must not have heard us then."

Max remembered now. Crinan and Bethoo had indeed flown over, and called to Gillamon and him, but Max had not heard what they said.

"Aye! I did see ye, but didn't hear ye. I were talkin' with Gillamon, tryin' ta figure out why the r-r-reeds by the loch hummed an' said 'Come ta Me. Follow the fire cloud,'" answered Max.

"I don't believe it. Did ye hear that, me love?" Bethoo said excitedly. "That makes four of us now. Five if ye count yer big orange friend."

Kate looked to Max, relieved to know he was heading her way.

Al grinned and kept quiet, waving at the seagull that smiled back.

"Well, so here we are," said Max. "Anyone got an idea where the fire cloud will lead us?"

"We were jest tryin' ta figure that one out when ye showed up," replied Crinan. "We were askin' a different sort of question. Now that we're at the water's edge, wha' do we do?"

Max stood in front of the little band of friends who were looking to him for an answer. The last thing he wanted to appear was uncertain, especially in front of Kate.

"Ah, well, let's look at the situation. Crinan an' Bethoo, wha' kin ye tell me aboot this land? Is it an island? Do ye see any land reachin' out ta where the fire cloud is movin'?" asked Max.

"It's indeed an island. A big island, mind ye. Down the east coast are huge white cliffs— 'tis a grand sight! Bethoo an' me been flyin' way up high into the clouds an' there be coastline as far as the eye kin see. Aye, the fire cloud is now over the other side of the sea. But there's no land across as far as we seen, lad," answered Crinan.

"Wha' aboot that little island we saw off the shoreline, dear?" asked Bethoo. "Would that help?"

"No, me love," answered Crinan. He turned to Max, "'Tis jest another island on the south of England, but it won't get ye far across the big sea. Plus it's ta the west. Not the direction we need ta go."

This isn't what Max wanted to hear. All eyes were looking to him for an answer and a direction of where to go and what to do. How was *he* supposed to know? He needed an answer. They needed a way across. And he needed to prove himself to Kate. Just then they all heard a rumble come from Al's belly, making them laugh.

"Is anyone else hungry besides me?" asked Al.

"Oh, Al, how kin ye think of food at a time like this?" asked Kate.

"Believe me, Kate, Al never stops thinkin' aboot food, no matter wha' kind of time it is!" said Max with a wink to Kate.

Kate smiled back. "Well, this is a good time ta eat," said Max. "I need some time ta think anyway. Al, help Kate find some lunch while I have a look around then."

Max trotted off down the beach, not knowing really where he was going, but making it look like he did. Kate and Al made their way over to a dune filled with delicious sea oats. Crinan and Bethoo followed along, picking at morsels in the wet sand.

The sun was bright on the sea, blinding Max. When he was a good way down the beach, he sat down in the soft, wet sand. He knew what he needed to do. He needed to talk to the Maker.

"It's me, Max, again. I'm grateful ta Ye for bringin' Al an' me ta this gr-r-rand shore. An' for helpin' us ta find me old friends. An' especially for introducin' me ta Kate. Ah, wha' a bonnie lass

51

she is! Me heart hasn't stopped beatin' hard since I laid eyes on her." Max's mind drifted for a moment.

"We're all followin' the fire cloud. This mystery keeps growin', an' I'm not sure where Ye mean for us ta go. But here we are on this side of the sea, an' there the fire cloud is on the far side. Water again! Water, water, water—of all things. Are Ye testin' me then? The first time Ye talked ta me it were at the water of the loch. The first challenge were crossin' water at the big cr-r-reek. Now here I am at this big body of water, needin' a word from Ye as ta wha' ta do with it. One of those r-r-revelations would be gr-r-rand aboot now," Max said out loud.

He caught his breath for a moment and hoped the Maker would respond. Max appreciated the fact that he could be himself with the Maker. The Maker never made him feel he had to act like someone other than who he was already.

Max continued, "Forgive me for sayin' it, but I KNOW there isn't a log big enough ta r-r-reach across this gr-r-rand sea of water. There isn't a log that big, is there?"

Max sat quietly and listened to the waves crashing at his feet. He felt the warm rays of the sun kiss his face and the sea breeze fill his nostrils with the energy he always knew from his beloved Scotland. He closed his eyes and soaked it up, allowing his mind to take him back home. The last time he was at the shore, it was with Gillamon on the morning he left the Glen. It seemed like forever ago that he had stood with him on the cliff overlooking the sea. His heart ached as he missed his friend, but what a surprise to be reunited with his other friends.

Crinan and Bethoo were always two of his favorite birds. They were ever considerate of others, a character trait that Max admired. And the love they showed to each other made Max wish that someday he could share that kind of love with someone.

His mind drifted to Kate. She was beautiful and strong, and had a sweet but spunky spirit. Could it be this grand journey was arranged for them to meet? There were always more questions.

Max remembered a Gillamonism: *"Sometimes a question grows into more questions rather than a single answer. 'Tis the way of life, Max. If there is a purpose for you beyond what you know, the Maker always has a way of making it known."*

Max opened his eyes and looked at the waves far out to sea. He squinted from the brilliance of the sun's reflection and watched the waves gradually move inland. He noticed how they crested as the water became shallow. He was wondering how that worked, when the Maker whispered to his heart.

"KEEP THINKING ABOUT YOUR FRIENDS FROM HOME. YOU WILL FIND THE RIGHT WAY FROM THERE."

Kate watched Max while she and Al sat chewing on the delicious sea oats. "Wha' is Max doin' doon there on the beach?" Kate asked Al.

"Oh, he's probably talkin' to the Maker," answered Al. "He does that when he needs to figure out what to do next. He learned to do this from his wise old friend, Gillamon. And I've never seen him lackin' an answer yet." Kate was drawn even more so to Max. He had character and a faith that made him strong and brave indeed. This is the kind of dog she could really love.

The afternoon wore on and nothing came readily to Max. He wrestled with his thoughts and with the Maker's instructions. He stared up at the fire cloud.

Why is this so hard? I don't like ta be the one ta figure things out. I'm much better at plowin' right ahead after the plan is made, not comin' up with the plan. I wish there were someone else leadin' this group of creatures besides me, Max thought.

Kate, Al, Crinan, and Bethoo left Max alone all afternoon, respecting his need for time by himself.

Max continued thinking and remembering his friends as the Maker instructed him to do. Suddenly, he jumped up with a start.

Of course! That will work. Aye, but I don't know how I'm goin' ta handle this. They'll all think I'm daft. I think I'm daft for thinkin' it. This will take courage I don't have. But I don't see another way, Max said to himself. He turned his thoughts back to the Maker. "Ah, yer a gr-r-rand helper. Thanks for the r-r-revelation. I knew ye would make the way 'come ta me.'" Max ran back down the beach toward the others.

"Crinan! Bethoo! I've got an assignment for ye," yelled Max.

The two seagulls flew over to Max and landed next to him on the sand while Kate and Al watched from a distance.

"I think I figured out a way ta cr-r-ross the sea," said Max with a big grin and a twinkle in his eyes.

"Go find Craddock."

54

CHAPTER 10

The Perfect Rock Jetty

Kate and Al saw Crinan and Bethoo take off flying toward the setting sun in the west. Al yawned and stretched out on the sand, clearly ready for sleep.

Kate was curious and started walking over to where Max sat looking at the two gulls in the distance. He looked up at her with a big grin on his face.

"Wha' is goin' on, Max?" asked Kate.

"I think I found a way across the sea," answered Max. "But I don't want ta tell ye jest yet wha' it is."

"Now why would ye be keepin' it from us then?" answered Kate.

"I need ye ta tr-r-rust me, Kate. I know wha' I'm doin' . . . I think," answered Max. "I have ta be extra careful with Al. He is a true scaredy cat an' this idea will be sort of hard for him ta take."

"Well, I'm not a scaredy cat. I kin handle it, Max! Tell me," pleaded Kate.

Max sat there and looked into the soft eyes of this beautiful little dog. How could he resist those eyes? After traveling so long with Al, he wasn't used to being around a brave animal on this journey. Perhaps Kate could handle it. After all, she had made the journey all the way from Scotland alone. She was a strong-willed creature. Still, he didn't want to concern her before it was time. Plus, he wanted to make sure the plan was going to work.

"Well, let me think aboot it. But ye kin help me find a r-r-rock jetty in the mornin'. We're goin' ta need one," replied Max.

"Wha's a rock jetty?" Kate asked, cocking her head.

"It's a bunch of r-r-rocks that sit above the water way out into the sea," Max explained. "Ye better get some good sleep now, lass. I'll guard things while ye get settled. An' I'll be nearby all night," said Max, now getting tired himself.

Kate, although miffed that Max didn't want to tell her about the plan, felt glad she could at least help with part of it. And because he was so thoughtful making sure she was kept safe, Kate knew she could trust Max completely.

"Good night, Max. I'm glad I met ye today," said Kate, smiling.

"Good night, bonnie lass. Aye, it were a gr-r-rand day," said Max.

The little Westie lay down next to the rocks while Max kept an eye out on the horizon. The fire cloud lit the night sky over the sea. Max had never seen anything more beautiful. That is, of course, besides Kate.

Max nudged Kate as the sun was making its way over the eastern sea. "Wake up, lass." Kate slowly opened her eyes to see Max smiling at her.

"It's a bonnie day," he said.

Kate got up and stretched. "Good mornin', Max. It is a beautiful day!"

"Aye! Let's get goin' ta find that r-r-rock jetty," said Max.

Max and Kate left Al snoring soundly on the sand. They walked down the beach about two miles and talked as they looked for a rock jetty.

"Al says ye talk ta the Maker. He also told me aboot yer friend, Gillamon."

"Aye, lass. Gillamon were me best friend. He taught me aboot the Maker an' the ways of life since I were a pup."

"Aye, the Maker helped me on me journey alone. He also led me ta meet ye," said Kate, blushing when she realized she actually said what she had been silently thinking.

Max smiled at Kate, making her feel self-conscious. "Uh, tell me aboot Gillamon," requested Kate, changing the subject.

Max told Kate all about Gillamon and their wonderful times in the Glen. They walked along the beach, talking until they had reached an outcropping of rocks going out far into the water. All along the jetty the waves crashed, sending sea spray to cover the rocks. The water swirled around the base of the rocks, creating foam on top of the water that rolled into shore. The jetty extended fifty yards into the sea. It was exactly what Max was looking for.

"This is it, Kate. This r-r-rock jetty will work. It's perfect. Come on, let's go get Al!" exclaimed Max.

Kate thought it was endearing to see Max get so excited about things. His Scottish brogue got thicker and his eyes got brighter.

"How will a rock jetty work? Wha' are we goin' ta use it for?" asked Kate, smiling at Max all the while.

"Ye'll see," said Max as they ran back down the beach.

Kate was somewhat frustrated now. She was confused and didn't understand what good could possibly come from the rock jetty to help them across the sea. Max wasn't talking. Kate was headstrong and didn't like taking no for an answer. She decided to race Max, just to challenge him. She wanted to see if Max could keep up with her. Kate went running fast ahead before Max knew what was happening. Max, not wanting to be outdone by a girl, picked up his pace.

Max was growling under his breath, "Ther-r-re's no way I'm goin' ta let this lass—pr-r-retty though she may be—get ahead of me!"

Kate looked behind and giggled as Max tried to reach her. A flock of sandpipers on the beach scurried into the air as Kate ran right into them. They circled around and flew right in Max's way. Kate was so light on her feet that Max never stood a chance catching her.

Soon they were back at the beach where Al lay sleeping. Both dogs were panting. They were having fun, enjoying the sheer delight of the other's company.

"Aye, yer a stubborn one, lass. I have no doubt ye kin handle anythin' that comes yer way. Ye kin certainly keep me on me paws, that's for sure," said Max, exhausted.

Kate jumped into the water to cool off, allowing the waves to splash over her fur.

"Wee, the water feels grand, Max. Come on in," shouted Kate.

"Ah, no thanks, Kate. I'll get cooled off enough here by the water's edge," replied Max.

Kate was puzzled as to Max's seeming aversion to water.

Max spied a sand crab crawling on his reed and took off running. "Get away from me r-r-reed, ye wee beast," he growled. The crab darted into its cavernous hole, out of sight. Max picked up his reed and brought it over to the water's edge.

"Is that yer reed? The one that talked ta ye then?" asked Kate.

"Aye. This reed has helped me out of tight spots, so it's special ta me. I don't want a pesky cr-r-rab tryin' ta get inside it then," replied Max.

Kate came out of the water and shook from head to toe. Sea spray went all over Max.

"Thanks, lass," Max said sarcastically.

"Happy ta help," smirked Kate.

They walked up the beach to get Al, who was still sleeping soundly on the warm sand.

"Al, wake up! Time ta go," said Max. Al continued to sleep, ignoring Max's call.

Max noticed a large sand crab hole right next to Al's head. He sniffed all along the sand until he came to another hole several feet away.

"Watch this," Max whispered to Kate with a wink.

Max started digging furiously in the hole, sand flying everywhere. All of a sudden a huge sand crab came darting out the hole by Al's head. Startled, it raised its claws and stood there in defiance of this big orange invader.

Max yelled loudly to Al, "Al, wake up! Time ta go."

This time Al woke up to see large pincers staring him in the face. "AHHHH!" cried Al.

The sand crab pinched Al on the nose, not letting go. Al went running around in circles with the crab hanging on for dear life. He finally flung the crab off and watched as it scurried off into another hole out of sight. Al went running after the crab and planted his face right in the sand. He looked up to find Kate and Max chuckling at the now very awake Al. His face and whiskers were covered with sand. Max was rolling on the beach with laughter next to Kate, and Al came over and joined them.

"Did ye see the size o' that monster?! It had me by the nose, it did. Sure, but I fought back," said Al, excitedly.

"Aye, lad. Ye were fierce, too! Look at the way ye went after it! Good goin' lad. I'm pr-r-roud of ye," said Max.

"I'm kind o' proud o' meself, too," said Al, spitting sand as he spoke. "Sure, but that were a rude awakenin'."

Kate laughed at the two of them, wondering what their journey together must have been like up until now. Al ran back to the crab hole to see if he could find his nemesis.

Kate whispered to Max, "Why did ye do that ta poor Al? Besides it bein' funny an' all?"

Max whispered back, "Al's been workin' on improvin' his courage. As he gets braver, he needs a greater test ta make him even stronger. I'm jest tryin' ta help him along."

The words were no sooner out of his mouth than Max thought of his own challenges and tests throughout this journey. The Maker was making him stronger with each one. He grinned as he looked up at the fire cloud, giving a nod of thanks to the Maker.

A shadow flew overhead. Another shadow came. The trio looked up to see Crinan and Bethoo coming in for a landing. Max jumped up and shook off the sand.

"Well, did ye find him then?" asked Max, eagerly.

"Aye, lad, we did. He's on his way," replied Crinan with a grin.

"Good work, me friends. Go tell Craddock ta meet us at the rock jetty two miles down the beach. That should be a good place," instructed Max.

The two gulls took off once again as Max turned to Kate and Al, saying, "Let's go!"

Al looked at Kate, and she answered his questioning face, "I don't know anythin' other than goin' ta a rock jetty, so don't ask me!"

"Max, what's this all about?" asked Al.

"Ye'll see, Big Al. Tr-r-rust me," replied Max, off trotting and calling behind him.

The three friends went running down the beach. They enjoyed the freedom of being on a wide-open shore with the sun shining and the sounds of the sea filling their ears. The fire cloud burned brightly in the sky keeping watch over them. And waiting for them.

CHAPTER 11

Dreams — the Cave

Noah put a few more sticks in the fire and stoked it until the blaze once again burned brightly, lighting up the walls of the cave. He walked over to where his father, Lamech, was sleeping. Noah reached into his own pocket for the cloth pouch he brought with him. Gently he touched his father's shoulder.

"Father," Noah quietly asked. Lamech stirred. "Father, Adah has fixed you some food."

Lamech opened his eyes. Slowly he struggled to sit up while Noah helped him turn slightly to prop his back against the cave wall. Noah then unwrapped some bread and pulled a skin of water from his belt. "Did you have a good sleep?"

Lamech nodded and smiled. "Dreams of my youth." Lamech touched the raindrop mark on his cheek and began to remember his dream. . .

A very old Adam and a young Lamech walk along a well-worn path. Adam uses his torch as a walking stick. "Are we going to the cave? Can we? Can we? Pleassse, great father! Can we please go to the cave?" young Lamech begs.

Adam grimaces at the exuberance of the young boy. "Lamech, I told you we are going to the cave."

"Do I finally get to see? Do I? Do I get to see?" Lamech keeps pleading when Adam suddenly stops in his tracks. "Lamech, We are here," Adam says as he pulls back some branches to reveal an opening to a cave. Adam lights two torches that had been hidden in the bushes. He hands one torch to young Lamech, and the two enter the cave. Adam walks slowly, cautiously, watching his steps. The boy respectfully follows slowly behind.

"It is not too far. Just around this rock," Adam instructs the young boy.

They round the rock and with the two torches burning bright. The walls of the cave light up with thousands of hand-drawn pictures. Lamech steps up to the nearest drawing, holding his torch close so that he might see the detail. He runs his fingers over the picture in awe. He moves to another picture and does the same. Studying and admiring in awe.

"You were right, great father. These are unimaginable. I have never seen animals like this," Lamech exclaims excitedly.

Adam looks thoughtfully at the pictures. "Some of these I have not seen since I named them."

"What is this, father Adam?" Lamech asked, pointing to the cave wall.

Adam steps over and recognizes the drawing of an ostrich. "That is a strange one. It thinks it can fly and roars like a lion! It's an ostrich."

"And this?" Lamech continues pointing down the wall.

"Bear . . . otter . . . kangaroo . . . and crab," Adam names as Lamech points.

"And this? Is it as big as your drawing, great father?"

"That is one I only saw once. The day that I named it—that is a whale," Adam said, marveling at the enormous creature on the wall.

Lamech holds up his torch and looks around the enormous cave, filled with years and years of drawings. "Great father, how long can we stay here?"

"Now that you know, you will have years to spend here," Adam replies, squeezing the young boy's shoulder.

Lamech smiles and spins around, scanning the thousands of drawings. He returns his gaze to the large one he'd been studying.

"Whale . . ."

CHAPTER 12

The Right Way

The animal friends reached the rock jetty in no time. Max stopped suddenly and turned to explain things to Al and Kate.

"Okay, now, ye asked me for a way ta reach the other side of the sea. I talked with the Maker an' did a lot of thinkin'. An idea came ta me that ye might think is daft, but ye got ta tr-r-rust me on this. I need ye ta come up with me on this r-r-rock jetty," said Max.

Al and Kate looked at the big, jagged rocks going out a short distance into the sea. Waves crashed all around making the rocks wet and slick. It wasn't very inviting, and it didn't seem to make any sense. Where would this rock jetty lead?

Kate looked at Al, who had a concerned look on his face, and said, "Lad, I know this doesn't look good, but I trust Max. Has he steered ye wrong yet?"

"No, he hasn't. But there's a first time for everythin'!" replied Al.

Kate frowned at Al. "Come on, Al. Ye kin do it. Ye handled that sand crab bravely, so surely ye kin handle this jetty. An' Max told me how ye like ta jump up on rocks. He said ye did so all the way across England."

"Aye, 'tis true, I like to jump on rocks. Sure, but DRY ones. These are wet and sharp and lead to the sea. It don't look good to me," said Al, not moving an inch off the sand.

Max jumped up on the first rock and asked Kate to follow him. This courageous dog was telling her not to be afraid but to follow him. She didn't know what he was up to, but how could she resist him? Up Kate jumped next to Max. He grinned and said, "That's me girl, lass! Okay, Al, yer next."

Al hesitated. He loved jumping up on rocks but this was different. Still, he knew he could trust Max. Kate was right. Max hadn't steered him wrong yet. He took a deep breath and jumped, slipping on the rock, at first, but then balancing himself. Max and Kate were moving down the jetty out to the sea. Al slowly followed behind, carefully watching his step.

Max tried not to look down at the water surrounding him. *Stay focused, lad. Ye kin do this. No fear. No fear. Remember yer loved an' yer able. Think Gillamon thoughts,* Max muttered to himself as he and Kate made their way along the rocks. They looked behind and Al was catching up.

"That's it, lad! Keep comin'," encouraged Max.

As the three of them reached the end of the jetty, Kate and Al both turned and said to Max in unison, "Now what?"

"Jest wait. He'll be here," answered Max, searching the horizon for any sign of Crinan, Bethoo, or Craddock.

Kate and Al just looked at each other, totally confused as to what could possibly be happening. Max kept scanning the horizon.

Out of nowhere a loud burst of sea spray came raining down, drenching them.

"AHHHHHH!" screamed Al, his eyes blinking away the salt water.

Max jumped up and went running to the edge of the rocks, calling, "Halloo, Craddock, me friend. Thanks for comin'."

65

Kate and Al then saw an enormous, dark gray form emerge from the surface of the water—a mammoth whale nearly fifty feet long—it was he who had sprayed them with water from his two large blowholes.

"Well, hello, Max, my good fellow," Craddock exclaimed with a proper English accent. "It's splendid to see you, old chap. I was so pleased when Crinan and Bethoo told me of your grand adventure, and I am delighted to render assistance to you. My, it has been awhile since I've seen you. Last summer, I believe?"

"Aye, last summer it were. How gr-r-rand ta see ye in these waters," said Max.

Kate wagged her tail with excitement. Al looked half his normal size now that he was wet with seawater. And he looked like he'd just seen a ghost.

"Let me introduce ye ta me friends. This sweet lass is Kate, from Scotland. An' this orange, wet creature is Al, from Ireland," said Max.

"Right! Pleased to meet the two of you. Craddock's the name. I hail from the west coast of England, Wales to be exact. I enjoy summering up on the coast of Scotland where I met Max years ago. Any friend of Max I count as my own. I'm at your service, fair lady and dear gentlemen," replied Craddock.

Craddock moved up close to the jetty so he could get a good look at the land creatures. He was a right whale. His large head was covered with white bumps on top and below his chin. One bump was just above one of his small eyes, giving him a very distinguished appearance. His beaklike jaw was shaped like a bow and adorned with large lips that curved precisely when he spoke. Under his lips were nine-foot black baleen plates that he used to skim the water for plankton. Craddock's flippers were enormous and made the water swirl as he reached out to touch the jetty. He was a majestic creature, but his large, warm eyes and generous smile made him totally approachable.

Max walked over to Craddock to look him right in the eye. "Ah, me friend. I kin't tell ye how relieved I am that ye came. We been followin' the fire cloud in the far southern sky for days on end. The problem is, when we reached this southern coast of England, it kept movin'. We're not really sure where it will lead, but feel the Maker has called us ta follow it, so that's wha' we're doin'. Have ye seen it in the sky?" asked Max.

"Right-oh, Max! Big, puffy clouds with fire in the center? Why, yes, I've seen it for days now. I enjoy watching the wonderful color it gives the sea at night. Utterly splendid," replied Craddock.

"Have ye heard a Voice tellin' ye ta follow it then?" asked Max.

"No, I don't believe I have, old chap. Just enjoying the view, you know," replied Craddock.

This confused Max. If there ever were a noble creature deserving of the Maker's call, it was Craddock. This just added to the mystery of this grand adventure.

"Well, I were tryin' ta figure a way across the sea ta continue followin' the fire cloud. I were thinkin' an' talkin' ta the Maker, an' He said ta remember me old friends an' I would find the right way. Then I thought of ye, Cr-r-raddock. Will ye carry us ta the other side of the sea?" asked Max.

"Jolly good show, old boy. I'm at your service and have traveled across this stretch of sea many times. I know it well. You were right to listen to the Maker. He's quite the wise One, you know," answered Craddock.

Max whispered to Craddock so Kate and Al wouldn't hear. "Um, Craddock? I'm not very good with water, see, so if ye could be so kind as ta not move suddenly, I would be much obliged ta ye."

"No problem, my good fellow. I happen to be a slow swimmer as whales go. I will give you a gentle ride," replied Craddock with a comforting voice.

67

Max got close to Craddock's large flipper, took a deep breath and walked across it and up onto his wide back. He turned and looked at Kate and Al. "Okay, here's the plan. Since we kin't swim ta the other side of the sea, Craddock here will carry us across. Kate, ye jest follow along like I did. Cr-r-raddock's strong flippers will hold ye tight as ye get on."

Kate was thrilled. "I'm delighted!" She gingerly walked across the last rock of the jetty over to Craddock. The large whale gave her a wide smile and a wink and said, "Me lady, your ride awaits. Mind the gap."

Kate carefully jumped onto the whale, mindful of the gap between Craddock's flipper and the jetty. She walked across Craddock's flipper and joined Max on top of the large whale.

Al sat motionless on the jetty, fear consuming his expression. His whiskers were shivering and not because he was soaked to the bone. He was scared to death.

"Al, come on, lad. It will be fine, ye'll see," encouraged Max.

"Noooooooo way am I goin' to ride on such an enormous swimmin' beast," Al responded. "What if he decides to go under? Sure, and I'll slide into his big jaws and be lost forever."

"Not quite, old boy. See here, as a whale, my mouth is large but only takes in very small plankton and krill. I wouldn't dream of scooping up a fine feline such as yourself. Besides, you can rest assured that I will carry you over the sea with great care. I won't let you fall. Nothing to fear," said Craddock, doing his best to convince Al.

Al may not have been comforted by Craddock's words, but Max certainly was.

"Come on, lad. Ye come this far, an' this is our way across. Ye kin do this. Don't leave us now." pleaded Max.

"No, I'm not goin'. I'll say me farewell to ye both here and make me way back home," said Al sadly.

"Al, if ye take a little of that growin' courage ye have an' trust the Maker, I'm sure ye kin do this thing. I know it looks hard. But nothin' is too hard when ye have good friends ta help ye," said Kate, trying to persuade Al.

Al remained unmoved. He hung his head low and got up.

"Farewell, Max. It were a grand adventure while it lasted. I guess I'm jest not up to this challenge. It's too much too soon, methinks. I'm jest not brave enough for somethin' so big. I'm sorry to let ye down. Ye been a good friend. Farewell, Kate. I'm glad I got to meet ye, and I know ye and Max will reach the fire cloud."

Al started slowly walking away along the rocks of the jetty back to shore. Max and Kate looked at each other, helpless to know what to say to change Al's mind. Crinan and Bethoo flew over in front of Al, begging him not to go. Nothing seemed to move Al. He was just too afraid. The gulls flew back to the others and landed on Craddock.

"The poor dear, there's no talkin' him out of it," said Bethoo sadly.

Craddock said, "Oh, dear me, how sad. I do say, I hope I didn't cause your little band to break up, old boy."

"No, me friend. Wasn't yer fault. Al has ta decide for himself wha' ta do. Ye kin't make anyone do wha' ye want them ta do. Creatures have ta make up their own minds," replied Max sadly.

Kate nuzzled her nose in Max's fur. "I'm sorry, Max. I know wha' a dear friend he's been." Max sighed and watched his friend walk away.

"Aye. I guess he'll have ta make his own way now. Let's go," said Max somberly to Craddock.

"Here we go," said Craddock as he moved his enormous flippers to shove them off the jetty.

The currents produced by Craddock's massive form in movement stirred the water into whirlpools all around them. The pairs of dogs and gulls sat on top of the great whale, crestfallen that they could not help their friend.

As he turned his head out to sea, Max heard a sound from behind that sent alarm rushing through him.

69

"AH-OOOOOOO. AH-OOOOOOO." It was the wolves. He saw them in the distance running down the beach. They were headed right for the jetty. And right for Al.

"Wait, Craddock. Don't leave. The wolves are comin', an' Al is out there alone. We've got ta help him," yelled Max.

"Right. Back to the jetty," said Craddock, turning his huge form around to the breaking waters around the large rocks.

Al was now jumping across the rocks down the jetty, getting away from the beach as fast as he could. No sooner had Craddock reached the jetty than Al jumped completely over his flippers, landing on Craddock's back next to Max.

"Welcome aboard there, old boy," exclaimed Craddock.

"Aye, glad ye could make it!" said Max with a wide grin. "Are ye okay, lad?"

"Aye! I'll choose a nice, wet enormous beast to a mean, howlin' one any day," said Al, digging his claws into Craddock's large back.

"I knew ye could do it, Al. Aye, but yer hurtin' Craddock with yer claws," remarked Kate.

"There's no fin to hang onto," answered Al.

"Just make yourself at home, Al. My hide is tough. You just hang on tight," said Craddock.

The wolves were making their way down the jetty. "Cr-r-rad-dock! Hurry! The wolves are gettin' close. Shove off!" yelled Max.

"RIGHT! I'm shoving off," said Craddock as he used his powerful tail to splash the jetty with a wall of water, drenching the approaching wolves.

The wolves shook off the sea spray and stood there, looking at the unlikely band of friends riding on top of the great right whale into the channel.

"Whew! That were close, Al, me friend. I thought ye might not have made it," said Max.

"Aye! I about jumped out o' me fur when I heard them beast-ies howl and start runnin' at me," answered Al.

"I guess ye figured which fear ye would rather face. I'm proud of ye choosin' ta come along. I were goin' ta miss ye, lad," said Max with a warm smile.

"Well, I were thinkin' about what ye had told me in the forest about not quittin' when I heard the wolves. I were feelin' like a real failure walkin' away like that. I were doubtin' meself. I were doubtin' ye. And I were doubtin' the Maker. But I had no good reason to doubt, not after all I already seen on this journey. When the wolves came, the fear o' the unknown on the sea were nothin' compared to the fear o' them. I guess ye could say the wolves were like a blessin' to move me onward?" said Al.

Max grinned. "Al, me friend, that sounds like somethin' Gillamon would say."

Al nodded his head as he and Max shared that knowing look that two friends do when words aren't necessary.

"I say, I don't like to interrupt your splendid conversation, but are you sure we should have left the wolves behind?" said Craddock.

"Aye, Craddock, we'll do jest fine without them. How kin ye ask that?" answered Max.

"Oh, you see I was wondering if they might possibly be following the fire cloud as well," replied the whale.

"I don't see how. Why would the Maker call *wolves*? No, it's best ta leave them be," said Max definitively.

"I see. Hmmmm. Well, how many wolves were there, old chap?" asked Craddock.

Max stood on this smooth swimming whale and looked back at the wolves that were now pacing back and forth on the end of the rock jetty, staring back at him.

"Two," he replied.

CHAPTER 13

The Crossing

The sea spray splashed all around Craddock as he carried Max, Kate, and Al into the channel. Crinan and Bethoo flew up above, their shadows darting back and forth over the whale and his passengers. Kate listened to the sea foam fizz as Craddock glided through the water. She grinned softly at Al, who was spread out flat across the huge back of their transporting friend. He was wide-eyed and drenched, spitting the sea spray out of his mouth and digging his claws into the whale as he hung on for dear life.

"Jest how big is this body of water an' where does it lead then, Craddock?" asked Max as he carefully inched his way to sit on top of the whale's head, just behind the two blowholes. He tried to keep his focus on the shiny surface of the whale and not on the deep blue water passing on either side.

"This sea is quite large, dear boy—about 350 miles long, 150 miles wide, but not too deep for me, I'm afraid. I enjoy going deep in the great ocean, and in this channel I can only dive just shy of 400 feet. I must be terribly careful in the narrowest part of this channel down by those large white cliffs in the distance. From here, we'll cross over to France to reach the fire cloud. I do believe it's about 80 miles across," explained Craddock.

"France? Wha' is that country like, Craddock?" asked Max.

"Oh it's a splendid country, old boy. Beautiful coastline and lush landscape. I've heard tell of a large, winding river that goes far into the countryside. I could not go there myself, of course, but I understand the scenery to be quite grand," replied Craddock.

"Aye, but nothin' could be as gr-r-rand as me homeland in Scotland," answered Max.

"So, Max, do tell me more about this adventure of yours. What do you think you will find when you reach the fire cloud?" asked Craddock.

"I dunno, me friend. It's a mystery, an' it grows with each passin' day. I were thinkin' I were the only one called ta follow the fire cloud at first. Then I met Al, who were also followin' it, then caught up with Crinan an' Bethoo, an' of course . . . bonnie Kate," Max said as he dreamily looked back to see Kate consoling Al near the rear of the great whale.

"I do say, old chap, you seem to be quite taken with Kate," said Craddock with lips curving into a smile.

"Aye, lad. Me heart's been beatin' fast ever since I laid eyes on her. She is the lass of me dreams. I think I'm fallin' in love with her. Craddock, do ye have a love?" asked Max.

"No, lad, I just haven't met the *right* one yet," said Craddock with a chuckle that caused his body to shake and the passengers to brace themselves. Al stifled a scream as he bit his lip and shut his eyes tight.

"Ha, ha, good one, Craddock. Ah, but kin ye please be careful of yer laughin' then? It tends ta make everyone shake an' I'm afraid Al kin't take much more of bein' scared," said Max, thinking to himself that *he* couldn't take much more, either.

"No worries. I'll try to keep my chuckles at bay. So, do you think that Kate is your right one?" asked Craddock.

73

Max looked back at Kate and replied, "Aye, lad. I think she's the right one for me."

"I think you two make quite the lovely couple. Utterly splendid!"

Just then a deep rumble came from Craddock's belly, and Max, Kate, and Al all felt their feet tingle. "I do say, I'm terribly sorry about that. I haven't had breakfast yet this morning, and I do need to eat, you know," said Craddock.

"Eat! Sure, and I want to eat, too!" said Al, his ears perked up at the mere mention of his favorite pastime. Suddenly he didn't seem as concerned about hanging on. To Al, eating was easily the most important part of his day. Sleeping was a close second.

Crinan and Bethoo swooped down to be eye level with Craddock. "Wha' do ye eat anyway?" they asked.

"A delectable diet of plankton and krill. I just open my mouth wide and in they come. Here, I'll show you. Ah, Max old boy, you may want to have your friends hold on tight," warned Craddock.

Max called Kate and Al to join him at the high point of Craddock's large head. Craddock proceeded to open his huge mouth as the others watched an enormous pool of water swirl in front of them, right into Craddock's mouth. Al eagerly looked for the plankton to see if any might wash up on top of Craddock's back.

"I don't see anythin'. Where's the plankton?" asked Al.

Craddock swallowed the plankton and told Max to move back a bit from the blowholes. He then let go a strong burst of seawater out of his blowholes, freshly drenching his passengers. Max and Kate proceeded to shake the water off their backs, down to their tails, while Al shut his eyes as their spray landed on his already soaked fur.

"Thanks-s-s-s a lot. Sure, I jest love water, yes I do. Why don't ye jest hold on to me tail and drag me alongside?!" said a very perturbed, soggy, hungry Al.

"Well, chap, if you'd like to try the plankton, that's precisely what you need to do. See here, let Max hold your tail while you hang on to my side and get your face in the water. Then open wide and enjoy the sweet delicacy of the sea," encouraged Craddock, following up with a resonating belch.

"But where's the plankton? I don't see anythin'," answered Al.

"It's invisible, old chap. It floats on the surface of the water. Just try it," eagerly exclaimed Craddock.

Al looked at the length of Craddock's large frame and decided that something that feeds such a huge beast must be good.

"Max, grab me tail so I can reach the water. Be careful o' me tail—don't bite too hard," instructed Al.

"Are ye sure ye want ta be doin' this, Al? Plankton may be good for whales, but not for cats, ye know," said Kate.

"I'm so hungry, I could eat a whale," answered Al.

"Max, be a good chap and lower Al down before he has any ideas," said Craddock.

"Aye, methinks yer daft, kitty, but I'll do it," answered Max, knowing full well the power of Al's stomach. He gently took Al's tail into his mouth, frowning as the soggy cat fur covered his tongue.

Al slowly clawed his way down Craddock's side, getting his face near the splashing water. He gingerly opened his mouth wide and placed it into the oncoming current. Al made a pitiful gargling sound as Max held on to the hungry cat's tail. Al's belly appeared to expand before their eyes as he swallowed at least a gallon of seawater. Max pulled Al up, seeing that he'd had enough.

Crinan started laughing as he flew down to get a closer look at Al, whose face was turning as green as Ireland itself. "Wha' a buffoon. I never seen such a cat so hungry as ta try somethin' so daft." He turned and flew up into the air to join Bethoo, who replied, "Oh, the poor dear."

Al slid onto Craddock's back, gagging and coughing up seawater as he faced backward on the whale. Max stifled a laugh when he got a warning look from Kate not to make fun of poor, hungry Al. After Al caught his breath, he spoke.

"How could ye have let me eat such a horrible meal, Max?" said Al, still spitting the salty water out of his mouth. "It were the worst thing I ever tasted, and I've tasted a lot o' things," whimpered Al.

"Me?! Ye were determined ta drink up the sea, lad. Don't be placin' the blame on me for yer worries! I guess ye figured out that plankton is for whales, not cats," said Max, not able to hold in a chuckle.

"Aye, lad, now I know. I think I'm goin' to be sick," moaned Al, who now was looking at the rolling sea swells behind him. His large belly picked up the rhythm of the sea with waves sloshing around inside.

"I do say, old boy, I'm truly sorry it was such a dreadful experience for you. I never considered a land creature trying such a sea feast. I didn't realize it would make you so ill," said Craddock.

Al kept belching up seawater, wishing he had never tried plankton as Craddock continued the long swim across the channel.

CHAPTER 14

The Sea Plan

The sun was high overhead. Max, Kate, and Al had settled in for the journey, resting on Craddock's back and trying to enjoy a period of calm after Al's debacle. Max was thinking about where they were headed, and how the Maker had faithfully provided a way across.

Aye, Ye said ta find the right way. Ye gave me the right answer, but it took me a while ta figure it out. I'm grateful for the thinkin' time. It makes me feel a little smarter than I were, thought Max as he stared up at the fire cloud, grinning.

Kate watched Max and her heart melted as she observed his big smile, thinking of how much he was coming to mean to her, and in such a short time. Al's eyes were closed, and he let out an occasional moan.

Craddock had been swimming for three hours when he began to laugh, and laugh hard, startling Max, Kate, and Al and forcing them to hang on tight.

"Wha' in the name of Pete are ye laughin' at, Cr-r-raddock?" shouted Max over the bellowing whale, his heart dropping with the sudden shaking.

"Do stop, Al! You're killing me, lad!" replied Craddock.

"Me? What did I do?" answered a still queasy Al, almost crying from it all.

"No, Al, not you," Craddock said as he continued to chuckle and rattle his passengers. "I mean Alexander. You rascal—stop tickling me."

Out of nowhere came a creature jumping out of the sea directly over Craddock and the others, giggling as it splashed back into the water on the other side.

"Wha' were that!?" asked Kate.

"Oh, that's my young dolphin friend, Alex. He takes great delight in skimming under my belly, tickling me," explained Craddock, still chuckling as he talked.

The dolphin came alongside Craddock, this time splashing Al by repeatedly slapping his tail fin on the water before submerging beneath the surface. Crinan was laughing from up above again at Al's expense as he watched the scene below.

"AHHHHHHHHHH! MAX! It's out to get me!" cried Al. "I don't think I can get much wetter, or any more scared! I were not meant to be one with the sea."

"Calm down, laddie. 'Tis jest a little dolphin now. He's jest playin' with ye then," Max said, this time not able to withhold a laugh.

Alex jumped up and over again before coming alongside the whale-weary friends for a better view. "What are you guys doing riding Craddock?" asked Alex, disappearing again beneath the waves, not waiting for an answer.

A big splash of water came from the opposite side once again drenching Al. Alex giggled and swam up to be eye level with Craddock.

"What's up, Craddock? Who's your friends back there? Especially the funny orange one?" asked Alex, continuing to frolic and swim back and forth around Craddock's large flipper. He was a bundle of pure, boundless energy.

"Just giving these friends a lift across the channel," answered Craddock.

"Whatcha doin' that for?" asked the dolphin, dipping again under the water, not waiting for a reply. He circled around and jumped back over Craddock, just grazing the top of Al's head before landing with another drenching splash. Al felt as if he couldn't hold on much longer before being lost forever in the surrounding sea.

"See here, dear boy, my friends are on a mission to reach the fire cloud. I do say, where are your parents?" asked Craddock.

"Oh, I got a little ahead of them. They're back there somewhere. I just saw your wake and had to check it out," answered Alex before disappearing from view once more.

The young dolphin was nowhere to be seen. Al was shivering with eyes shut again, just bracing for another surprise attack. Max and Kate scanned the water for the little dolphin, but it appeared as if he just vanished. Craddock continued his slow, steady glide through the water as Crinan and Bethoo looked from above.

"I say, do you lovebirds see our little friend?" Craddock asked the gulls.

"Not a trace from up here," answered Bethoo. "Do ye think he were afraid he'd get in trouble with his parents?"

"I sure hope so," said a sour Al, feeling a glimmer of satisfaction as he considered Alex getting punished.

Suddenly two large dolphins emerged at the surface, blowing spray from their blowholes. They swam up near the whale but respectfully kept their distance. Kate admired how elegantly they sliced through the blue water, never having seen such beautiful creatures up close. Their deep gray bodies glistened in the sun as they gracefully swam in arcs on top of the water. They had warm, gentle eyes and curved mouths that seemed kind.

"Well, hello! Splendid to see you two. I do say, Alex is growing into quite the boisterous lad," greeted Craddock.

"Hello, old friend. Yes, we have our hands full with him these days. I hope he didn't cause any trouble," said the father dolphin.

"HA! I'll tell ye what he did," said Al before Kate slapped her paw over his mouth.

"Hush, Al. He's jest a boy, not meanin' any harm. Don't be rude ta his parents. Nothin' happened ta ye but a little splash of water. Shake it off, lad," said Kate with a forceful whispering voice.

Al quickly realized he was the only one attending his pity party and promptly buttoned his lip.

"See here, no harm done, old chap. Just a splash or two you know," Craddock answered with a grin. "I'm transporting these friends. They are following the fire cloud."

Alex popped up beside Craddock, swimming behind his parents, eyeing Al but behaving himself. Al's eyes narrowed as he looked at Alex, daring him to splash and make trouble.

"Are there other creatures following the fire cloud as well?" asked the mother dolphin.

"Craddock got me thinkin' aboot that," said Max. "We left some wolves behind in England an' Craddock were wonderin' if they were tryin' ta get across the channel. I have me doubts that the Maker called *wolves*, but maybe there are other noble beasts in need of passage. How far do ye dolphins travel then?"

"Oh, we go all up and down the ocean boundary, traveling great distances sometimes," answered the dolphins.

"Aye, an' I know Craddock an' his whale friends roam the seas far an' wide. Hmmm," muttered Max.

"Wha' are ye thinkin' then, Max?" asked Kate.

"I'm thinkin' that if the Maker did call other creatures like us, from other lands, it could be they need a way across the great waters an' oceans. The dolphins are swift an' kin reach places quickly an' communicate with the whales. The whale beasties are slow but large an' steady. They kin carry passengers like us. Craddock, do ye think other whales might want ta help carry land creatures like yer doin'?" asked Max.

"RIGHT! Smashing idea, old chap. I do believe you are on to something here, and I know other fellows such as myself would be honored to assist in this endeavor," answered Craddock. "Perhaps the Maker intended to use us sea creatures in this mysterious journey."

"Alr-r-r-ight then. Crinan an' Bethoo, kin ye fly along the coast an' help spot land-bound animals needin' some transport? Dolphin beasties, kin ye swim near the shores an' let the whale beasties know where ta go?" asked Max.

"Aye! We'll do our best then. An' we'll meet up with ye when we all reach the fire cloud," said Crinan as he and Bethoo took flight to soar above the dolphins.

"Thanks, me friends. I'm grateful ta ye. We'll see ye down the journey," answered Max.

Crinan and Bethoo soared up high into the sky, looping in circles as they caught the gusty sea breeze currents above the channel. The dolphins began calling other members of their pod with sonar, and Max saw other fins breaking the surface as more dolphins joined the procession.

Kate beamed with pride at her new beau, watching him take charge and help deliver other creatures.

"Good luck to you all. And Max, I think you've found a way to help many creatures. If you're right and the Maker has called creatures near and far, this could be bigger than we all know. Farewell!" said the father dolphin as he swam alongside and waved his fin to Max, Kate, and Al. He disappeared beneath the waves, along with his family.

"Good riddance," mumbled Al under his breath when he no longer saw the pesky young dolphin.

He had barely uttered those words when out of nowhere Alex burst out of the water and landed next to Al, drenching him once more. Alex stood up tall on the end of his tail, moving backward calling out, "My mom said I forgot to tell you goodbye. So, goodbye!" Alex took off jumping high out of the water as he once again joined the pod of dolphins.

Kate came over to Al. "Oh Al, the wee beast is gone then. All should be quiet now," she said as she attempted to calm the poor cat down.

Al sat there saying nothing for a moment, water dripping from his whiskers, and one eye closed from the sting of salt water. He just looked back at Kate and finally said, "So help me, Kate, I will never ride on the sea again! I thought the land beasties were bad, but this were the worst scare I ever had."

"Be careful of wha' ye say, lad," interrupted Max, now at Kate's side. "Never is a mighty strong word. Ye don't know wha' might be up ahead on the journey," said Max with a grin.

"Buck up then! Maiden voyages just help you get your sea legs to be all the better prepared next time!" said Craddock, trying to affirm the pitiful Al.

82

"Humph. I can't see how things could get any better until me paws are on the Maker's good green earth," replied Al.

"Well lad, ye should be feelin' better real soon then. I think I see land," said Max, looking at the growing shoreline of France.

Kate and Al stood up quickly, joining Max in scanning the horizon and gazing on the far shore. They saw extensive beaches and green hillsides, dotted with fields of yellow.

"How much longer? How much longer?" pleaded Al.

"Oh, I suppose another hour will do," said Craddock.

"Hang on lad, yer almost there," encouraged Max. He continued his thoughts to himself, *Aye, but wha' awaits us on that shore? An' how are we supposed ta land on it? I don't see rock jetties anywhere.*

As Al was experiencing some relief, Max began to worry. If Craddock couldn't get close to shore, how in the world would they make landfall?

CHAPTER 15

The Landing

Max noticed the color of the water change as they neared the shallows off the coast. He looked toward the land and saw the beautiful green grass on the hillside. And of course nice, dry sand at the water's edge. He felt a jolt of energy go through him as they neared the end of their channel crossing. They were landing on a beach called Normandy. Max felt this was a place full of destiny.

Al looked up from his distasteful bath, licking the salt off his fur. "Land! Land! We're almost there. 'Tis the most beautiful sight I ever saw."

"Aye, lad. We're almost there," Max replied, wearing a fake smile for Al's sake. He moved up further on Craddock's head and whispered to him.

"Cr-r-raddock, I think we got a problem."

"I'd say so, dear boy. This is as far as I can go. The tide is high and rushes quickly in to the beach at Normandy, but it will soon retreat. I'm afraid I can't bring you any closer," Craddock explained, trying to keep his voice low. He understood the value of not giving Al unsettling news before it was time. Al's ignorance was bliss for all.

Kate joined Max on Craddock's head, clearly recognizing something was up. She looked back at Al with a smile before whispering to Max, "So, wha' is happenin' then?"

"Seems we have a wee problem, lass. Craddock kin't take us any further inta shore, an' 'tis a bit far for us ta swim," Max said, turning to Kate. Too late—Al was right behind her.

"I knew I shouldn't have gotten on this whale beastie. I should have taken me chances with them wolves. Whatever will we do? I'll be lost forever to the sea!" cried Al.

"Hush, laddie. If ye would stop the whinin' I could think of a way ta get us off Cr-r-raddock an' on ta shore," Max scolded, pacing back and forth on top of the whale.

"Don't even think about callin' any more friends of yours, like dolphins or sea turtles to take us ta shore. I'm done with rides, I tell ye. Done with 'em," cried Al, dramatically holding his paw over his eyes.

84

"Al, old boy, do me the favor and take a step slightly to the right, please," Craddock said, drawing curious looks from Kate and Max.

Al, thinking Craddock might be uncomfortable for some reason, obliged and slowly took a step left.

"Excuse me, old chap, I meant to my right," Craddock corrected.

Al took a step in the other direction.

"Another, if you would. Most kind," Craddock said again.

Al took one more step, his face growing more puzzled. Max, unable to take any more of this strange behavior said, "Craddock, 'tis no time for games . . ."

"Now one step forward, my good man," Craddock said, ignoring Max.

Al obeyed.

"Cr-r-raddock, if ye hadn't noticed we have a situation her-r-re," Max shouted, but before he could complete his sentence—

PPPWOOOOOOOOOOOOOOOSH! The moment Al took the last step forward he positioned himself right over Craddock's blowhole. Al went flying high into the sky.

"AHHHHHHHHHHHHHHH!" Al screamed as he flailed his limbs in midair.

But soon he fell right at the shore's edge in the soft, wet sand. Al started grinning from ear to ear, wet sand all over his face as he scooped up the sand in his arms, trying to give it a hug. He rolled his back in the watery sand, happy to be on land.

Max and Kate were astonished at Al's sudden departure, and started laughing at the humorous scene. They also felt relief. Craddock had figured the best way for them to reach the shore.

"And now Max, would you kindly take the young lady's paw?" Craddock asked. "I believe I can assist you both at the same time."

Max and Kate paused for a moment, then also positioned themselves over the blowholes.

"Craddock, how kin I ever thank ye enough for all ye done? Ye been a gr-r-rand fr-r-riend," said Max.

"I was utterly delighted to help, old boy. I'll be helping others across, I'm sure," replied Craddock.

Kate kissed Craddock on the head, "I'll miss ye. Thanks for everythin'."

"You're welcome, dear lass. And Kate, you and Max be careful once you get to shore. The tide rolls in quickly on this beach. Don't let it catch you," Craddock instructed. "Cheerio now, my merry little band. Go find where that fire cloud leads. Ta-ta."

Craddock then let out another PPPWOOOOOOOOOO-OOOOOSH! Max and Kate went flying into the air on the large spray of water. Kate was laughing, but Max shut his eyes tight, not wanting to see the deep water that they were flying over. The two landed with a thud in the shallow watery sand.

Max and Kate turned to wave at Craddock as he winked his large eye and slapped his tail on the surface of the water to say farewell before sliding back into the depths of the sea.

"There's none like him," Max said as he watched the waters swirl where Craddock went under the waves. He had been the right way indeed.

Max and Kate walked through the soggy, soft sand. The tide was rolling in quickly, and they had quite a distance to cover before reaching dry sand. If they didn't get moving, they could be in trouble. Max and Kate picked up speed, passing Al, who was still rolling around in the wet sand. "Come on now, Al. Get a move on before the water gets ye," said Max, not looking back but striving to get to dry land.

Kate looked back and saw the water coming in even faster. Al wasn't going to be able to outrun the tide if he didn't get up and moving. "Al, get up! Hurry! The sea is comin' in. If ye don't get movin', it's goin' ta take ye back out to sea."

Those magic words woke Al out of his dreamy glee. He sat up and saw a surge of rushing water nipping at his paws. He jumped up and started running. His paws were sinking in the sand at first but finally, he made his way to firmer sand. Kate grinned at Max as Al came bolting past both of them. Al was not about to let the sea reclaim him. Up he went onto the dry sand. But he didn't stop running. Up he went to the green hillside. Up, up, up to the top of the cliff he went, not stopping to look where he was. Al disappeared from view into the countryside.

Max and Kate came out of the water and shook off their wet coats. Max collapsed on the warm, dry sand and exclaimed, "Ye-hee! We made it, lass." He proceeded to roll in the sand, wiggling his back as if to become one with the land once more.

Kate grinned and said, "Aye, we did, an' it's all thanks ta ye, me brave Max. I'll follow ye anywhere."

Max stopped rolling and looked at Kate. They sat for what felt like an eternity, just looking at each other, feeling gratitude for their safe journey, feeling the warmth of the sun warming their wet fur, but feeling even greater warmth from the love that now grew inside their hearts for one another.

"Kate, I never known a lass so strong an' beautiful. Ye might think this is too early for me ta ask. We haven't known each other long, but Bonnie Katelyn Maitland, would ye think aboot bein' me forever lass?" asked Max, eyes full of warmth and hope.

Kate's heart leapt. Max was asking her to be his! She looked at this brave Scottie dog who had captured her heart. "Aye, me love. I will be yer forever lass. Maximillian Braveheart the Bruce, I do!"

The two dogs put their heads together and nuzzled in the warmth of their love. Up above, the fire cloud stopped to hover over them as if approving of this new pair of forever loves. Max and Kate had landed safely on the other side of the sea. Their hearts had landed safely in the love of each other. And all was right with their world.

87

CHAPTER 16

Eden

N oah stoked the fire again, adding a few more sticks as his mind raced. His father had told him so many remarkable things today. He was overwhelmed with the responsibility before him. His great father Adam had named the animals. Now, Noah would be responsible for saving them.

"I must get back to work while there is still light. And you need to rest," said Noah as he knelt down by Lamech.

"There is so much more to tell, that I must tell," Lamech protested.

Noah adjusted the blankets over his aged father. "I'll return in a little while, father."

Lamech grabbed Noah's arm and shook his head, "I must tell you—"

As Adam and young Lamech continue walking down a wooded path, Adam suddenly stops.

"Why did we stop, father?"

Adam takes a deep breath and sighs. "I've not been here in a very long time."

"But where are we?" Lamech persists, looking around.

"We're at the beginning, Lamech. We're at the Garden," Adam responds, a sad look in his eyes.

Lamech's mouth drops open in disbelief. He whispers, "Will He be here? Will He walk with me like He walked with you?"

Adam doesn't answer.

"Great father, will He be with us?" Lamech continued.

Adam looks down into Lamech's pleading eyes. "He is always with us."

"But will He walk with us?" the young boy asks.

Adam sighs once more and looks back toward the Garden. "It's your choice."

He motions with his walking stick to move onward. Lamech follows. Slowly. Cautiously. The young boy whispers, "I don't understand."

"There are rules, young Lamech. Observe from a distance. We may approach but be careful not to get too near," Adam explains.

Before Lamech can respond, Adam has made his way around the outcropping of rocks and there before them is the Garden of Eden. A vast expanse of green like Lamech has never before seen. Flowers of every kind imaginable in bloom. Full healthy shrubs line the paths. A crystal clear river runs through the Garden, its banks flanked by gently swaying reeds, humming in the wind.

At the grand entrance to the magnificent Garden stands a fierce-looking angel wielding a fiery sword. He swings it back and forth as a skilled swordsman, sparks flying each time as he cuts the air.

Lamech stands in awe, never having seen such an incredible sight, when a pair of hummingbirds flit around his head. The boy laughs and jumps while Adam laughs with delight as the young boy half-heartedly tries to catch them. But Adam's laughter turns into caution as Lamech has inadvertently approached the entrance to the Garden.

Lamech yells in pain and clutches his face. He races back to Adam, throwing his arms around the old man, burying his face in Adam's robe.

"*Lamech! Let me see,*" *Adam says urgently.*

Lamech slowly raises his face and looks into the eyes of Adam. A seared mark appears under Lamech's right eye. He had neared the angel and suffered the consequences of the sparks from the fiery sword.

"*I didn't mean to, father.*"

Adam drops his head and clutches the young boy. "I understand, Lamech," the old man says as he looks at the Garden where he once dwelled. A tear runs down Adam's cheek. "I understand."

The angel continues to wave his sword and the hummingbirds continue their play.

PART TWO

LIZ AND THE
FIRE CLOUD

CHAPTER 17

The Garden

The little hummingbird buzzed from one flower to the next, wings moving so fast—almost imperceptible. The sun shone on his metallic green feathers, making them iridescent in the bright light. His throat was the color of sun-drenched rubies and his needle-like beak effortlessly sucked up the sweet nectar of the flowers. His head darted up and around between sips so he could keep an eye on his surroundings as he drank. As quickly as his beak plunged into an open blossom, he was up and out of it again, flying sideways, backward, forward, up and down as he danced among the flowers and sampled the variety of wonderful blooms available in this beautiful garden.

A gentle breeze was blowing. All was calm. Not a sound was heard but the soft mouse-like squeaks coming from the little hummingbird as he called his mate to join him. She was slightly larger in size, measuring three and a half inches long, but her colors were not as deep as her mate's. The green on her tail and wings was not shiny and bright, but with white on the very tip of her tail. Her throat was a dappled gray, lacking the impressive ruby red of her mate. She flew to his side, cheering him by her loveliness.

"Rosie, come try the trumpet creeper over here—it's delicious." said Rudy as he twittered around his mate with enthusiasm. "We've got to keep up our energy, so drink up, *bonita* love."

"Hmmmm, *muy bueno*. I'm hungry after our long flight over the great sea. I still don't see how we made it," said Rosie as her slender beak tasted the long tubular flower. She closed her eyes in delight as she sipped the nectar.

"*Sí*, I didn't know we could fly that far. It seems impossible now. Argentina to Brazil is one thing—Brazil to wherever we are across the great sea is another. I wonder where we are anyway," said Rudy, zipping over to some petunias that were lower to the ground.

"*Monsieur*, you are in France, of course. Where else could you be with such delicious food as this, no?" answered a gruff, deep female voice with an exaggerated French accent.

Rudy and Rosie met in the air, hovering together over the garden to see who had spoken to them. It was a hen. A big, fat, white hen looking quite pompous, almost as if she had eaten her fill of this garden as well. She had red plumage on her head, eyes, and cheeks. The feathers on her back and wings were a deep brown, and her hind feathers a golden yellow. She held her chin up proudly as she spoke.

"*Buenos días, señora. Sí*, this is a wonderful garden and we are enjoying it very much. I'm Rudy and this is my wife Rosie," answered Rudy as he and Rosie hovered around the hen.

"*Bonjour. Je m'appelle . . .*" and it was then that the hen noticed they didn't understand a word she was saying.

"Pardon, nice to meet you. My name is Henriette. What could possibly have caused you to fly all the way from Argentina?" asked the hen, clucking her tongue as she considered the distance these two tiny birds had flown.

"We've been following the fire cloud up there. We heard the Maker say to 'Come,' so we did. It was a long journey over the great sea, but we had to follow His Voice. We don't know why we would be called to make such a long journey, but we are here," answered Rudy.

"*Bien sûr*—of course. The owner of this garden has been studying the fire cloud. We all heard the same Voice ourselves. I do not understand what this means, but Mademoiselle will figure it out," answered Henriette.

"Mademoiselle?" asked Rosie. "She owns this garden?"

"*Oui.* Mademoiselle Brilliante. She owns and tends this garden with great care. She is very smart and studies things very carefully. My husband Jacques and I live nearby the Mademoiselle. We help her keep watch for pests that would harm her garden—her 'masterpiece' as she calls it. She is quite proud of it, no?"

Rudy and Rosie looked around the garden. It was perfectly manicured with straight rows of plants aligned in order by type of plant. There were flowers, herbs, and vegetables, all healthy and robust. Clearly this garden had been well planned and well nurtured. It was a masterpiece of beauty indeed. At the edge of the garden was a tall border of sunflowers, towering above the masterpiece below.

"I see, but you said you have also heard the Voice?" questioned Rudy excitedly.

"*Mais oui*, but yes. Mademoiselle has been studying the fire cloud, and says we are to leave soon," answered the hen as she sadly looked around the garden. "Mademoiselle does not wish to leave her garden. It has been her favorite project, so she has hesitated on deciding when we will go."

"When you leave, would it be possible for Rosie and me to join you since we are headed in the same direction?" asked Rudy.

"*Je ne sais pas* . . . I don't know. I will have to ask Mademoiselle," said Henriette with uncertainty. "She is the one who makes the decisions of what is best. We will ask her, no?"

As the three birds were delightfully enjoying conversation in the garden, out of nowhere came a blundering beast, causing alarm and mayhem just with his entrance. It was Al.

"FOOD! REAL FOOD!" said Al as he ran past the hen and the hummingbirds and went diving into a pile of greens. He was oblivious to anyone or anything other than food. He proceeded to stuff his mouth full of the aromatic herbs. Tears of joy streamed down his cheeks from the fact that he finally had something to eat other than plankton, salt water, and sand.

Unfortunately, the fuzzy, gray-green herb plant that Al ate first was catnip. As Al bruised the leaves with his big paws, an irresistible oil was released that drove him crazy with excitement. Al proceeded to trample all the neighboring plants as he went on a feeding frenzy. He ran over to the cabbage and ate several leaves before trouncing to the nearby thyme. Next were the carrots and the chives. Al was a whirlwind of destruction, finally jumping on top of a tomato plant, bringing it crashing down, splattering red, juicy tomatoes all over his orange fur. He looked like a big fat tomato himself. Throughout his garden rampage, Al didn't hear Henriette yelling at him.

"*SORTEZ! SORTEZ!* GET OUT! GET OUT! WHAT IS WRONG WITH YOU? *LE CHAT EST FOU!* THE CAT IS CRAZY!" screamed the very ruffled hen.

Rudy and Rosie hovered nearby, watching this drama unfold and growing worried about Mademoiselle's garden. By the time Al had finished trampling everything, there was not one plant standing that had not sustained some damage. The garden was utterly destroyed, except for the row of sunflowers at the edge of the garden. They remained tall and untouched.

Al, finally flattened on his back and looking like he would be sick, noticed the big, irritated hen, who continued her tirade of mixed French and English exclamations toward him. The hen moved closer until her beak was two inches from Al's nose as she let him have it. He quivered with dread. What had he done? Al looked around at the destruction of the once beautiful garden. Branches were bent, plants were uprooted, and dirt covered the bruised flowers.

"Ah, sorry miss, I didn't mean to ruin yer garden," a submissive, weak Al uttered.

Henriette would hear none of it. She continued ranting and raving, flapping her wings to add emphasis to her remarks, pointing out each and every plant Al had destroyed.

"Just wait until Mademoiselle sees this! She will be *très malheureux*—very unhappy!" scolded Henriette.

Al couldn't get a word in edgewise so he gave up and just laid there, taking a verbal beating from this hen and wondering who the "mad moiselle" was and what she would do to him when she saw what he had done. A name beginning with "mad" had to belong to a mean creature. A feeling of fresh fear came over Al, greater than any bat, wolf, or sea beastie had given him before. He knew he was doomed.

Rudy and Rosie saw another bird approach the ranting hen who towered over the cowering cat. It was an elegant rooster, strutting along to see what had happened. He was much taller than Henriette, with beautiful, metallic blue-green tail feathers that swayed as he strutted. His neck seemed to propel him forward as he stuck it out with every step. He, too, had red plumage on the top of his head and cheeks, but had deep brown feathers with a touch of white right below his eyes.

"Henriette, what has happened?" asked her husband, Jacques the rooster, loud enough for her to hear as he perused the garden.

"What has happened? Can't you *see* what has happened? This crazy cat has destroyed Mademoiselle's garden, that's what has happened!" angrily replied Henriette before turning her rage back on Al for another round of accusations.

Jacques looked at poor Al. The rooster sympathized with the humbled cat lying at the feet of his wailing wife. Tomato juice dripped off his whiskers, sprigs of lavender stuck to his fur, and his eyes were filled with terror. "*Quel dommage.* What a pity," said Jacques. But he wasn't referring to the garden. He was referring to Henriette's diatribe of Al. He knew, all too well, what it was like to be henpecked by Henriette. He had lived with it for close to five years now.

"Henriette, why not stop your yelling? It is not going to fix Mademoiselle's garden. I think this cat has heard your message loud and clear, and I'm sure he is sorry, no?" Jacques said to Henriette.

Al looked at Jacques with tears welling up in his eyes, "Aye, aye! I tried to say I were sorry but I couldn't seem to get the lass to hear me."

"Ah, *oui.* I know the feeling well, *mon ami,*" Jacques said to Al with a sympathetic voice.

"I can't believe what I'm hearing. You're actually feeling sorry for this . . . this . . . imbecile?! *C'est ridicule!* Nonsense!" scowled Henriette.

"Well, it's evident to me that this cat didn't mean to destroy the garden. Now he feels ashamed for what he has done. Of course, he will need to make amends to Mademoiselle, but it is her garden. There is nothing we can do to fix it now. Let her handle this," said Jacques with a firm voice.

"You seem to forget that Mademoiselle asked us to watch over her garden. How dare you suggest I let this cat off so easily!? You're as crazy as this cat!" Henriette fired back at her mate.

Jacques shrugged and looked at Al, "Ah, well, I tried, *mon ami.* My wife is quite the stern one. You will have to endure her until Mademoiselle comes." The rooster leaned in close to whisper in his ear, "And I would pray that she comes soon."

Al's momentary hope for an ally in this battle melted away as Jacques abandoned him to his wife's rage. Meanwhile, his stomach ached. He had eaten way too much, and his stomach lashed out at him as much as Henriette.

CHAPTER 18

A Brilliante Encounter

The quiet hummingbirds looked over and noticed a petite, jet-black cat sitting up on a ledge, her back to the garden, bathed in the warm orange glow from the fire cloud, listening. She furrowed her brow in response to what she heard.

"*Oui*, You want me to leave my garden," the petite cat said. She paused a moment. "You know how hard I have worked on it. I carefully planned each row. I tilled it, planted it, weeded it, and nurtured it. And now I am enjoying the fruits of my labor, no? Please do not fault me for wishing to enjoy it."

The small cat sat for a moment longer, listening before responding. "*Mais oui*. Yes, Maker, we will gather the seeds. *Oui. Je comprends*. I understand."

The cat then turned and gazed at the garden below. She just sat there, watching the scene with deep golden eyes, studying all the players involved, observing the condition of the garden, her tail twitching from side to side as if perturbed. Yet she appeared calm and collected. Rudy and Rosie buzzed over to where the cat sat, asking if she knew the Mademoiselle and how she would react when she discovered her garden was destroyed.

"*Oui*, I know her quite well," was all the cat said in reply as she looked at the two hummingbirds with great interest. "Your accents—Spanish, I believe?" she inquired as she began to walk down the ledge, jumping onto the path below that led into the jumbled mess of the garden. Rudy and Rosie flew after her, hovering just above her ears. The cat's ears twitched back as if being lightly touched by the breeze their little wings made.

"*Sí, señorita*, we just flew in from Argentina. My name is Rudy and this is my wife, Rosie."

The petite cat came closer to the hen, the rooster, and the pitiful orange cat.

"Argentina? *Oooh la la.* This is a great distance for ones so small to fly. *C'est impossible.*" the cat replied as she kept walking.

"Oh, but it's true. We heard the Maker call us to follow the fire cloud and somehow we made it across the great sea," Rosie said.

The cat stopped in her tracks and looked at the tiny birds with a wrinkled brow. She tilted her head to one side as she studied them, yet said nothing. Onward she walked as the little birds quietly followed behind, looking at each other and shrugging their tiny shoulders. She stopped from time to time, inspecting the damage to various plants, shaking her head with a "pfft" muttered under her breath.

Jacques looked up and saw the cat walking toward them. He walked over to meet her as Henriette continued to scold Al. Al didn't realize there were so many ways to tell someone they had done something wrong. He felt heartsick as well as stomach sick.

"*Je regrette.* Your garden is no more, but Henriette has scolded the one who did this," said Jacques to the cat.

Rudy and Rosie looked at each other and said, "Mademoiselle?"

"*Oui.* Allow me to introduce *Mademoiselle Lizette Brilliante*," said Jacques to the hummingbirds.

The black cat walked over to where Henriette continued to rake Al over the coals and said, "*C'est assez,* Henriette. That's enough."

Henriette turned to see Mademoiselle sitting calmly, looking directly beyond her to Al, who was crouched down and shivering in the dirt.

"Mademoiselle, you see what *le chat fou* has done to your precious garden. I saw the whole thing," Heniette blurted out in her gruff tone.

Liz looked at Henriette and replied, "*Oui*, Henriette. You have done a fine job of scolding the crazy cat that did this. I will handle it from here."

Jacques looked smugly at Henriette, who ruffled her feathers once more before walking over to the rooster, still mumbling under her breath in French. Al's eyes were closed. He was afraid to look at the "mad moiselle" who surely would be a creature to be reckoned with.

"M-m-m-mad . . . moiselle, I can explain. Please do not be angry with me! I'm jest a tired, hungry fool o' a kitty who needed somethin' to eat. Yer garden were so delightfully captivatin' that I jest jumped right in and all o' a sudden I were tearin' the place apart. I dunnot know what got into me, lass! I'm sorry," groveled Al, eyes still shut as he trembled with remorse and fear.

"*Nepeta Cataria*," is all Mademoiselle replied with a calm, certain voice.

Al stopped shivering, daring to open one eye to see what the mad moiselle looked like after answering him with such a strange word and in such a calm manner. There before him stood not a horrifying, mad creature, but a gorgeous, black, petite female cat with deep golden eyes.

"There's no need to call me names, lass," Al said, holding his side. The sight of this incredibly beautiful creature calmed his heart. She did not appear to be mad, nor likely to destroy him on the spot.

"*Nepeta Cataria* is what got into you and caused you to become *le chat fou* or "crazy cat". It's the horticultural term for catnip. This is a wonderful herb that all cats love, but should be taken in moderation. If a cat eats too much, he will go wild. Which is precisely what you have done," responded Mademoiselle, in almost a matter-of-fact tone.

Henriette was incensed. "Mademoiselle, why are you not furious with him?! Aren't you going to continue scolding him?"

"*Non*. You've scolded him enough for both of us, I think. *Oui*, I am upset, of course. My masterpiece is destroyed, no? But the destroyer has been scolded, and he is sorry. Further scolding will not accomplish anything. This was not an intentional act, but resulted from too much catnip. And as you will see, there are consequences for such poor behavior," answered Mademoiselle.

Jacques continued to smile smugly, taking great satisfaction from seeing his henpecking wife put in her place. Finally, Henriette was speechless.

Mademoiselle looked at Al's pitiful condition. Despite his sloppy appearance and his cowardly manner, there was something endearing about him. He was vulnerable and dopey, yet humble and genuinely sweet.

"What is your name, *Monsieur*?" Mademoiselle asked Al as she calmly sat and studied him.

Al, catching his breath, looked up at this mystifying cat, and said, "Albert Aloysius I'm sorry."

Mademoiselle looked at Al with doubt, "Pardon? Your name is Albert Aloysius I'm Sorry? What kind of name is this?"

"Oh, no, no, no, lass. Only the first part is me name. The last part is how I feel after ruinin' yer lovely garden. I feel so sorry and sick, and I jest want to make it up to ye."

"Ah *oui*, I understand how you must be feeling. But your name—Albert Aloysius—do you know what it means? I can tell you are Irish, but your name is not," said the black cat.

"Me mum never told me what it meant. She only said I were named for a long, lost uncle who she loved," replied a humble Al.

"Your first name means 'noble' and your last name means 'famous warrior'," explained the cat.

Al looked down at his paws. "Well, I'm not livin' up to me name. I'm a nobody, fraidy worrier."

The black cat walked over to Al, lifted his chin with her paw, saying, "Sometimes we must grow into our names, no? Do not dismiss yourself yet, *mon ami*. The fact that you feel bad for what you've done means you have character and integrity to admit your mistake and a desire to make it right. Many creatures do not do this. So, I believe you are at least noble. Give yourself time for the other meanings to grow."

Al smiled at this beautiful cat. She not only wasn't going to destroy him, instead she was lifting him up to a place he had never been before in his heart. He was noble! This cat whose garden he destroyed believed him to be noble. Was he dreaming?

"Thank ye, lass. Ah, I mean, uh, Mad Moiselle. Ye don't live up to yer name either, but in this case it's a good thing, methinks. Ye don't seem mad at all," replied Al with a heart full of gratitude.

The black cat looked at Al and began to giggle. Henriette looked at Jacques in disbelief. Never had she known Mademoiselle to laugh like this. In fact, Mademoiselle never showed much emotion at all. She was always so intellectual. Why was she acting so strange? Henriette was ready to open her mouth when Jacques got right in her face and told her not to peep a word. Rudy and Rosie grinned at the turn of events below. Something lovely was happening despite the destruction of the garden.

"Oh, Albert, you make me laugh. Mademoiselle, not 'mad moiselle'! It is the French term for your word 'lass.' It is not my name, nor does it mean I am mad," said the black cat, still laughing as she spoke.

Al, feeling silly, laughed anyway at himself. "Aye, maybe I am '*le chat fou*'? What is yer name then, lass?"

"I am Lizette Brilliante, but you may call me Liz," replied the black cat with a smile.

Henriette jabbed Jacques in the side, "Mademoiselle never told us to call her 'Liz.' But then this imbecile comes crashing through

103

her garden and she laughs and tells him to call her by her first name. *Je ne comprends pas.*"

"It is not important for you to understand. Nor is it any of your business, Henriette. Now be quiet!" said a firm Jacques, ruffling his tail feathers to finally assert his authority over his mate.

"Aye, lass, 'tis a beautiful name. What does it mean?" asked Al.

"*Merci.* My first name means 'the Maker's promise' and my last name means 'illuminated' or 'bright.' In other words, 'intelligent,'" replied Liz.

"Well it is true ye are a very smart lass—the smartest I've ever met," said Al, feeling better in his heart all the time, but feeling far worse in his belly.

"Albert, you are looking as green as Ireland itself. Let me get you something to eat," suggested Liz.

"Oh no, lass! Me belly feels like it could explode, and part o' me wishes it would. I can't eat anythin' more," said Al, holding his stomach.

Liz walked over to the edge of the garden and pulled some leaves off a plant that had been trampled, but not eaten. She carried them over to Al and laid them gently in his lap.

"*Mentha X Piperita.* Peppermint. Eat just a small amount to ease your stomach. Then rest a while. Later we will discuss this mess," said Liz as she looked forlornly around her once magnificent garden.

Liz slowly walked away from Al, up and down the rows she had so carefully planted. Henriette followed Liz, uttering suggestions for how Al should be dealt with. Liz politely ignored the bossy hen, examining each plant and studying what could be salvaged. Rudy and Rosie hovered above the two, but remained silent. Jacques walked over to Al.

"Go ahead, *mon ami.* Eat it. Mademoiselle knows what is best," said Jacques with warm encouragement before turning to join the others.

Al took the peppermint and slowly lifted it to his mouth. The last thing he wanted to do was eat another bite, but he felt he had better do what Liz said. As he slowly chewed the mint, the sick feeling in his stomach eased. His eyelids drooped, and he soon fell into a deep slumber. He dreamed of being a warrior fighting off mighty beasties . . . wielding a carrot.

CHAPTER 19

The French Connection

Max and Kate were so wrapped up in each other that it took some time for them to notice that Al wasn't around. Love has a way of blinding hearts to the things that would take away from moments such as this. The two dogs were laughing and talking about the mystery of how they met, and what their future might hold. Time seemed to stand still, but the sun overhead did not. It was late afternoon before it dawned on Kate that there was a reason why their time together was so perfect. Al was missing.

"Max, I forgot all aboot Al. We haven't seen him in hours. Where could he be?" said an anxious Kate.

"Yer right, me love. Ah, not ta worry. He wouldn't go very far alone. We'll find him. An' I guess we'd best find some food then. Kin I find me sweet lass a bite ta eat?" said Max reassuringly with a grin.

"Aye, dear Max. Let's go see where the kitty is. How I would love some greens ta nibble," replied Kate.

Max picked up his reed, and he and Kate looked around before heading in the direction where Al had run up the side of the cliff. When they reached the top of the hill, they looked back over the sparkling sea channel they crossed, amazed at how the Maker had delivered them from England. They couldn't believe how far they had come and were relieved that the fire cloud had stopped, giving them time to rest.

Max's large head moved back and forth through the swaying field grass, his nose sniffing and snorting as he walked. Suddenly he stopped, sniffed intensely, popped his head up and exclaimed, "Got him, Kate!" Max had picked up Al's scent.

Kate trotted behind Max as he led the way. France was indeed beautiful and romantic as well. The dogs walked through fields of yellow flowers, munching a few along the way. The flowers had a distinct taste unlike anything they had tasted before. Kate looked at the blue sky above and the glowing yellow field below, marveling at the setting in which she followed Max. She felt like she could fly, her heart was so happy.

Al's scent carried them zigzagging across the meadow, typical of Al in a food foraging mode. Max and Kate chuckled as they looped around and around and back and forth, envisioning Al going before them. Soon they reached the edge of the meadow that narrowed near a high wall of green shrubs leading to a path. They followed the path that was bordered by thick, dark green hedgerows on either side. Before Max started feeling small from looking skyward, he saw an opening up ahead.

Max and Kate came to a garden. This garden was a mess, clearly not one that was well cared for—but wait. These plants were recently destroyed and uprooted. What kind of creature could have caused this? Max furrowed his brow, as he grew worried about Al. What if Al had encountered the beast that had destroyed this garden? Max went trotting down the rows of the garden. Al's scent was everywhere.

"Ah, lass, I'm worried aboot Al. A beast must have chased him all around this garden as he were tryin' ta run away," said Max to Kate.

107

But Kate wasn't there. She wasn't behind him. He didn't see her anywhere. Where was she? Had the garden beast gotten to Kate?

"KATE! KATE! Where are ye, lass?" shouted Max.

Max listened and heard her distinct laughter coming from behind a row of sunflowers standing tall on the far border of the garden. Relieved, Max trotted toward the sound of Kate's voice. He walked around the tall flowers stretching to kiss the sun, their thick stalks supporting the huge blossoms of golden yellow petals with black-seeded centers.

Max peeked around a flower stalk and saw Kate, her back to him. She was talking to someone, giggling about something. What could be so funny? Had Kate found Al? Just then a pair of hummingbirds grazed Max's head, lighting on a nearby flower stalk.

"Kate, who are ye talkin' ta? I were worried the garden beastie got ye!" said Max firmly.

When Kate turned around Max could see a small black cat in front of her. "Max, Al is the garden beastie! He is the one who did all this damage an' destroyed this nice cat's garden," explained Kate.

"Then why are ye laughin'? Seems ta me ye'd be so mad at that fat cat ye'd give him a r-r-real piece of yer mind!" replied Max, feeling relieved but mad about Al at the same time.

"Oh, I'm not laughin' at the destruction of the garden, dear. Liz were tellin' me how Al thought she were mad since her name begins with Mad— 'Mademoiselle.' He were terrified of her. An' that were after a big hen scolded him," replied Kate.

Max looked at this petite, black cat and chuckled at the thought of Al being terrified of her name, much less her frame. "I see wha' ye mean, lass."

"Max, allow me ta introduce Mademoiselle Lizette Brilliante," said Kate with a sparkle in her eye.

"*Enchanté*, Max. Please call me Liz," said the cat as she walked over to greet Max.

"Nice ta meet ye, lass. I'm r-r-real sorry aboot yer garden. Al got away from us an' we didn't know where he were. It looks like he jest went crazy," said Max.

"*Oui*, that he did. But he is very sorry. In more ways than one," replied Liz as she, Max, and Kate looked over the garden.

"Aye, he better be sorry, lass. Where is he anyway?" asked Max.

"He is asleep over in the far side of the garden, under a lavender bush. He felt quite ill after eating so much. I gave him some peppermint and told him to rest," replied Liz.

Kate noticed a slight glimmer in Liz's eyes as she talked about Al. She and Max were amazed at how calm this cat was after such a terrible thing as losing her garden.

"Kin I ask ye why ye don't act mad then, lass? Yer takin' this all in a gr-r-rand way," said Max.

"Ah *oui*, I am, how you say, 'put out,' no? But there is nothing I can do to fix this now. Albert did not mean to destroy my garden. Besides, this is the very thing I needed," answered Liz.

Max and Kate exchanged questioning looks, wondering what Liz meant.

Liz continued, seeing their confusion. "It is difficult for me to leave my garden. After working so long on my masterpiece it is only logical that I would wish to enjoy it. I also do not wish to leave this garden to fall into disrepair. Now, those reasons no longer exist. It is logical for me to go now." The petite black cat picked up a bruised flower and held it to her nose. "I can now follow the fire cloud."

Max and Kate felt a new surge of excitement. The Maker had called Liz as well.

Liz began pulling a few weeds around the sunflowers as she said, "I assume you two are following the fire cloud from Scotland, as well?"

"AYE! Yer a smart kitty, I must say, lass. Quite a far cry from Al," said Max.

"Al is followin' with us," said Kate to Liz with a knowing grin.

109

"*Sí!* So are we," piped in the hummingbirds as they flew over to light on the sunflower stalk where Liz was grooming the ground.

"And so are my hen and rooster friends. We have all been called by the Maker—all eight of us," observed Liz.

"Do ye have any idea wha' this could be aboot then?" Max asked Liz.

"Hmmm . . . I'm still studying the facts. Tell me, do you know of any other creatures called by the Maker?" asked Liz. She continued to inspect each and every sunflower stalk as she waited on an answer.

"Aye, our seagull friends, Crinan an' Bethoo, have been called as well," quickly answered Kate.

"But where are these friends now?" asked Liz. She snapped her front paw out in front of her and began licking it to clean off the dirt from her weeding as she listened to Max.

"Ye see, lass, we crossed the sea channel on a whale ta reach France. I were thinkin' there might be other creatures who were needin' a way across water that were also called by the Maker. The seagulls are helpin' ta find other creatures on the shore who need ta cross. They'll let the dolphins know, an' the dolphins will get the whale beasties ta pick them up an' carry them across," explained Max.

"Interesting. Tell me, *mon ami*, what do you know of the sea creatures? Are they following the fire cloud?" Liz asked as she began to wash her face with her clean paw.

"That be the str-r-rangest part. Me friend, Craddock the whale, is a gr-r-rand beastie—one of the finest I know. But the Maker did not speak a word ta him. 'Tis a mystery ta me," answered Max.

"An' don't forget the dolphins, dear. They weren't called ta follow the fire cloud either," Kate joined in.

"Aye, no sea creature we met were called," said Max, hoping for an explanation or an insight from Liz.

"Hmmm. Were there any other creatures you encountered on your journey that were not called?" asked Liz.

"There were two wolves that chased Al down the beach an' looked like they wanted ta get on Craddock an' ride across the channel with us," said Kate.

"What happened?" asked Liz.

"We left the wolves pacing on the rocks. Max didn't think they would be called by the Maker, bein' such mean beasties," explained Kate.

Max then felt a lump in his throat as he thought of Gillamon. "I have a dear friend who helped me ta understand that it were the Maker callin' me, an' he is the one who told me the fire cloud had come. But he weren't called hisself. Gillamon is an old mountain goat, an' is not well. He could never have made the journey," said Max sadly, lowering his head and looking away as he remembered how sick Gillamon had been.

Liz ceased washing her face and stared intently at Max for a moment, not saying a word. When he looked back up at her, their eyes locked for a moment. Liz seemed to be studying Max and all he had said. He felt as if she was peering into his mind and his heart.

"I see," said Liz as she stood up and began walking to the other side of the garden.

"Wha' do ye see?" Max called after Liz. Turning to Kate, he said, "She sounds like Gillamon, Kate! He did this ta me all the time."

Liz didn't respond, but kept walking with tiny, ordered steps down the path, tail up in the air, sun shining on her black fur as she sauntered. Rudy and Rosie buzzed over to Max and Kate as they looked at each other, deciding to just follow this little cat to wherever she was headed.

111

CHAPTER 20

A Pattern Emerges

L iz stopped to lift up a broken blue iris, shaking her head saying, "pfft" as she looked at the mass of blue and gold flowers now lying on the ground. "*Quel dommage*, the beautiful *fleur-de-lis* is lost."

Liz left the flowers and continued walking toward the far side of the garden, calling, "Henriette. Jacques. Come here, *s'il vous plaît!*"

Rudy and Rosie hovered above Max and Kate as they walked, explaining, "Henriette is the mean hen that scolded Al for destroying Liz's garden. Jacques is her rooster husband."

Liz stopped and turned to Max. "May I have a word alone with you, *mon ami?*"

"Certainly, lass," said Max as he winked reassuringly at Kate, who told Rudy and Rosie to join her down the path.

Liz sat down and invited Max to join her. They sat next to a wounded plant with red heart-shaped blooms on a stalk of blue-green leaves. Max waited, not saying a word as he watched Liz inspect this once beautiful flower, knowing that she must be struggling with the demise of something so delicate that she had carefully cultivated. He had watched her go silently with a heavy heart about the garden.

"*Dicentra*. How appropriate, no?" Liz finally said. She saw Max look at her, his head cocked to one side, not understanding what she meant. "Pardon, *Dicentra* is the horticultural name for this flower, but you may know it as Bleeding Heart."

"Aye, lass. I be truly sorry for the sadness ye feel. Gillamon once told me that gardenin' kin be painful," said Max in sympathy.

Liz looked up at Max, "How so? What did Gillamon say?"

"Well, he said a good gardener must prune the plants he cares for ta help them grow stronger. It may be painful for the plant, but it's necessary ta get rid of the branches that keep it from bein' all it were meant ta be. It may even look cruel when the gardener cuts the branches down ta where the plant looks like nothin' but a stump. But a wise gardener knows there is more inside that plant waitin' ta burst out."

"Hmmm . . . Gillamon was right. Pruning is a necessary part of good gardening. But I don't see how that applies here to my garden. Albert wasn't pruning, but destroying. It wasn't for the good of the garden, but for the good of a hungry, crazed cat," Liz replied, not emotionally, but with a very rational tone of voice.

113

"If ye look at it on the surface, aye, that's wha' happened. But ye yerself said losin' yer garden helped ta make yer decision ta leave an' follow the fire cloud a bit easier," answered Max.

"What are you saying, Max?" asked Liz.

"Perhaps the Maker were the gardener, an' ye were the plant needin' the prunin' ta get ye movin'," answered Max, not sure how this intelligent cat would respond.

Liz looked at Max thoughtfully but did not say anything right away. "Those are indeed wise words, *mon ami*. There may be some truth to your hypothesis, but I have to look at what happened logically. As I explained, Albert destroyed my garden because he first ate the catnip, which induced a predictable behavior for a cat. Now the logical thing to do is to proceed and leave this place," answered Liz.

"Well, they weren't my words, lass. I'm jest repeatin' wha' Gillamon told me once when I were havin' a rough go of it. Don't ye have faith that the Maker kin allow things ta happen that are for yer good?" asked Max.

"I believe in the Maker, of course. It would be foolish not to. There is too much evidence of His existence, no? But I must be able to explain things logically. I need things to make sense so there is order. And I've found there is a logical explanation for everything that happens," answered Liz in response, putting her petite nose in a bloom to smell the fading fragrance.

"Then ye must be smarter than I thought there, kitty lass. That's a pretty tall order ye live by. I couldn't begin ta try an' explain everythin'. But in a way, it must be harder for ye," said Max, moving from a chuckle to a thoughtful tone.

"How so?" Liz said, looking him in the eye.

"Well, Gillamon told me that ye kin never know everythin' an' livin' with faith in the Maker is the only way ta have any peace aboot things. If ye have ta explain everythin', that doesn't leave much r-r-room for faith," said Max.

Liz wrinkled her small brow as she thought about what Max said. "Well, when the day comes when I abandon intellect for faith, that's the day that amazing things will truly happen. If I can't explain it, then I'll just have to believe it in faith, no?" Liz said.

"Okay, lass. We'll jest see. We'll jest see," Max chuckled.

"Now, on to more immediate matters. From what I can tell, you are clearly the guardian of this little group that has traveled from Scotland. It is evident that you are brave and smart to have figured out a way across the sea channel," said Liz.

Max tried to interrupt and say he found the way by praying to the Maker, but Liz kept going.

"You are a formidable animal—quite capable of protecting us as we travel. I am too small for defense. My strength is my intellect. I know a great deal about the lands we will most likely travel through, having been there myself. Of course, I do not know where the fire cloud will ultimately lead us, but I do know it is currently heading southeast. I propose that we work as a team in leading this group of animals. I will be the primary leader on how we will travel, whereas you will be the primary leader on keeping us safe and lending the muscle behind our movement. Does this sound reasonable to you?" asked Liz.

"Aye, I do like the way ye think, even if I think ye could do with a little less thinkin' sometimes. I gladly will let ye lead us, an' I'll protect us," said Max.

"*Très bien!* Very well! Then we must talk to the others. I'm glad you came my way. It is wiser to travel in a large group," Liz replied.

"Funny how we came yer way, isn't it, lass? Must be jest a coincidence then?" said Max in a sarcastic tone and a grin.

Liz ignored his comment, walking ahead to join the others. Max followed along behind. They soon rejoined Kate, Rudy, and Rosie.

115

"Why don't you go wake up your friend Albert? He needs to hear this," Liz said as she pointed to the lavender bush where Al lay. He was on his back, a big, goofy grin spread across his face as if he was dreaming of grandiose things, but he was a mess.

"Oh, dear, Al needs a bath! Let's wake him but do it gently," Kate said as Max walked over to where his destructive friend was dreamily sleeping.

Max looked at Al and decided that he needed a firm awakening. He leaned over the sleeping, drooling cat and put his mouth right in his ear, "AL! HENRIETTE IS COMIN' FOR YE!"

Al's eyes popped wide open, and he sat up with a start. Max started laughing at the look of fear on Al's face. Al heaved a sigh of relief when it was Max he saw and not the mean hen. He put his paw up to his head, holding it to get his balance.

"Max, am I glad to see ye, lad. Oh, me achin' head. Oh, me achin' belly. Max, I done a terrible thing," said Al as he shook his head.

"I alr-r-ready heard all aboot it, lad. Ye were a bad kitty. Shame on ye for destr-r-royin' a whole garden. An' a garden belongin' ta a bonnie kitty lass, too!" Max scolded Al.

"Sure, and ye don't have to tell me, Max. I feel so bad about it all, and I already had a tongue lashin' from the mean hen. But in spite o' it all, it were amazin' how Liz were so kind to me! Aye, she is a beautiful sight to see," said Al with a broad smile on his face.

Kate and Liz watched Max and Al from a distance. Kate turned to Liz and said, "Al really is a sweetheart. He is jest very fearful sometimes, an' he does have a large appetite. But I think ye will like him when ye spend some time with him."

"*Oui*, I know. I can tell he is all of those things," Liz smiled as she replied.

Henriette and Jacques walked toward them from up above on the path. Henriette commanded their conversation, talking continually all the way. Jacques' head looked forward as if not listening to his bossy mate. Liz introduced her new friends to Henriette and Jacques.

"So the crazy cat is with you?" Henriette inquired of Kate.

"Well, it's more like we are all with each other. We've traveled across the sea channel an' now into France followin' the fire cloud," explained Kate.

"Mademoiselle, did you hear this? These other creatures are following the fire cloud, too. They heard the Voice, no? *Je ne comprends pas*. What is happening?" rambled Henriette.

"Henriette, please calm down. I'm sure Mademoiselle will explain everything," said Jacques. Then, looking at Kate, "*Bonjour*, Kate. It is indeed a great pleasure to meet you. Please excuse my wife's brashness. She is really harmless." Jacques reached down to kiss Kate's paw as she instinctively lifted it, blushing.

"I be delighted ta meet ye, Jacques. Ye have a beautiful country—I jest love France. An' yer wife is quite colorful as well," replied Kate thoughtfully, trying to engender good feelings with Jacques.

"*Attendez un moment,* Henriette. I will explain everything as best I can," said Liz patiently as she looked over to see if Al was up.

Max and Al were still talking. Al bowed down low on his front legs for a long stretch and a broad yawn. Then he shook vigorously, trying to rid his fur of the pieces of garden that clung to him. His stomach sloshed with the still undigested food, almost throwing him off balance. He looked at Max with a weak grin.

"Lad, ye need ta go on a diet methinks! Maybe the slim French kitty kin help ye," teased Max as he looked at Al's big belly.

"Aye, that I should, and that she could," replied Al. He looked over to see Liz staring in his direction and smiled. Then he saw Henriette and cringed. "Max, please protect me from the fat hen—she doesn't like me nary a bit."

"Yer on yer own with her, lad! Ye r-r-reap wha' ye sow, an' ye done some sowin' in this garden!" said Max as he trotted over to join Kate, Liz, and the others.

Liz jumped up on a ledge so everyone could see and hear her. She looked at Al and smiled warmly, "It is good to see you up, Albert. Do you feel better?"

"Aye, thank ye, Liz. That peppermint ye gave me really did the trick," said Al, smiling back at Liz but losing his smile when he glanced at Henriette, who gave him her mean look. Al moved behind Max.

Rudy and Rosie landed on a nearby branch so they could hear Liz. All the others huddled in close so they could do the same.

"It has become obvious to me that what I thought may have been a single directed mission from the Maker is, in fact, something quite large in scope. I have studied the fire cloud for days now. It appeared after the Maker distinctly told Henriette, Jacques, and me to '*Come. Follow the fire cloud.*' From what you have shared with me, each of you received the same message.

"Rudy and Rosie flew all the way across the great sea from Argentina. Max and Kate came from Scotland, and Albert from

Ireland. There is a single message given to multiple creatures on different continents. A clear pattern is emerging, no? Look at the eight of us. Pairs—male and female—of young, healthy, diverse creatures. Birds of the air and creatures of the land have been called, but not the creatures in the sea." Liz stopped there, looking at the little band of animals below, wanting to explain more, but not having anything further *to* explain. It frustrated her not to have all the answers. She wasn't used to working this way.

"She's giddy right. Now why didn't I see that? Two of each creature is wha' we've seen so far. Air beasties an' land beasties, all with the same message. Yer a smart one, lass," exclaimed Max, feeling a sense of relief that he didn't have to be the brains of this mission anymore. Not that he minded learning as he went along, but he was glad to have some help with a partner to whom ideas and insights came easily. Still, he realized he would have to remain the leader who operated primarily on faith. Faith appeared to be a secondary guiding force for Liz. Max wondered if her intellect, seemingly her greatest strength, could also be her greatest weakness.

118

"But why do ye suppose we've been called? An' why not the sea beasties?" asked Kate.

Liz hesitated as she thought for a moment. "I do not yet have enough facts for an accurate answer, Kate, but I would make the assumption that the reason either has nothing to do with the sea or everything to do with it."

"What do you suppose the Maker is up to, *señorita?*" asked Rudy.

"I would never presume to know what the Maker is doing, especially without more facts. All we can go on now is what we know so far. The fire cloud is moving in a southeasterly direction, but is still for the moment. When it moves again, we will all follow it—together. I predict that it will once again move at daybreak," explained Liz.

"Max and I have discussed our situation. I have traveled far and wide and know much about this land and lands beyond. I will be able to guide us from what I know. And Max will be able to guard us on our way," Liz replied, looking at Max with a smile.

"Aye, and so will I!" said Al. All the animals looked at Al as if he were crazy, which was really nothing new.

"You see, what did I tell you!? *Le chat est fou,*" huffed Henriette.

"Ye think ye kin guard us then, kitty, when yer terrified of this big hen?" Max asked Al in a sarcastic tone. He then looked at Henriette, "No offense, lass." Henriette stuck her beak in the air and grunted, "Humph."

"Liz told me that me name means 'noble, famous warrior.' She thinks I'm noble but need to grow into the other two words. I figure I best start tryin' to become 'famous' and a 'warrior.' And I figure this journey is probably a good way to learn," Al explained.

Max was speechless. He couldn't believe what he was hearing. Al? A noble, famous warrior? It wasn't possible!

Max looked up to see Liz smiling at Al, her tail slowly curling up and down. "Kin ye tell me wha' 'Maximillian' means then, lass?"

"Hmmm . . . I believe it means 'greatest,'" replied Liz.

"There, ye see! I'm still the gr-r-reatest, so let me take the lead then, warrior kitty," Max said with a wink to Al.

"Oh, Liz, wha' does me name mean?" asked Kate, intrigued with all that Liz knew about names, and apparently everything else.

"Kate is a lovely name, *mon amie.* It means 'pure,'" Liz responded with a smile.

Kate grinned her peppy grin and wagged her tail with enthusiasm. She liked her name, which was pure like her beautiful white coat.

"And what about 'Henriette?'" asked Jacques, curious to see if names really mean things.

"Well, it means 'ruler of the house,'" said Liz in a shy tone, worrying about offending the puffy hen or embarrassing the proud rooster.

With that, everyone started laughing. How funny it was that the names matched up with the personalities of these creatures. Even Henriette liked the meaning of her name because frankly, it was true. Jacques pecked her on the cheek. She might be bossy, but he loved her all the same. She always meant well even when she didn't behave well.

"Now, I would suggest that we all eat a good meal and get a solid night of rest for our travel tomorrow. And since we are leaving my garden—or what is left of it—we must enjoy it. Eat up, and *bon appétit!*" said Liz as she jumped off the ledge and walked over to Al.

Max and Kate were starving, so they trotted off into the garden to enjoy the fruits of Liz's labor. Rudy and Rosie continued buzzing around the flowers, sipping the wonderful nectar, and Jacques and Henriette headed for the corn.

Liz, knowing full well that Al had no interest in food at the moment, went to give him his assignment. He had said he wanted to make everything up to her. Now it was time for him to do just that.

CHAPTER 21

Au Revoir

It had been a cool night in the garden, and a soft mist hung low between the rows of plants and flowers. The sun was about to break onto a horizon of brilliant blue sky filled with pink clouds resembling cotton. All the animals were sound asleep, enjoying peaceful rest, when they were rudely awakened.

"COCK-A-DOODLE DOOOOOOOO! COCK-A-DOO-DLE DOOOOOOOO!" screamed Jacques, stretching out his neck, his colorful feathers ruffled as he strutted around the garden, repeating his scream, "COCK-A-DOODLE DOOOOOOOO!"

"Wha' in the name of Pete is all that r-r-racket?!" asked a very startled Max, sitting up abruptly.

"Ah, that would be Jacques. He is a rooster, after all, no? He is doing what comes naturally," replied Liz, daintily walking toward Max, Kate, and Al.

Kate nudged Al to get up, as he slept through Jacques' wake-up call. Rudy and Rosie flew over to the rousing animals, saying, "*Buenos días!* It is a beautiful day for travel."

"*Oui, mes amis,*" Liz replied. "The fire cloud has started to move again. We must get ready to leave soon. Jacques, *merci* for waking us."

"You are most welcome, Mademoiselle. Henriette and I are ready to leave. She said her farewells to our home. Do you think we will ever return?" asked Jacques.

"I would like to return here, *mon ami*. But I do not know. We should assume we will not, so as not to build up our hopes, no?" answered Liz, a tinge of sadness in her eyes. She did not wish to leave her beloved France. She guarded all such hopes with realism.

Henriette came waddling down the garden path, wiping her eyes with her feathered wing. But when she saw the eyes of the others looking at her, she quickly straightened up and ceased being so emotional. She didn't wish to appear anything but strong and in control. It wouldn't do for the ruler of the house to be seen crying, after all.

"Ah, Henriette, *bonjour*, I am glad you are here. Would you do me a favor and please wake Albert?" Liz asked Henriette, wisely giving her something to do so the hen would not feel self-conscious.

"*Oui*, Mademoiselle," sniffed Henriette as she walked over to Al, who refused to get up. She leaned over the cat, clucking her tongue at how she rarely saw this imbecile cat do anything other than eat or sleep. "GET UP, CRAZY CAT!" she screamed into Al's ears.

Al's fur stood on end as he jumped up and moved away from the loud, ruffled hen. He sat next to Max, his fur all mussed. Max just looked at Al and shook his head.

"Listen closely, *mes amis*. The fire cloud is now moving, as, of course, I said it would. It is time to leave. Please eat a quick breakfast and we will be on our way. Albert, I will ask you to carry the sack, *s'il vous plaît*," said Liz as the animals dispersed to eat.

"Wha' sack, lad?" Max asked Al.

"Liz asked me to help her last night, to make up for what I did. She had me fill a sack o' seeds from all the plants and flowers in her garden. I had to climb way up high on the sunflowers, too. Liz wanted samples from each and every plant here. Sure, and it took me most o' the night," explained Al, yawning. "That's why I'm so tired, lad." Al pointed to the little sack that Liz wove together from cornhusk. It had a strap that Al could slip over his shoulder, making it easy to carry on his back.

"Well done, kitty! It were good of ye ta make it r-r-right," replied Max, patting Al on the back with his burly paw.

"It were the least I could do," answered Al, yawning even wider and rubbing his eyes.

"As long as yer carryin' that sack, could ye carry me r-r-reed as well?" asked Max.

"Aye, I'll carry it for ye," answered Al.

"Yer a gr-r-rand fr-r-riend. I'd say Liz were right—I kin see some noble in ye," answered Max.

"Hurry, ye two! Let's eat so we kin get goin'," called Kate.

"Aye, I finally have an appetite again. Let's eat," said Al, perking up at the mention of food. Al left the seed sack sitting on the ground and went looking for breakfast. When he was a good distance away, a shadow entered the seed sack.

Liz sat up on a rock waiting for the animals, licking her paws to clean up after her breakfast of berries. The hummingbirds flew over to Liz, and the others gathered around.

"It is time. As we leave, Rudy and Rosie will keep an eye up above and will serve as scouts on our journey. I will be in the front, and Max will bring up the rear as our protector. Are there any questions?" asked Liz.

"When can we stop for lunch?" asked Al, drawing smirks from the others.

"You silly *chat*. You just ate breakfast," scolded Henriette.

Liz giggled. "We will eat when we have put a good distance behind us, *mon ami*."

With that, Liz jumped off the rock and led the eight animals out of the garden. It was an exciting moment, and all the animals felt a rush of energy as they embarked on the next leg of the journey. Liz didn't look back at her garden. There was nothing left for her here. So she left it behind, looking only ahead.

123

CHAPTER 22

Adam's Journal

Noah knelt down next to Lamech and softly whispered in his ear, "Father. I have brought my sons as you requested."

Lamech's eyes struggled to open and he smiled. He reached out a weak hand and Ham, Shem, and Japheth approached the dying man.

"Grandfather, you should come see what father is building," Shem said, taking the old man's fragile hand into his own. He held it for a moment, gently squeezing it and willing the dear man to hang on.

Lamech returned the hand squeeze and smiled. "I've heard. Shouldn't it be completed by now?"

The men laughed, sharing knowing glances with each other. If only their grandfather knew.

"We could carry you there if you'd like to see it," Ham suggested.

"There is not time. Japheth, did you bring the cart?" Lamech asked.

Japheth took a step forward in response. "Yes, grandfather."

"Shem, take the torch. Find the niche in the cave wall," Lamech instructed, coughing.

Shem hesitated at hearing his grandfather cough, but obeyed and crossed to the opposite side of the cave to where Lamech's gaze fell, searching.

"It is hidden," Lamech instructed. "Behind that sharp rock. The one that is eye level."

Ham and Japheth joined Shem in the search while Noah and Lamech shared a final moment.

"Protect them," Lamech said, closing his eyes and opening them again.

"What is it, father?" Noah asked, his face full of grief for his ailing father.

"It is His story," Lamech said as he squeezed Noah's arm. "Protect them."

"Here it is. Bring the torch, Shem," Ham said.

The three brothers looked around the jutting rock to find a small, deeply hidden hole. Shem held the torch over the hole to reveal many slabs of clay stacked inside. Ham reached in and struggled to pull out a heavy tablet. Dust and dirt from the cave showed decades of settling, and Ham tried his best to brush it away.

125

"What does it say?" Japheth asked, trying to see the tablet in the dim light.

Ham finally cleared away the thick coating that covered the symbols, pictures, and other various markings. "These are the generations of Noah . . ."

"What is this?" asked Shem.

The three sons turned to question their father and saw Noah pull the cover over Lamech's head. Noah laid his own head on the chest of his deceased father, and wept.

CHAPTER 23

Questions with Answers, and Answers with Questions

The group of animals and birds made their way through the green meadows of France. Liz set the pace, wanting them to make good time, but trying not to tire Henriette and Jacques, who weren't equipped for long-distance walking. Kate looked up at Rudy and Rosie, amazed at how fast their little wings flapped. Their wings seemed to disappear while in flight. Their tiny bodies zipped along carefree above the meadow where the animals walked.

"Liz, how is it that Rudy an' Rosie kin fly so fast?" Kate asked Liz, grinning up at the two small birds.

"Energy. The Maker supplied hummingbirds with an extraordinary ability to use energy," replied Liz, glancing briefly up at Rudy and Rosie while maintaining her steady walking pace.

"Where does energy come from?" asked Kate.

"Hmmm . . . well, the sun gives most of the energy to the earth, and it exists in everything you see. If there were no energy, nothing would exist. The sun would not shine, the winds would not blow, the rivers would not run," Liz explained as she looked at the animals around her, "and the birds and animals would not fly, walk, or run. Jacques would not crow, Henriette would not scream, Max would not trot, and Albert would not jump."

Kate picked up her pace to walk right next to Liz. She was fascinated by what this intelligent cat was explaining, and she wanted to learn more.

"How does the sun make wind? Or make rivers run? Or make Rudy an' Rosie fly?" eagerly asked Kate.

Liz smiled at Kate, happy to share her wealth of knowledge with one interested in learning.

"You see, *mon amie*, as the sun heats the earth, it does not happen, how do you say, 'evenly?' Certain areas of the earth heat up faster than other areas, causing differences in air pressure. There must be balance in all things, so the high pressure moves to become balanced with the low pressure, and *voilà!* Wind is born," explained Liz as she looked to see if Kate understood her.

127

Kate furrowed her brow as she tried to understand Liz. She looked up at the sun now getting brighter as it rose higher in the sky. "So yer tellin' me that the sun makes wind?"

"*Oui*, isn't that fascinating!? And to answer your other question, it also makes water move. The sun warms the seas and rivers, causing some of the water to evaporate—ah, turn into a mist that leaves the water and rises into the air. When much of the water gathers in the air, clouds form. You see, the puffy clouds over there came from the rivers below," Liz said as she directed Kate to the skies.

"But how does that make water move?" asked Kate, not fully getting it.

"Ah, let me help you figure this out, *mon amie*. What happens when many clouds come together and become very thick and dark?" asked Liz.

"Well, it usually rains," Kate replied.

"Exactly. Rain. The clouds first have small amounts of water in them, but those small amounts turn into greater amounts.

When the clouds get too heavy, the water falls back down to earth as rain. Tell me what happens when rain falls on the ground." Liz continued.

"Oh, in Scotland the rain sometimes falls lightly, an' sometimes drops in buckets. When it falls fast, we call it a real gully-washer. It makes streams of water run fast, an' . . . oh, I see wha' ye mean," said Kate as she suddenly understood how the sun ultimately caused the water to flow.

"*Très bien,* Kate. You understand how this works now?" asked Liz, delighted at how quickly her pupil learned.

"Wha' aboot lightnin' then, lass?" asked Max, who had walked ahead to listen to their conversation, obviously interested in what Liz was explaining.

"Lightning is energy, too, Max. It happens when electrical energy builds up in the clouds as charges begin separating. When the separation gets large enough, a large amount of energy causes a spark that reaches from the cloud to the ground. It is very exciting, no? The energy becomes heat, light, and also, sound," explained Liz.

"Sound?" asked Max.

"*Oui!* Thunder—you've heard it, no? *C'est magnifique,*" asked Liz.

"Aye, aye, thunder," said Max in an almost loathsome tone. "I've heard it, lass," said Max as he walked back to where Al dragged his feet at the end of the line. Max nudged Al along, encouraging him to pick up the pace. Max had heard enough for now.

Kate and Liz continued their discussion. "But wha' aboot us? Wha' aboot Rudy an' Rosie's energy, an' our energy ta be walkin' here now? Where does that come from?" asked Kate.

"Why do you suppose I told everyone to eat a good breakfast today?" asked Liz, glancing back at Al, who was clearly heavy on his feet from all he ate.

"Well, food always makes me feel grand—like I have energy for the day ahead," said Kate, stopping short as she realized that food was energy. It was obvious, of course, but in light of their conversation, it took on a whole new perspective.

"Correct, Kate. And where do you suppose food gets *its* energy?" asked Liz, wanting Kate to really think about things, to figure them out.

"Yer sure stretchin' me mind, Liz. I would say that the berries I ate this mornin' got their energy from the Maker's good earth, an' from . . . the sun?" asked Kate, unsure of herself.

"Brilliant! *Oui!* The plants get their energy from the nutrients in the soil, *oui*, but they store energy within from the sun. Do you remember how my beautiful sunflowers faced toward the light? If you watch them, they follow the sun's direction all day. It is quite wonderful to watch them soak up the sunshine, no? Sunflowers are the most visible followers of the sun, but all plants do the same. So as you ate the berries today—"

"I see. I got the energy from the plants, an' that came from the sun," said Kate, grinning as she understood the process.

"*C'est bon,* Kate. Very good. You are an excellent student, *mon amie,*" answered Liz affirmingly. "So, Rudy and Rosie get their energy from the nectar they drink, and the Maker has equipped their bodies to use that energy to help them fly quickly. You see, there is an explanation for the way things work."

Kate pondered these things for a moment as they walked on. "But how did Rudy an' Rosie fly so far across the great sea when they would use up the energy they ate in South America?" asked Kate, suddenly finding a wrinkle in the equation.

Liz furrowed her brow and didn't respond immediately. She looked up at the two hummingbirds. That very question had bothered her since she met them in the garden. It really was impossible that they were able to make it that far. She needed an explanation.

"Rudy and Rosie, please come here," Liz called to the hummingbirds. The two birds flew down to hover above Liz and Kate.

"Tell me, did you make any stops along the way across the great sea? Were you able to find food on your journey?" Liz asked.

"*Sí, sí, señorita.* When we left our home we were able to eat as we flew across South America. But as we left Brazil, we were over open water for a long time. When we thought we couldn't make it any farther, we came across an island about seven hundred miles northeast of Brazil, right on the equator. We stopped and rested while we enjoyed the delicious hibiscus flowers there," answered Rudy.

"But there was still a large space of ocean to cross. Did you stop anywhere else?" asked Liz.

"*Sí,* the next stop was twice as far. I still don't know how we made it to the island of Fogo, as the local insects called it," replied Rudy.

"I thought my wings would fall off, but we made it just in time, *señorita,*" piped in Rosie, smiling brightly at Kate.

Liz thought a moment. Seven hundred miles was a stretch to begin with for their first stop. But another thirteen hundred miles for two little hummingbirds to fly was just not possible. She became frustrated as she searched for an answer. "Were there wind currents that gave you thermal lift on your flight?" she asked the birds.

"*Sí,* there were winds that came to lift us up," replied Rudy before Liz interrupted him.

"So you see, the winds provided the lift you needed to carry you to the next island, and to other islands along the coast of Africa until you reached Spain and then France. I knew there must be an explanation. There always is," said Liz, feeling confident that she had the explanation she needed.

"Well, the winds did come up under our wings to help carry us, that is true, but the mystery of it is where the winds came from. For you see, at the point of our greatest exhaustion, where we didn't see how we could fly another mile, we were in the doldrums. There is no wind in the doldrums. The water below was still and breathless. Yet a mighty wind carried us still," explained Rudy. "We're just grateful we made it at all."

"I think it's wonderful how you made it. Wha' an exciting adventure it must have been. The Maker were definitely watchin' out for ye, in givin' ye wha' ye needed at jest the right time," said Kate, wagging her tail.

Liz was stumped. While Kate easily accepted things in faith, Liz hated not knowing why things happened. Wind in the doldrums? It wasn't possible. From a place dead to wind came the sustaining winds the little hummingbirds needed, and at just the right time. She remained quiet as she kept walking, her brow wrinkled in thought.

"Liz, there must be a grand amount of energy in the fire cloud. I never seen fire in a cloud before. Do ye suppose it's the Maker Himself who travels along inside the cloud, givin' it the energy ta make fire?" Kate asked.

Liz looked up at the fire cloud. It was true, she had seen lightning in clouds but never fire. Could it be? Could the Maker inhabit the fire cloud? If He made the sun, the source of almost all the earth's energy, she deduced, then He could surely be in the fire cloud itself. Liz then glanced to the sun, squinting her eyes as she tried to look at it. The sun was made of fire as well.

Using her logical train of thought, she then realized something profound. The Maker was the source of all energy. And of life itself. If He made all of life, couldn't He sustain it, however He chose? Even bring wind where there was no wind to help two little hummingbirds cross the ocean?

Liz watched Rudy and Rosie fly effortlessly up above. But why would a Creator so vast and powerful be concerned with the needs of such small creatures? It didn't make logical sense. Liz had to ponder this for a while.

"*Oui*, Kate. You may be right. You may just be right," Liz replied.

CHAPTER 24

Running with the Bull

I'm starvin'. Can we stop now?" asked Al.

This was a phrase that the little band of eight creatures had become used to hearing frequently. The animals were making good time. The fire cloud had moved steadily over the past few days, stopping only in the late evening so the animals could eat and rest. And of course, each day began with Jacques' wake-up call. Max couldn't seem to get used to the rooster's early morning crowing. His large ears were sensitive to loud noises, and Jacques' amazing lung power was just plain annoying. Max hated waking up like that.

Liz continued to explain things to Kate and the other animals along the way. She pointed out the various plants found across France, including the yellow mustard flowers that Kate and Max had eaten when they first arrived. Liz was well familiar with the terrain and the animals that roamed the countryside, as well as the birds that nested in the trees. She never ceased to amaze the others with her knowledge. And Al was growing enamored with her.

"I suppose we can stop now," replied Liz. There was a creek nearby to provide water, and the land here was lush and green. It was a perfect spot to rest. "Don't go too far away, *mes amis*. We have made excellent time on our journey, and we are nearing the end of the border of France. I wish to enter Switzerland before nightfall."

"Switzerland?" asked Max. "That's where Gillamon is from."

Liz walked over to the creek bank to sip some cool water. Al, Kate, Henriette, and Jacques followed Rudy and Rosie to a cluster of wild strawberries growing nearby. Max joined Liz at the creek bank. Liz was careful not to muddy the waters with her paws. Max, on the other hand, plopped his paws just under the water to sloppily lap it up, turning the water cloudy with mud. Liz stopped drinking and gave a perturbed look at Max, saying, "Pfft."

"Wha'?" was all Max said, water dripping from his chin as Liz stepped away. He was oblivious to his muddy mess. He didn't understand the ways of this tidy cat. She liked things orderly and clean. Max didn't see the point.

133

Liz walked back to sit under a big weeping willow tree whose branches hung low over the water, as if it were looking at itself in a mirror. Max continued to lap the water when he noticed the reflection of the clouds on the water's surface. The clouds took on the shape of Gillamon's face. Max smiled.

Kate joined Max at the water's edge. "I know ye'll be glad ta see Gillamon's home."

"Aye, lass. It'll make me feel close ta him again," Max said, when he became distracted as he glanced over Kate's shoulder. Al was jumping up and down, chasing some butterflies across the meadow when suddenly he bolted across the countryside.

"Did Gillamon ever tell you about the mountains in Switzerland?" Kate asked Max.

"Aye, that he did, lass. He said they were some of the most beautiful peaks in the world. Gillamon is a mountain goat, so he should know," replied Max, still looking over Kate's shoulder.

"Liz were tellin' me the climate should be comfortable. This time of year we shouldn't run into a whole lot of snow," Kate was saying. She noticed Max was distracted.

Al was now running back across the meadow, and in the distance, a large bull was chasing him.

". . . except for the higher elevations, that is," Kate continued.

"I'm sorry, lass. Wha' aboot the higher elevations?" Max said, half listening to Kate.

"Snow. Liz says we shouldn't have a problem with snow until we get high up in the mountains," Kate explained. Max didn't respond. "Max?"

Kate turned around to see why Max had so rudely tuned out their conversation, when they both saw Al running as fast as his chubby legs would go, an enormous bull right on his tail. The two thousand pound beast snorted as he was bearing down on Al. His black shiny hide revealed strong, sculpted muscles. The bull's nostrils were flaring and his sharp horns were aimed right for Al's behind.

A black-and-white cow came slowly walking into the pasture behind them, biting off chunks of grass and chewing, her head lazily moving side to side. She looked over to see the bull chasing Al, stopped chewing briefly, then lowered her head again to bite off another chunk of grass.

"Max, wha' should we do?" Kate asked, panicking.

"We should try ta find a pass ta cross before we get ta the top of the mountain," Max calmly replied.

Kate turned to give Max an incredulous look. "Excuse me?!"

Max looked at her and then at Al and then back at Kate. "Oh, ye mean aboot Al here? I guess Maximillian Br-r-raveheart the Br-r-ruce will have ta handle this."

Max took off running in the direction of the cat and the chasing bull. Kate joined Liz under the willow tree.

Max was fast on his feet, blazing across the meadow to catch the bull. He stopped in the center of the field, just as the two sped past him. The bull's hooves dug into the ground, kicking up grass and dirt into Max's face.

"STOP! I ORDER YE TA STOP R-R-RUNNIN' NOW!" Max shouted after them.

Al and the bull ignored Max, changed courses, and ran back through the field right at him.

"STOP, I SAY! STOP!" Max yelled.

They whizzed past, ignoring Max again. This angered Max and he took off running. He came alongside the bull, nipping at his heels.

"He's *loco*," came a voice from behind the animals who sat watching Max, Al, and the bull. It was the cow, chewing her cud as she walked up to them. "My husband, Don Pedro. He is normally very calm and gentle. But if he sees a creature moving wildly, it sets him off, and he runs after it. When this happens he falls into a trance, not knowing what he is doing. He becomes a *loco*, angry bull."

Max, Al, and the bull started slowing their pace.

"I would not say this to my husband, but Don Pedro, he is not the young stud he used to be," Isabella the cow continued.

"No, no, no! This will not do," said Liz, walking quickly over to the center of the field with Isabella, Kate, Henriette, and Jacques following her. Liz was worried about Al.

Max, Al, and the bull stopped running, all three panting heavily with hearts pounding.

"Listen up, ye daft beast," Max said, huffing with breaths between words. "How dar-r-re ye run after me friend. If ye ever come near him again, I'll pull yer tail off," shouted Max, angry at this bull as the realization came that he could have lost Al.

The bull was breathing heavy, snorting as a cloud of dust swirled around his massive form. Max couldn't believe what he heard next. This massive, mean bull was crying? He shook as he heaved up and down with heavy sobs.

"I . . . I . . . I'm so, so, so . . . sorry," sobbed the bull, tears running down his cheeks. "I . . . (sniff) . . . I . . . couldn't control myself. The cat was (sniff) jumping *loco* all over the field and it set

135

me off," whimpered the bull in a deep voice.

Max looked back at the cow, not understanding what was happening.

"I told you. He's really gentle when he's not *loco*," said the cow.

Max looked up at Al. "Are ye hearin' this lad? This bull is aboot a bigger baby than ye are when yer afraid then!"

Max walked over to be eye level with the bull. "Me name is Maximillian Br-r-raveheart the Br-r-ruce. An' that kitty ye aboot tr-r-rampled is named Al. Get yerself out of this dir-r-t an' go tell him yer not goin' ta tr-r-rample him again."

The big black bull raised his head. He looked at Max, who stood right in his face, then at Al, who sat cowering on the ground. He stood, towering over Max, and walked over to Al, his head hung low. Finally gaining his composure, he said, "My apologies, *gato*. I was out of my mind when I was chasing you. I have anger issues. Sometimes when I see things move I lose my head. I'm sorry."

136

Al looked at the bull, shocked at the difference in this beast. A few minutes ago this bull was dead set to gore him. Now he was apologizing? Al looked at Max, who told him, "It's okay, laddie."

"Ye nearly scared me out o' me skin, bull! Don't ever do that again!" Al said.

Don Pedro nodded his head in agreement. "*Sí, señor*. I won't, as long as you don't jump around like you did."

"But I can't help me jumpin'," answered Al with a frown.

"Well, I can't help my running," answered the bull with a scowl.

"When I see a bull runnin' toward me—" scowled Al.

"And when something jumps in front of me—" snorted Don Pedro.

Just then the argument was suddenly interrupted when Isabella let loose a loud, discordant sound—*PPPPPTTTTT.*

The group of animals stopped and looked around, holding their noses and feeling awkward at this surely embarrassing moment for the cow. Al gasped for air, Jacques crowed with laughter, Don Pedro stopped arguing, and Liz went into a state of shock.

Isabella leaned in and whispered to Kate, "If you ever need to get a man's attention . . ." The cow gave Kate a wink.

Max mumbled under his breath to Liz, "Methinks it were his wife's gas that made Don Pedro run away."

"Ah-hem," Liz said, trying to regain her composure. "What we have here is a clash of animal behaviors that are incompatible, no? Before we address the problem, we first need to determine if a solution is even needed. That is, if we will part company or spend more time together. I am fairly certain, but tell me, cow and bull, are you following the fire cloud?" said Liz, calm and collected as always.

"*Sí, señorita*, how did you know?" answered the cow, amazed at the instinct of this petite black cat.

"Mademoiselle knows everything, silly *boeuf!*" Henriette responded with a shrill voice.

"We eight creatures are also following the fire cloud, and have come from diverse countries. You clearly are another pair of land creatures from Spain, I assume. It is only logical to conclude that you are on the same journey," replied Liz.

"*Sí, señorita*. You are correct. My apologies for my behavior. I am tired from our travels, and a little more on edge than usual. I just snapped," said Don Pedro to the group of animals clustered around, feeling embarrassed.

Liz studied the bull for a moment. Her gaze then drifted to Al as she made sure he was unharmed. She smiled at Al, relieved that he was okay. Liz returned her gaze to Don Pedro. "Well, if you intend on joining our group, you must realize that such behavior is not acceptable. It is in the nature of a cat to jump and run erratically. And it is in your nature to become wild with anger at such movement. The cat's behavior is acceptable and harms no one. But your behavior—*ooh-la-la*. I suggest you receive training in anger management," said Liz in a matter-of-fact tone.

"Anger wha'?" asked Max, not knowing what Liz was talking

about.

"The management of anger," explained Liz. "Don Pedro must learn techniques to control his temper when under stress. He must learn not to overreact when faced with irritation. And I can think of no one better to assist in this training than Henriette."

"*Moi?* How so, Mademoiselle?" asked a surprised Henriette.

"You see, *mon amie*, since you are naturally good at giving instructions and being, um, so abrasive, you will provide the proper dose of anger generation where Don Pedro can learn to react in a positive fashion. *Comprenez vous?*" asked Liz.

"*Oui!* I will be glad to help this silly *boeuf* learn to control his temper! Don Pedro, you are with me!" said Henriette.

"Better do what she says, *mon ami*," said Jacques to the humbled bull. "I've been on the receiving end of her yelling and you don't want to stay there longer than you have to."

"Ah well, let us all regroup before we head over to Switzerland." said Liz. "We now have ten in our party, so the travel will be more cumbersome. Henriette will, of course, need to be with Don Pedro to train as we go. Henriette, you and Jacques ride on the bull's back, since you are tired from walking. Albert, I suggest you walk behind Don Pedro in case you get the urge to jump."

"An' lass, kin I suggest that Isabella bring up the rear of the group? I'll walk jest in front of her. I think it could be a dangerous place walkin' behind her then," said Max, again drawing snickers from the group. "Besides, maybe the cow will be our best defense from creatures tryin' ta follow us."

Liz giggled, "Of course, *mon ami*. As long as you keep an eye on things back there, you may walk in front of our flatulent friend. Now, everyone get a drink of water. The fire cloud is still moving, and we have some ground to cover before nightfall."

Don Pedro gave a nod of his head in agreement and followed Henriette as she waddled across the meadow back to the creek, already cackling ground rules for the training.

Max, Kate, Jacques, and the hummingbirds followed after

them. Isabella grazed her way in their direction as well.

Al and Liz remained there in the meadow. "Albert, I am sorry you were chased by the bull. But you recovered very bravely, no?" Liz said as she rubbed her chin on Al's whiskers, purring. She could finally let her relief show that Al was okay.

"Oh, lass. It did take me by surprise and gave me a scare, but all is well now. I have to give some understandin' to the bull. After all, I were *loco* after eatin' the catnip in yer garden, and you gave me understandin'. I guess grace makes for more grace," said Al with a grin. "And Don Pedro is in good hands, methinks. If he misbehaves, Henriette can put him at the end of the line behind his wife!"

Al and Liz shared another laugh before turning to walk back to the creek with the others.

Al felt great satisfaction that Henriette had a new target for her rants. But he felt even greater joy from seeing Liz's concern and affection for him. It made running with the bull worth it all.

CHAPTER 25

The Mountain Pass

The scenery before them was astounding. Even Max had to admit that these snow-capped mountains overlooking glacier-born blue lakes gave Scotland competition for beauty. The mountains of Switzerland seemed to go on forever, rising and falling on the horizon and plunging into sparkling waters below. The air was fresh and crisp. It also affected them in a strange way.

"WHA' DID YE SAY?" shouted Max to Kate, who had asked him something.

"I SAID, DID YE SEE THOSE BIRDS FLYIN' OVER-HEAD?" shouted Kate in reply.

"DID I SEE THE HERDS DYIN' IN A BED? WHA' KIND OF NONSENSE ARE YE SAYIN', LASS?" Max shouted in reply, shaking his head to try to clear his ears.

"NO! THE *BIRDS*. DID YE SEE THE BIRDS?" Kate shouted again, feeling flustered.

"DID I TREE BY THIRDS? I LIKE TA TREE PESKY BEASTIES BUT USUALLY JEST ONE AT A TIME," said Max, thinking Kate was asking about his pest-rounding abilities.

Kate shook her head. Max made absolutely no sense. Suddenly the animals all came to a halt. Liz had stopped walking up ahead, jumping onto a rock where everyone could see her.

"YOU NEED TO CLEAR YOUR EARS. THEY ARE PLUGGED UP FROM THE CHANGE IN ELEVATION," Liz shouted.

"WE NEED TO SEAR OUR FEARS? AYE, SHE IS A WISE LASS, AND QUITE PROFOUND!" exclaimed a very loud Al, not understanding what Liz said.

"MADEMOISELLE SAID DEAR ARE THE YEARS," interjected Henriette, who rocked back and forth on top of Don Pedro as he walked, smiling at Jacques as she thought of their years together. Jacques beamed back, enjoying the fact that he could not hear Henriette for once.

"CHEER AT JEERS?" asked Don Pedro, thinking those words were just more anger management advice from Henriette.

Rudy and Rosie seemed to be the only ones not affected by the change in elevation on their ears. They were used to flying at high altitude, after all. The hummingbirds enjoyed a good laugh at the absurd conversation among the animals. Finally, Rosie flew over to Liz, putting her beak inside the cat's ear, saying, "They can't understand you, *señorita*. No one can hear a thing, so the words are all nonsense."

"*Merci*, Rosie," Liz replied. With that, she began to yawn. She said nothing, but repeatedly yawned. As the animals watched Liz, they couldn't help but yawn as well. With every yawn, they noticed their ears popping and clearing. They could hear again.

Max's ears finally popped clear. He turned to Al and said, "Kin ye hear me now?"

"Liz, wha' happened ta our ears?" asked Kate.

"You see, *mes amis*, we are now entering higher elevations in this mountain pass. As this happens, the air pressure in our ears gets how you say, 'out of whack' and needs to adjust. Yawning helps reduce the pressure. When you could not hear me, I simply began to yawn. It is quite contagious, no?" asked Liz.

"Aye, I can hear ye fine now. It's amazin' how jest a little bit o' misunderstandin' can change the meanin' o' things," said Al.

"*Oui*, that is why it is very important to make sure we always understand each other on this journey. If you do not understand something, just ask. And if you cannot hear, then just yawn," replied Liz, looking to see that everyone understood her.

"I heard everyone just fine. You should have heard yourselves," laughed Isabella, while letting loose her usual *PPPPPTTTTT.*

"Ah, *oui.* Yawning helps the ears to pop clear, but also chewing. And since cows continually chew their cud, Isabella's ears stayed clear. *Magnifique*," Liz replied.

It was nearly nightfall, and they were in a good place to rest. "As you can see, the fire cloud has stopped, and so will we for the night. Everyone find a bite to eat and let us sleep close together since it will be quite cold tonight. A word of caution, *mes amis.* We must be careful to keep our voices down as much as possible. We are in avalanche territory," said Liz. They had climbed into a heavily snow-covered area, and the temperature would quickly drop when the sun went down.

Al and Isabella discovered they shared a passion for food and soon found a nearby clump of buttercups poking out of the snow to devour. Liz had explained that cows can spend up to eight hours a day eating, and that their stomachs were made up of four sections. As for Isabella's gas problem, Liz said that cows can produce two hundred pounds of gas a day from all they eat, being expelled through burping and other unpleasant noises. Al was jealous at how much a cow could eat. He and Isabella talked frequently about various foods, likes and dislikes. Still, Al was ever careful to stay upwind from the cow.

"So the air pressure, an' the snowy cold an' avalanches are part of journeyin' through these mountains. Wha' else should we expect then, lass?" asked Max.

"*Ooh-la-la*, these mountains are full of wonderful sights, like the golden eagles that Kate saw earlier. Many beautiful creatures live here. And *oui*, wolves are known to roam these mountains. But of course, seeing the flora is what I like best," replied Liz, snapping out her paw for her routine pre-meal bath. She never ate before washing.

"Aye, of course. The plants are yer favorite thing, bein' the gardenin' lass ye are," said Max. "Well, time for me ta inspect the area an' make sure all is secure for the night. I'll sniff out the wolf beasties if they be here." Max got up and trotted away from them, ears perked up attentively now that they were clear, to check out their surroundings. Max was a fine watchdog, and Kate smiled as he trotted off, watching him shake his back paws from the cold snow.

"Tell me aboot some of the pretty flora here," said Kate, always eager to learn.

"Well, as you can see around us are wonderful woods filled with pine and spruce trees. As you go up the mountains, there are short pine trees and then further up you see dwarf shrubs. Now for acid soils, one typically finds *Rhododendron ferrugineum,* but of course on the more basic soils you find *Rhododendron hirsutum,*" Liz explained, always excited to discuss vegetation.

Kate wrinkled her brow, indicating that Liz was talking above her head again. Liz stopped and simplified her explanation. "Above that line are the meadows and the higher you go, the more sparse vegetation becomes. At such high altitudes, plants form into isolated "pillows." It is fascinating to observe that the most brilliant colors of plants are found at the highest elevations, which are exposed to the most severe weather. Wonderful wildflowers and brilliant lichens and mosses are plentiful way up high where the fierce winds blow and the storms rage. The lichen are soft and well formed. It is fascinating, no?" asked Liz.

"Aye, that is fascinatin'. The lichens an' mosses in sheltered places in Scotland are rough an' ugly rust colored. Wha' do ye suppose makes the difference?" asked Kate.

143

"Perhaps it is the strength of the little plant that comes through when it is tested by the severe conditions. The winds sculpt to make it soft, and the sun brings out the brilliant color," said Liz pensively.

"That's kind o' like life, then," remarked Al, joining Kate and Liz, some buttercups still hanging from his mouth.

"What do you mean, Albert?" asked Liz.

"Well, it's the goin' through the hard times that can make a soul beautiful. Storms cause smoothin' around the edges, jest like water smoothes stones over time. And the struggles make ye stronger, and wiser," explained Al, yawning to keep his ears clear, and thinking about that life lesson he and Max had shared.

Liz sat silently and pondered what Al said. It was a fact of nature that trees up on the mountain peaks have the strongest roots to withstand the winds. And the battered mountaintops produce the most beautiful flowers. She smiled as she realized that this fact of nature also applied to life. This seemingly simple cat was right. He had a depth to his heart that drew Liz to him. She may have the facts on how things work, but seeing the meaning behind things often escaped her. And the meaning many times was far more important.

"So tell me aboot the wildflowers," asked Kate, enjoying all she was learning from Liz.

"Albert and Isabella are enjoying some *Ranunculus glacialis,* or glacier buttercup," said Liz, smiling at Al, who walked back over to graze with Isabella. "There is another flower I have heard of but have never seen. Few ever do see it because it is so hard to reach, but I hear it is a flower of incredible beauty. How I would love to see it!" said Liz.

"Do tell me aboot it! It sounds intriguin'," said Kate.

"*Leontopodium alpinum,* which is part of the Asteraceae family. It has woolly white leaves and beautiful blooms of five to six small yellow flowers surrounded by a star of leaflets. It thrives in rocky limestone places that are very inaccessible. It is a very special flower. Ah, how I would love to see one, just once," sighed Liz.

"Wha' makes it so special?" asked Kate.

"It has long been known as a flower that a lover would risk his life to get for his true love. It symbolizes bravery and love. It's known as *Edelweiss*, from the German *edel*, which means 'noble,' just as someone else's name here means 'noble'," explained Liz, smiling at Al, who smiled back with yellow flowers in his teeth.

Isabella leaned her head over to Al and whispered, "*Señor*, have you been listening?"

"I'm sorry. What were ye sayin'?" replied Al, chewing.

"Not to me. To the *señoritas*. You told me how badly you still feel about tearing up Liz's garden. I think I know how you can make it up to her," Isabella said, looking over at Liz.

The cow smiled. "Every woman loves to get fresh flowers."

145

CHAPTER 26

Noble, Famous Warrior

I must be completely daft. I cannot believe I'm doin' this. Me, the scaredy kitty, leavin' the safety o' our camp to wander the mountains in search o' flowers! Love makes ye do daft things," Al muttered to himself as his paws crunched through the snow.

At least the moon was full, giving a silvery sheen to the snow-covered mountain. And the fire cloud brilliantly illuminated the sky. Even though Al could see well in the dark, he still was afraid of being in it all by himself, and appreciated the lunar and fire-cloud nightlights. He had waited until everyone was asleep before venturing out in search of edelweiss for Liz. Al watched Max fall into slumber, checking that his feet were running in his sleep as the signal that it was safe to leave.

Up and up he climbed, frequently yawning to pop his ears and adjusting the seed sack he carried on his back. He tried not to think about the fact that he was all alone and could meet up with a wolf or two or three. But Al was tired of being so afraid all the time. And if he were ever to face his fears and grow into his name, he needed to fight as a warrior fights in battle—for fear is a powerful enemy for any creature.

The further Al climbed, the less vegetation he saw, just as Liz had described it would be. Ah, Liz. What an incredible creature she was. He didn't know if she could possibly ever love such a simple-minded cat as himself, but perhaps proving his love for her this way would make him worthy. Al lost track of time, and it took most of the night to reach the peak. When he got to the top, he looked over the scene below. What an amazing sight.

The moon sparkled on the crystallized snow all the way down the mountain until the moonbeams landed on the lake. Al couldn't believe he had reached the top. He felt proud of himself and just seeing this view was reward enough for his hard climb. The wind was blowing briskly, dusting his fur with the already fallen snow. He shivered in the cold night air; he knew he had better hurry and find the edelweiss so he could get back down the mountain before the others noticed him missing.

As Al began to inspect everything, he put the seed sack on the ground and loosened the tie around it. A shadow, unseen by Al, emerged from the sack and moved slowly up the slope.

147

Al's paws felt the soft lichen growing on the rocks, and he pulled some off to put in the seed sack. Wouldn't Liz be happy to see the lichen as well? Then he spotted what he had come for. There, between some rocks, were the wooly white leaves of the edelweiss. He gingerly pulled the flower from the rocks and stood to study the small yellow petals. The colors of the fire cloud bathed Al in yellow. He stood there, rapt in the beauty around him.

The shadow moved across the mountain and suddenly a solid sheet of ice started sliding in Al's direction, completely covering him, the seed sack, and the edelweiss. Al's life flashed before his eyes, and the greatest regret he had was not putting the edelweiss at Liz's feet.

The sun was just about to break the horizon, the pink sky making the introduction of a new day. Liz snapped to attention as she realized it was sunrise. "I must stop him before he . . ." was all she was able to say before they all heard the loud, "COCK-A-DOO-DLE DOOOOO! COCK-A-DOODLE DOOOOO! COCK-A-DOODLE DOOOOO!"

Liz couldn't reach Jacques in time to keep him from crowing. Everyone woke up and looked around, ready for the new day. Liz went running over to Jacques to clamp her paws over his beak just as he was about to belt out another round of cock-a-doodle-doos.

"STOP, JACQUES! You must be quiet. Contain yourself," urgently said Liz.

"But why, Liz? This is what I do, no?" replied a calm Jacques.

"As I told you yesterday, we are in avalanche territory! Any loud noise could set the snow crashing down the mountain!" explained Liz.

It was too late. Up above them, they could hear the rumble on the mountain.

Jacques stood there, jaw hanging open, looking at the rushing snow just as Henriette noticed Al was missing. "Where is *le chat fou?*"

"Oh, dear. It's my fault. I sent Al on an errand," Isabella said when she saw that Al was gone.

"You did *what?*" Don Pedro snorted.

"May I make a suggestion?" Max asked.

Suddenly, the ground began to tremble and shake. Up above them they saw the avalanche coming, crashing down the mountainside toward them at incredible speed.

Henriette looked at Jacques with a scowl on her face. "Now look what you've done."

"No time ta argue. Everyone MOVE or ye'll be bur-r-ried alive!" shouted Max.

It was total chaos. The creatures fled as fast as they could. The hummingbirds flew up high to get out of reach of the hurtling snow that was quickly gaining ground toward the fleeing animals. Max made sure everyone was ahead of him before he took off running.

He yelled for them to keep moving, and not to look behind. It seemed unlikely that they could outrun the avalanche. It appeared that the entire mountain was falling down on top of them.

Don Pedro tripped on a rock and rolled before quickly getting up again, almost knocking Isabella off her feet. Henriette was screaming all the way down the mountain, her wings spread out in a panic, with Jacques right behind her—feeling sick that he had caused the avalanche. Kate and Liz were running in front, gasping for breath as they plunged through the deep snow. The snow was beginning to overtake the animals.

Suddenly Max saw a gully up ahead. He yelled for the creatures to dive into the ravine, and the animals did so just as the avalanche went crashing by, the powdery snow flying all around them.

Almost as quickly as it started, it was over. The snow ceased racing down the mountain, and all was still. The animals were breathing heavily, exhausted from running and emotionally frazzled from the experience. One by one they dusted themselves off and looked at each other to make sure everyone was okay.

"Is everyone alr-r-right?" asked Max, making sure they were all there.

"*Oui, mon ami,*" said Liz, with labored breathing. "We are all here."

"Except for Al, Mademoiselle," said Henriette, actually concerned about him.

Liz's head lowered as she replied, "I am afraid that Albert was missing from our camp before the avalanche. Now I do not know how we can find him." Liz's eyes welled up with tears.

"But we must look for him," ordered Henriette. "Everyone up, up, up. Look for that crazy cat until we find him."

Kate walked over to Liz and nudged her, "There is always hope, dear."

Liz sniffed and said, "Hope? Hope is too risky for me. The likelihood of Albert surviving on his own, and especially if he were caught in this avalanche, is . . ." She shook her head in doubt.

"I won't let ye give up. Stay with me while we search," said Kate.

It was a surreal feeling that the once violent snow now lay silent, looking beautiful as it covered the landscape. How quickly things can happen. All the animals felt vulnerable. Rudy and Rosie flew over to the little band of animals and joined in the search for Al. They looked everywhere, while Max and Kate used their noses trying to sniff out Al's scent. But it was no use. The fresh snow covered everything, including any sign or smell of Al. No amount of digging led to anything but snow, snow, and more snow.

Liz looked skyward at the fire cloud, which was moving once again. "We cannot leave and follow you now! We have to find Albert! I do not understand why you led us through these mountains when there are other ways to travel in this direction. Why could we not have journeyed through the south of France to avoid this mountain pass? Why has this happened?"

All the animals stood silently by as Liz plopped down on the ground in despair, unanswered questions spewing out of her. This time her lack of understanding cut to her heart. It wasn't just facts or information she was missing. It was Al. Even Liz did not realize how deeply she felt about him until this moment when he was no longer there. Kate and Max shared a pained look, as did the other pairs of animals, not knowing quite what to say. Sometimes, nothing is the best thing to say.

Liz looked at the ground, her head low. Her vision was blurred from the tears in her eyes, but finally she opened them. There, next to her on the ground, was something peeking out of the snow. Woolly white leaves and beautiful blooms of five to six small yellow flowers surrounded by a star of leaflets.

Kate walked over to Liz as she saw the cat looking at the flowers. "Liz, this looks like wha' ye described as edelweiss. Is that wha' it is then?"

"*Non,* it is impossible. We are too low on the mountain for this flower to grow here. It must be something else. It does not matter," Liz said as she got up to walk away. She needed some time alone.

Liz heard Kate call to her, "Liz! The flowers moved! Come see!"

Liz looked behind over her shoulder and remarked, "It must be the wind."

Isabella rushed over to look at the flowers sticking out of the snow. "No, no! Come see!" she urged.

Liz stopped and turned, walking slowly back to Kate, Isabella, and the flowers. Sure enough, the flowers were moving. And the wind wasn't blowing. Curious, Liz used her paw to gently dig the snow away from the flowers, and they moved even more. Kate looked at Max, cocking her head, then at Rudy and Rosie, who shrugged their tiny shoulders.

Liz expected to find some roots at the base of the flowers. But she discovered something orange. It was furry. It was Al's paw.

151

"Albert! Albert! Albert! It is you!" Liz said as she saw his paw clenching the bunch of edelweiss.

Max ran over to Liz and began to furiously dig Al out, shouting, "STEP ASIDE, LASS, I'LL DIG THE KITTY OUT." Max proceeded to dig through the snow to reveal a very soggy, shivering Al. His paw remained tightly clenched around the bunch of flowers.

Al shook his head and opened his eyes to see Liz standing over him, smiling with relief. With a stiff upper limb, he slowly extended the edelweiss to Liz, and with chattering teeth said, "Th-th-these are f-f-for ye." He sneezed hard, snow falling off his fur.

"Oh my . . . Albert. They are beautiful. *Merci beaucoup!* But I am most happy that you are safe," replied Liz, kissing Al on the nose as she took the flowers into her paws, beaming with joy.

Max pulled Al out of the snow and slapped his burly paw on his friend's back. "LADDIE, THAT WERE SOME FEAT. IT

WER-R-RE A DAFT FEAT, AN' YE BEST NOT DO IT AGAIN. BUT I'M PROUD OF YE," he shouted because his ears were again plugged.

"You, Albert, are a noble warrior. And because your name means 'famous' we will name these mountains in your honor," Liz said with the warmth of hope burning in her heart. Turning to the other animals, Liz exclaimed, "Because of Albert's bravery in climbing to the top of this mountain to get this edelweiss, and facing multiple dangers, I hereby name these mountains 'The Als.'"

"WHA' DID SHE SAY?" asked Max, shaking his head and his stuffy ears.

"She said we'll name these mountains after Al. We'll call them 'The Als,'" Kate explained.

"AYE, THE ALPS. 'TIS A FINE NAME INDEED. THE ALPS," Max continued to shout. He yawned and his ears popped.

All the animals erupted in shouts of joy, hugging each other and celebrating that not only was Al safe, he had accomplished what no one thought he could. He grew into his name.

Al was a noble, famous warrior.

152

CHAPTER 27

The Wedding

I propose a toast," exclaimed a member of the wedding party, slurring as he spoke.

"Another toast to the happy couple. May you always be rich, may you always have everything you desire, and may you have many children who try and take their inheritance early."

Laughter abounded at this wedding, as did heavy drinking. The guests had been celebrating for two days, and they were just getting started. Shem felt uncomfortable, and couldn't wait to leave. But it was his best friend who had married this foreigner. He wanted to join in celebrating his friend's happiness, but still he knew that this marriage was not God honoring. He was torn. How could he congratulate his friend on what he knew in his heart to be wrong?

It had become increasingly difficult for Noah's family to co-exist in this society that plunged further and further into wicked-ness as the years went by. Shem held on to this last good friend, who had walked in the ways of God when they were children. But now his friend rejected God to pursue what he wanted in life.

Shem frequently questioned who was really right. Was his father right? Or was the rest of the world right? It was hard being such an outsider.

"Hey, we haven't heard from the crazy ark builder," shouted a drunken guest.

Others joined in the heckling, asking Shem to say something. Shem knew they were mocking him. They didn't really care about anything he had to say. But he felt he would honor his friend nonetheless. What did he really have to lose?

"I'm here today to wish my good friend Avi well in his marriage. May God . . ." Shem hesitated as he looked at the audience of guests, their eyes boring into him. "May God bless your marriage and may you seek God and follow Him so He can indeed bless you with true happiness."

"Sounds like his crazy father! Always talking about God," another guest shouted. Others joined in to taunt Shem.

"I heard him say that God is going to destroy us if we don't shape up."

"Yeah, why would we want to shape up when we're happy the way we are?"

"Noah has been building that boat for one hundred years. Any nut like that isn't worth listening to. If God were really coming to get us, don't you think he would have done so by now?"

Avi couldn't stand the ridicule of his friend any longer. "Silence! Shem is my guest and my friend. Stop this banter before I ask you to leave." Avi motioned for Shem to go outside with him. Shem looked around the room at the smiling faces filled with avarice. Yet he knew their smiles weren't from happiness, but from delight in seeing yet another blow come against the family of Noah.

Avi took Shem to the garden behind the house to sit down under the shady grapevines. "Shem, I'm sorry about all that. Everyone's drunk, and they don't know what they're saying," Avi said apologetically.

154

"No, Avi, they do know what they are saying. This is all I hear from people in our city, whether drunk or sober. I've heard it for so long that I'm used to it by now," said Shem with a sad smile on his face, running his fingers through his jet-black hair. He looked at Avi, piercing his friend with his deep blue eyes, which were full of concern. His gaze of compassion made Avi squirm.

"I know you don't really approve of my marriage. But I can't resist this girl. She's the most beautiful thing I've ever seen," Avi said, smiling and putting his hand on Shem's shoulder, longing for him to agree.

"Yes, she is indeed beautiful, Avi, but God has made it clear that His people are not supposed to marry godless foreigners. You will not be happy, unless you turn back to God. Please, there is still time! Turn from this path you are headed down, and bring your wife into our beliefs. God is going to bring His wrath down soon, and I want you and your household to be saved." Shem pleaded with Avi, his heart longing to reach his friend.

155

With that Avi straightened up, the smile leaving his face. "You don't understand, Shem. You are too stuck in your beliefs and your ways. I choose a new way of thinking and living. I'm free to do whatever I want, and I choose my bride and her ways. There are no restrictions. I'll be happy, you'll see. I'll be happy. Now go, you don't belong here. I wish it could be different between us, but we are on opposite paths now. So go," Avi said as he turned and left Shem in the garden.

Shem stood and called to Avi, "If you have a change of heart, know I will be waiting to be your friend."

Avi shook his head sadly and went in the house to rejoin the wedding party. Shem sighed and looked at the ground. That was it. Shem bid his last farewell to Avi, and to anyone he could consider a friend, outside of his two brothers, Ham and Japheth.

Shem started walking home, his heart heavy. The streets were full of violence. Two young boys went running down the street carrying a canvas bag. A market owner was yelling after them, "Thieves! Stop them! They stole my money."

It was dangerous to be out past dark. Thugs abounded in the streets, and would kill anyone for just a few spare coins. Murder was part of the daily news in this city. And God was nowhere to be found here—He didn't enter the thoughts of a single soul outside of Shem's family.

Godless. The people chose to be godless. How empty, thought Shem. God provided such meaning to life. How could people so easily write Him off in pursuit of people, places, and things that would never satisfy? Shem pulled his cloak further around his head and picked up his pace to get home.

As he walked along, he thought about what the people had said at the wedding. It was true; his father had been building the ark for more than one hundred years. It was all Shem ever knew as a child, growing up to the sounds of hammering and sawing, and the strong smell of pitch used to coat the inside and outside of the boat. His father explained to Shem and his brothers that God had told him to build the ark. Shem never got tired of hearing the story, for it was so amazing, and it gave him comfort to see a purpose behind what seemed foolish to the world.

Noah was about five hundred years old when God spoke to him. For four centuries Noah and his wife, Adah, had farmed the land here. She was a solid and a faithful mate, and together they followed God and tried to honor Him in all they did.

One day God came to Noah and said,

"I'M GOING TO PUT AN END TO THIS CORRUPT AND EVIL WORLD AND ALL THE PEOPLE IN IT. I CAN'T STAND THE VIOLENCE ANY LONGER. BUT YOU, NOAH, YOU ARE THE ONLY RIGHTEOUS MAN I SEE. YOU AND YOUR FAMILY WILL I SAVE. YOU ARE TO BUILD AN ARK OUT OF GOPHER WOOD. MAKE ROOMS IN IT AND COVER IT WITH PITCH INSIDE AND OUT. YOU NEED TO MAKE THE ARK 450 FEET LONG, 75 FEET WIDE, AND 45 FEET HIGH. MAKE A ROOF FOR THE ARK AND PUT A WINDOW AT THE TOP, 18 INCHES FROM THE ROOFLINE. PUT A DOOR IN THE SIDE AND GIVE THE ARK THREE DECKS.

"I'M GOING TO BRING FLOODWATERS TO DESTROY THE EARTH AND EVERYTHING THAT HAS BREATH LIVING UPON IT. EVERYTHING ON EARTH WILL PERISH. BUT WITH YOU, I WILL ESTABLISH MY COVENANT, AND YOU WILL ENTER THE ARK—YOU, YOUR WIFE, AND YOUR THREE SONS AND THEIR WIVES. YOU ARE TO BRING INTO THE ARK TWO OF ALL LIVING CREATURES, MALE AND FEMALE, TO KEEP THEM ALIVE WITH YOU. TWO OF EVERY KIND OF BIRD, ANIMAL, AND CREATURE THAT MOVES ALONG THE GROUND WILL COME TO YOU TO BE KEPT ALIVE. YOU ARE TO STORE UP ALL THE FOOD THAT YOU AND THE ANIMALS WILL NEED."

Noah was floored with this word from God, but he faithfully obeyed. He believed what God had told him would come to pass. So, instead of planting wheat that year in the south field, he staked out the dimensions of the ark. And he began to build. As Shem, Ham, and Japheth grew older they helped as well. They cleared the forest around them, felling tall trees and shaping the wood into perfect planks. After a few years, the boat began to take shape.

Whenever Noah and his family worked on the ark, they always had an audience of people from the city coming by to check out this crazy spectacle. As they laughed and jeered at Noah, he was ever full of grace toward them. He repeatedly preached to them to change their ways, repent of their sins, and leave the violence behind to follow God. Noah tried to share the hope that they, too, could be saved when God destroyed the world, but no one ever listened. All they did was laugh at the crazy old man and his crazy family—the city's resident God-loving fools.

Shem was grateful that he had met his wife, Nala, when he did. She was so pure, so good, and her heart was inclined to God's. Ham and Japheth also found godly wives. God had indeed blessed Noah's family with faithful women. Shem uttered a word of thanks to God as he walked along the dusty road leading home and to Nala.

As Shem took the turn off the main road, there in the distance he saw the magnificent structure sitting securely in its strong cradle. The ark was bigger than life. It may have looked foolish to the world, but every time Shem drew near to the ark, he felt wrapped up in the unmistakable feeling of safety. He felt the presence of God because God Himself had ordained and designed this ark. While Shem didn't see how it was possible for this ark to ever go anywhere, as they were miles from the sea, he felt safe inside its hold.

Shem smelled the wonderful aroma of garlic and herbs as he approached his small home built in the shadow of the ark. Nala and the other women were preparing dinner, and Shem's mouth watered at the thought of one of their delicious meals. "Hello, I'm home," he said as he entered the house.

"Thank the Lord you are here. I missed you. How was the wedding?" Nala said as she kissed Shem on the cheek.

"Predictable," Shem answered as he walked over to the fire where sat Noah and his brothers.

Noah was whittling a stick by the fire, and looked up at Shem with a twinkle in his eyes. His long white hair flowed to his shoulders, and wood shavings stuck to his long white beard. Noah's face was full of wrinkles but his face was soft nonetheless, as was his heart. He knew what Shem must have encountered at the wedding. He shook his head and chuckled, "More 'crazy' arrows hurled at you, I presume?"

"Yes, father. And I tried once more to talk to Avi, to help him see that he is on the wrong path, but his mind is made up. He no longer wishes to follow God," Shem said, poking at the fire with a long stick.

Noah didn't respond right away, and everyone waited for him to speak first. Oh, how his sons respected him. The Creator had spoken directly to their father. His integrity was beyond reproach, his goodness unmatched. They would ever be obedient to whatever their father instructed them to do. How they loved him, for their father had taught them love. Noah told his sons about God's love, and he lived out that love in how he treated every member of the family. Yes, this six-hundred-year-old man was ridiculed and rejected by the world, but loved beyond measure by his small family. They were his world now.

158

"Well, you tried, Shem," Noah finally said. "God only asks us to share the truth with others. Each person must decide for himself or herself whether to respond to God or not. The free will He gave to each heart is a precious gift, yet it comes at a painful price when a heart chooses to reject the only source of hope, the only source of true love and happiness."

Shem sat thoughtfully and looked around at his brothers. They shared smiles as they sat there, the fire crackling and spreading warmth around them. "How grateful I am, my brothers, for you and your friendship. Were it not for you, I would have no one to call friend."

Ham and Japheth smiled before Ham decided to lighten the mood. "Yeah, you say that now. Wait 'til Japheth here drops another hammer on your foot!"

"You're right," laughed Shem as he thought of his aching toes, which carried the bruises of Japheth's hammer. Shem shoved Japheth with his muscular hand, remembering how that accident, days ago, left him screaming with pain.

"Hey, it was an accident!" Japheth exclaimed in his defense. "Besides, I don't leave nails sitting in chairs like some people I know," Japheth said accusingly at Ham.

"Well someone's got to provide a little entertainment around here! It gets boring from time to time, and there's nothing like nails in a chair to stir things up!" laughed Ham.

Noah looked at his sons and how they carried on together. How faithful they had been to do as they had been told all these many years. They had sacrificed friends, social status, and any hope of ever being anyone important in the world. What a high price to pay. Still, he knew that what they had done was the right thing. It was the obedient thing.

When God gave instructions, there was only one right response. And his sons had chosen to obey.

"So, father, we finished the last stall on deck 3 today. I think all we lack is completing the pitch on the upper deck and we'll be finished. What will we do then?" asked Japheth.

Noah thought for a moment and then replied, "We gather supplies for the ark. And we wait on the Lord. I don't know if the completion of the ark means that God will be ready to act. But be sure that we will know when the time is upon us."

"How will we know?" asked Ham.

"The animals. The animals will come to us. God said they would come to us to be saved. When they begin to arrive, the time will be near," said Noah, continuing to whittle his stick.

"How many animals do you think will be in our care?" asked Shem. "We've never cared for more than our farm animals. How will we know how to handle every beast that roams the earth?"

"Well, given the size of the ark, and the stalls we've built, I estimate thousands upon thousands," said Noah, looking each son in the eyes. They were overwhelmed with such a large task.

"That many? How will we ever be able to feed them, and take care of their waste?" Ham said, clearly upset at the seemingly impossible job before them.

"Do you forget who ordained this venture? If God has ordained it, He will enable us to do it. He is the Maker of all creation, and He knows how to care for every creature. He will give us the wisdom and the way to make it happen," Noah replied calmly.

"But how could we ever gather that much food? And how long will we be on the ark? What if we run out of food?" said Ham, getting more worried as the conversation continued.

"Our God shall supply all our needs, Ham. Trust Him. In all things, trust Him," said Noah, standing up and stretching his legs. He heard Adah calling them for dinner. "Now, God has provided our food for this evening, so let us be content and go enjoy it."

As Noah left the room, Shem, Ham, and Japheth were speechless as their minds swirled with the reality of what was heading their way. Thousands upon thousands of animals, birds, and insects would soon come to them, and they would be in charge of their care. Shem thought of what the city people would say. He could only imagine their jeers as the Noah family became not only ark builders, but animal keepers as well.

"God help us! May He bring animals to us who know what they're doing anyway. They'll have to help us help them is all I know," said Japheth as the sons followed Noah into the other room for dinner.

Shem held out hope for his friend. When finally Avi saw the animals, then maybe he would believe that what Shem said really was from God. Maybe then.

161

CHAPTER 28

The Raging River

Suddenly the ground beneath him disappeared, and he was in midair for a split second as he fell off the rock face. Violently he rolled along the rocky slope, hitting every outcropping on the way down. He felt a searing pain in his left leg before he landed with a breath-stealing thud on the hard ground below. He could feel the warm blood oozing from his leg, which would only serve to further arouse the wolves. They smelled his blood and sensed his fear.

A violent boom of thunder crashed into his ears after the jagged bolt of lightning lit up the dark sky. The instant flash illuminated three scowling wolves on the rock face, looking down at him. They growled, teeth snarling and pungent breath stinking up the air around them. Their yellow eyes stared menacingly at him. There was nowhere else to run, even if he could have run away. He was cut off. He knew it. And they knew it. The leader of the pack lifted his head high, nose turned toward the sky. He howled at the storm to declare victory and the end.

As the wolves made their way down to where Max lay bleeding and breathless, he slowly backed up to the edge of the cliff. His instinct for survival made his mind race, surpassing the speed of his pounding heart. The thunder continued laughing at Max, confirming his hopeless thoughts that he was doomed. One of the wolves landed with a grunt next to the small, terrified dog, a low chuckle coming from his throat. The other two wolves joined him in short order, all moving in close. Instinctively, Max suddenly rolled over the edge of the cliff and fell downward, his back arched with nothing under him but air. The wolves watched from up above as their prey was lost to the black night, out of their reach.

Max's breath was knocked out of him as he hit the water. After falling for what seemed an eternity, he plunged deep into the raging river before struggling to reach the surface for air. The water was wild and cold, carrying Max along with the rushing current.

His momentary relief of escaping the wolves was short lived as the water pulled him down again and again. He panicked, struggling to keep his head above water. The pain in his leg intensified when cramps overtook his exhausted muscles. It was no use. He could not swim against this raging river. It would be easier to give up than fight. Max allowed himself to slip into the depths. Still, he desperately held his breath. His mind started to get fuzzy. He blacked out, lost to the darkness that engulfed him.

163

CHAPTER 29

A Land Flowing

"Max, ye had a bad one last night. Yer paws were movin' like I never seen them before. Are ye aright then, me love?" asked Kate with eyes full of concern.

"Aye, lass," Max said, yawning from the restless night of sleep. "It were a bad one. But it is mornin' now."

Max squinted when he heard Jacques' loud wake-up crow, his head aching from lack of sleep. "I tell ye, Kate, if I could r-r-reach in an' pull that voice box out of that bir-r-rd, I'd do it faster than Al kin eat a melon."

Kate giggled, "Well, at least we don't have ta worry aboot avalanches anymore. Jacques is jest makin' up for lost time. He had a rough go of it, not crowin' for so many mornin's. Jest shake it off an' let's get goin'. At least those paws of yers kin run on the ground an' not in the air then."

Max looked at Kate, smiling whether he wanted to or not. She always had a way of finding the bright side of things. That was one of the things he loved most about her. It was, indeed, a relief that they were out of danger of avalanches. The band of animals had traveled through the Alps, taking the mountain pass taken by the fire cloud. Everyone was relieved to reach the lower meadows of easy rolling hills after the formidable mountains that challenged every fiber of their bodies. Looking back at the Alps in the far distance, they marveled that they were able to cross them without loss.

Now that they were in flat terrain, the animals no longer suffered from popping ears or freezing, snowy cold. Travel was easier now and spirits rose. The bond that these unlikely pairs of travelers shared also grew. Having experienced so many hardships and challenges together, it was only natural for them to share mutual camaraderie as well. Of course, each one had some idiosyncrasy that caused irritation, but even those traits had to be accepted. Irritation is part of the blessing of diversity. So onward the animals traveled throughout the sunny day, laughing at each other and at themselves as they recounted the stories from their adventure.

"So where are we now, lass?" asked Max as he trotted alongside Liz, surveying the low green meadows filled with lush grass and occasional wildflowers.

"From the topography I assume we are in Hungary," Liz replied, also looking around the area for some recognizable feature.

"Ye can say that again! I'm starvin'," Al piped in.

"No, dear Albert. *Hun-gar-y*, not hungry," Liz said with a giggle. Al never ceased to make Liz smile. "Hungary is a country."

"Well, whatever the name o' this place, I'm still starvin'. Sure, and I say we stop to eat," replied Al, not allowing his lack of knowledge to deter him from his prime objective.

"*Sí, el gato* is right," chimed in Isabella, already grazing on the tall grass.

"It appears that we must stop for a while, whether we are hungry or not. Look up ahead," said Liz, directing the others to the end of the meadow.

In the near distance was a river. It wasn't as wide as the English Channel, nor was it as narrow as the creek Max had traversed.

But it was a wide body of rushing water to cross. And that sent alarm coursing through Max. "Not water again," he murmured to himself.

"Ooh, it is a beautiful blue river. Do ye know wha' it's called then?" asked Kate, appreciating the beauty of this scenic place.

"I am not certain, Kate. I have reached the end of where I have personally traveled, but I have heard that a beautiful blue river winds through this continent and is called the Danube. I believe this is the same river. Ah, but it is *très belle*, no?" asked Liz, sharing Kate's enthusiasm at seeing the beauty of the winding river.

"Let me down now, bull," Henriette ordered Don Pedro. Nodding his head out of respect, he slowly knelt so Henriette and Jacques could jump off his back. Henriette went waddling over to Liz and Kate, rustling her feathers as she stretched her wings. "Mademoiselle, and just how are we to cross *la rivière?*"

Liz didn't answer, her tail slowly curling up and down as she studied the river and the surrounding landscape. The fire cloud was moving ahead on the other side of the river, bringing into question how were they to follow the fire cloud.

"Rudy! Rosie! Come here, *s'il vous plaît*," requested Liz, not taking her eyes off the sparkling blue water.

The hummingbirds flew over to Liz, ever eager to help. "At your service, *señorita*," exclaimed Rudy. Then Rosie corrected him, "No, but it is *señora* now." Liz smiled as she looked at Al grazing the fields alongside Isabella, realizing that she had found her mate for life. Her heart belonged to him now, so *señora* was, indeed, the proper Spanish title for this cat.

"*Merci*, Rosie. I need you two to fly over the river and tell me exactly how wide it is. See if you can locate a narrow place for us to cross. Meanwhile, we will need to discuss our situation."

The two hummingbirds took off to inspect the river while Liz turned to discuss things with Max. "Well, *mon ami*, you figured out how to cross the channel from England, no? Perhaps you have an idea for crossing the Danube as well?"

Max frowned. He didn't have an idea. There were no logs big enough for this river. And surely whales didn't inhabit landlocked, freshwater rivers. No, he didn't have an idea. But he knew how to get one. "Liz, I think ye best be talkin' ta the Maker on this one then. He is the One who showed me how ta cross water before."

Liz kept her gaze on Max, thinking about what he said. "Why don't you ask the Maker for us while I look at the logistics of our situation? Perhaps we can work together on a solution?"

"Aye, lass," Max said, smiling, "I'll have a chat with Him then."

Liz nodded and turned to walk to the riverbank. Henriette and Jacques waddled along behind her. Kate turned to Max, "Okay, me love, I'll be prayin' too. May the Maker give ye the answer we need." She kissed him on the nose and then went to join Liz as she inspected the area.

Max sat there, feeling the weight of the world on his shoulders. Not only was he responsible for spiritually leading this group, he was once again faced with one of the things he hated most—crossing water.

"Aye, here we are again, then. Maker, I wish I knew why I have ta keep takin' this challenge with water. Ye know how hard it is for me, after wha' happened so long ago. Still, ye have shown me the way before, an' I know ye'll do it again. Max prayed as he watched the others make their way to the riverbank. He sat a long while, praying and waiting on an answer, fearful, but confident that the Maker would provide a way.

CHAPTER 30

When Cows Swim and Horses Dance

Rudy and Rosie twirled in the air, hovering just above the cool water of the Danube. They observed deep churning currents, suggesting a formidable challenge for crossing. Up and down they flew along the river, popping into an occasional flower to sip the nectar. Soon they flew back to Liz to report their findings.

"*Señora*, this river will be a challenge for any creature to cross, as the currents are very strong. We did locate a narrow area to cross, but still it looks to be about two hundred feet," reported Rudy. The animals looked at each other with concern. Two hundred feet was a long distance for any creature, much less all ten of them.

"*Merci*," Liz replied as she sat and stared across the Danube. No one bothered to ask her what they were going to do. They knew Liz was thinking, and would provide a solution in due time. Liz walked over to Don Pedro and began studying his legs.

"Uh, *señora* . . . what is it?" asked Don Pedro, watching the petite black cat curving around his legs, her tail grazing him.

"Just checking, *mon ami*," Liz replied. "Don Pedro, pardon, but would you swish your tail for me?"

An odd request, but Don Pedro obliged, swishing his tail back and forth, not understanding why Liz had asked him.

"*Merci*, now please raise your left front hoof," Liz requested, studying Don Pedro's every move, and taking mental notes. "Now your back hoof, left first, *s'il vous plaît*. Then let me inspect your horns." Don Pedro silently did as Liz asked, even though he felt somewhat silly as he bowed his head to the ground.

"*Très bien*, Don Pedro," Liz finally said as she completed her inspection and walked away from the bull over to where Isabella and Al grazed.

"Ah, Liz, ye should try some o' these field onions," exclaimed Al, his oniony breath violating Liz's nose with its stench. She wrinkled her nose and turned her head to the side.

"No, *merci*, Albert. I am not hungry, but you go ahead and enjoy. Never mind me. I am just looking at Isabella," Liz replied, slowly walking around the cow. Isabella casually chewed her cud, following the same directions Liz had given Don Pedro. Finally, Liz remarked, "*Très bien*. I see now. *Merci*, Isabella."

"What do ye see, me love?" Al asked, burping at the same time he talked.

"Good one, Al," exclaimed Isabella, admiring Al's belch as she let loose a *PPPTTT.*

"Never mind. Enjoy the onions," Liz said as she walked away from the funny pair of gassy cat and cow. She made her way over to Max, who was still sitting alone in the meadow.

"Am I interrupting you, Max?" Liz asked softly as she approached, not wanting to disturb her good friend.

"No, lass, come have a seat with me," answered Max as he patted the ground next to him.

"What have you discovered? Has the Maker given you a solution?" asked Liz, sitting down, her tail curled up around her small feet.

"Not exactly. In fact, He's given me a strange r-r-revelation. He said I have ta waltz ta cross. But I have no idea wha' a waltz is!" said Max, looking at Liz.

Liz smiled, but gave Max a curious look. "But a waltz is another word for dance, no? Why would the Maker tell you to waltz? How is this supposed to help us cross the river? It is not logical, *mon ami!*"

"Things sometimes don't make sense at first when He tells me, but they get clearer with time," replied Max, wanting to convince Liz that the Maker knew what He was doing, even when it appeared illogical.

Liz sat a moment, struggling to understand how dancing could help them cross the river. She was stumped. It made no sense.

170

"Well, while we try ta figure it out, did ye come up with anythin' then, lass?" asked Max.

"Ah, *oui*, partially. Rudy and Rosie have reported that strong currents run in the Danube, and it will require great strength to cross. The narrowest part they located is two hundred feet across, which is still a considerable distance. I have thoroughly examined Don Pedro and Isabella, and am convinced that they are capable of swimming across the Danube," Liz explained.

"Aye, they kin swim, but wha' aboot the rest of us then?" asked Max, not seeing how this could work.

"This is why I said I have partially figured out the way across. While Don Pedro and Isabella swim, their backs will be submerged under water, but their heads will not. This, of course, provides limited carrying space. I have calculated that Jacques can ride on Isabella's head, and Henriette can ride on Don Pedro's. Since Albert and I are small creatures, we can fit onto Don Pedro's horns and hang on while he swims," Liz explained, suddenly turning her gaze to the ground.

"But wha' aboot me an' Kate?" Max asked with a frown. "There's not enough room for us then."

Liz didn't reply immediately, but put her gaze into Max's concerned eyes. It was true, there was no room for Max and Kate to ride, and this frustrated her. They could not leave the two dogs behind.

"I do not know. I have not figured this out completely. But we will not cross without you and Kate, *mon ami!*" Liz said, putting her paw under Max's chin, a determined look in her eyes.

"Thanks, lass. Ye've done a gr-r-rand job at figurin' things out. Now all we have ta do is see where the Maker's directions of waltzin' fit this mystery," said Max. "An' the Maker hasn't let me down yet."

Liz smiled. "I'm glad you're here, Max. And I'm grateful for your faith, *mon ami*. Perhaps you will teach me something, no?"

The two friends shared a moment of strength, thankful that they weren't alone in this process. They had each other. And they had the Maker.

Out of the corner of Liz's eye she saw something in the distance. A cloud of dust swirled on the horizon. She turned her gaze and then saw two large horses running in their direction, their hooves kicking up the dust. They were running at breakneck speed right toward Kate.

"KATE! KATE! KATE!"

Kate was napping in the grass, unaware of the trampling danger headed her way. Max ran as fast as his short legs would carry him. The horses were closing in, and Max didn't know if he could intercept them before they reached Kate. She was so small and low in the grass that he doubted the horses would even see her lying there.

Max continued shouting to her, "KATE! KATE! WAKE UP! WAKE UP!" Kate's ear twitched as if trying to hear Max, but she was in such a deep sleep from exhaustion that her body didn't want to listen.

The other animals were on the other side of the meadow, and looked up to see what was happening. "Oh no! Little Kate is in harm's way!" shouted Al.

"Better let Max reach her, *amigo*," said Isabella, also with grave concern.

Henriette needed to control Don Pedro in this crisis. She had to keep him from seeing the movement of the horses so he wouldn't take off running after them. She got right in his face while standing on the ground below. "Look at me, *boeuf!* Keep your eyes right here!" she said, pointing to her eyes with the tip of her wing. Jacques stood next to Henriette, spreading his wings in an attempt to block Don Pedro's view.

"Almost ther-r-re!" Max said to himself as he closed the gap between Kate and the horses. He ran by Kate, quickly nudging her with his paws, shouting, "KATE! GET UP AN' MOVE!"

With that Kate snapped awake but was confused as to where she was and what was happening. Then she saw Max running toward two charging horses headed straight for her. Kate jumped up and ran to the side of the field where Liz sat, her mind and body trying to wake up to comprehend the scene taking place.

"Liz, Max will be trampled," Kate screamed, watching Max run directly in the path of the powerful horses.

"Max doesn't need size to control these beasts. He needs mind power," she replied. Liz had judged the distance and placed herself close enough to where the horses would intercept Max, but she remained out of harm's way.

Max started shouting at the horses as he ran closer to them, "STOP! STOP, YE BEASTIES! R-R-RIGHT NOW!"

The horses were bearing down on top of Max, their eyes catching a glimpse of the small black dog barking at them. They were startled to see a creature right under them. The lead horse was an enormous jet-black stallion with a long black mane and tail blowing behind him in the wind, his nostrils flaring as he snorted with every breath. The other horse was a beautiful brown mare with black mane and tail, running close behind him. As the stallion reached Max, he reared up on his hind legs and neighed loudly, startling his brown companion and pawing his hoofs at the air.

Max stood his ground, growling and ordering the horse to settle down. Liz was nearby and began yelling instructions: "MAX! YOU MUST MENTALLY DOMINATE THIS BEAST! YOUR SIZE DOES NOT MATTER; IT IS A MENTAL GAME. MAKE HIM HEED YOUR DIRECTION."

Max held his ground in front of this upset horse that continued to rear up on his powerful hindquarters. The horse was poised to stomp the small dog. Max stood up on his back legs to get a better position and locked eyes with the horse, commanding his attention and ordering him to stop.

"WHOA, HORSIE! STEADY NOW, STEADY. CALM DOWN, LAD. JEST LOOK AT ME AN' CALM DOWN," Max said with a firmness that let the horse know who was in control.

173

Just then the mare slowly walked up to Max and said, "*Signore! Spicciati*—hurry. Now that you have his attention, you must sing to him."

Max didn't take his eyes off the stallion for an instant, but replied back to the mare, "Wha' are ye sayin', lass? Sing ta the beastie?!"

"*Sì!* He is asleep, and singing is the only thing that wakes him. Because his attention is on you, you are the only one he hears," the mare replied.

"This beastie is asleep. Wha' in the name of Pete am I supposed ta sing then?" hoarsely whispered Max, not taking his eyes off the still upset stallion.

"*Non importa!* Anything, even a lullaby will do. Just make some sort of music," the mare instructed, urging Max on.

All Max could think of was a Scottish lullaby his mum had sung to him as a puppy. He cleared his throat and started to sing:

"Hush a bye, don't ye cry,
Go ta sleep little bay-bee,
When ye wake, ye shall have
All the pretty little hor-ses."

The horse began to settle, slowing his anxious rearing as he kept his eyes on Max. Soon the stallion stopped rising up and stomping his front hooves. He stood still, his tail swatting back and forth as he kept his gaze on Max. The stallion's eyes blinked, and he shook his head as he looked at the unknown landscape around him. He then saw the brown mare smiling at him. He looked down to see Max at his feet, and then back to his mate with a look of question on his face.

"Pauline, tell me I didn't do it again, eh?" said the black stallion in a deep, accentuated voice.

"*Sí,* Giorgio. You were sleep-running again. This little dog stopped you from trampling his mate, and then sang to you," the mare replied.

"*Buon giorno, Signore. Grazie* for stopping me and waking me up. I'm sorry for almost hurting your mate and causing trouble. I have a sleep-running problem, so *scusate,*" explained Giorgio as he bowed in apology to Max.

"I never hear-r-rd of such a daft thing. A horse that sleep-runs," said Max, not believing what he was hearing.

"Ah *oui,* you run in your sleep, too, Max. But you do not actually go anywhere," said Liz as she walked over to join Max and the horses. Kate followed close behind Liz. Rudy and Rosie were perched on top of Don Pedro's horns and Henriette and Jacques sat on his back as he walked from the field to join them, along with Al and Isabella.

"It's true, me love. I watch ye run in yer sleep most every night when ye dream," said Kate to Max, drawing a wrinkled brow from her mate.

"But I don't get up an' r-r-run across the meadow like a daft beastie!" said Max in his defense.

"Horses sleep while standing, *mon ami*, so it is only logical to see how a horse who is dreaming of running could then take off actually running," Liz explained. She turned then to the stallion. "What I do not understand is why you wake up with music. And with a lullaby at that? Lullabies usually put creatures to sleep, no?"

The big black stallion looked at Liz with embarrassment. "*Sí, Signora,* I am backwards. I fall asleep so quickly that I never needed a lullaby to put me to sleep when I was young. Now, it is the music that wakes me. It is my weakness. *Capisci?*"

"Well, I cannot say that I totally understand, no. But I think it is a fascinating condition you have, *mon ami*," Liz replied, looking at the situation from a purely scientific standpoint.

"I'd say it's a danger-r-rous condition ye have there, laddie! Ye almost r-r-ran over me wife, Kate," said Max with a frown and a growl in his throat.

"*Mi dispiace, Signore e Signora.* Please forgive me, and allow me to make it up to you somehow," the stallion replied, again bowing low to Max and now Kate at his side.

"I forgive ye, Giorgio, is it?" replied Kate with a warm smile. "Ye couldn't help it, I know. I was amazed at how active ye were while asleep. When Max stopped ye an' raised up on his hind legs ta get yer attention, an' ye were up on yer hindquarters—it almost looked like ye two were dancin'."

Max and Liz looked at each other, both realizing that this was the dance the Maker meant. They smiled as they realized they had their way across the Danube.

"Well, it jest so happens that Kate an' me need transport across the river here, along with our other friends, who kin ride the cow an' the bull. Kin ye swim then, laddie, or do ye need ta be asleep ta do that, too?" Max said with a bit of sarcasm.

"*Prego.* Of course we will help! And no, I can swim when I am awake, as can my wife Pauline," the stallion replied, not catching Max's jab.

"Tell me, *mes amis,* which part of Italy are you from?" Liz asked, already knowing their country of origin.

"We're from the southern tip of Italy, and have traveled a long way. You see, we are following—" Pauline began, before she was interrupted.

"The fire cloud," the entire group of animals exclaimed.

"*Sí, Signora!* But how did you know?" Pauline asked with amazement.

"We all are following the fire cloud and have come from many countries. Since you agree to help us cross the Danube and I hope stay with us as we travel, we will be able to make much better time on our journey," said Liz, realizing that the smaller animals now all had faster transport.

176

"*Mes amis*, it is time to cross the Danube, no? I have determined that Don Pedro and Isabella will be able to swim the distance, and they will carry Henriette and Jacques. Albert and I will hold onto Don Pedro's horns as he swims. Kate, you will ride on Pauline and Max, on Giorgio. Rudy and Rosie, of course, will fly. Are there any questions?" Liz asked as she explained the river crossing.

All the animals got into position as they reached the water's edge, waiting for the signal from Liz. "*Bonne chance,* everyone! Here we go!" said Liz as Don Pedro slid into the Danube with his load of passengers. Max had to laugh at the sight of Al being completely wet and hanging onto the bull's horns. Al's lower lip was trembling and he was scared to death, but Max admired how he kept up a brave front as best he could. Liz and Al kept their heads close as they clung to Don Pedro's horns. Henriette was clucking, not used to being wet, instructing Don Pedro to keep his head up as high as possible. Jacques sat on Isabella's head, exhilarated with the river crossing, and chuckling as he saw Henriette out of her comfort zone. Kate was excited about riding Pauline, the beautiful brown horse, as she always loved splashing in the water. Rudy and Rosie flew above the animals, amused and amazed by what they saw.

Max felt sick to his stomach as he eased into the river on this Italian stallion. He just prayed the horse would not let him drown. He held tight to Giorgio's mane with his teeth while keeping his eyes firmly shut. The Maker had helped him cross other bodies of water, and he knew he would get across the Danube as well. So even though he was afraid, he trusted the Maker anyway.

The strong swimming animals gradually made their way across the broad river. It was strenuous but they soon climbed onto the shore. Everyone cheered as they reached the other side, grateful that they were on solid ground again. As the sun began to set, the fire cloud stopped. At this point, Liz began experiencing a sense of wonder that completely overwhelmed her.

The Maker had told Max that he would need to dance in order to cross the river. While it didn't make sense at the time, Liz now understood what the Maker meant. He was faithful to provide a way for them in an unexpected way. And not only did He provide a way across the river, He provided a new, fast way to travel until they reached their final destination.

Liz looked up at the fire cloud and smiled. "You have given Max the answers he needed, and You have provided for all of us when I did not see any logical way. *Merci*. I never would have thought that dancing could be an answer to prayer."

Liz paused and then continued her solitary conversation with the fire cloud. "I do not dance very well, *Monsieur*. Nor do I pray very well. Perhaps, I am now willing to learn, no? Please . . . teach me how."

The fire cloud burned warmly, and Liz felt a stirring in her heart. Maybe this was a new beginning of her journey in faith as well.

177

PART THREE

WORLDWIDE ANIMALIA AND NOAH'S ARK

CHAPTER 31

God's Plan

Noah sat in the dark, his face barely visible by the torch in front of him. The memory of his father's voice echoed in the cave:

"Walk with Him, Noah. Always walk with Him."

The final words of his father faded deep into the cave and were replaced with the Voice, which spoke through the fire:

I SEE HOW GREAT MAN'S WICKEDNESS ON EARTH HAS BECOME AND THAT EVERY TENDENCY, EVERY THOUGHT OF HIS HEART, IS CONTINUOUSLY EVIL. I AM GRIEVED THAT I HAVE MADE MAN. AND MY HEART IS FILLED WITH PAIN.

Noah thought of the villagers. What God said was true, but Noah had never thought of God feeling pain. He knew father Adam felt it when he and mother Eve sinned in the Garden. And he knew that pain was part of man's and woman's existence ever since.

But God? God's heart knew pain?

"I WILL WIPE MANKIND, WHOM I HAVE CREATED, FROM THE FACE OF THE EARTH FOR I AM SORRY THAT I MADE THEM. I AM GOING TO BRING FLOOD-

WATERS TO DESTROY THE EARTH AND EVERYTHING THAT HAS BREATH UPON IT. EVERYTHING ON EARTH WILL PERISH. BUT YOU, NOAH, I HAVE FOUND FAVOR WITH YOU. WITH YOU, I WILL ESTABLISH MY COVENANT."

The flame from the torch flared up with intense light, illuminating the walls of the cave.

"STUDY THESE WALLS, NOAH. THE HAND OF ADAM MADE THESE DRAWINGS. THESE ARE THE ANIMALS I BROUGHT TO HIM SO THAT HE MIGHT NAME THEM. EVERY CREATURE, WHETHER LIVESTOCK, BIRDS OF THE AIR, OR BEASTS OF THE FIELD, ADAM DID NAME THEM. STUDY THESE WALLS, NOAH. JUST AS I BROUGHT THESE ANIMALS TO ADAM, SO SHALL I BRING THESE ANIMALS BACK TO YOU."

The interior of the cave now lit up completely. Hundreds of thousands of drawings covered the walls. As Noah scanned each picture, the animals seemed to come to life as they migrated across the cave walls, directly toward Noah's torch.

CHAPTER 32

Worldwide Animalia: Canucks

"Murray, you can't stay in there forever," said the mosquito as it landed on the moose's large antlers. The moose's body was submerged in the shallow, dark pond. He kept his large head just above the water so he could breathe.

"Well, I'm not coming out 'til your wife stops biting me. She's deadly, eh?" said Murray. "I'm just glad you don't bite. How do you stand living with her, Tito?"

"She doesn't bite me. It's just what female mosquitoes do. Sorry about that. I promise to have a word with her, but we've really got to get going. The others are waiting for us on the path behind the pond," answered Tito.

Murray looked both ways to make sure the coast was clear before standing up tall. Water dripped off his 1,500-pound body as he walked out of the pond. His six-foot antlers shone in the sun as the water drained off them. His brown hide glistened and his muscles twitched, as if anticipating another bite from the large, irritating mosquito.

"So, the fire cloud's moving again, eh?" Murray asked as he lumbered his way over to the path to join the others.

"Yep. Racket flew up above the tree line to inspect the path, and it looks clear," answered Tito.

Just then Racket descended on Murray's antlers and gave him a triple-speed peck. "Hey, Murray, whadda 'yat?"

"You're such a hoser, Racket," Murray said to the woodpecker with a disgruntled look as he shook the bird off his antlers.

"Sorry, just can't resist your antlers. They look like wood." Racket flew to a nearby tree and rapidly banged his red head, as if to get the urge out of his system.

Murray gave a half-grunt, half-laugh as he watched the red head banging away at the tree. *I'm glad I'm a moose,* he thought to himself as he caught up with his traveling companions.

184

Bogart the beaver was talking to Mel, a black bear who was chewing on some red berries, juice dripping from his chin. Tito flew over to talk with his wife about laying off the biting.

"So, I hear the fire cloud is moving again, eh?" said Murray as he joined Bogart and Mel.

Just as Bogart opened his mouth to reply, tears filled his eyes from the horrific smell that suddenly engulfed them all. They all began holding their noses, shaking their heads, shouting, "UGH! SHOO! RODNEY COOKED IT!"

The small skunk casually walked over to the group of animals, his eyes squinting in the sunshine, his black-and-white-striped tail moving side to side. "What? Well don't blame me. I can't help it if I don't see what's flying toward me. I shoot first and ask questions later," said Rodney, not at all affected by the smell he had shot into the air.

"I didn't mean any harm, Rodney. I was just coming to tell you we're off again," said Racket, landing on the branch of berries that Mel was grazing on. "I can't help it if you guys can't see past your nose."

"Hey, let's calm down, eh? Racket, just give Rodney a warning call the next time you swoop down to his level," suggested Bogart with a big, bucktoothed smile.

"Between the mosquito bites, Racket's pecking, and Rodney's stink, I've just about had enough of this great companionship," exclaimed Murray.

"Ah, come on, Murray. It's not so bad. We men out here in the rugged wilderness, journeying together on a mysterious adventure. It's the stuff legends are made of, only this is for real," said Mel, standing on his hind legs to get eye to eye with the moose.

Murray grunted in reply. Still, the bear was right. This was a spectacular journey through beautiful Canada. He wondered where they could be going and why the Maker had called them. Murray wanted to find out as much as the rest of them what this was all about.

"Let's get going," said Mel as he grabbed another clump of berries, knocking Racket off his perch. "We can make good time today, eh? I'm so hungry from hibernating all winter, but I'll keep traveling as long as there's something to eat on the way."

"That's easy for you to say. I travel better in water than on land," said Bogart, his bucky smile fading as he began wringing his hands. "Now I feel like a real land gorby, eh?"

"Nah. You aren't a dorky tourist, Bogart. You're a real Canuck after all. A genuine Canadian. I bet you can ride on Murray's antlers. Whadda ya say, Murray?" Mel asked the moose.

"Sure, eh? But you're the only rodent I'll carry up there. Rodney needs to stay on the ground behind me," Murray answered. Bogart walked over to Murray, who lowered his head so the beaver could climb onto his antler. Racket came over and landed on the unoccupied antler.

"Hey, watch it up there, hoser. No more pecking at my antlers," instructed Murray.

"No problem, moose. Westward, ho," exclaimed the loud woodpecker as he looked at the beaver next to him. Bogart shook his head at the obnoxious bird. Racket came by his name honestly, making for a noisy journey through the great white north of Canada.

The sun was up and shining bright over the Canadian Rockies as the small band of animals slowly made their way by a pristine blue-green lake below. The fire cloud burned brightly in the sky, leading them onward to an unknown destination.

CHAPTER 33

Worldwide Animalia: Aussies

Crinan and Bethoo were admiring the incredibly blue water of the Coral Sea when they noticed a group of animals hugging the shoreline.

"There's another bunch. We'd better go have a look then, me love," Crinan said to Bethoo.

"Oh, how wonderful, dear. More beasties ta help," answered Bethoo as she followed Crinan in his downward spiral to reach the shore.

The Scottish seagulls set down in the middle of the white beach where was congregated the strangest group of creatures they had ever seen. Two kangaroos, two koalas, two bearded dragons, two duck-billed platypus, two crocodiles, and on top of one croc's nose, two praying mantises. As the birds landed, the bearded dragons' necks flared out in surprise, revealing spike-like scales. The koalas kept sleeping in the sun.

"Good mornin' ta ye. I'm Crinan an' this is me wife, Bethoo. We've come all the way from Scotland on a mission ta help stranded beasties. Are ye followin' the fire cloud then?" asked Crinan, looking at the duck-billed platypuses, with great curiosity.

"G'day, mate. How is it you came to be all the way down under?" answered the crocodile.

"Yeah, that's a back of Bourke way to fly," piped in the male bearded dragon, his neck returning to its normal state.

Crinan and Bethoo looked at the dragon, not understanding what he meant. "Come again, lad?" asked Crinan.

"He means you flew a long way to get here," Itchy responded. "G'day, now. I'm Itchy and that's my mate, Spike. We're from the bush—uh, the outback here in Australia," explained the female bearded dragon.

"Oh, I'm sorry ta hear yer itchy, dear," answered Bethoo.

"No, Itchy is my name. But no worries, love. Thanks heaps for coming. How is it you know we're following the fire cloud?" asked Itchy.

Bethoo blushed from not understanding this very different culture. She had not yet gotten used to meeting bizarre creatures with unusual names, languages, and customs. She always felt silly when she misunderstood. Still, she felt blessed to be exposed to the vast expanse of the Maker's creation.

"We've been helpin' creatures worldwide. The fire cloud is showin' up all over the globe, an' we been helpin' animals find passage from land across the sea ta reach it," explained Crinan.

"Ace, he's no Aussie, but he sure rocked up at the right time. G'day, my name's Boomer and this is my wife, Sheila," said the male kangaroo, sitting on his hind legs, balancing on his large tail. He was about six feet tall with a reddish coat. Sheila was a bit shorter with a blue-gray coat. She had a sweet smile as she echoed, "G'day."

"But how are you two small birds supposed to help these creatures?" asked Sydney the crocodile. I mean, me and Alice here can swim, but these others are stuck on land. And the fire cloud is moving northwest.

"Our wise friend, Maximillian Braveheart the Bruce from Scotland, came up with a plan ta help beasties who kin't swim ta reach the fire cloud. We locate creatures needin' passage, then tell nearby dolphins, who bring whales ta help transport them. It's been workin' everywhere. Trust us. Somethin' big is happenin' in the world, an' ye best let us help ye," explained Crinan to the group of creatures gathered there.

"I'm totally stoked, mate," Boomer explained. "I think it's a spiffy plan. I say we give it a fair go."

"I don't know. I think we should pray about this. We wouldn't want to come a guster," piped in the male praying mantis. His mate thoughtfully shook her triangle-shaped head in agreement. Their long green bodies were stretched out, with front arms folded in what appeared to be a praying stance.

"Come a guster?" asked Bethoo, confused again.

"Means to make a mistake," Boomer explained to Bethoo. Then turning to the uncertain mantids, he said, "Oh, you say that about everything, Stewart. I believe the Maker brought us this far, and now He's given us a way across the sea. You, yourself, said yesterday you were praying for a way off this land."

189

"Old man's right, you know. Sometimes the Maker answers prayers in unusual ways," said the female platypus, Quilpie. "We've all been ready to give up going any farther and here comes a way— unusual as it seems."

The praying mantids shook their heads as they realized that this, indeed, was the answer to their prayer. One of the koalas rolled over and moaned. Bethoo couldn't get over how cute these bear-like creatures were. They had fuzzy light gray fur with white chests, round heads, big black noses, and large rounded ears. They looked peaceful as they slept.

"Well, if yer willin' then, we'll contact the dolphins an' arrange transport. There's a chain of islands from here all the way up the northwest direction the fire cloud is goin', so ye'll be able ta stop an' get food along the way. Ah, if ye kin wake the koalas before they board the whale, that would be best," said Crinan as he and Bethoo got ready to take off.

"Hooroo! And thanks heaps. We'll be ready. Me and Alice can bring the mates out to the whale so they can get on board, and then we'll follow along," said Sydney the crocodile.

"Yeah, I reckon. Thanks, mates," chimed in Boomer the kangaroo.

As Crinan and Bethoo took flight, the group of animals gathered around the sleeping koalas and looked at each other. They knew they would have to wake them sooner or later.

"I think we should wake them up now so they can prepare to get in the water," said Quilpie the platypus.

"Nah, let them sleep. Don't want them to worry about being shark biscuits too early," laughed Sydney, his wide mouth of sixty-eight teeth showing. "Besides, I say just stick them in Sheila's pouch for the journey—they won't even wake up. I've never seen creatures sleep so much."

The little Australian group looked skyward at the seagulls and then to the fire cloud. How incredible that the Maker had sent them a way to keep following the cloud, just when they had given up.

Soaring high above the deep blue sea, the seagulls searched below for bottle-nosed dolphins. "I don't mean no disrespect," Crinan said to Bethoo, "but wha' in the world were the Maker thinkin' when he made that duck-billed platypus? That's the strangest beastie I ever seen."

"Aye, me love. 'Tis a strange creature. The Maker has such a creative imagination. He never ceases ta amaze me," Bethoo replied with a smile.

CHAPTER 34

Worldwide Animalia:
Russians

"T*ebye zharko,* Peter?" asked Pearl as the two polar bears slowly made their way across the thawing tundra. Pearl noticed beads of sweat all over Peter's face.

"Of course I'm hot, Pearl. This thick coat of mine vasn't meant for such varm temper-ratures. It must be for-rty degrees here," replied the huge polar bear with his thick Russian accent. With that, Peter collapsed on the ground with a thud, rolling on his back in the snow to expose his belly to the breezy air, exclaiming, "Ah, this feels nice, my little jewel. Stop a vhile and take a r-rest."

Pearl stopped to look at her big lug of a husband, feeling sorry for him. After all, he weighed almost one thousand pounds more than she, and his four inches of blubber was keeping him hot as they traveled into this warmer zone. Peter liked cold temperatures, always happy back home in the blowing arctic snow. But here in lower Russia, it felt to him like the tropics. Pearl wondered how far south the fire cloud would actually lead them, and how hot it would be before they arrived at their unknown destination. She began to worry about Peter. She knew he could only go so far south on land. She breathed a silent prayer to the Maker for help.

It felt good to stop. The two bears traveled about twenty miles a day, so frequent stops helped to break up the trip. They had been traveling for weeks now, after that incredible day out on the ice floe when the Voice spoke to them on the wind. The bears knew they had to leave and follow the fire cloud. Their hearts gave them no choice but to go.

"Vat's the matter vith him?" said a voice from behind. Pearl looked to see two arctic foxes sitting in the receding snow.

"*Privyet*—hi. He is ver-ry hot and tir-red," Pearl replied to the male fox, surprised to see how the foxes had just appeared next to them.

"*Tochna.* Exactly. This is vat I tell my vife, I am hot and bothered! Let's stop, I say. Vat's the r-rush?" said the fox as he, too, plopped down in the snow next to Peter to cool off. "I'd give anything for a good tventy-below day."

"*Da.* This is vat I vish for, too. You must be from the nor-rth like us. I am Peter and this is my vife Pearl," replied Peter with a big smile on his face to share some male bonding with another miserable beast.

"*Privyet.* I am Yuri, and this is my vife, Dessa. Ve've been valking for days and days. Since you are out of your usual territory, can I assume you, too, are following the fir-re cloud?"

"*Da.* This is vat ve are doing. Pearl, did you hear-r this? Ve are not the only ones on this long, hot jour-rney," exclaimed Peter, even happier knowing they weren't alone. He had felt like they were crazy for doing this strange thing. Perhaps it wasn't that strange after all.

"Dessa, I am happy to meet you," Pearl said to the female fox. The fox's sweet white face glowed with joy at meeting another female companion. Dessa weighed only seven pounds; her short legs and ears gave her a petite presence next to Pearl, who towered over her by about five hundred pounds.

"It is vonderful to meet you, Pearl. I vas just telling Yuri that I hoped there vould be other cr-reatures on this journey and there you vere."

"Vat do you suppose this is all about?" Pearl asked Dessa, lying down on her stomach to be eye level with the small fox.

"I'm not sur-re, but it is a good thing to know that ve veren't the only ones called," Dessa replied with a smile.

Just then Pearl and Dessa noticed two white birds circling above them against the white sky. Everything was white. "Do you ever get tired of all the vhiteness, Dessa? For once I vould like to see some color, you know? Do you think ve vill see come colorful land on this jour-rney?" asked Pearl as they watched the birds circle in closer.

"Vell, it vould be nice. But at least my coat changes from vhite to br-rown vith the spr-ring. It is nice to have a change, I know," replied Dessa.

Peter started making snow angels as he stretched his huge body out on the snow. "Ah, isn't snow the gr-reatest thing ever? I can never get enough." But as Peter's arms moved back and forth, he rubbed much of the snow away, revealing brown scrub growth beneath.

Suddenly one of the birds dive-bombed right at Peter's head with a loud, "HOO-UH, HOO-UH, HOO-UH, WUH, WUH, WUH!" causing Peter to roll over and almost squash Yuri, who jumped up to get out of the way. The bird's large, heavily feathered claws just missed Peter's arm as they grasped at the brown scrub growth before the bird turned back into flight.

"Vat ar-re you doing?" Peter yelled up to the swift bird that soared back into the sky.

After a minute of circling, the birds turned to come in for a landing next to the animals below. Their huge five-foot wingspan displayed white wings, dotted with soft brown spots underneath. As they landed, Pearl was struck by their big yellow eyes and black bill. They were two large snowy owls.

"Now ther-re's some color," whispered Dessa to Pearl.

"*Ne boysa.* Do not be afr-raid. I thought I saw the gr-round moving and came in for a closer look," said the male snowy owl to the surprised animals.

"*Ne boysa?* Why should I be afr-raid of you?" asked Peter of the bird as he stood over him.

"I thought you vould be fr-rightened vith how I svooped down on you," explained the owl. "I am not called 'the vhite terror of the nor-rth' for nothing. But please, allow me to intr-roduce myself. I am Ivan and this is my vife Natasha. Ve have been flying vith the fir-re cloud for days and have followed you fr-rom above."

"You, a terror? That's funny. I am the lar-rgest beast in R-rus-sia, so if anyone is a terror of the nor-rth, that vould be me! I am Peter, and this is Pearl, Yuri, and Dessa," offered Peter, standing in what he hoped would be an intimidating stance over the snowy owl.

"But you did not see me coming—I have the best eyes and ear-rs of the gr-reat nor-rth," protested Ivan.

"So how is it you thought the gr-round vas moving?" asked Yuri in Peter's defense.

Ivan opened his mouth to speak, but nothing came out.

Pearl stepped in to break up all the male competition and arguing. "Enough of this. Let us all discuss how ve can vork together to follow the fir-re cloud, and not ar-rgue about who is gr-reater than the other," Pearl bellowed.

"Ivan, vat can you tell us about the landscape? The fir-re cloud is heading south, so ve have been following it but are getting ver-ry hot. Is there another vay to go?" Pearl asked, grabbing every-one's attention with her loud voice.

Ivan, grateful for Pearl changing the subject, replied, "There is a r-river just up ahead that flows south."

"*Da*. The Volga R-river. It flows south through R-russia to the Caspian Sea. Ve could get in the r-river and svim it, no?" eagerly replied Peter. "I love to svim and it vould be much cooler than valking on this hot land."

"*Da*. Peter is r-right. I say ve do as he says," agreed Yuri. "Of course, Dessa and I vould need to r-ride on your backs. Is this okay?"

"It's a splendid idea! I say ve go now," answered Pearl, Dessa smiling in agreement.

"Let's go! Ve vill fly above and lead the vay," exclaimed Ivan as he and Natasha took off in flight.

Peter stood there looking at the snowy owls flying south toward the Volga River, grunting that he had to walk. They soon reached the river and the bears climbed into the water with the foxes on their backs. Peter was grateful for the cold water. He hated to admit it, but he was glad that Ivan had come along to lead them to the river. Pearl, too, was grateful and offered a silent, "Thank you," to the Maker.

195

Peter and Pearl sometimes swam fifty miles from shore off the northern coast of Russia, so swimming this river was nothing to them. But what could it mean? What could be so important as to call these creatures to leave their cold habitats and venture into the warm unknown? Whatever it was, Pearl hoped this river would lead them to a worthy answer. And soon.

CHAPTER 35

Worldwide Animalia:
Africans

The early morning sun was already so hot over the savanna that the horizon appeared to be melting as waves of heat rippled the landscape. The fire cloud was up and moving to the north, and the animals, insects, and birds of the African plain were all coming to life. Bugs were swarming over the low grasses, irritating Iggi the zebra as he tried to eat his breakfast.

"Of all the stripes I could have had, why'd I have to get ones making a big arrow pointing to my backside? I can't graze without these bugs bothering me. I'm going to go crazy if they don't stop," said Iggi, swishing his tail to ward off the pesky bugs.

"Come on, now, Iggi. Going whacko won't help a thing. Okay, bugs. Break it up, break it up," said Iggi's wife, Zula, as she brushed her nose over Iggi's back, trying to get the bugs off her husband. "Just try to ignore them and graze this new grass we found. We'll be chucking out of here soon anyway when everyone wakes up, so maybe the bugs will stay here."

"Hmmph! They better stay here," mumbled Iggi, spitting grass out of his mouth as he spoke.

Zula looked over at the grove of mimosa trees nearby to see their giraffe friends also eating breakfast. She couldn't help but chuckle as she saw Upendo pulling the leaves off the tree with his powerful tongue. He was never happier than when eating, because his mind was temporarily distracted from his problem. It was a very big problem and led to other problems with his nerves, such as high blood pressure. If ever there was an aptly named animal, it was Upendo. More than anything he wished he could be upended and live low to the ground. Poor giraffe. He was afraid of heights.

Upendo's long neck stretched high in the air, the sun glistening on his beautiful brown patchwork coat. He was enjoying the tasty leaves. He closed his eyes with delight, grunting with satisfaction as to how fresh they were. "You gotta try these top branches, Chipo. Best mimosa I ever tasted."

"*Is it?* That's great! But you're able to stretch your neck to reach those taller branches better than me," Chipo replied while bending over to eat from a lower tree nearby. She was considerably shorter than Upendo, who loomed over her at eighteen feet.

"No, I'll get some for you. Come on over here and I'll pull off the leaves," said Upendo. He may have had a height problem, but he was one of the most thoughtful animals anywhere. He was always thinking of others and meeting their needs, despite his own problems. Perhaps it helped him focus on others, rather than on himself.

Upendo stretched his neck even higher and tore off a huge cluster of leaves. As he pulled the small branch away, there in front of him was a huge pair of eyes, and below them, a giant mouth of teeth opening wide and grunting.

"Ah, Chipo. Help!" cried Upendo, dropping the leaves.

Chipo ran to his side to see what had startled the giraffe. She looked up and then saw a tawny tail swishing from side to side.

197

She chuckled and said, "Calm down, Upendo! It's only Jafaru. He's been sleeping up in this tree. You just happened to get eye to eye with him as he yawned."

Jafaru poked his huge head out between the branches and greeted the giraffes, "*Howzit*? Good morning, hey? Didn't mean to give you a fright there, Upendo."

Upendo's heart was racing a mile a minute, but he was relieved to see it was just Jafaru. Still, it would take him some time to settle down.

"Upendo, look at me. Keep your eyes right here—don't look down, don't look down. Deep breaths, deep breaths," said Chipo, coaxing the rattled giraffe with her gentle voice.

Jafaru climbed from branch to branch until he hit the ground, dust flying up around him as his 400 pounds of muscle hit the earth with a thud. He lowered his brown front legs into a long stretch, yawning once more and showing his sharp, two-inch canines. A beautiful female lion came walking up to him, rubbing her head firmly against his dark mane. "Good morning, love."

"Good morning, Sasha. What had you up so early today?" asked Jafaru, lovingly nudging his wife back.

"Oh, I thought I'd check the area ahead to see how things look for our travel today. The fire cloud has turned to the northeast a bit. We should leave just now. Good morning, Upendo and Chipo, how are you today?" asked Sasha as she noticed the unnerved giraffe.

"N-n-never better, Sasha," Upendo replied with a weak smile, trying to act like all was well. He didn't want to make Jafaru feel bad again.

"You did it again, didn't you?" Sasha asked Jafaru.

The male lion looked down at the ground, avoiding Sasha's wrinkled brow. This was not the first time the lion had startled the giraffe. "I just like sleeping as high in the trees as I can get. I don't mean to give him a fright. He's just always up and eating before I get down," answered Jafaru.

"Shame that it happened again. I wouldn't blame those giraffes if they stopped traveling with us. Tonight we'll find a nice high rock for you to crash on so Upendo can have a peaceful morning tomorrow," said Sasha before turning to Upendo. "Sorry, friend, we'll do better tomorrow."

With that, the lions walked over to the zebras while Chipo worked to calm her mate. "It's a hot morning, hey?" asked Jafaru, slapping Iggi on his backside as he saw a big fly land there.

"OUCH! *Oke,* you don't know your own strength, but thanks for swatting that fly away," said Iggi, smarting from the lion's huge paw slap.

"I couldn't help but notice you startled Upendo again," Zula said with a smile to the muscular lion.

"Yeah, Sasha's going to find me a good rock to crash on tonight, so I don't do that again," replied Jafaru as he licked his paw to remove the squashed fly.

"I've been out checking ahead this morning. The fire cloud is headed northeast. We should get going. You ready?" Sasha asked the zebras.

199

Before they could answer came a loud "R-R-ROAR! R-R-ROAR!" from another lion a couple of miles away. Jafaru's fur stood on end and a snarl came on his face as he echoed the roar with his own, making the other animals cringe. Jafaru was a supreme protector, even though he sometimes irritated the others. He never let other lions get near his friends or his territory. He took off running to deal with this intruder. Sasha, Iggi, and Zula followed along behind, not able to keep up with the fast beast.

"R-R-ROAR! R-R-ROAR!" bellowed the unwelcome lion again, causing Jafaru to pick up his speed for another mile. Up ahead was a clearing in the brush, so Jafaru slowed down and crouched behind the tall grass to assess his opponent. His shoulders moved from side to side, ready to pounce. There in the clearing he observed a pair of large white rhinos. They were so wide that he couldn't see around them. The lion must be on the other side, in front of them. But these rhinos were standing their ground. Funny, they didn't seem to be disturbed at all. In fact, Jafaru shook his head to clear his ears. Were the rhinos laughing?

"Do it again," Jafaru heard the female rhino say.

With that, the lion let forth another "ROAR!" and set the rhinos off laughing. Had they gone mad, wondered Jafaru? He kept trying to get a view around the gray-brown thick legs of the rhinos but it was no use. Finally, he decided to jump out and take the other lion by surprise. He poised his body for strike mode, power surging into his back legs as he pounced from behind the tall grass out beside the rhinos.

"ROAR! WHO DARES COME IN MY TERRITORY?" roared Jafaru as he landed with a thud.

The two rhinos just sat there looking at him, startled but calm. And in front of them stood an ostrich. They all looked at Jafaru, speechless and taken aback by his sudden entrance.

"Where is the lion? Did he run in fear of me?" asked Jafaru, assuming he had scared his rival off.

The rhinos looked at each other and then at the ostrich before they all burst out into a fit of laughter.

"What's so funny, hey?" asked Jafaru, not getting what was happening. The animals couldn't catch their breath, they were laughing so hard. Tears rolled down the male rhino's face as he fell on his back.

"Shame, that's funny," said Tumo the male rhino. "This lion has been tuned by an ostrich!"

"What do you mean?" demanded Jafaru.

"Do it again, Kirabo. Show him," said the female rhino, Kamili, to the ostrich.

With that the ostrich closed his eyes and let forth a mighty, "ROAR!"

Jafaru's jaw hung open a moment before sitting down to scratch his head. "You mean to tell me some ostrich has been roaring? I thought it was another lion."

A female ostrich came and joined the others. "My husband is the best lion impersonator in the savanna."

"Glad my performance was so believable to you," said Kirabo, bowing gracefully as the others cheered on his performance.

"How in the world can an ostrich roar like a lion?" asked Jafaru, stumped but quite impressed with this large bird.

"It's just another funny skill the Maker gave me, *oke*. I'm the biggest bird on the planet, but I can't fly. I can outrun an antelope any day, and roar like a lion, but I can't fly," said Kirabo. He stood eight feet tall, twice as tall as Jafaru.

"Well, I'll be. Things aren't always what they seem. I never would have believed it if I hadn't seen it for myself. Sasha won't, either," replied Jafaru, shaking his head.

"Who's Sasha?" asked Kamili the female rhino.

"She's my wife. We're from the southern plains, headed north with a pair of zebras and giraffes," answered Jafaru.

"Don't tell me you're following the fire cloud," asked Tumo, looking down his four-foot long horn at the lion. "We're headed that way ourselves."

"*Is it?* Well Sasha will be glad to hear it. She's been questioning every creature we see about it, and so far, you are the only ones we've met who also got the word to follow it," said Jafaru with a smile.

Sasha called from behind the tall grass, "Is it safe to come over there, love?"

"Yeah, come on over. You're not going to believe this," answered Jafaru.

Jafaru introduced the newfound friends to Sasha and the zebras, and they were thrilled to meet up with other animals on this fire cloud safari through Africa. The giraffes slowly caught up with the others. Chipo continued to encourage Upendo not to look down, but keep his gaze on the horizon. With that, they were off heading northeast toward the fire cloud. Jafaru told Kirabo that as the real lion, he would be doing all the roaring from now on. After all, there was only room for one king of the beasts.

CHAPTER 36

Stuffed Turkeys

Liz's assessment was right. With the addition of the two horses to their travel party, the animals made much better time. The fire cloud continued to draw them southward, gradually shifting to the east as the animals trekked through Romania and then Bulgaria. Challenges were continually placed before the animals on their journey, including another scary encounter with wolves in the Romanian forest. But somehow, the Maker always came through for them, enabling them to overcome whatever challenge or obstacle blocked their way.

The animals reached a beautiful sea and enjoyed traveling along the coast for days. Al, swept up in a moment of romantic passion for Liz, decided to return her gift of naming the Alps for him. He decided he would name this sea after Liz's beauty. Being simple-minded, he just called it the "Black Sea."

"Oh, Albert, you shouldn't have. How sweet of you to think of me," said Liz as she rubbed her head against his long whiskers. They were sitting on top of Isabella the cow, who smiled at all she heard.

"The big, beautiful sea reminds me o' how big me love is for me beautiful, black Liz," said Al with a goofy grin on his face.

Max rolled his eyes at Al and Liz. "Aye, do ye really think any-one would call those mountains 'The Alps' or that sea 'The Black Sea' jest because ye named it yerselves then?"

"But someone has to name these things, *mon ami*. Like your beloved Scotland. Who named your fair land?" asked Liz, know-ing she would stump Max on this one.

Max wrinkled his brow as he started to speak, but couldn't think of a reply.

"Well, I'm sure a fine, intelligent creature gave Scotland its name. Who's to say that we have not marked the Alps and the Black Sea by name for all time?" asked Liz rhetorically.

"Of course the creature who named Scotland were intelligent. Ah well enough, I won't argue with the two of ye. Enjoy yer name gifts ta each other. 'Tis a sweet gesture then," said Max, smiling as he sat up on top of Giorgio the horse. *Let them have their fantasies*, Max thought to himself. *No harm with that. Their intentions are ta honor their mates, not themselves.*

203

Max decided it was time to get down to keep his legs from cramping. "If ye don't mind, laddie, would ye please let me off yer back so I kin stretch?" asked Max.

"*Sí, Signore*," replied Giorgio, stopping and kneeling down so Max could jump off the horse's back. Max stretched out long and then gave a good shake from head to tail. Kate giggled at how fluffy Max looked right after he shook like that. His black fur stuck out in all directions—like Al looked after a terrific fright. Kate sat on top of Pauline, the brown mare, and looked lovingly at Max.

"I think I will name the next big shrub I see 'The Shakin' Max,' " said Kate, "because that's how ye look, me love."

Max looked up at Kate and had to laugh, "Well, I think we've had enough of namin' places an' things today. Besides, I don't think ye'll be seein' many big shrubs here. This land we're in looks dry. Any idea of where we are, Liz?"

Liz looked around from atop the cow. The land had indeed turned arid and much more rugged the farther inland they traveled from the Black Sea. They were now entering a desert region, and it was getting hotter by the day. In the distance loomed a huge snow-capped mountain high above the horizon. Liz felt a chill up her spine, but not at the thought of the snow on top of that mountain. It was something she couldn't quite put her paw on. She had a sense of destiny yet foreboding about it. They had traveled around the mountain from a distance for several days. The more Liz studied it, the more she felt a shared destiny with that mountain. It didn't make sense. The fire cloud wasn't over that mountain, so it obviously wasn't their destination. Liz shook it off and asked Isabella to let her down. Al jumped off, too.

"We are somewhere in Asia and this is a desert climate. We must conserve our energy and travel only in the early morning hours and evening time so we can rest during the hottest part of the day. Water will be increasingly difficult to find here," said Liz. "And Isabella, stay out of that seed sack, *s'il vous plaît.*"

They had strapped Liz's seed sack around Isabella's neck when they were in Austria. Food had been plentiful so the seeds posed no temptation to the ever-hungry cow. But now there would be little grass to chew in this rugged, arid land.

"You heard Madame. If I see you so much as sniff too hard at those seeds, I will peck at your hooves," threatened Henriette, getting eye to eye with the big cow. The fat hen sat next to Jacques on top of Don Pedro. Jacques and the bull both rolled their eyes.

"Aye, an' that means me r-r-reed, too. No nibblin' on it then," added Max.

"*Sí,* I hear ALL of you. I will leave the seeds and the reed alone. But what will I eat?" the cow asked Liz. The same question was on the mind of every animal there. Rudy and Rosie flew over to land on Don Pedro's horns, waiting for an answer as well.

"I will need to inspect the landscape and study our situation," replied Liz. *And pray,* she thought to herself. "Everyone stop and take a rest for now. Ah, but Giorgio, please stay awake, *mon ami.* We don't want you running off again, no?"

The black stallion lowered his head in agreement. His "sleep running" problem made him bolt away from the group at times, embarrassing him. Max had developed quite a repertoire of songs to have ready to sing to the big horse in order to wake him. There certainly was never a dull moment with this group.

The sun was high in the sky. Liz looked up and couldn't help but think that the sun and the fire cloud looked like partners. Both burned brightly and in harmony against the blue sky. Both served as guides; the sun for time and the fire cloud for place. As Liz silently talked to the Maker while looking skyward, two dark shadows flew over her.

"Hey, it's a pair of . . . of . . . ," said Kate eagerly, not quite knowing what to call the large birds who awkwardly landed in their midst. Clearly they weren't the best of fliers.

"TURKEYS," said the male turkey as they landed and flapped their large wings on the ground, obviously out of breath and gobbling.

"*Bonjour, Monsieur et Madame,*" said Liz, amused by the appearance of the birds.

Their feathers were dusky brown with an iridescent bronze sheen and black lines. Their side feathers were a white, checkered pattern. Their heads and necks were rather bare and bluish-red, looking as if the feathers had just been plucked off, revealing mottled, bumpy skin beneath. Their tails were shaped like fans, spread out to reveal chestnut feathers tipped in white. The male looked down at Liz with beady little black eyes, puffing up the long feathered beard on his breast. Liz couldn't stop staring at the snood, the fleshy blue-red wattle that hung from their beaks. She tried not to be so obvious, but it was rather distracting to look at.

"Allow me to introduce myself. I am Lizette Brilliante, and these are my friends. We have traveled for weeks from Europe, and are following the fire cloud. May I ask your names?" Liz asked, trying not to stare at their snoods.

"Yumay," the female turkey replied with a tone of superiority.

205

Liz looked at them and then at Max, who shook his head, and at Rudy and Rosie, who shrugged their tiny shoulders. "Well then, what are your names?" she asked again.

"Yumay. My name is Yumay and this is my husband, Can," said the female turkey.

"Oh, I see. *Pardon.* And can you tell me where we are?" asked Liz, trying to keep a straight face.

"Why yes, I can," said Can, flipping his snood over his beak, appearing smug. "You are in Turkey, of course."

"More daft beasts namin' places after themselves," mumbled Max under his breath.

"Shhh! Be polite, Max," said Kate. She was always delighted to meet new creatures, and didn't want to appear rude. The turkeys, however, didn't seem concerned about being impolite. They were rather haughty as they talked to the animals.

"We are in Turkey? And you are turkeys?" Liz asked, studying the large birds. "May I ask which name came first?" Liz was tickled by these birds but ever curious to gather new information.

"We named it, of course," said Can.

"I knew it," muttered Max before addressing the turkeys, "an' I suppose that creatures everywhere will be callin' this land 'Turkey' jest because ye named it?"

"Our great land is deserving of a name that reflects majesty and beauty. Have you traveled through our land and seen the lush coastal areas and the beautiful forests? We have mountains, valleys, plains, beaches, rivers, lakes, and beautiful woodlands. A land so remarkable can only have a name that describes its grandeur. So we have named this land after ourselves, for we are obviously the most majestic, exotic, beautiful creatures in the land," said Can, flipping his snood to the other side of his nose in a gesture of snobbery. "Much better than any of the other inhabitants here, especially those humans."

Max was chuckling under his breath as the pompous bird spoke, but stopped when he heard that humans lived in Turkey.

He looked at Liz and they exchanged a moment of silent concern. Max had shared with Liz everything Gillamon told him about the humans. Liz also was well familiar with the troubled race, having heard the stories passed down from her ancestors. They knew that the presence of humans would mean trouble.

"Humans? Did you say humans live here also?" asked Liz.

"Yes, but we try to stay clear of them. Such boring creatures, they are. All humans are the same. There's no diversity in language, culture, or even color," Yumay explained.

"Wha' do ye mean then, lass?" asked Max.

"Well, I assume you animals are from different countries, as you have different accents. We in the animal kingdom enjoy variety. We have different languages, looks, cultural traditions, and unique traits. But these humans are all the same—one language, one culture. One bad culture, I might add. They are a hostile bunch," Yumay said as she looked down her nose at Max.

"And I submit that we in the animal kingdom are much smarter than humans, too. We often know when things will happen, even before they do, like the frequent earthquakes here in Turkey. We feel them sometimes a day before they happen. The humans are always caught by surprise, panicking whenever the earth rumbles. I'm telling you, these humans could learn much about life by watching us," added Can.

"Hmmmm. There is some truth to what you say, *Monsieur*. So, what do you recommend to avoid encounters with these humans?" asked Liz.

"An encounter with humans is inevitable now that you are in this land. But you will soon be out of Turkey. The land just beyond is the border with Persia. We're headed that way now," explained Can, pointing to the border lined with jagged rocks.

"Why don't ye two join us then?" offered Kate with her peppy grin. The self-righteous turkeys didn't offend her. She thought them to be rather interesting, and funny.

207

"Why join you? Why would we want to? We prefer to travel by ourselves, and can reach the destination sooner by leaving now," answered Can, oblivious of how insulting he was.

"Well, be off with ye then, turkeys," growled Max, not liking these birds a bit, especially after that degrading reply to Kate.

"May I ask one more question before you leave?" asked Liz as the turkeys readied for flight. "Is there a name given to that mountain in the distance there, the one capped with snow?"

"Ararat. It's called Mount Ararat," Can said as he and Yumay took off flying toward the fire cloud. Their bodies looked awkward in the air, and it took them a while to get steady as they flew.

"Good r-r-riddance. Those birds' heads were stuffed with delusions of gr-r-randeur. I never seen such ar-r-r-rogant beasties. Turkeys. It would serve them r-r-right if the humans got a hold of them," complained Max.

Liz wasn't listening. She continued to stare at Mount Ararat, still feeling disturbed in her spirit about that place. But what did it matter? The fire cloud had led them around the mountain, not to it. Now that they were headed into Persia, there were other pressing matters to think of. There were humans in this land. It was obvious that the fire cloud was leading the animals to a certain encounter with humans. *What,* Liz wondered, *will happen when we encounter them?*

CHAPTER 37

Arriving Day

Noah was up early this morning. He just couldn't sleep with so much on his mind. God had spoken to Noah in Adam's cave last night, telling him that in seven days he would send a flood to wipe out every living creature on earth except for Noah, his family, and the animals that would come to enter the safety of the ark. God gave Noah instructions to get his family and the animals on board over the next week.

The gravity of what God told Noah was overwhelming. Even though Noah had prepared for this event for a century, he still didn't feel mentally or emotionally ready for what was to come. How could he? It was a burden to carry such divine revelation of coming calamity. Only his family listened to his words as he told them of the Lord's pending action. He was burdened for the unbelievers. He was burdened for his family and the coming ordeal. He was burdened for the animals that would be in his care. He couldn't stand just sitting and thinking any longer. He decided to inspect the ark again.

Noah slowly walked along the central corridor of the ark on the lower level. The first rays of sunlight poured in through the windows at the top of the ark. Beams of light and swirling dust filled the air. He could hardly believe they had finally finished building and supplying this huge, floating vessel. A century of his life was invested in this massive boat, and as he walked through the stalls, he found visual reminders of the passage of time.

A wooden beam rising to the middle deck bore the marks of Noah's hammer from a bad day several decades ago. He had been working on the ark for forty long years and had grown weary. One day he became so tired and angry at the whole process that he hammered the wood over and over, venting his frustration and leaving deep indentations on the beam. Noah smiled as he remembered his talk with God that night. The Lord eased his mind that he wasn't crazy for building the ark. God also validated Noah's heart. Noah was a simple human with normal emotions, yet given a God-sized task. The ridicule he endured for building the ark, coupled with the seeming impossibility of his task, caused Noah to mentally and emotionally collapse. But after a few days of rest, Noah's perspective returned. His spirits were lifted and he went back to work. Noah never let the ridicule bother him again after that day.

Noah noticed artwork in one of the stalls where, as children, his sons painted pictures of the animals that would someday inhabit this floating zoo. Stick-figure cows, horses, and chickens with happy faces were whimsically drawn. Noah smiled at the picture. He hoped the animals in his care would, indeed, be happy. He and his sons tried to consider every possible need the animals would have, and a way to meet those needs.

God had instructed Noah to outfit the ark with enough food for Noah's family and the animals. But how much was enough? Noah wasn't even sure how many animals would come, although he knew it would be thousands, based on the dimensions God had given him for the ark. And he had no idea how long they would be living aboard this floating box. All he knew to do was fill the supply rooms to capacity and trust God to provide the rest.

His thoughts then turned to his family. How could they possibly be happy with what was going to happen? Everything they knew would be taken from them, and they would become animal caretakers for an unknown period of time. His family had sacrificed their lives to support Noah in this endeavor. Had he done the right thing by his family? All these questions circled in Noah's mind as he walked alone in the silence of the ark. Yet he knew without a doubt what God had told him to do. He knew that all the decisions he made were based on that reality alone. Then why was it so hard and painful to do as God asked? Noah knew the answer. Pain and hardship weren't part of God's original plan. Humankind's choice was the root of all pain—not God's.

Noah looked around the ark. It was a true masterpiece of engineering. Each of the three decks rose fourteen feet high and held three hundred stalls of varying sizes. Multiple pens were stacked in some stalls for small creatures. The lower deck where Noah walked was designated for the large animals. They felt impressed to build an entire section of large stalls that were open to the deck above, making them twenty-eight-feet tall. Noah wondered what animal could possibly need that much space.

The middle deck held supplies and would accommodate mid-sized animals, and the upper deck housed living quarters for Noah's family and all the birds. The stalls faced the central corridor, with railings or full bars facing out and a walkway in front of the stalls. Noah's family would be able to see into all the stalls, and the animals would also have a view of their ark neighbors.

Ramps led from both sides of the central entry door on the middle level to the upper and lower decks. Lanterns were hung all along the central corridors to provide light, dim though it was. Shem had even rigged an irrigation system to provide slowly dripping water into barrels for each pen. He devised a holding tank topside for their water supply.

Noah smiled as he thought of his sons. Each had contributed ideas for a system vital to making this floating habitat work. Shem

211

provided ideas for water. Japheth provided ideas for how to best organize and feed the animals. Ham provided ideas for storage supply and how to efficiently clean the pens. Noah's special project was to provide a kitchen for his wife, Adah.

How Adah loved to cook. Noah was determined that she have the comfort and haven of a cozy kitchen aboard the ark. He brought in stonemasons to construct her oven with a ventilation shaft up to the roof. He built her a huge pantry with shelves from floor to ceiling full of spices, dates, nuts, and cooking supplies. Noah also brought in massive stone jars filled with oil and grain. Noah surprised Adah the day they completed the kitchen. He had her cover her eyes as he led her to the upper deck. She was thrilled, as were the daughters-in-law. It gladdened Noah's heart to do this for his wife. He had asked so much of her. She deserved the best he could give her in return.

All the stalls and pens were full of clean water and straw and awaited their occupants. Noah shook his head with a chuckle as he realized that the sound of silence he now experienced in the ark would end once those occupants arrived. It would be loud, and it would smell. Thank goodness the Lord had instructed Noah to build those windows up above. Fresh air and sunlight were crucial for their survival. Yes, it was going to be a wild experience. There would never be a dull moment—that was for certain.

The silence was broken when Noah heard Ham call him from above decks. "Father! Hurry! Come see what is happening."

"What is it, son?" Noah asked as he looked up to the open windows.

"It's . . . it's moving. Come see," replied Ham excitedly.

Noah made his way to the upper deck and opened the ark roof to join Ham. "What is this all about?" he asked as he stepped outside. Ham didn't reply but pointed to the sky above them. A single cloud was swirling in the air, moving toward them. As Noah and Ham stared at the cloud, Shem and Japheth ran up the ark ramps and joined them to see what was happening.

The white puffy cloud moved toward them, turning in circles until it was directly over the ark. Suddenly the cloud split in two, with the top half swirling clockwise and the lower half swirling counterclockwise. There was energy in the cloud and a sense of power about it. In a flash, fire burst from the center of the cloud and filled the sky with heat and a light as brilliant as the sun.

"What is it, father?" asked Shem. He and the others stood mesmerized by the spectacle hovering above the ark. They didn't know whether to be afraid or to be in awe, whether to stay put or to run, but they couldn't run. The cloud had a magnetizing presence about it that kept them standing there . . . speechless.

"This is a sign from God. He spoke to me last night that the flood would come in seven days. I do not know what this . . . this fire cloud signifies, but it is not of natural origin. It is supernatural, and the powerful presence we feel is from God," replied Noah.

He was not afraid, but his heart caught in his chest. What did this sign mean? Was it a blessing for the completed ark? Was it a warning of some kind? Noah half expected to hear God's Voice come from the fire cloud, but it swirled silently in the sky, growing to cover the full length of the ark. The only response Noah could give was to fall down on his knees and worship the Lord. His sons joined him on their knees as Noah prayed, asking God's blessing and protection for the ark, his family, and the animals. It was a holy moment, and each of the men felt a surge of energy course through them as they knelt in the presence of God.

Finally, Noah stood and turned his gaze from the fire cloud to the southern horizon. He squinted as he saw something he'd never before seen. Two massive animals were walking in his direction. They stood ten feet high on columnar legs and had a grayish-brown hide. Their ears were massive, looking like huge fans as they flapped back and forth. They had strange, elongated noses coming from their huge heads, and one of them had two long, white tusks growing out of its face.

213

Noah looked at his sons, puzzled looks on their faces, as they watched these two beasts head directly for the ark. Noah had spent much time in the cave, studying Adam's drawings of the animals. God had revealed the names of the animals to him, but Noah wondered if he could possibly remember them all.

Noah had no sooner thought those words than he heard God speak to his mind,

"ELEPHANTS, NOAH. THEY'RE ELEPHANTS. REMEMBER? THEY ARE FROM THE FAR EAST."

Noah felt relief. God would give him the knowledge he needed as this mysterious event unfolded. Noah turned to his sons and said, "These animals are elephants. God has brought them to us, so let's make ready to receive them."

"Look! Behind the elephants are two of the most beautiful birds I've ever seen," exclaimed Ham.

"And some sort of funny bull, too," added Japheth.

"Wait, there's also some kind of very tall goat?" said Shem.

There, walking slowly behind the elephants, was a pair of peacocks. Their iridescent green and gold feathers were ornamented with beautiful blue, eyelike markings. The male peacock's long upper tail feathers were spread out in a glorious display of color as he stuck his blue head in the air. The female peahen was less colorful and showy, but beautiful nonetheless.

Noah stood amazed at the beauty of these animals, struck with the wonder of God's variety. *Peacocks, water buffalos, and antelopes,* thought Noah, as he smiled and led the way down the ark as the humans prepared to greet their first arriving passengers.

"I really wish you would stop strutting like that, Raja. You're causing a scene," said Duke the elephant as they walked the road leading to the fire cloud.

"Make a grand entrance, I always say," the proud peacock said as he continued to strut with feathers in full array, his chin held high.

"I think these people are bad—just look at them. They've got evil written all over their faces," said Vijay the antelope. "Varada, just stay close to me," Vijay said to his young wife. The antelopes pressed close together as they walked past the staring crowd.

The people of Noah's village could not believe what they were seeing. Where were these animals coming from? And where were they going? No one moved, terrified of the huge beast leading the way. They watched as the animals turned and headed in Noah's direction.

Duke looked up to see the fire cloud in a stationary position over the ark. He had never seen the cloud appear so large. It was three times the size it had been on their long journey from India. The elephant grew excited as he realized they had arrived at their intended destination. "This must be the place. Our long *yatra* is finally over," Duke said as his trunk reached over to hold the trunk of his wife, Fareeda.

"How wonderful. Finally. I'm so tired from our journey. I don't think my feet have ever been so sore," said Fareeda. Her warm, sweet eyes smiled back at Duke.

"What about those humans up ahead, Duke? Do you think they look okay?" asked Ballari, the female water buffalo, chewing her cud as she spoke. "I hope they're not like the villagers. Those people were creepy." She and her husband, Jag, had six-foot-across horns that curved upward at the ends. Their traveling companions tried to steer clear of walking near them to avoid getting skewered.

Duke looked at the humans and spotted an old man holding a staff, surrounded by a small group of men and women. The big elephant immediately felt at ease. This was a good man, he knew in his gut. He could tell by the man's eyes. Duke looked at the others gathered with him. Yes, they too looked like good, kind humans.

"There is nothing to fear here. The Maker has called us to these humans because this is where the fire cloud has stopped. They look like good people. Be gentle and do as they say," instructed Duke. Everyone respected the wise elephant's opinions. Raja still kept his feathers fanned out to make a good impression.

Noah and his family gently walked over to greet the animals, smiling and speaking in calm tones. Noah went up to Duke and looked him in the eye while gently patting the front of his long trunk. "Welcome, my big friend. You must be tired. We have a place prepared for you and will take good care of you."

Duke shared a look of agreement with Noah and touched the end of his trunk to Noah's shoulder to reassure him that he understood.

"Did you see that? It's as if he knows what I said," Noah remarked to his wife, Adah, who laughed with joy for her husband.

Ham called out, "Look! There are more animals coming in the distance! I see a pair of black bears and a pair of birds flying above them. There are two huge brown beasts with funny looking antlers that look like rakes."

"Wait—it looks like they are each carrying a small brown animal in their antlers. And there's two black-and-white-striped animals walking behind all of them," added Japheth.

216

Noah ran over to have a look. Sure enough, here came another group of foreign animals headed straight for the ark. God once again reminded him about these animals from a cold, northern land. Noah's pulse raced with excitement. Things were happening quickly. He looked up at the fire cloud. Of course, this must be the beacon that the animals followed to reach the ark. It was a sign for the animals. Now he understood.

"Everyone look lively. This is going to be a long day," exclaimed Noah.

Adah felt overwhelmed with what was happening, but happy in her heart for Noah. The word from God to Noah had been true. All the years of building and supplying the ark were complete. What God said He would do was finally taking place. The animals were coming to Noah, just as He said they would. And here, Adah knew, they would be safe from what was about to come.

CHAPTER 38

Finally

Noah and his family were ready to begin boarding the animals onto the ark when God gave Noah an odd instruction.

"WAIT, NOAH. DON'T BOARD THE ANIMALS YET."

This didn't make sense to Noah. The animals were now arriving in a steady stream and the ark was ready to house them. So why wait to lead them onto the ark?

"WAIT. I WILL TELL YOU WHEN,"

was all Noah heard God say. So he told his family to provide water for the animals outside the ark, and to organize them as best they could. While confused, they did as instructed.

It didn't take long for the people of the village to gather around Noah's ark to see what was going on. Strange animals were making their way to the crazy ark builder from every direction. Thousands of birds and insects were also flying in to land on the ark, looking like an eerie storm darkening the sky. The sound of the animal life congregating was almost deafening. And it was as if Noah and his family were expecting them! But why? That was the burning question in the minds of those who came to watch the animals parading up the road and flying in the air to Noah.

As the people hurled their questions and teasing comments at Noah and his family, Noah remained steady and consistent in his reply. "These animals have come to us to be safe from the calamity that will soon sweep over the earth. It is not too late for you to be saved, also! Come, follow the one, true God and you will be safe from harm as you join us."

The people didn't believe Noah. They responded with ridicule and sarcasm.

"How is your ark supposed to save these animals and us? From what? If these animals are coming to you, why don't you put them on board?"

"You've built a boat, Noah. We're over one hundred miles from water."

"Not only is it a boat, it's a boat that you can't navigate. Where are the sails, Noah? What about oars?"

"It's just a big, wooden box. You can't make it go anywhere. Looks more like a coffin than a boat."

The people didn't pay attention to Noah's words. Nor did they pay attention to the signs that something divine was taking place. It didn't matter that these animals of unknown origin were voluntarily coming to Noah. It didn't matter that the fire cloud burned brightly in the sky. Nothing mattered but how big a laugh the next heckler could get out of the crowd. Soon the people grew bored and left Noah and his family to themselves.

"Let us know how you make out there, Noah."

"Yeah, bring us something back from your big voyage."

A trail of laughter followed the crowd as they wandered down the road back to the village. Noah kept his family focused on the task at hand. He knew the truth, and his family knew the truth. The blindness and hard-heartedness of the people didn't cause Noah and the others to lose faith or lose sight of their mission. It saddened them, but they had to let the people choose to reject Noah's words of warning. No one was sadder than Shem.

There in the distance stood Avi, Shem's friend. He had followed the crowd to check out the animals and the ark, yet he remained silent. As the people dispersed, Avi stayed behind, watching and thinking about what he saw and heard. Shem saw Avi and went running over to him. Maybe a personal appeal could persuade his friend to embrace the truth.

"Avi, hi! How are you, my friend?" Shem asked, wiping his hands on the towel tied at his waist. He was filthy from handling so many animals. His sandals even smelled, having stepped in the wrong place more than once.

Avi looked at Shem from head to toe before answering, "Well, I'm a lot cleaner than you are today, that's for sure."

Shem looked down at his feet and laughed, "Yes, this is not a clean job." He smiled and looked into Avi's eyes before continuing. "Avi, do you see all that is happening? My father isn't crazy. He's been given a mission from God, and everything that God told him is taking place. God even told him as recently as last night that in seven days He will cover the earth with a flood. Surely you must see that my father's words are credible."

"Credible? How could they be credible when they make no sense? Sure, it's amazing that these animals are coming, but it's also strange. I just can't accept that safety lies in something so . . . so odd. And God gives your father specifics like 'seven days'? If it were so urgent, he would be trying harder to convince us," replied Avi, gazing at the ark.

"But you must believe us. The word of the Lord is true. We're *not* making this up," Shem said, pleading for Avi to believe him.

Avi looked at the ground and kicked a rock away. "I've never known you to lie to me, Shem. You've always been a true friend. But as I told you at my wedding, I have a new life now. I've married into a new family, and they look at your father and this ark,

219

and think it's just crazy. I can't go against what they say, no matter how much I want to believe you just because you're my friend," Avi said, clearly resigned to the fact that he was not going to change his mind.

"Avi, please . . ." Shem started to say before Avi held up his hand to stop Shem from speaking.

"There's nothing more to say. I better get going. Good luck with this project," Avi said, as he turned to go. "Hey, if you prove me wrong in a week, I promise I'll never disbelieve you again." Shem thought he saw a passing look of sadness in his eyes. Avi shook his head and walked away, leaving Shem standing there alone in the road.

There truly was nothing more to say. Shem had tried to reach Avi. But Avi made his choice. He chose not to listen. It weighed heavily on Shem's heart. His final hope of Avi seeing the animals come to the ark as a convincing sign of their words was gone. Shem had to let his friend go, free to experience the consequences of his decision.

As Shem turned to walk back to the ark, he saw two animals struggling on the road. They were huge white bears, and they could barely walk. Something was wrong. Shem ran to the bears and saw that there also were two small white animals and two white owls with them. They didn't look well, either. Just as Shem reached the bears, one of them collapsed and began breathing heavily. Shem put his hand on the huge, white beast and gently stroked his fur. *This animal is overheated,* Shem thought to himself. *He can't make it any farther on his own.* "Hang on, big guy. I'll get you some help. Just stay right here," Shem said as he took off running back to the ark.

"You see, Peter. You are going to make it. These humans vill help us now," said Pearl the polar bear as she comforted Peter.

"Yes, ve are finally here, my friend. You have made this impossible jour-rney and now you vill be okay," said Yuri the arctic fox, chiming in to encourage the exhausted, overheated bear.

Peter closed his eyes, feeling relieved. The heat had been too much for him. The group traveled from Russia down the Volga River, swimming all the way south through the Caspian Sea to Persia. But it had been a hundred-mile walk in the searing heat from the sea to reach the ark. Peter wished for even the warmest of Russian temperatures compared with this heat.

Shem ran toward the ark, calling to his brothers to come meet him in the shed. There he pulled the supply cart from the shed and emptied the scrap wood out of the back. The family used the cart to transport wood and heavy items, and Shem figured it could transport the bear as well.

As Ham and Japheth came over to Shem, he told them to each take a handle and pull the supply cart. Shem loaded two large jugs of water and bowls onto the cart as he explained what was happening. The brothers were concerned. They had not yet encountered a sick or injured animal. They hoped they would know how to help.

When the brothers reached the animals Shem set the water in front of them. Pearl and the foxes lapped up the cool water as Shem slowly poured water from a ladle into Peter's mouth. Peter closed his eyes and swallowed the water, sighing with relief.

"Okay, we need to get this bear on the cart," Shem instructed. "I'll try to coax him."

Shem patted Peter on his side. "Do you think you can stand up to get into the cart, big guy? We'll carry you to the ark but we can't lift you ourselves."

Peter opened his eyes and looked at Shem. Little did Shem know that Peter understood every word he said. As Shem, Ham, and Japheth got behind Peter and gently rolled him upright, Peter cooperated. The big bear stood on shaky legs and walked onto the cart's ramp. The brothers were excited, each exclaiming, "He's doing it. He must understand that we're trying to help him."

Once Peter was in the cart, the brothers heaved with all their might on the wooden handles but could not get the leverage to

221

balance the heavy bear with the cart's wheels. They strained with all their might, but realized the bear was just too heavy. How were they going to do this? Then Ham had an idea. "What about the elephant? He's strong and could pull this cart."

"Great idea, Ham. Go get him," said Shem as he patted Ham on the shoulder. Ham ran off to get Duke while the others stayed behind. Soon Ham was leading Duke back with a harness that he strapped to the front of the cart. Duke spoke to Peter, "We'll have you to the ark in no time. Just hang on."

"Thank you! Oh thank you for helping us," said Pearl. The humans heard the animals grunting at each other as they got ready to move the bear.

Ham started pulling Duke by the harness. "Okay, come on now, Mr. Elephant, pull, pull!"

With that, Duke pulled and lifted the cart with ease, the wheels rolling as Duke slowly walked back up the road to the ark. "It's working," Japheth shouted, slapping Shem on the back. Shem's broad smile drifted from Duke to Peter, then to Pearl and the other animals. It helped his spirit to be able to render assistance to these animals, after feeling rejected by Avi, who didn't need or want Shem's help. Shem put his energy in helping those he could help.

As they reached the ark, Noah praised his sons for helping the poor bear. He patted Duke on the trunk. "Thank you, my big friend." He then reached his hand over to gently touch Peter. "You will be okay now." At that moment, God spoke to Noah.

"NOW, NOAH. IT IS TIME. BRING THIS BEAR AND HIS COMPANIONS ON THE ARK FIRST. THEN THE OTHERS MAY FOLLOW."

Noah closed his eyes and offered thanks to the Maker. Then he addressed his family. "God has told me it is time to board the animals, beginning with this bear. Shem, you and I will bring the bear inside and try to make him as comfortable as possible. Ham, you and Japheth work with your mother and your wives to begin boarding the other animals. Praise God! Finally, we can realize the results of our work on this ark as we bring these animals inside."

The humans cheered and hugged each other as they set about to do as Noah instructed. Noah took Duke by the harness and together they entered the ark.

CHAPTER 39

The Miracle

Duke pulled the cart up the ramp into the ark and then down to the lower level, carefully watching his step along the wooden walkway. When they reached the lower level, Noah stopped at a large stall that would accommodate the polar bears. Peter's breathing was shallow; he was about to pass out from the heat. He was not well, and Noah and Shem were concerned that he would not make it.

Noah looked over the heat-exhausted animals. The animals could now enter their stalls, but what was the use? Even though it was slightly cooler in the ark, it was still too hot for them to be comfortable. God had told Noah that these animals were from the cold, snowy north, so he understood that they were not used to this heat. Noah closed his eyes and prayed, "Oh, God, please. How do we help these suffering animals? What else can we do?"

"YOU CAN DO NOTHING, NOAH. BUT I CAN. MOVE THE POLAR BEARS INTO THE STALL."

Noah opened his eyes. "Guide the bears into the stall, Shem. Help the large white bear get up and move."

Shem gently spoke to Peter, "Okay, big guy, here you go. Come on into your stall and rest." But Peter didn't move. He had no more strength left in him. He lay there, unable to open his eyes.

"Oh, Peter, please get up. Come, ve vill be fine here. You vill be okay. Just get up and come vith me," Pearl said as she nudged Peter with her nose, but Peter didn't respond. He was overcome with heat exhaustion and had passed out.

"Move the female bear into the stall. Maybe we can get the male to follow," Noah suggested.

With that, Shem put his hand on Pearl's back and gently coaxed her toward the stall. Pearl didn't want to leave Peter's side, but felt she must follow this human. Maybe Peter would wake up and follow her. She walked slowly, her head down and her heart full of worry.

As Pearl crossed the threshold into the stall, they all heard a cracking sound. It was a sound that Noah and Shem had never before heard. But Pearl knew the sound well. She jerked her head up to see something she had not seen in more than a thousand miles. The wooden beams of the stall started to glaze over with ice.

225

The ice spread quickly, swirling along the wood in an intricate pattern made up of millions of unique ice crystals. The wooden beams groaned from the added weight as the ice became thick with layer upon layer of multiplying crystals. Pearl's feet felt cold as the temperature in the stall plummeted below freezing. She exhaled slowly and saw a puff of her icy breath float in the air. She could taste the cold air. It was fresh. It was arctic. It tasted like home.

Pearl looked back at Peter, her heart racing. Excitement filled her eyes as she bellowed, "PETER! VAKE UP! IT'S FREEZING IN HERE! COME QUICKLY!"

Noah, Shem, and even Duke fell back a step with how loud this polar bear called to her mate. They were speechless at what was happening, looking at each other in amazement. It was a miracle! Yuri and Dessa the foxes ran into the stall and jumped for joy, and Ivan and Natasha the owls flew inside and spread their wings to feel the cold air. It wasn't possible! This was an arctic habitat.

Shem stepped inside the stall and stood with his arms outstretched, exclaiming, "I can't believe this, father. I've never felt so cold in my entire life."

Noah looked toward heaven and chuckled, "Only You could have done this. Only You." He quickly joined Shem, laughing in awe at what was happening. Their teeth began to chatter as they shivered, folding their arms over their chests and rubbing their hands over their upper arms to warm up. They blew into the air, and their breath turned into puffs of icy mist. Suddenly there was light gleaming from the ice, illuminating the stall. The ice mysteriously glowed yet did not emit heat.

A huge ice shelf formed in the corner that was large enough for the bears to lie on. The foxes jumped on the shelf and spread out on their bellies, calling to the owls to join them. The owls flapped their wings and drifted onto the shelf. The male owl waved his wings as he swayed back and forth, closing his eyes in delight, clearly enjoying his new habitat.

Noah looked up to see a long row of thick icicles hanging from the ceiling. "Look at those, Shem." Shem looked at the icicles and then at Peter. He jumped up to knock one of the icicles off, catching it as it fell into his hand. It felt cold in his grip as he ran over to Peter and rubbed the ice over the bear's face, hoping to revive him. He would be okay if he just got up and entered the stall.

Peter slowly opened his eyes. Pearl continued to bellow for him to get up. He couldn't believe what he saw. "Vhat is this? Ice? Am I dr-reaming? Have I died and gone to heaven?"

"You're not dr-reaming, love. Come quickly and see vhat the Maker has done for us. Ve have ice. Ice! Come see!" Pearl said excitedly, hope filling her heart.

The stall was now completely white with ice. Shem put the icicle in Peter's mouth, and he sucked on it to awaken his senses. It was enough to help Peter lift his head. He was only a few feet away from the thing he had longed for. If he could just muster up the strength, he could get to the ice and be okay. Peter looked at Pearl. The foxes and the owls smiled and laughed with joy. He looked at Shem and slowly stood. The bear was shaky, but Shem held him up as best he could to guide him into the stall.

Peter walked over the threshold, felt the cold ice under his feet, and breathed the cold air into his lungs. He closed his eyes and said, "Ahhhhhhhhhhhhhhhhh, now this is vhat I have needed." Peter dropped to his back and rolled around on the icy floor, feeling life pouring back into his body.

"Now there is von happy bear," exclaimed Ivan the owl.

"Da! You can say this again," said Peter, sliding his arms back and forth over the snow and ice, making a snow angel. "I feel like I am home."

"Ve made it. And the Maker made sur-re ve have vhat ve need," Pearl chimed in, sitting down next to Peter. "Even the humans seem happy for us."

Noah and Shem were dancing around on the ice when Shem slipped and fell on his backside, laughing. Noah extended a hand to help Shem up and said, "Whoa, watch it there, son! You're not in Persia anymore."

The animals and humans were celebrating God's provision for the arctic animals when they heard Nala shouting above them from the middle level of the ark, "Shem! Shem! Please come quickly!"

"Nala! I'm coming!" Shem yelled back and then turning to Noah, said, "I hope she's okay." He carefully walked over the ice out to the corridor before running toward Nala's voice. She was petite and had been pushing herself to help with the animals and the ark. Sometimes she lifted things way too heavy for her small frame, but she never complained, finding joy in the most menial tasks.

Shem ran down the corridor, then up the ramp to reach the middle level. Noah started to follow Shem, instructing Duke to wait by the polar bears, when he heard Ham calling from the

227

opposite direction. "Father! Hurry! Come to the end stalls on the middle level!"

Noah hesitated for a moment, then turned and walked quickly in Ham's direction.

Shem reached the middle level and heard Nala laughing with Adah saying, "I know. I can't believe it."

"What can't you believe, Nala? What is it?" Shem asked, winded from running. He was relieved to see that she was okay. But as he walked over to his wife and his mother, he couldn't believe it, either.

There in the ceiling of the stall was a strange light coming from an unknown source. It looked like the sun yet staring at it didn't hurt the eyes. Intense heat poured from the light into the stall, making the air dry. All moisture was sucked out of the self-contained atmosphere, creating a hot, arid desert. The floor of the stall was completely covered in hot sand. A gentle wind blew in this desert stall, causing the sand to shift and form ridges.

228

Standing in the center of the stall was a pair of large camels, chewing their cud and using their extra eyelids to shield their eyes from the blowing sand. A pair of light brown scorpions scurried over the sand, leaving a trail before climbing under a large rock that had appeared in the corner.

Shem stood staring in disbelief. An arctic zone? Now a desert zone? Was this really happening?

"Look over here, Shem," Nala said as she led him to the next stall.

A desert zone had formed in this stall as well, but was slightly different. Growing within the stall there were scrub brush, grasses, and a few succulent flowering plants. A pair of bearded dragon lizards basked in the hot sunlight on a dead tree branch. As Shem walked closer to look at the lizards, one started slowly waving his arm in a circular motion, no expression on his face. He then switched to the other arm, slowly circling his hand in a waving motion. Shem looked at Nala, who smiled and said, "I think he or she likes you!"

Also in this stall were two kangaroos that sat and gazed back at the humans. The male was scratching his tummy while chewing on a clump of grass. The female sat up on her hind legs, looking quite content. Suddenly right next to her a flower bloomed from one of the plants. She looked down at the emerging flower and then back at the humans. Was she smiling? She then leaned over and pulled off the flower, taking a bite and holding the remainder in her paw while she chewed. The male kangaroo hopped over to the water and drank. He looked up, water dripping from his chin, and grunted, looking pleased.

"How . . . is this happening?" asked Adah as she held her hands to her cheeks and slowly shook her head in disbelief.

"Did it begin when the camels and the kangaroos walked over the threshold into the stalls?" Shem asked. A pair of flies buzzed around the male kangaroo's ear, and he shook his head to shoo them away.

"Yes! How did you know that?" Nala replied, surprised but delighted.

"We just saw the same thing happen with the polar bears, but their stall turned into a cold, frozen zone. It happened just as the female walked over the threshold. You should see it. There are ice shelves, icicles, and a strange light coming from within the ice, but it's not like this light that gives off heat. It's just a *miracle*," exclaimed Shem, hugging Nala and Adah as they shared in the wonder of the impossible.

"God is causing the natural habitats of these animals to form around them, providing the conditions they need for survival," said Noah as he walked up behind them. "It's happening all over the ark, with varying temperatures and climates. You've seen ice and desert. Come with me. You will not believe what I will show you next."

Japheth and his wife Lillie walked along the lower corridor of the ark, herding along a strange collection of animals. Most were beautiful, of course, but some were quite odd.

"It looks like the Maker put the knees of these birds on backwards. Look how they bend when they walk," said Lillie as the flamingos gracefully walked down the corridor, looking at one another and rolling their eyes.

A pair of crocodiles slowly walked along behind them, their massive tails swishing from side to side as their bellies dragged on the floor of the ark. Walking next to the crocs were by far the strangest creatures the people had ever seen. They had flat tails and webbed feet, brown fur, and a nose that looked like a duck.

"I'm sorry, but what was the Maker thinking when He made these creatures?" laughed Japheth.

"Oh, but they are so cute. I know they are strange, but how could you not love a face like that, I ask you?" said Lillie, picking up the female and putting her cheek next to the platypus's duckbill. Lillie's chestnut brown hair matched the color of the little animal. Lillie gently put the platypus down, and the small creature smiled at her mate.

The band of animals followed the humans and looked at the plain, wooden stalls they passed, wondering how they could be happy cooped up in such drab living conditions. Although the corridor was lit with oil lamps, the stalls were dark. The living quarters were clean and roomy but devoid of anything similar to what they were used to. They soon reached an area of extra large stalls. The stalls reached up two decks high, towering above them. The animals looked at one another, wondering what could be so big as to inhabit those stalls.

Lillie looked back at the animals, then at the double deck stalls. Clearly, these weren't the right animals to inhabit the twenty-eight-foot-tall stalls, but she felt an impression to stop. "Japheth, don't ask me why, but I feel like we should put the crocodiles in this stall."

Japheth held up his hands to gesture how tall the crocodiles were. "But Lillie, the crocs are only this high. There's no way they'd need all that room."

Lillie looked at the large crocodiles that sat there smiling up at her with mouths filled to capacity with pointy teeth. Funny, there were two small green insects sitting on the crocs' heads. They had triangle-shaped heads and long arms folded in at their sides. She smiled back at the crocs and their small green insect passengers.

"I know it doesn't seem to be the sensible thing. I just have a feeling they should be in this stall. It couldn't hurt to see for a minute, could it? We can always move them again."

Japheth looked at Lillie and then at the crocodiles. She had such a big heart for animals, especially the outcasts. Perhaps that's why she had gravitated to this group of strange creatures . . . and these two big reptilian beasts! What did she see in them that so attracted her heart? She was smiling at them, and they at her. Lillie turned her gaze to smile at Japheth, cocking her head as if to say, "Come on, do it for me?"

"Okay, I don't think this is a great idea, but I'll go along with you," said Japheth, grinning and shaking his head. His wife had a way of captivating him with those eyes and that smile that he just couldn't resist. Lillie clasped her hands together in excitement and gave Japheth a kiss on the cheek before moving to the crocodiles.

"Here we go, my toothy friends. Let's see how you like this stall," Lillie said as she gently cleared the other animals from their path so they could walk through. The flamingos, armadillos, and platypuses moved aside for the crocodiles, who looked at each other and then up at the huge stall. The green insects also looked up, and then bowed their heads. *Are they praying?* Lillie wondered. *How curious.*

Sydney the crocodile looked at his wife Alice and said, "Okay, love. Here we go. Looks like a beaut of a place."

Alice smiled back at Sydney, "It's not Australia, but it's so tall in there, it will feel like we're down under."

"I don't know," Stewart said from atop Sydney's massive head. The praying mantis looked uncertain as ever. "I've prayed for a miracle to help us have a place as good as home. This doesn't look anything like home."

"Oh, Stewart, I say we give it a fair go. I think you've prayed enough for the Maker to provide for us. He got us to the ark, didn't He? That alone was a miracle. Time to *live* in it," said Cookie, the female praying mantis.

"Cookie's right, Stewart. You've got one smart Sheila, there. No worries, mate!" said Sydney as he started walking slowly across the floor to follow Lillie into the stall, Alice right beside him.

Lillie walked into the stall. "Come on in. That's right, let's see how you like it here."

As Sydney's small, clawed feet crossed the threshold, a rumble began to shake the stall and caused the wooden planks underneath to roll, as if an earthquake were exploding under their feet. Lillie was knocked to the floor and Japheth called her name in panic, "LILLIE!" But the rumbling noise drowned out his voice. Something incredible was happening.

Lillie sat on the floor, the crocodiles next to her, as they watched a massive rock push up through the wooden planks. The rock grew, and grew, and grew, soaring high into the double stall as a loud thundering sound filled their ears. The rock looked like it would not stop growing before soaring into the upper deck, bringing it crashing down on top of them.

All eyes were gazing upward at the rock when suddenly it stopped. The rumble ceased and all was quiet.

Japheth rushed inside the stall and sat next to Lillie. "Are you okay?"

Lillie could only shake her head, yes. She was in awe of what had happened—stunned speechless.

Lillie then felt something under her hands on the floor where she leaned back on her arms. It was soft, gooey, wet, and ticklish. She quickly pulled her hands back and stood up to see an amazing sight. Marsh grass was growing out of the floor, which had turned to a gray, muddy bottom. Lillie and Japheth jumped back in alarm as they watched the grass spread around the middle of the stall, forming a perfect circle.

Sydney started laughing. "Ace, that tickles," he said as the wet grass grew under his belly. Stewart sat there covering his eyes with his long front arms, afraid to look at what was happening.

"Look, Stewart. It's marsh grass. Marsh grass, growing *here!*" exclaimed Alice. "There's nothing to fear—open your eyes, love."

Cookie flew over to Stewart and pulled his arms back. "You asked for a miracle, Stewart. You got a rip-snorter of one."

Stewart opened one eye, then the other. He blinked twice at the spreading marsh grass and then breathed in to smell the distinct aroma of marshland. Could it be? It smelled like the banks of the river he so loved back in New Zealand.

"I . . . I can't believe it," Stewart said as he clasped his hands together. "It's almost like home. If only there was some flowing wa—" Stewart's words were cut off when a huge rumble began again, this time from the top of the rock.

All eyes quickly turned to the top of the stall. It couldn't be. It just couldn't be!

233

CHAPTER 40

A New Creation

Noah led Adah, Shem, and Nala down the corridor to join Ham and his wife, Mabir, at the opposite end of the ark. As they approached, their skin started feeling wet from the humidity. The sounds of squawking birds, howling monkeys, and buzzing insects filled the area with energy and life.

Suddenly they saw something swinging above them in the air. It was a pair of red howler monkeys, clearly having the time of their lives. But what were they swinging on? As the people looked closely, their jaws dropped. It defied explanation. There in mid-air swung the monkeys on strong, green vines. The vines were rapidly growing all along the frame of the stalls, curling around beams and branching off into hundreds of other vines. A thick canopy of vegetation filled the stalls throughout this entire region. Nala reached her hand out to touch the vine as it moved along the railing next to her. As her hand touched the vine she felt the soft petals of a flower open under her fingers. She jumped back with a giddy, "Oh!" as the flower tickled her.

Mabir ran over to Nala, a beautiful flower tucked behind her ear. "Can you believe this?! We were just standing here with the animals in the corridor, and the next thing we knew—" she started to say.

"The monkeys crossed the threshold into the stall and the vines started growing," interrupted Shem, laughing at yet another spectacle as he allowed a small vine to curl around his finger. He could hardly contain his excitement.

"But look up there, it's not just vines, it's trees. Real trees are actually growing," said Ham, talking fast and pointing to the ceiling of the stall.

Shem, Nala, and Adah turned their gaze to see a lush forest of leaves and trees, so thick there was no wood to be seen. But there dancing between the branches was light. It was as if sunlight was just above the tree canopy, finding its way through the tangle of branches and leaves.

The girls jumped as the red howler monkeys screamed a loud, "OOH-WA-OOH-WA-OOH-WA-OOH-WA-OOOOOH!" The monkeys were joined by a pair of black chimpanzees who swung in the trees with them.

235

The male chimp stopped to swing by one arm toward a tall, thick stalk. He sniffed at the stalk when suddenly he screeched. There next to the chimp sprouted a cluster of long, green-yellow bananas. He called to his mate, who joined him on the branch, along with the red howler monkeys. The monkeys looked at each other, then simply sat and stared at the bananas.

"Ah never see more. Dem bananas just popped out of nowhere. Should we eat dem?" said Rufus the red howler monkey, swinging by his tail.

"I think we should check the bananas to see if they do anything else," replied Keb, the male chimp. "I wouldn't want to graze on something without checking it first." He kept his gaze on the bananas while scratching his underarm.

"Let's eat, hey? Only the Maker could make these fruits pop out of nowhere for us," said the female chimp, Okapi. She shook her head in Keb's face for emphasis.

"And dat's why I say it's okay to eat dem. Go ahead, Keb. Give me one of dem bananas. I'll eat it first if allyuh don't want any," exclaimed Jovita, the red howler monkey, also swinging by her tail and jabbing Keb in the arm.

"Okay, friend, I'll get you one just now. Shame if we don't eat them. They look so good!" answered Keb, pulling a banana off the bunch.

The humans watched as the male chimp started pulling the bananas from the clump, passing them around to the monkeys there. A pair of huge, red orangutans swung over to where the monkeys sat and waited their turn. They all sat, peeling the tasty fruit, eating, and screeching with delight between bites.

Noah's family pointed and laughed with joy at this miracle. "But look at the really big monkeys," Ham shouted, directing their attention to the next stall.

There in a thick grove of trees sat the largest of primates, a pair of gorillas. The male was massive, with huge muscular arms and broad shoulders. The female was smaller but still quite large compared with the other primates. Together the gorillas sat in a nest of leaves in the middle of a bamboo grove, pulling off stalks next to them and chewing the bamboo with great satisfaction.

Ham went over and tried to break off a stalk of bamboo but couldn't bend it. The plant was incredibly strong. He looked back at the gorillas, marveling at the massiveness of their bodies. *Are they laughing at me?* Ham thought as they looked at him with grins on their faces.

"Did you see that, Mashaka?" the male gorilla said, laughing at the weak human who couldn't bend the bamboo. "He's a *moffie* boy!"

"Now Katungi, don't you go off like that. Shame that the human is so weak but you don't have to go make a scene about it. He knows you're stronger," replied Mashaka, knowing her husband had a tendency to show off in the jungle. Sometimes his strength gave him a big head, and that was his weakness.

236

"I'm not going to make a scene, just want to have a little fun showing off to this *oke*," said Katungi. Suddenly he stood up, lifted his long arms, and beat his chest with his fists. He made a hooting sound, acting genuinely excited. Mashaka the female gorilla just sat there, rolling her eyes, not impressed with her mate's performance.

Mabir tried to suppress her laughter as she watched Ham and the gorilla. Ham suddenly felt like an eighty-pound weakling compared with this beast, who pulled off another stalk of bamboo as easily as snapping a dry twig.

"Humph! Are you satisfied now? Seems to me you'd be mindful of these humans. So shape up and I best not see you give that human a fright!" Mashaka ordered her big silverback mate.

"I'm just having fun with that *moffie* boy. I'll shape up," Katungi said to his wife with a grin. The gorilla sat down and continued his meal, smiling at Ham from his perch. Ham looked back at the gorilla and gave a weak smile in return, hoping he'd never have to match strength with this beast in anything that mattered.

It was hard for Noah's family to know where to look next. Insects buzzed all around them, landing here and there. A pair of toucans flew about, going from branch to branch, eating berries that popped out on the limbs. One of the toucans flew right into the trunk of the tree, bonking her beak before unsteadily landing on a branch. The colorful bird shook her long yellow beak as if to clear her head.

A beautiful black and orange butterfly landed on Noah's shoulder before taking flight again. Noah smiled as Adah stretched out her hand to beckon the butterfly to land on her fingers. The butterfly softly landed in her hand and spread her wings up and down as if to say "hello" before flying back to the growing rain forest.

"Wait, do you hear something?" Shem asked.

"Which 'something' could you possibly be talking about, Shem? There's so much noise in here, I can't make out much of anything!" said Mabir, still giggling at how the gorilla showed up Ham with the bamboo.

237

They stopped and listened. Slowly they began to hear the sound of rushing water. They looked at each other and all around to determine the origin of the sound. Ham ran a long way down the corridor to one of the twenty-eight-foot stalls and called back to the others, exclaiming, "It's a waterfall!"

The others gasped as they ran down the corridor, overwhelmed at the thought of another miraculous event occurring in the ark. They had already seen more than they ever could have imagined. And now a waterfall? They soon gathered around the top of the stall and gazed over at this inexplicable spectacle. The waterfall flowed at the top of the stall from an invisible reservoir behind a well-formed rock that appeared to have come from the deck below. The water cascaded down twenty-eight feet, crashing into a pool of water that filled a circular pond in the middle of the lower stall, leaving a sandy bank around the edge. Marsh grass was visible around the edge of the pool, and amazingly, the water did not

238

overflow its banks. Sitting on the edge of the bank was a pair of crocodiles, sitting half in, half out of the water, eyes closed, content to let the world go by.

Cool spray from the waterfall misted their faces as the humans looked to see cranes, ducks, and all manner of waterfowl flying down from the upper deck to enjoy the water in the pool. Frogs were croaking and jumping on the rocks and a pair of chameleons slowly walked along a branch that overhung the waterfall, licking the water drops from the leaves.

Japheth and Lillie waved up at Noah and the others from the lower deck by the pool. They had just guided a pair of flamingos in to join the other animals. "This is impossible!" Ham shouted, holding his head in disbelief.

"You should have seen it happen," shouted Lillie.

"Did you bring all these creatures in with you?" shouted Noah, seeing all manner of birds, reptiles, and other animals gathering there.

"No! We brought some of these animals, but now all sorts of creatures are creeping down the corridor, finding their way to the waterfall. It's like they are following the sound of their home—they know right where they belong," answered Japheth, holding up a turtle that wriggled his legs in the air. Japheth set the turtle down and it sauntered into the pool of water, disappearing in the marsh grass.

"And look, plants and vines are growing everywhere. It's like . . . a whole new world forming inside the ark!" shouted Lillie, giddy and happy from all she saw around her.

The people looked at one another with mouths wide open; they were witnessing a miraculous transformation of the ark. Even though just building the ark seemed like a miracle, it never occurred to them what God would do *inside* the ark.

"Look how the Lord has provided for the needs of the animals—from the cold to the desert to the rain forest. He has made the impossible happen within the walls of the ark. We are seeing a new creation happen right before our eyes," Noah said, smiling broadly.

239

Adah put her hand on Noah's arm. "Not a single need of these creatures has been overlooked. They even appear to have their favorite foods. How could God do all this—care for so many different creatures at the same time?"

"My mind just can't take all this in," Nala said, twirling a bright pink flower in her hands then lifting it to her nose to smell the sweet fragrance of the bloom. "There is beauty here—it's like a paradise."

Shem suddenly had an idea. "Father, perhaps if the people from the village saw the miracles happening inside the ark, then they would believe," Shem said hopefully, thinking of Avi.

Noah looked at his son, knowing how burdened he was for his friend. His wise, gentle eyes filled with understanding and compassion. "No, Shem. The people have not believed the clear evidence of God's work outside the ark, which alone was miraculous.

They have not believed our words of warning and now their hearts are hardened to the truth. Nothing more is going to persuade them." He gestured to a trumpet vine that curled its way along the railing where he stood. "Not even this."

A pair of colorful macaws flapped their wings and landed on the railing as Noah reached into his pocket and pulled out a handful of nuts. One bird bobbed her head up and down and started mimicking Noah, cackling loudly, and saying, "Not even this, not even this, WAAA."

The humans clapped and laughed at the talking bird. This was one of the most amazing things yet. "Who knew birds could talk," exclaimed Mabir with sheer delight.

Noah chuckled and gave the bird another nut. "The miracles of seeing God work the impossible like we've seen here come to those who believe and trust Him *before* seeing such signs as these. It's because we first believed the word of the Lord and did as He said that He has granted us the privilege of seeing Him do the impossible."

"The Lord asked us to build an ark filled with empty wooden stalls. Was that our faith then?" asked Shem.

"Well, that's how we acted on our faith. He has now taken our small work and added the impossible. He's taken a seed of faith and grown a miracle. The gift of miracles is available to anyone—whoever first has faith in what He says. Because we have entered into the ark, we have experienced a new creation," Noah said, feeding the birds, who gobbled up the nuts.

"New creation, new creation," squawked the loud bird, bobbing her head up and down excitedly.

Shem understood what his father was saying. Faith yields its own rewards, but belief must exist before the impossible is shattered. Nala came over and hugged Shem from behind, silently consoling him.

Japheth and Lillie walked up from the deck below to where Noah and the others were—standing in awe of the miracles.

Noah brushed off his now empty hands and smiled as he spoke to his family, "Let's celebrate the gift of the miracle. We have witnessed God's creative handiwork, including seeing light come from darkness. Only He could do this."

The family looked at the rain forest and then the waterfall. It was true. Light was everywhere in the ark. It was in the ice. It was in the desert. It was in the forest. The light had no visible source, but they knew without a doubt that the light source was God Himself. He was the light of the world.

"We have been blessed to see the entire world of creation in one place—inside the ark. This will be a season of discovery and learning as we watch these animals and see how they live. We'll learn to care for them, as we better understand what sustains them, and how they interact with one another. And it has only begun, for what we've seen today is just the beginning. We've got a lot more ark to fill."

Noah's family erupted in laughter and awe, already over-whelmed with what they had seen on this first day of the arriving animals. *What more awaits us to witness?* they wondered. As the day came to a close, they danced and sang in the corridor, celebrating God's creation and provision. The animals, too, seemed to join the celebration, exclaiming the wonder of the Maker with the unique, joyful noise He had given to each and every creature.

PART FOUR

THE HERO AND
THE FLOOD

CHAPTER 41

Reunion

The seagulls flew playfully in the sky around the fire cloud, looping up and down and feeling the incredible force that radiated in the air—they were celebrating. After endless weeks of traveling coastlines in search of animals needing transport, Crinan and Bethoo were elated. Their mission was complete. They followed the fire cloud that now hovered larger than ever over the ark and were amazed at what they found inside.

Crinan and Bethoo had seen all manner of creatures since their arrival three days earlier and enjoyed a daily series of miraculous events aboard the ark. They flew up and down the corridors, greeting the animals they had helped from various places around the world, so happy that they had arrived safely over the sea to reach the ark. As they watched the stalls transform, the gulls wondered how these animals had brought their habitats with them. They could hardly wait for Max, Kate, and Al to see this gigantic, miraculous ark. And everyday, the gulls spread the word about Max. Soon all the animals would be able to meet the one whose idea had saved so many of them.

Crinan and Bethoo still wondered what it could all mean. Animals, birds, and every kind of creeping creature made their way to the ark. Now what? What was the reason the Maker had called the animals here? They frequently discussed this mysterious mission on their long flights, but the questions always led to more questions rather than answers. Hopefully they would know what this was all about soon.

Today the gulls viewed a new parade of animals heading toward the ark. "I kin't wait ta see Max, Kate, an' Al," said Bethoo excitedly. She missed her friends and wondered how they had fared in their journey here.

"I kin't either, me love. I suppose Max will have many a grand tale ta tell us aboot their travels. An' jest wait 'til we tell him how his idea spread around the world ta help so many beasties—won't he be surprised then?" answered Crinan, scanning the sea of creatures below for any sign of Max.

246

"Aye, that he will, dear. But—" Bethoo answered, suddenly looking sad, "I dread tellin' him the bad news. He'll take it hard."

Crinan glanced over at Bethoo, a solemn look in his eyes. "Aye. It will hit him hard, but maybe his heart will lift when he sees how many creatures he helped." The gull directed his gaze back to the ground below, continuing his search.

"The ark is gettin' full. I hope there's room for them when they get here," said Bethoo.

"Don't worry. Why would the Maker have them make the long journey only ta not have room in the ark? Let's have a closer look ta see if they're here," Crinan said. With that he dove toward the ground and Bethoo followed. They swooped down over a crowd of animals when suddenly Bethoo spotted Kate.

"There's Kate. I see her. It looks like she's ridin' a horse? An' there! There's Max walkin' in front of a big group of animals next ta a little black cat. Al, I see Al. He's ridin' on top of a cow." Bethoo was so excited that she flew ahead of Crinan.

"Wait for me, love. Wait for me," answered Crinan, who was also excited to see their old friends.

Bethoo landed directly on the horse next to Kate, a huge grin on her face. "Kate, ye made it. I'm so happy ta see ye. We've been waitin' days for ye."

Kate was delightfully startled. "Ah, Bethoo. Me sweet bird friend. It's been a long time." The terrier and gull embraced and held on to each other for a moment, filled with gratitude to see the other again.

Al saw the two friends hugging and made a huge jump over from Isabella to Pauline to join the embrace, his big paws squeezing them tightly. "Top o' the mornin' to ye, Bethoo!" Bethoo and Kate exchanged pained looks from Al's tight hug.

"Hello, Al dear," Bethoo replied when she finally could breathe.

Crinan came in for a landing next to Max. "Mission accomplished, Max," he said with a grin.

Max stopped in the road and slapped Crinan on the back with his burly paw, making a few of Crinan's white feathers fly off. "Well if it isn't me old friend. It's good ta see ye, laddie."

Crinan, staggering from Max's greeting, said, "Aye, it's good ta see ye, too." He then spoke to Liz, "Excuse me, lass, I'm Crinan. Me wife, Bethoo, is up there with Kate an' Al."

"Ah, *oui!* But Max has told me so much about you. I am Liz. Lizette Brilliante. *Enchanté,*" said Liz, coming over to nudge Crinan with her head. She knew how important Crinan and Bethoo were to helping Max, Kate, and Albert get across the channel by finding Craddock the whale. And she knew of their important mission to help the other animals. She couldn't wait to ask the gulls about their journeys.

"We met Liz an' her friends when we landed in France. An' ye might say Al were love-struck the minute he laid eyes on this lass. I guess ye figured that the Maker called animals two by two[*] ta follow the fire cloud," Max said, his smile bright to see his old Scottish friend again. His heart felt a twinge of homesickness. How he missed Scotland, the Glen, and of course, Gillamon.

"Good for the big, orange kitty. He picked a bonnie lass, I must say. I never would have thought he had it in him," said Crinan, winking at Liz. "Aye, every creature we helped has a mate. Two by two is how it were. An' ye won't believe wha's inside the ark."

"Two by two to reach the ark," Liz said, her gaze fixed on the enormous structure in front of them. Liz sat staring at this marvel of manmade construction. She was instantly fascinated and couldn't wait to get inside and explore. She was also relieved. She looked at the animals in their group and announced, "*Mes amis,* we have finally arrived. Our long journey is over. As you can see, the fire cloud has formed in a grand way overhead, and along with the arrival of the hundreds of other animals you see here, we can clearly conclude our destination is this ark."

"She's a bit of a brainy one, then, eh?" Crinan whispered to Max.

"Aye, never could have made it here without this smart lass," Max whispered back.

"Ye mean no more walkin'? No more travelin' for days on end? No more scroungin' for food? No more crossin' water?" asked Al, bubbling over with relief as he realized their journey was at an end.

"*Oui,* at least for the walking and traveling. We will need to see about the food. But I assume there will be some inside," Liz replied, smiling at Al and the others.

"Aye, ye need not worry aboot food. I never seen so much food! Anythin' ye kin imagine is inside that ark!" offered Bethoo, happy to give good news to everyone.

---

[*]God instructed a select number of animals to come on board in pairs of seven. See Genesis 7:2-3. In this book, we are focusing only on pairs of animals.

Al and Isabella exchanged looks. "AYE! *SÍ!*" they both said at the same time, their mouths watering at the thought of bountiful food.

"Wha' aboot the water then, lass?" asked Max, hoping there would be no more water crossing either.

"Well, we can't rule water out since we are, in fact, getting ready to board a boat. And boats are constructed to float on top of water," Liz replied matter-of-factly, her logical train of thought rolling off her tongue.

Max gulped. "But I don't see any water here, an' we haven't seen any for miles. Maybe this ark is a land boat."

Liz looked at Max with a wrinkled brow. "Now that isn't logical, Max. Of course boats are made for water. True, we haven't seen a body of water for miles around, and looking at this structure I do not see a way to transport this ark to the water. I will need to study this situation further, no?"

Henriette came flapping down to the ground from Don Pedro's back, with Jacques right behind her. "Don't question Madame, *chien*. She knows what she is talking about. Madame, should we go get on the ark now? I will need to direct this bull so he won't get too excited with so many animals moving about," said the bossy hen, glaring back at Don Pedro.

Liz looked over the entire area, observing the movement of animals up a huge ramp into the middle of the ark. Then she spotted them—humans. The fur along her back rose in alarm. But her mind grew calm as she observed behavior she had not witnessed before with humans. She watched one man gently guide a pair of striped, horse-looking animals up the ramp, softly patting them on the back. She couldn't believe what she saw next. Another man helped two incredibly tall creatures with necks that rose ten feet in the air. *These animals must be eighteen feet tall,* Liz estimated. One of the creatures appeared to be quite nervous, and Liz observed the human trying to calm the strange, brown-patched beast. Two women laughed as they guided a pair of lions and horned beasts into the ark, and another female guided a pair of huge birds up the ramp—the biggest birds that Liz had ever seen.

They had encountered some humans after crossing the border from Turkey into Persia and had found them to be most unkind, just as the turkeys had warned. A group of dirty men had chased Albert around a field and almost caught him before Henriette turned Don Pedro lose to charge the men. For once, the bull's charging came in handy as he snorted and ran after the men, causing them to scream in fear as they ran away. Henriette praised her pupil for saving Al, a welcome response for Don Pedro.

Another time a group of humans tried to capture Giorgio and Pauline, but the horses outran the men. Again, it was fortunate how Giorgio's sleep running problem actually worked out for their protection since the humans didn't know how to wake the sleeping horse.

There were other human encounters as they neared the ark, and Liz observed that humans always looked angry. Her spine bristled whenever they came near one. The animals had not yet encountered one decent human. Max shared what Gillamon had told him about humans.

"They are troubled creatures with hard hearts. Be kind to them," Gillamon had instructed. "Every human struggles with some sort of pain."

While Liz pondered what Gillamon had said, she was still logically concerned. She tried to reason things in her mind: *Why would the Maker call the animals to this ark and to the care of humans? Could it be that these humans are different somehow?* Suddenly one of the humans spotted Liz and the others. He had jet-black hair, and smiled as he looked in their direction. *He's smiling,* Liz thought. *These must be different kinds of humans. I haven't seen a human smile yet.*

"Okay, *mes amis*. Listen to me. It appears a small group of humans will be helping us onto the ark," Liz started before the animals gasped in fear.

"Do you want me to chase them, señora?" eagerly asked Don Pedro, drawing a look of approval from Henriette.

"No, Don Pedro, chasing won't be necessary. I've observed these humans, and they are definitely different from ones we previously encountered. It only makes sense that if the Maker has called us to them, then they are responsible to provide for our welfare," explained Liz.

"Oh, the man walkin' our way looks very nice," said Kate, wagging her tail. She was ever the optimistic one, always happy to meet others and to give them a chance.

"*Oui*, but Kate is right. This man does look kind. Do as he instructs and stay close," said Liz.

Max looked at the man walking toward them, and was instantly drawn to him. There was something about this human that made Max feel at ease. He walked toward the animals, arms open in greeting, and a smile on his face. He stopped as he met Max in the road.

"Well hello there, little guy. Welcome. Aren't you a nice looking animal?" said Shem as he leaned over to pat Max on the back, then scratched him on the side at his "tickle spot." Max rapidly twitched his back leg as a reflex to the scratching, making Shem laugh. It felt good. He liked this human.

"Where is your mate?" Shem said as he looked around before spotting Kate on top of Isabella. "Now isn't that something? How did you get up there?" he asked as he walked over and gently lifted Kate from Isabella's back, rubbing her fur before putting her on the ground next to Max. Kate wagged her tail excitedly and licked Shem's hand.

Shem noticed the seed sack hanging around Isabella's neck that also held Max's reed. Curious, he went to touch it when Liz meowed up at him. Distracted, he directed his attention to the petite cat at his feet.

"Well, well, and what a beautiful creature you are," Shem said as he picked Liz up to hold her. Liz stared into his eyes, fascinated by this human and the sensation of being lifted into the air. Shem stroked her beautiful soft fur and she purred. She had never experienced this before; and it was obvious that his human hadn't either. Al meowed from below, clearly jealous as he rubbed Shem's legs with his tail. Shem reached over to pet Al. "Okay, big guy, I see you, too." He stroked Al under the chin, and Al closed his eyes in delight, purring loudly and drooling with delight.

"Let's see here, now I do know what some of you animals are: a bull, a cow, two horses, a hen, and a rooster," said Shem, going over to each one to made physical contact—a touch here, a pet there. Rudy and Rosie flew over to buzz around Shem's head, landing on Giorgio's back. "Wow, I've never seen such tiny birds before! Welcome, little ones," Shem said, smiling at the two hummingbirds, who shrugged their tiny shoulders as he petted them.

Max, Liz, and all the other animals felt immediately comfortable. Yes, this was clearly a different type of human. This one was special: warm, kind, and inviting. They would be okay under his care. As Shem led the animals to the ramp of the ark, Crinan and Bethoo grinned broadly. They weren't going to tell Max and the others about what was happening inside. The surprise was part of the fun. The gulls flew ahead of them and into the ark. They had some announcing to do.

CHAPTER 42

The Hero

When they reached the entryway of the broad door of the ark, the animals heard a symphony of noise coming from inside. Squawks, roars, chirps, and bellows brought the ark alive with sound. Shem looked back at the animals and said, "You see, you aren't the only ones who've come to the ark. You'll have lots of friends here."

Liz smiled pleasantly and thought, *He has no idea about how much we animals know. Humans must not understand animals very well. Hmmm.* This thought alone was intriguing to Liz. She would enjoy educating them.

"Here we go, lassie," said Max to Kate, grinning a mile wide. And then to Liz, "Okay, Liz, let's see where this jour-r-rney's led us then."

Liz and Max exchanged smiles of anticipation. Henriette pecked Al in the back as he stood there, holding up the line, his jaw dropped in awe of the ark's massive size. "Ouch! That hurt me backside," said Al as he frowned and picked up his pace. Jacques put his feathered wing over Al's back and apologized for his hen-pecking wife as they walked along. Giorgio and Pauline went clop,

clop, clop up the ramp, as did Isabella and Don Pedro. Rudy and Rosie buzzed around excitedly, hovering just above the group, but not wanting to fly ahead of them.

Max walked directly behind Shem and was the first of the group to step foot inside the ark. As the animals followed and came in the door, a hush fell over the ark. Not one creature made a sound. And all eyes were staring right at Max.

Noah came up to Shem and stopped as he, too, perceived the sound of silence. He and Shem looked around and studied the stalls: silence, stillness, and staring were universal among the animals.

Noah looked down at Max and the others, an eyebrow raised in question. "It seems our new friend here is having quite the effect on the ark," Noah said to Shem as he crouched down to be eye level with Max. "Welcome, my little friend. My, what influence you have for one so small!" Noah petted Max on the back and then petted Kate, who wagged her tail, eager to meet this nice man.

"What do you suppose the animals are doing, father?" Shem asked as he looked around. "Do these animals know something we don't?"

It was all Liz could do to keep from bursting out laughing. *What a silly question,* she thought as she walked up to greet Noah. She was curious to meet yet another human who for all practical purposes appeared quite trustworthy.

Noah gently stroked Liz and remarked, "What a beautiful— ["CAT," God whispered]—Cat." Liz purred and looked right in Noah's eyes, studying him. "Doesn't she look intelligent, Shem?" he said, chuckling, taken in by her big golden eyes.

Well, perhaps he knows more than I thought if he perceived that obvious truth, Liz thought to herself.

Max felt all eyes on him, and he soon became very uncomfortable. "Liz, why is everyone starin' at me?"

"I kin answer that one," Crinan said as he flapped over to land next to them. "Bethoo an' me have spread the word aboot ye, Max.

We've told them aboot how it were yer idea ta rescue the water-trapped beasties. They've been waitin' for ye, jest ta get a glimpse of ye!" Crinan smiled as he looked around at the staring animals.

"It appears you are quite the hero, *mon ami*," said Liz, smiling at Max, happy for her friend.

Max lowered his head in humility. "But I didn't do anythin'! The Maker showed me how ta get across the channel. I jest figured it were a good idea ta help others. That doesn't make me special."

"Of course it does," said a voice from behind. It was a beautiful, long, reddish-brown snake that slithered up next to Max and the others. His scales had an iridescent sheen to them as he rose up to greet them with a smile. "I can't tell you what a privilege it is to meet you, Max! May I call you Max? Your fame has spread around the world. And we all have you to thank for it. If it weren't for you, we'd all still be sitting on the seashores of our various lands, wondering how to follow the fire cloud. Yes, you are a hero."

"Uh, well, thank ye. I'm honored ta have helped. Where did ye come from?" asked Max humbly, yet wanting to know about one of his "fans." "An' I'm sorry, I didn't get yer name."

"Call me Charlie. From Borneo—quite a long way, I assure you. I just had to be the first to greet you and say welcome. And thank you, Max. Thanks for what you've done," said the snake, genuinely pleased to meet Max. He turned to the ark inhabitants and shouted, "Everyone, let's hear a cheer for Maximillian Braveheart the Bruce—our hero."

With that the entire ark erupted in noise again. Cheers echoed throughout the ark for Max.

"Oh, Max, I'm so proud of ye. Ye've always been me hero. Now yer the hero for the world!" Kate said as she kissed Max on the cheek.

Noah and Shem shook their heads and laughed in wonder at the reaction of the animals. They had seen so many new animal behaviors over the past three days that nothing seemed to surprise them anymore. Shem then turned to lead Max, Kate, Liz, and Al down the middle corridor while Noah took the cows and horses with him to the lower deck, but failed to notice the seed sack and reed around Isabella's neck.

Henriette squawked and followed Don Pedro down the corridor, her wings spread as she waddled behind him. Jacques fell in line and followed his wife. Noah looked at the hen as she flapped her wings and flew up to ride the big bull. Chuckling at the unusual relationship of these creatures, he said, "I guess you don't have to go to the bird deck if you'd rather stay with the bull. It looks like you are good friends."

Henriette sat smugly on top of Don Pedro while the bull looked painfully at his wife, Isabella. The journey was over, but evidently, the training was not.

Rudy and Rosie instinctively flew to the noise of the waterfall, finding their way to a trumpet vine filled with flowers. They were in heaven as they sipped the sweet nectar. The hummingbirds began to meet the other birds and creatures gathered in the rain forest, telling them "yes," they had traveled with Max. Everyone wanted to hear about their journey, and the brave hero they had heard so much about. Rudy and Rosie were the center of attention by the waterfall that afternoon.

Walking down the corridor, Max and the others passed stall after stall of admiring creatures who shouted their thanks to Max.

"G'day, mate. You sure were an ace leader to help us. Name's Boomer, and this is my wife, Sheila. We're from the northern territory of Australia. We'll be seeing you around. Thanks heaps," said the big kangaroo. The bearded dragons also waved and echoed Boomer's remarks.

"*Konnichiwa*, Max," said a pair of rats who bowed low in respect as they greeted him, smiling with big front teeth and heavy Asian accents. A pair of giant flying squirrels flew over to land next to them, and chimed in, "*Domo arigato*. Thank you very much for helping us make it here. We've come from Japan," the squirrels said as they also bowed to pay honor to the great dog hero.

Max nodded respectfully back at the animals, saying, "Yer welcome," as he walked along, feeling a little embarrassed by all this attention. Kate just nuzzled her mate with affection, soaking up this big moment for him, proud to be at his side.

They came to a stall with a group of animals perched on what looked like a gently rolling green pasture. Max's heart caught in his chest. It looked almost like Scotland. There in the stall was a pair of small goats, but they were different from Gillamon. They clearly weren't mountain goats. As they approached, the goats fell over on the floor, their legs stiff and straight in the air.

"Wha' in the name of Pete is wrong with them?" asked Max as he walked by.

"Hello, Max! Never mind them—they're fainting goats. If they get startled or excited about the least little thing, they just up and faint for a couple of minutes. Doesn't hurt them, but it took us forever to get here from America. Anyway, name's Patrick and this is Sallie. We never could have made it across the Atlantic if you hadn't been so smart. Thanks a lot," said a plump raccoon, his wife sitting next to him, waving.

Max and Kate looked at each other. They had never seen creatures like this. Fainting goats? And the other two looked like they were wearing masks. And where was America anyway?

On and on it went. Soon they were greeted by a pair of emperor penguins standing in the middle of an ice-filled stall, clapping their fins in appreciation of Max. "Way to go, Max! We floated on an iceberg as long as we could. But it grew quite small when we entered the hot tropics. It would've been way too far for us to swim all the way from Antarctica. The whale came at just the right time." Two leopard seals barked their appreciative remarks, joining the penguins as they clapped their fins. When these animals spoke, their icy breath made puffs of steam rise in the air.

"Liz, are ye hearin' this?" Kate said to Liz, caught up in the wonder of seeing all these grateful animals. But Liz wasn't listening. She was staring in disbelief at the stalls that had mysteriously transformed into the natural habitat of each animal they passed. There were desert and arctic zones, green pastures, forests, and rocky areas. The stalls all appeared to have a light source as well. This wasn't possible—it defied all logic. Liz walked along with her brow furrowed. Liz had no earthly explanation for what she saw in front of her, but she was gloriously fascinated at the same time. She was surrounded by untold scientific exploration and discovery—just waiting for her. Al simply walked along, but she noticed he had tears in his eyes.

"Why, Albert? Why the tears?" Liz asked.

Al sniffed, then smiled and said, "Look at all the food."

"Okay, here you go," said Shem as he stopped in front of one of the stalls. "I think you'll be comfortable in this stall. Of course, you're welcome to come and go as you please, being such small, tame creatures." Shem opened the stall gate and stepped aside.

Liz walked to the head of the line and stared into the dark stall. It was plain wood with nothing but a water barrel and dry hay sitting in the corner. She had seen these elements in the other stalls as well, but those stalls also had natural habitats. Curious, Liz proceeded to walk into the stall. Max, Kate, and Al followed right behind her.

When the four animals entered the stall, they felt grass sprout up under their tired paws. Rocks emerged from the grass all around the stall, and Al cried out in fear. "What is happenin'? The earth is shakin'," the big, orange cat said as he lay down on all fours, grabbing the grass with his claws. Liz was too awestruck to respond right away. So were Max and Kate. They just stood there speechless until the rocks stopped forming and all was still. Mist clouds swirled and danced about. A warm light glowed from an unknown source, illuminating the stall.

"Ah, it looks like you're from a beautiful, green part of the world," Shem said, smiling as he walked into the stall. He looked

258

down at Al, who was about to die of fright, and bent over to pick him up. Al scrambled to put his head up on Shem's shoulder, shivering as his heart pounded. Shem gently stroked Al's back, orange fur flying off as he did so.

"It's okay, orange fella. God has provided your natural habitat to live in aboard the ark, that's all. I know it scared you but there's nothing to fear. You'll love it here. Look, I'll show you," Shem said as he walked over to where a hedge of bushes grew. They were covered in berries. He picked a few and put them under Al's nose since the cat's eyes were closed tight.

Al sniffed and opened one eye. "Berries!" he yelled and then took the sweet fruit from Shem's hand. Shem laughed and set Al down on the soft grass. He looked at Max, Kate, and Liz and folded his arms. "You see, you won't have a single need here on the ark. God has thought of everything. I'll leave you for now to check things out." Shem left the shocked animals alone in the stall, staring at each other in disbelief while Al proceeded to gorge himself on the berries.

259

Kate looked around, wide-eyed and grinning, "Oh, Max, it looks jest like home. It feels jest like home. I kin't believe it."

"Aye, lass! This is somethin' I never would have dr-r-reamed of. The Maker has surpr-r-rised me again," Max replied, turning to Liz. "So there, missy, wha' do ye make of all this?"

Liz sat there silently, her tail slowly tapping the floor. She was in deep thought, reviewing the series of incredible events. Max called loudly again to Liz to break her train of thought, "I said, wha' do ye make of all this?"

"Oh, *oui*. I'm sorry, but I was thinking. It is obvious that the transformation took place as we entered the stall. Beyond that, I am certain of nothing," Liz replied with a wrinkled brow.

Kate walked over to Liz. "Ye must be so excited, Liz! Ye kin study all of these amazin' things an' help us understand it all." Kate stood there, tail wagging and eyes grinning at Liz.

Liz returned a weak grin, "Well, I shall do my best, *mon amie*. It will take some time, no?"

"Well, I hope time is wha' we have plenty of then. I'm ready for a r-r-rest. But first I think I'll join me friend Al an' try those berries," Max said as he walked over to the hedge.

Al smiled up at Max, berry juice dripping from his chin as he grinned and said, "Max, these berries taste jest like the ones from home. Try some!" Together the two devoured a cluster of berries, laughing with joy and relief as Kate joined them.

They had made it! Finally, their long journey was over. They were safe aboard the ark. Max was a hero. And they had all the comforts of home. What more could they possibly want?

Everyone was content except Liz. She wanted answers. She walked over to inspect the threshold of the stall, studying it for any clues of how the transformation began. Her gaze then drifted to the stalls across the corridor. She smiled back at the animals that were still hovering in their stalls to get a glimpse of Max the hero. She marveled at the tropical climate in front of her. There stood a pair of huge Galapagos tortoises, heads raised to get a peek at Max. A pair of green iguanas climbed on top of the large tortoise shells to also get a good look, smiling and waving at Liz.

Liz nodded her head in "hello" before her gaze drifted down the dark end of the corridor to the one stall where there came no cheers for Max. This dark stall was filled with rocky ledges and a cave. And standing silently in front stood two creatures, glaring at her. There was no "hello" or greeting—just icy, cold stares from yellow eyes. Liz shivered.

It was the wolves.

CHAPTER 43

A Hard Day

Max and everyone in their travel group collapsed from exhaustion from the long journey, and chose to sleep a long time. Everyone, that is, except Liz.

Liz spent the next two days exploring the ark. She saw incredible habitats of places she knew of but had never been to. Her mind was thirsty for knowledge about the creatures that inhabited these places. She continued to be stumped by the transformation of the stalls. Liz spent hours introducing herself, getting to know various animals, and yes, explaining how she had traveled with the now-famous Max. The animals she met were instantly charmed by her beauty and grace, and marveled at her wealth of knowledge. Liz came to realize that it would take her a long time—possibly months—to study the thousands of ark inhabitants. She hoped she would have ample time to conduct her research.

Despite Liz's interest in her ark neighbors, she stayed clear of the wolves. While her intellectual side wanted to understand them, her experiential side was so repelled by them that it kept her away from their stall. She would not venture down to the end of the dark corridor where they were. For now, what Max had told her about the wolves, and her experience with them on the way to the ark, was sufficient. She didn't need to know more.

While Liz was energetic from research, Al was sleepy from exhaustion. The long journey finally caught up to him, and he slept for hours on end, waking only to nibble a berry or two before falling back to sleep. It was late in the afternoon when he finally stayed awake long enough to realize that Liz had been gone awhile. Al decided to go looking for her. Max and Kate were snoozing in the corner. He tiptoed out of the stall and headed down the corridor in search of his black beauty.

Al decided he'd go see Isabella and Don Pedro first. Maybe Liz was visiting with them. Plus, he wanted to see what kind of food Isabella, his best eating companion, had enjoyed since coming to the ark. He leisurely made his way to the lower level, enjoying the sights and sounds along the way.

Crinan and Bethoo flew in to perch on the railing in front of Max's stall. They had been waiting for the right time to talk with him; they had something important to tell him.

"Shhh, looks like they're still sleepin'," Bethoo whispered to Crinan.

"Aye, I know they're tired from their trip," Crinan whispered back. "I guess we best come back when they're awake."

"I hear ye, laddie. I'm awake," said a very groggy Max. He stood up and stretched out long and hard, yelping and giving a thorough all-over body shake. Kate awakened as well, yawning as she came out of her deep sleep.

"I didn't know I could sleep so long. I feel like a cat for doin' so," said Max, yawning again as he walked over to the two gulls. But then he noticed that both cats were gone. "I even out-slept the cats then."

Crinan flew into the stall to land on a rock next to Max, and Bethoo followed. "Aye, we also slept for hours on end when we arrived. Ye've got nowhere ta go then so jest enjoy it, lad," Crinan said with a smile. "Ye've done enough journeyin' for a lifetime."

Max wondered if Liz had even slept. "Has that kitty lass been in this stall at all since we got ta the ark? She is the most curious creature I ever met."

"She's been all over the ark talkin' ta the beasties an' learnin' aboot them. Al's been asleep most of the time," said Bethoo.

Kate looked around and noticed Al was missing. "Maybe Al's gone lookin' for Liz."

"Ah well enough, that lassie will not rest until she figures out how the stalls came ta be transformed. I tried ta tell her it were the Maker's doin', but she still wants ta know how He did it. Curiosity will be the death of that kitty, I kin tell ye that right now," said Max, stretching and giving another yelp. "So wha's up with ye two?"

The smile left Crinan's face and he and Bethoo lowered their heads, not saying a word. Kate scooted over to Max's side, a look of worry on her face as she observed their seagull friends. "Wha's the matter?" she asked, concerned.

Crinan closed his eyes, took a deep breath and exhaled, then opened his eyes to look at Max. "Lad, I'm afraid I've got somethin' hard ta tell ye."

"Well get on with it, lad. Wha's wrong?" Max questioned, his brow furrowed.

Crinan looked at Bethoo, suddenly at a loss for words. Bethoo flew over to Max and put her wing across his back. "It's aboot Gillamon, dear," she said softly.

Max grew anxious and animated, his ears alert and tail up. "Gillamon? Wha's wrong? Is he sick then?"

Crinan flew over to join Bethoo next to Max. Looking into Max's eyes, he knew he had to find the courage for both of them. "Max, Gillamon . . . Gillamon died."

"Oh!" Kate exclaimed, tears rushing to her eyes as she put her head over on Max. "Oh, me love, I'm so sorry, I'm so sorry." Kate softly wept.

Max's heart caught in his throat. He felt hot tears fill his eyes. His mentor, his dear friend was gone. He couldn't believe Gillamon had died—it didn't seem real. Max couldn't find any words for a few moments, and his friends surrounded him in consoling silence. Bethoo was crying, and Crinan held his wing firmly across Max's back. After a while, Max spoke.

"I were so worried aboot him when I left. He . . . he wasn't well. How? How did he die?" Max asked, his jaw clenching as he tried to hold back the tears.

"He died in his sleep, Max. We went ta see him on our last trip home before we headed ta the ark. He weren't well, an' were coughin' somethin' terrible. We stayed with him our last night in Scotland an' the next mornin' he were gone," Crinan explained gently, feeling Max's pain. Crinan and Bethoo felt it, too, for they were friends with Gillamon. But no one was as close to the wise old mountain goat as Max.

Max shut his eyes tight, and tears ran down his face. "Well," he said as he opened his eyes, "I'm grateful ye were there with him so he didn't die alone."

Bethoo smiled and said, "We were able ta tell him aboot how ye met Al an' then Kate, an' how ye had the grand idea ta help other creatures cross the sea after callin' for Craddock. Gillamon an' Craddock were always good friends, so he were happy aboot that. Oh, Max, Gillamon were so proud of ye. He knew ye had been called for an important reason. I think he almost were waitin' for a word aboot ye before he died."

Max's heart was breaking, but he was glad that Gillamon was proud of him. In the midst of his pain, Max felt gratitude.

Crinan joined in, "An' Max, Gillamon gave us a message for ye. He must have known he were dyin'. He made sure I could repeat it word for word back ta ye."

Max smiled. *That sounds jest like Gillamon,* he thought.

Crinan continued, "This is wha' Gillamon wanted me ta tell ye."

"Max, I am so very proud of you. Please don't be sad for me, for I have lived a long, happy life. I asked the Maker to help me live in a way so I would use everything He gave me to the full. I will be able to stand before Him and say that I left nothing here undone. I've completed all I was meant to do, including helping you grow, Max. An old goat could not want more.

"There is more to this mission you are on than you realize now. The Maker has a way of bringing multiple purposes out of singular events, and they will all become clear with time. Always remember to look to the Maker for direction as those purposes unfold. Without His revelation, you will surely lose your way.

"I'm so happy to hear about Kate. She sounds like a beautiful lass. I hope you will have many wonderful years together. Go now and be happy. Remember all I taught you. And remember that you are loved and that you are able. Farewell, Max."

Crinan's voice cracked with emotion as he finished. All eyes were full of tears, and all voices were silent as they grieved over the loss of someone so dear. After a while, Max told the others, "Thank ye, me friends, for bein' with Gillamon, an' for bringin' me his dyin' words. They mean so much ta me. Now I think I'd like ta be alone."

Kate softly kissed Max and rubbed her head under his chin. "We understand, me love. Take all the time ye need." Crinan and Bethoo softly echoed Kate's remarks. They wanted Max to have space to grieve privately in his own way.

Max sniffed and nodded his head. "Aye, time is wha' I need then." Max turned and walked out of the stall and down the corridor, his head low and his heart heavy.

The number of animals daily coming to the ark had slowed dramatically. Noah was amazed at the timing of it all. Here these animals had traveled from all over the world to reach the ark, and had arrived within a few days of one another. *God's timing is always perfect,* Noah thought. He stood looking down the road where the animals had trod, and surmised that they would not see many more creatures walk this path. The ark was nearly filled to capacity. Noah knew that just as God's timing was perfect, the exact number of animals He called was also perfect. There would be room for all who were meant to board the ark.

Adah joined Noah, rubbing her hands together with the lavender oil she and the girls had pressed earlier in the spring. She held her hands to her nose and closed her eyes as she breathed in the soothing aroma. Even in the midst of the busy, hard work, Adah took time to take "mini-vacations," as she called them. She felt it was important for everyone to stay refreshed and energized. In her wisdom, she modeled the balance of work and rest. It had been a long day, and now it was time to put aside the cares of the day.

"So, my fine zookeeper. How do you think things look in the ark now?" Adah asked, smiling and tickling Noah's chin.

Noah smelled the lavender oil and smiled, "It's beautiful with you on board, that's what I think." He took her hand in his and kissed it. "Thank you, Adah. Thank you for believing in me and working so hard for this mission. I know all you've missed by helping me."

Adah placed her hand on Noah's cheek and softly held his face. "Oh, Noah, I wouldn't have missed working by your side these many years for the world. I have missed nothing."

Noah and Adah turned to look at the village down below and shared a moment of silence. Their minds drifted to what would happen to their world. "I feel guilty somehow. Here we know the truth and what will happen in two days, yet we are secure. My heart is heavy for the people. They have no idea what is coming," Adah said, a pained look in her eyes.

Noah put his arm around his wife. "Well, it's not because they weren't told what was coming. I know your heart goes out to the people, but don't carry guilt because you are safe. You and I have both tried to spread the truth. We've preached for over a hundred years, and even told them this week that the time of God's judgment was coming in a matter of days. They have listened to the truth, but have not heard it. You can't make people believe, no matter how your heart longs for them to."

Noah paused and took a deep breath. "God respects their freedom to choose and so must we. It will not be easy, but you must rest your heart in the fact that you have chosen God while trying to spread the truth to others. I can't tell you how many sleepless nights I've had, as I've worried for these people. But I know I've done all I can do."

"I suppose you're right. Shem needs to hear these words, Noah. Try and have this talk with him. He's really struggling, and it's only going to get worse in two days," Adah said.

"I'll have a word with him. But for now, focus on the task at hand. I need you to be strong for the others. Tomorrow we need to get our few remaining things from the house, and welcome any final animals that come. It will be our last day on dry ground for a while. Let's make the most of it," Noah said.

He kissed Adah on the head as they stared off at the setting sun on the horizon. It was sobering to realize that tomorrow would be a day of "lasts."

Their last time inside their home on land. Their last time to board animals, and their last time to see the village.

CHAPTER 44

The Last Day

CAW-CA CAW . . . CAW . . . CAW!
COCK-A-DOODLE DOO!

CAW-CA CAW . . . CAW . . . CAW!
COCK-A-DOODLE DOO!

CAW-CA CAW . . . CAW . . . CAW!
COCK-A-DOODLE DOO!

CAW-CA CAW . . . CAW . . . CAW! CAW-CA CAW . . . CAW . . . CAW! CAW-CA CAW . . . CAW . . . CAW!" screamed Ricco, the Mexican raven at the top of his lungs.

"COCK-A-DOODLE DOO! COCK-A-DOODLE DOO! COCK-A-DOODLE DOO!" answered Jacques at the top of *his* lungs, his throat feathers spread out and vibrating.

"Stop this right now!" chimed in Henriette. "*C'est ridicule.* I will not have it."

"But I am the one who is supposed to wake everyone up, no? And here comes this . . . this garbage-eater trying to outdo me," complained Jacques. His rooster pride was threatened, and he was not about to back down. He had been competing with the loud Mexican bird every morning since they got to the ark. Jacques and Ricco found themselves waking up a minute or two earlier each day, just to beat the other bird to the punch.

"Garbage-eater? Is that what you called me, *señor*, garbage eater? *Sí*, I may not have as picky tastes as you . . . you French, but I am proud to be a Chihuahuan raven. And I am the first to wake all the creatures in Mexico, so why don't you give up and let me wake the ark like I'm sure I am meant to do," squawked Ricco back at Jacques.

Tempers were flaring, feathers were flying, and it wasn't pretty.

"ENOUGH! The French hen is right. I will not listen to this, and I know the rest of the ark agrees with us," chimed in Ricco's wife, Maria. Her deep black feathers were just as ruffled as Henriette's. The hen and the raven stood in the corridor, wings on hips, glaring at their husbands.

"Well, I will not give up my post. Humph," said Jacques, putting his nose in the air.

"Neither will I," answered Ricco, crossing his wings and looking the other way.

"Aye-aye-aye. Men. *No entiendo*," said Maria to Henriette.

"*Mais oui*. These men are being ridiculous. Why they each insist on being the one to wake the entire ark, I will never understand," replied Henriette, enjoying the complaining company of another female, feathered friend.

"*Sí, sí, gracias* for seeing things like this! I'm glad we agree," replied Maria, also warming up to Henriette. "Why don't we leave these two *loco* birds and get some breakfast? *Por favor*, come to my stall, *amiga*."

"*Oui*, I would love to," said Henriette as she waddled down the corridor next to Maria, who hopped along next to her.

269

Jacques and Ricco looked at each other, feeling mutual disgust as rivals. Each bird thought the ark was his territory, and this arrangement was going to be difficult. But for now, this morning had begun. The war would continue the next morning.

"*Adios*, Frenchie—until tomorrow," Ricco squawked, flapping his wings.

"Humph! I will be ready and crowing ahead of you, *Monsieur* garbage-eater," replied Jacques.

Both stopped suddenly when a massive shadow passed over them. It was Don Pedro the bull.

"I suggest you *amigos* learn to sleep in on this cruise. Otherwise, you might find yourselves running with the bull," Don Pedro said with a wicked grin on his face.

Ricco and Jacques looked at each other and gulped. They dropped their heads and slowly hopped down from the railing. The war would have to stop . . . for now.

270

Upendo heard the crowing down the corridor, but was up anyway, early as usual. He loved his surroundings here on the ark. He and Chipo had been given a twenty-eight-foot tall stall so their long necks could fit. Upendo was afraid of the tall ark when they arrived, but Ham had gently guided him up the steep ramp, speaking words of assurance to the scared giraffe. Once they got into the stall, an incredible thing happened.

A cluster of tall mimosa trees erupted from the floor, filling the top of the stall with a canopy of delicious leaves. Upendo was immediately at ease, and began to pull off the leaves with his strong tongue, closing his eyes with delight at the delicious flavor. It was one of the best mimosa trees he had ever tasted. Perhaps it grew so tasty because of the moisture from the rain forest in the stalls next door. But the most amazing thing of all was that the leaves appeared to grow back! The more Upendo and Chipo ate, the more leaves there were. Yes, Upendo liked it here. And Jafaru, the lion, slept in his own stall, high up on a rock that had formed there, so he wasn't a concern to Upendo anymore. Life was good. Upendo felt safe and secure aboard the ark.

Upendo reached high into the tree branches and pulled away a big cluster of leaves. As he pulled the branch away, there in front of him was a huge pair of green eyes, and below them, a big mouth of teeth opening wide and screaming, "AHHHHHHH! IT'S OUT TO GET ME!"

Upendo started to scream back at the other screamer, for he was just as startled and terrified, "Help! Chipo!" The giraffe felt his blood pressure rising.

Chipo looked up to see Upendo screaming his head off like he always did in the savanna. It could only mean one thing—Jafaru.

"Calm down, Upendo. Look, I'm sure it's just Jafaru come back to visit, that's all," said Chipo, walking over to the mimosa tree.

But the scream coming from the leaves was not the deep voice of a lion—unless he had laryngitis, that is.

"Jafaru, you come out here this instant. What do you mean coming back and giving Upendo a fright like that? You've got your own stall! And what's the matter with your voice anyway?" scolded Chipo.

As Upendo and Chipo peeked into the shaking leaves, they saw a curious sight—an orange cat. The two giraffes looked at one another, questioning looks on their faces.

"I think Jafaru went and shrunk himself, hey?" Upendo whispered to his assertive mate.

"What kind of crazy thing is this?" Chipo asked the shaking leaves.

"I'm s-s-s-orry, lass. I didn't mean any harm. I jest fell asleep up here last night. When I awoke, I saw this tall beastie, and was afraid he were goin' to eat me," said a very startled Al. Chipo laughed, shaking her head. Upendo looked at her and then back at Al. He didn't understand what was going on.

271

"He looks like Jafaru, only smaller. Are you telling me this isn't Jafaru?" asked Upendo, still rattled from Al's surprising presence in the tree.

"No, Upendo. This is just a small cat. It's not Jafaru," she chuckled. "Who are you, *oke*?" she said to Al.

Al poked his head out of the leaves and jumped down a branch to be eye level with the giraffes. "Me name's Al. I'm jest a plain kitty from Ireland. I went lookin' for me mate last night and ate so many bananas next door that I were full to burstin'. I got so sleepy I jest crashed on the first tree I found. Sorry about that," said Al, relieved that he wasn't going to be eaten by the giraffe, and glad to hear Chipo laughing.

"Well, no harm done, Al. I'm Chipo and this is Upendo. You see, our lion friend Jafaru used to sleep in the trees and scare Upendo in the mornings, so that's who we thought you were."

The three shared a laugh. Al was flattered that the giraffes had thought him to be the king of the beasts. He sat a little taller, remembering that he was, indeed, a noble, famous warrior.

"There you are, Albert," said Liz as she jumped up on the railing of the giraffe stall, slowing waving her tail up and down.

"Liz, me love, I came lookin' for ye yesterday and got lost in the rain forest. Well, actually, I met some monkeys and they introduced me to the best fruit I ever tasted—bananas. Ye got to try them, Liz," Al said as he jumped from branch to branch down to Liz, finally kissing her on the cheek. "I ate so much that I fell asleep up here in this tall beastie's tree."

"I can see this, no? *Bonjour, Madame et Monsieur*. I am Liz, Albert's mate. I am sorry if he upset your morning routine," Liz said as she introduced herself to the giraffes.

"No harm done. It's nice meeting such small cats. I never knew cats came in any size but extra large," said Chipo, bowing her head low to greet Liz. "Wow, and you're a different color, too. You're a pretty cat."

"*Merci*. And yes, I am discovering all sorts of creatures I never knew existed before. What kind of animals are you?" Liz asked inquisitively.

"Giraffes, from Africa," Chipo replied.

Liz continued to question the giraffes on their eating habits, and various other aspects of life as a creature from the savanna. Finally, she remembered why she was looking for Al and returned to her current train of thought.

"*Merci*, Chipo." Then turning to Al, she said, "Oh, Albert, I've been looking for you. I returned to our stall shortly after you left, and learned that Max got some terrible news from Crinan. Kate told me that Gillamon died."

"Oh no. Max must be broken up somethin' fierce," said Al sadly.

"*Mais oui*, he left to go be alone with his thoughts but never returned last night. Have you seen him?" Liz asked, pulling off a leaf that was stuck to Al's fur.

"No, I haven't seen him, love. I were lookin' for ye at Isabella's and then wandered down here. Oh, that reminds me," said Al, jumping up and back into the tree.

Liz and the giraffes watched Al climb into the branches, shaking things up as he looked around for something. Chipo then asked Liz, "So you're the two cats who traveled with Max? We've heard about how brave he was, and how he saved many animals. We traveled by land and didn't need to ride a whale, but I would very much like to meet this hero."

"We must find him first," Liz answered.

Al popped out from the tree branches, grinning. He had the seed sack and the reed in his mouth. He jumped down the branches to Liz. "I almost forgot, lass. I got yer seeds back. And Max's reed," he said, now sad as he grew concerned for Max.

"Oh, Albert, *merci*. Let's make our way back to the stall and see if perhaps Max has returned. We can drop off his reed and my

273

seeds, and then continue our search for him," Liz suggested. "Chipo, Upendo, it was a pleasure meeting you, *mes amis*. We will see you soon. *Au revoir*."

With that, Liz and Al made their way down the corridor looking everywhere for Max.

"Mother, do you want this stack of bowls?" Japheth asked Adah as they packed up another load from their house.

"Well, my kitchen is getting tight on board, but we better bring all we can fit onto the ark. Yes, Japheth. Bring the bowls," Adah answered as she folded a pile of clothes she had brought in from drying outside. They smelled like sunshine. Adah wondered how long it would be before she could dry their clothes outside in the sun again.

Noah's family had been packing up their house all morning. It was a sad day for them. They knew that tomorrow they would board the ark to live for an indefinite period of time. They would spend their last night here in this house as a final farewell to the place that had been home to them for more than a century. All the happy memories made in this house were invisibly imprinted on the walls, but the family could see them with their hearts.

"Father, looks like a few late arrivals coming down the road," Noah heard Ham shout. "These could be the last of the animals!"

Noah put down his small reed brush that he used to paint on the clay tablet. He had kept a daily journal of animal arrivals, carefully marking their species and origins. Adam's journal inspired Noah to have a record of the extraordinary events with the ark and the animals. But now his writing would have to wait. There were a few last animals to care for. "I'm coming, Ham," Noah said as he got up from the table.

Together they went to greet a group of giant panda bears, Siberian tigers, and white ducks. Behind this group were two rein-

274

deer and two walruses, struggling to make it down the dusty road. The weary animals from China and Greenland were relieved to reach their destination.

"Get the cart, Ham. Looks like we have some more cold-weather friends needing assistance," Noah instructed.

The last of the animals had arrived, and not a day too soon.

CHAPTER 45

Max's Hero

s the wolves made their way down to where Max lay bleeding and breathless, he slowly backed up to the edge of the cliff. His instinct for survival made his mind race, surpassing the speed of his pounding heart. The thunder continued laughing at Max, confirming his hopeless thoughts that he was doomed. One of the wolves landed with a grunt next to the small, terrified dog, a low chuckle coming from his throat. The other two wolves joined him in short order, all moving in close. Instinctively, Max suddenly rolled over the edge of the cliff and fell downward, his back arched with nothing under him but air. The wolves watched from up above as their prey was lost to the black night, out of their reach.

Max's breath was knocked out of him as he hit the water. After falling for what seemed an eternity, he plunged deep into the raging river before struggling to reach the surface for air. The water was wild and cold, carrying Max along with the rushing current.

His momentary relief of escaping the wolves was short lived as the water pulled him down again and again. He panicked, struggling to keep his head above water. The pain in his leg intensified when cramps overtook his exhausted muscles. It was no use. He could not swim against this raging river. It would be easier to give up than fight. Max allowed himself to slip into the depths. Still, he desperately held his breath. His mind started to get fuzzy. He blacked out, lost to the darkness that engulfed him.

Something was bumping him. With every bump came fresh pain, bringing him back to consciousness. Max felt his body being pushed against the current, not flowing with it. Something was keeping him from floating downstream. He was too delirious to fight against it, and submitted himself entirely to whatever had control of him. Maybe the wolves finally had won.

His head was above water, allowing him to breathe. Bump, bump, bump. Max cringed from the searing pain, but soon the bumps stopped. Max lay shivering on the bank of the river, out of the clutches of the raging water, but he didn't know how. He was now safe from drowning, but would he still meet his doom? He passed out without needing to know.

When Max came to, the sun was shining and warming his fur. His eyes were closed. He wondered if he had died. He wasn't in a hurry to find out.

He listened to the sound of birds, and he could still hear the river, but the sound was more of a gentle stream, not gushing whitewater. He was in a quiet place. He must be dead. The last place he remembered being was anything but quiet. It was chaos; it was danger; it was fear, but this place was peaceful. Max summoned all his courage, but would only open one eye to take a peek.

He saw nothing but white. Yes, he must be in heaven. His eyes were fuzzy and not wanting to focus. He opened the other eye. Everything was white. But then the whiteness moved. It was hair? White hair? Max blinked his eyes hard and tried lifting his head, but invisible hammers beat his head back to the ground. He opened his eyes again, slowly.

There in front of him was a white goat. A big, white, hairy, horned mountain goat. The goat stared back at Max with warm, gentle eyes but didn't say anything. The goat waited for Max to focus his eyes. Finally, the goat spoke.

"You've had a rough time, my little friend. But you're safe now." The goat spoke in a soft voice that Max greatly appreciated. His head was throbbing. "Don't be afraid. I'm taking care of you. You must have wandered quite a way from your home. I don't know how a small puppy as yourself could have gotten way out here on the edge of the Glen." The goat smiled at Max, and Max breathed a sigh of relief. "My name is Gillamon."

"M-m-me name is Max. I got lost last night. How? How did ye find me?" Max asked, his throat dry.

"I heard the wolves in the distance and knew trouble was brewing. I came down to the river to confirm my belief that it was overflowing its banks from the rain. As I stood in the shallows, I saw that you were unconscious as you floated along the current towards me. I reached out and bumped you out of the current with my horns and was able to push you to the riverbank and out of the water. You're quite fortunate, little one, for you could easily have died."

"I thought the wolves had me. I were runnin' an' they chased me for miles ta the edge of a cliff. It were there that I rolled over the edge ta escape the beasties an' landed in the river. Me leg were bleedin' an' the pain were so bad, I couldn't swim. Thank ye, Gillamon. Ye saved me life," Max said, feeling a sense of relief as he realized that he did not die.

"You are very welcome. Tell me, what made you run to begin with?"

Max closed his eyes. He didn't want to tell this gentle animal why he was running. He was too embarrassed, but he knew he owed Gillamon his life. If he could trust him with his life, he could trust him with the truth of his faults.

"I'm embarrassed ta tell ye. I'm . . . I'm . . . terrified of thunderstorms. This isn't the first time I've run away when the lightnin' started strikin' an' the thunder started boomin'. I ran away from home one night a few weeks ago durin' a storm like last night," Max stated. He then started to weep. "Me mum ran after me, tryin' ta find me."

"Don't be afraid to tell me. There is nothing to be ashamed about. Please, go on when you're ready," said Gillamon, his wise, deep voice filling Max with comfort.

Max slowly lifted his head and moved from lying on his side to lying on his stomach. He rested his head on his front paws. His lip trembled as he remembered what happened that first bad night.

"She . . . she came after me, knowin' how scared I were with thunder, an' lightnin' an' pourin' rain. She didn't want me ta be afraid. But I were afraid. I kept runnin' even when I heard her callin' me in the distance. I kin't explain wha' happens ta me when I first hear the thunder. It jest makes me want ta run away from it," Max explained, keeping his eyes focused on the ground.

"I understand. Storms can be very frightening, especially to one so young. What happened next?" Gillamon encouraged.

"I found a cave ta hide in, out of reach of the storm. I ran in there an' me heart were poundin' in me chest. I listened ta me mum, but little by little, her voice got softer until I couldn't hear her anymore. In the mornin' I went back ta the burrow, an' she weren't there," Max said, tears flowing freely from his eyes now.

"I never saw her again," Max said as he began to sob.

Gillamon sat and said nothing for a few moments, allowing Max to just grieve. He was afraid of storms, and his fear caused him not only to get lost in a storm, but also caused his mother to get lost as well. Something happened to her in the night. And Gillamon wondered if the wolves that chased Max tonight had encountered his mother.

This young puppy was carrying the weight of the world on his shoulders. Max was scared, grieving, and alone. Gillamon took his time before he spoke.

"Oh, young one, I'm so very sorry about your mother. But you must know that whatever happened to your mother is not your fault. Don't carry that burden, or you'll spend a lifetime in agony," Gillamon said, firmly but gently.

"But it *is* me fault. If I weren't so afraid, me mum wouldn't have had ta come find me!" Max protested, allowing the bottled-up feelings of guilt in his heart to come out.

"Protecting children is what parents do. And if that means laying their lives down to save their children, that's what they will do. That's how much parents love their children. It is of no consequence to them. They love with a fierce love that knows no boundaries. I suspect that your mother loved you so much that she would have chased you all the way to China to get you back," Gillamon said, smiling.

"She did, oh, she did love me! She told me so all the time. But that night she didn't find me. I hid, an' she never came back so . . . so somethin' must have happened ta her," Max said solemnly.

"You don't know what happened to your mother, but you need to trust her," Gillamon said, drawing a confused look from Max's face.

"Trust her? How?" asked Max.

"Trust that she knew what she was doing when she came after you. Trust that her love for you was worth more to her than whatever she had to go through out there to protect you. Trust that she would have done what she did whether you deserved to be rescued or not. Trust that whatever happened to her wasn't in vain," Gillamon instructed, trying to get Max to understand.

"That's hard for me ta understand. I kin't imagine that kind of love. I know she loved me, but she loved me enough ta die for me?" Max asked. He began to weep all over again.

Gillamon sat down next to Max, nuzzling him with warmth. "I know it's hard to take in a love like that, but that's how parents are, little one. If she had never come after you, she could not have lived with herself. Don't be afraid to let your emotions out. You've lost someone you loved. You need to grieve. Never stuff your feelings down in your heart. If you do, they will come back up to bite you one day when you least expect it," Gillamon said, giving Max much to consider.

"For now, know that you are safe. I assume that you have been living alone since you lost your mother. You can now come and live with me. I will take care of you and help you until you are strong enough to be on your own," Gillamon continued, looking at Max, whose broken heart ached with the relief of knowing he didn't have to be alone anymore.

"Well, okay. I will come with ye. Thank ye for rescuin' me an' for takin' me in. I were needin' rescuin'," Max said, sniffing and taking a deep breath. "An' Gillamon, where is China anyway?"

Gillamon chuckled and began to explain the first of many things to Max. The two stayed by the riverbank until Max had the strength to walk again; then Max went to live with the wise, old mountain goat who had saved him from the wolves and the river.

But perhaps, most importantly, Gillamon would save Max from himself—from the guilt and pain he carried inside. Gillamon taught him the way to live life—a life dependent upon the Maker. Max matured and overcame his guilt about his mother. And he grew strong and brave, daring any beast to make him afraid again. Max was soon fearless of any creature, but not of storms. Gillamon told Max there are some weaknesses that remain with everyone, but they, too, can serve a purpose for our good.

Gillamon was Max's *hero*. Never would there be anyone more worthy of that title in Max's mind. Never!

Max was sobbing, crying in his sleep. The floor felt like it was shaking. Was he crying that hard? Max had found a quiet place to hide and grieve. He fell asleep thinking about Gillamon, and the mercurial dream had come to him again. Now he woke to find himself crying as he realized anew how much he would miss his hero.

"Are you okay, Max?" came a voice in the darkened storage room.

Max started and looked around, asking, "Who said that?"

"It's me, Charlie. I was going by this supply room and I heard someone crying. I thought I'd check in to see if someone was hurt. Are you hurt, Max?" asked the snake with a calm voice and a look of concern on his face.

"Only me heart, Charlie. I got some bad news from home. Me dear friend died, an' I came in here ta be alone for a while," Max answered.

"Oh, I'm so sorry, Max. How did your friend die?" Charlie asked, coming over to sit with Max.

"He died of old age, I guess. He were an old mountain goat. He rescued me when I were a pup an' raised me. He taught me aboot life an' how ta do the right thing. Ye called me a hero, Charlie, but I'm not a hero. Not compared ta Gillamon, I'm not," Max said somberly. He was actually a little relieved to have some company. He had been alone for too long.

"He sounds like he was a remarkable friend. I wonder why he wasn't called to come to the ark. It seems to me that Gillamon would have been the perfect choice for a mountain goat," Charlie replied.

Max sat and thought a moment. It was true. Gillamon should have been chosen to come to the ark. If there ever were a creature deserving to be called by the Maker, it was Gillamon. "I think yer right, Charlie. Gillamon should have been able ta come. But I don't think he could have made the trip," said Max, remembering how hard their journey was.

"But can't the all-knowing One do anything He chooses? He could have healed Gillamon and given him the strength to make it. Well, what's done is done. I'm sorry for your loss, Max," said Charlie, trying to help Max feel better.

"Thanks, Charlie," Max said, smiling. Then he felt the vibration again. "Did ye feel that?" Another vibration. It wasn't Max's sobbing that made the floor shake. Something was happening.

"Yes, I did feel something. What do you think it is?" said Charlie, looking all around the storage room.

"I'm not sure, but I best get back ta Kate an' the others," Max said, getting up and heading toward the door. "An' Charlie, thanks for checkin' in on me. Thanks for listenin'."

"You're welcome, Max. I'm happy to listen anytime," said Charlie, smiling.

Max turned and headed down the corridor. He felt more vibrations, and he wasn't the only one. Animals all along the corridor were feeling it, too. They were restless and worried. Max began to run. Something was happening—something big.

283

CHAPTER 46

The Flood

M ax's short legs took him lightning fast down the corridor. He heard the animals shouting, nervous with the mysterious vibrations, asking what was happening. Pairs of animals held on to each other, looking around for an explanation for what they were feeling. Upendo was about to have a heart attack. "I feel like I'm going to fall! What's shaking me?" he asked Chipo. But the female giraffe had no answer for her frightened mate. Every animal on board was nervous.

Strangely enough, the humans were unaffected. Max ran past Ham and Japheth as they brought a final load of supplies into the storage area. "What's up with the animals? They seem on edge about something," remarked Ham. "Look at the little dog. Something's got him spooked."

"I don't know. Nothing is happening that I can see. We better let father and the others know," Japheth replied.

Max made it back to his stall and found Kate, Liz, and Al relieved to see him. Crinan and Bethoo flew in and landed on the railing, calling, "There ye are, laddie. We wondered if ye got lost."

"Oh, Max! I'm so happy yer back. Are ye okay?" Kate asked as she rushed over to greet Max.

"Aye, lass. I had a bit of a hard night, but I'll tell ye aboot it later. Somethin's happenin' now that we need ta figure out. Liz, wha' do ye think is causin' the vibrations?" Max asked, panting from running down the ark.

"I've been studying the animals all along the corridor, and each one seems affected by the vibrations. But objects in the ark itself are motionless, so these vibrations must be coming from deep inside the earth for us animals to feel them," Liz replied. "Did you notice the humans, Max? Are they aware of these vibrations?"

"I heard them talkin,' an' they're wonderin' why we animals are nervous. I don't think they feel it," Max answered.

"Hmmm," Liz said as she thought a minute. "There is a phenomenon called an earthquake that may be causing this. We are in a part of the world where these happen quite frequently."

"An earthquake? How bad does it get?" asked Al, feeling nervous but trying to be brave.

"Well, an earthquake can be very small or very big, depending on what is happening deep in the earth. We will have to wait and see if this is indeed the cause of the vibrations," Liz explained, trying to reassure Al and the others.

"But aren't we safe here on the ark?" asked Kate. She looked worried but tried to remain hopeful about the situation.

"It would not be logical for the Maker to call animals from around the world to come to the ark only to have them harmed by an earthquake. *Oui*, Kate, you must be right. We will be safe here," Liz said reassuringly, drawing the series of events to a logical conclusion. She hoped her logic would prove true.

"NOAH, IT IS TIME TO BOARD THE ARK. GET YOUR FAMILY INSIDE, QUICKLY."

Noah's body quaked with a sense of urgency as he heard God speak to him. He got up immediately from the table and called to his family.

"Adah, Mabir, Lillie, Nala! Girls, hurry, we must get to the ark," he shouted. "Nala, where is Shem?" he said, walking

285

into the room where the women packed their few remaining items.

"I haven't seen him in a while. He said he was going to the village for some rope. He said something about needing it for the door. What's happening?" Nala responded anxiously.

"God just told me that we must board the ark. Things are getting ready to unfold," said Noah, his hand on Adah's arm, urging her to get going. "Don't worry, you four get to the ark. We'll find Shem. Now go! Hurry!"

The women gathered up their woven baskets and ran to the ramp of the ark. Ham and Japheth met them coming the other direction. "Something is happening to the animals. They are all nervous and restless. Where is father?" Japheth asked the women.

"He's in the house. He said God told us to board the ark," Adah replied, concern on her face.

"Shem isn't here! He went to the village. Someone has to go get him!" Nala said as she gripped Japheth's arm. "Please, find him!"

"We will, Nala. Don't worry," Japheth said, looking Nala in the eye with confidence.

"You women get inside the ark. We'll be right behind you," Ham said, putting his hand on Mabir's shoulder. "And don't be afraid." Mabir touched his hand. Her eyes were full of fear.

Lillie put her arm around Nala's waist. "Come on, Nala, let's go. Shem will be here, you'll see." Nala sluggishly agreed, looking back over her shoulder as she walked with the women up the ramp, hoping to see Shem coming up the road toward the ark.

When Ham and Japheth reached the house, Noah met them outside, wrapping his clay tablet in a piece of cloth. "Father, the animals are all nervous—they know something is happening. Nala said it's time to board the ark, but Shem went to the village. We've got to go find him," Ham said urgently, worried for his brother.

Noah had prayed for wisdom to know what to do. God said to board the ark now. If they went to look for Shem, no telling what that could mean if they were not where they should be when God acted. But they couldn't leave him alone outside the ark.

"Ham, go get the stallion. Ride into the village at top speed and find Shem. You must not stay long. We have to board the ark quickly, so you must hurry back. We'll pray that Shem will be nearby so you can bring him back. Hurry! Go!" Noah instructed.

Ham ran as fast as he could back to the ark and down to the lower level to the horses. Giorgio and Pauline were shuffling their feet, nervously pawing at the floor and snorting. Ham entered the stall, and placed a guide rope around Giorgio's neck. He looked at the tall, strong stallion and pleaded, "Come on, boy. I need to ride you quickly into the village to get my brother. I need you to be swift. Our lives depend on it."

Giorgio looked at Pauline for a brief instant and then back at Ham. He stood still while Ham climbed up on the railing to get over onto the horse's back. Ham gently squeezed Giorgio's side with his feet. "Let's go, boy!"

287

When they reached the exit ramp, Ham leaned over and spoke in the horse's ear, "Okay, now run like the wind. HA!" Giorgio neighed and took off running down the ramp to the road, kicking up dust behind him. Noah and Japheth watched as Ham rode toward the village. "Oh, God, please help Ham find Shem in time," Noah silently prayed as he and Japheth made their way to the ark. Up above them, the fire cloud started swirling in the sky.

Avi was tired of this wedding party. It had gone on for three days now, and he just wanted to go home. This wedding was for his new wife's sister and followed on the tails of his own wedding. Avi was sick of the celebrating. He wanted to rest.

"Come on, Zena, let's go. I'm tired of all this. I just want to go to our home and be with you," Avi said, pulling on his new wife's arm. She would have none of it.

"No, I'm not ready to leave. My sister and I are new brides, and we have a lot to celebrate. Don't be such a bore," Zena replied, obviously caught up in the festivities.

Avi dropped his hand from her arm as she walked away toward her sister, who was laughing and talking a mile a minute. Avi breathed out a heavy sigh and decided to step outside for some air. He couldn't stand it in there anymore. He went out into the garden and sat on a low, stone wall. It was much quieter outside. He shut his eyes for a moment of solitude, but then he heard a horse galloping down the road, and a man shouting. Avi silently fumed, *Can't I just have a minute of peace?*

"I must see what is happening outside. I will go to the upper deck. If you wish, you may join me, *mes amis*," Liz said as she walked out of their stall. Al followed right on her heels. He didn't want to be apart from Liz at a time like this. Kate and Max decided to follow, so the four animals walked down the corridor to the upper ramp. Crinan and Bethoo flew along above them.

"Max! Help us! What is happening?" shouted the animals as Max strode by. They wanted the hero to offer some kind of explanation. They wanted to feel safe. Max didn't know what to say. He was just as nervous inside, but he didn't let it show.

"Just tell them to remain calm and stay in their stalls," Liz hoarsely whispered to Max.

"Aye. Uh, listen up, everyone. Jest r-r-remain calm. There's nothin' ta fear. Jest stay in yer stalls while we check on things," Max said with his loud, Scottish brogue. He repeated the instructions up and down the corridor, appearing brave and in charge. It helped the animals to know Max was on the case.

Liz led them to the upper deck and up to the row of windows so they could get a good look outside. The windows ran along the entire roofline of the ark, eighteen inches from the top. "Lass, why don't we jest look out the front door then?" Crinan asked as the animals jumped up on some crates to see out the windows.

288

"The main door of the ark only gives the view in one direction. I wish to view the entire perimeter of the ark," Liz explained, looking out the window.

"Aye, I understand. So wha' do ye see then?" Max asked, looking but not noticing anything out of the ordinary. All looked calm in the village below.

Liz didn't reply but kept gazing out the window. Finally, jumping up, she began to walk along a skinny railing on the window ledge. She was so petite that she could easily maneuver the narrow ledge on her dainty paws. She wanted a more complete view and this ledge went along the entire length of the ark. Al, Max, and Kate stayed behind because they couldn't fit on the narrow railing.

"We'll jest wait here, me love," Al called as Liz walked away. Crinan and Bethoo flapped their wings as they perched on the window ledge. The friends looked out the window and tried to find anything out of the ordinary that would explain the vibrations they felt. The group hoped Liz would find an explanation soon.

"Shem! Shem! Where are you? Answer me!" Ham shouted as he and Giorgio galloped down the main road in town.

One woman threw a bucket of dirty water out the window of her house, narrowly missing him. Some men were running down the street with an angry merchant screaming after them. Giorgio's ears went up and he snorted as stone jars crashed in a house nearby. A brawl was underway inside.

Ham's heart was racing. He didn't see a sign of Shem anywhere. Where was the rope merchant? Ham had to think. Where did Shem go to buy the rope for the ark? Suddenly he remembered and squeezed his heels into Giorgio's side. "Come on, boy! I know where he is." The horse obeyed and picked up his speed as he ran down the dusty road.

"That should be enough," Shem said as the merchant measured out the rope.

The merchant had dark circles under his eyes and deep lines in his face. He had spent much of his life on the sea, and his weathered face held the clues to a life lived hard. Being inland these past few years hadn't softened his skin or his demeanor. The merchant didn't say anything to Shem. He just grunted and took his knife out to cut the rope. He'd charge this son of the crazy ark builder double price. He just wanted him out of his shop and hoped he would never return.

Shem heard Ham calling him outside, "Shem! Hurry!"

Shem, startled, looked at the merchant and said, "Hang on, I'll be right back." He ran outside to see Ham riding the black stallion toward him.

"There you are. Shem, hurry! Climb up, we've got to get back to the ark," Ham shouted, giving Shem a hand to get up on the horse.

"But I'm just buying the rope we need," Shem said, pointing back at the merchant's shop.

"No time! God told father we have to enter the ark immediately. Things are getting ready to happen, Shem. The animals are restless. Hurry, just get on. We've got to go!" Ham said urgently.

Shem looked back at the merchant and then grabbed Ham's arm, pulling himself up onto the back of the horse as they took off down the street. Giorgio now understood the urgency. The Maker was getting ready to do something important. They had to be in the ark where it was safe. He picked up the pace and ran faster than he ever had back to the ark.

Avi's eyes were now open wide. The stone wall where he sat backed up to the rope merchant's shop. He heard every word that Ham said. He sat up, alarmed.

Nala and Mabir stood nervously at the door, holding Noah's arm. Noah's calm presence gave them strength. "Steady, girls. They'll be here. Have faith," Noah said firmly.

"There. Down the road. I see the dust from the horse," shouted Japheth from the upper window. He had climbed up high to get a better view.

Noah and the girls looked to see Ham and Shem riding toward them. They all sighed with relief. "Okay, now, get inside. Get up to the living quarters with Adah and Lillie. We'll join you shortly," Noah instructed. Nala and Mabir smiled and hurried inside.

Noah smiled as Ham led Giorgio up the ramp. "Shem, I'm glad you are safe. Hurry, let's get this horse into his stall and get inside. I feel we don't have a moment to lose."

Shem jumped off the back of the horse as the men entered the ark. Ham rode Giorgio down the corridor back to the lower level.

"I'm sorry, father. I didn't realize," Shem said, feeling bad that he had caused his family such alarm. "Father, I know God said to enter the ark, but what about the door? I wanted to buy some rope to complete a pulley system so we could pull the door closed. Ham was in such a hurry that I left the rope behind. How do we close the door?"

291

Noah put his hand on Shem's shoulder. "Never mind the rope. God will help us figure a way. The important thing is that you are here, safe inside."

As Noah and Shem shared a moment of gratitude, they felt a jolt that almost knocked them off their feet. The jolt was followed by the sound of wood creaking. They stood, trembling at what they saw. The ramp that led to the ground below was actually the door of the ark. Noah and Shem watched in amazement as the ramp door lifted from the ground and rose toward them by itself.

"God is shutting us in," Noah said, barely a whisper. Shem looked at Noah, grabbing his arm as he realized that the hand of God was moving the door. He couldn't speak.

The door creaked and groaned as it rose, dust flying off it and swirling in the air. Noah and Shem watched as their view of the outside world was cut off. The door came to the top and closed with a powerful thud. At that same exact moment, there was a deafening clap of thunder that shook the entire ark. The animals were all shouting, while the humans were shaken by the jolt.

Noah and Shem prepared to make their way to the upper deck, but a blinding light stopped them. The men shielded their eyes from the beam of light that moved all around the edges of the door.

"God is sealing the door shut. Nothing can enter now," said Noah, holding his hand in front of his eyes as he tried to gaze at the power of God's work.

After the light completely sealed the door, it suddenly vanished. Noah and Shem heard explosions in the distance, and the sound of something hitting the roof. "Hurry, let's get upstairs to the others," Noah urged. He and Shem ran down the corridor, breathless with what was happening.

292

Avi looked up to see the strange fire cloud that had hovered over the ark now spreading like a blanket across the sky above him. It expanded in all directions, growing at a menacing speed. The sky grew dark as the fire cloud grew toward the distant horizon. A chill ran up Avi's spine as the temperature dropped and the wind began to blow.

He knew he had to get inside. As Avi ran toward the house, a huge explosion of water erupted right in front of him. A geyser hurled water more than a hundred feet into the air. Avi fell backward from the force but quickly scrambled to his feet. He had to get to Zena. Another explosion came—this time right under the house itself. Walls exploded with jets of water tearing the stones apart as if they were made of straw, and at the same time the roof collapsed down on the people inside. Avi could hear them screaming. Water started pouring from the house. And Avi was swept away by the current.

Again he got up, trying to walk against the current, but the force was too strong. There was no way he could make it back to the house. Suddenly thunder clapped from the heavens and light-ning struck from the fire in the center of the cloud. The heavens opened up and a deluge of water fell from the sky. What was hap-pening?! Avi panicked as the water carried him further down the road. The village was in chaos. More explosions sounded, and gey-sers of water sprayed into the air.

Shem was right. This is God's judgment! I have to get to the ark! Avi's mind swirled as he tried to make sense of it all. He allowed the current to carry him down the road. It was flowing in the direction of the ark.

"AHHHHHHHHH! LIZ! COME QUICK!" Al shouted as he and the others viewed what was happening in the village below. The skies turned an ominous dark as the fire cloud spread quickly across the horizon. They saw the lightning repeatedly strike the ground, heard the thunder, and spotted explosions of water burst-ing throughout the village.

Liz came running up behind them. "Geysers. The vibrations we've been feeling are not from an earthquake but from geysers. They are exploding in all directions—not just in the village." Liz saw the look of fear and question on their faces. "Geysers come from springs of water deep beneath the surface that explode to expel huge amounts of water into the air."

A loud boom of thunder clapped and shook the ark. Max stood behind the others, trying to keep his composure. But his fear of storms was coming to the forefront. Panic was now at a breaking point inside him. He slowly moved back as Liz contin-ued talking.

"Rain is pouring from the sky. Underground springs are erupt-ing in the earth. It appears that the Maker is causing a flood," Liz said, staring out the window, unable to take her eyes off the scene unfolding in front of them. Crinan and Bethoo couldn't believe the expanse of the fire cloud and how angry it looked. Kate and

293

Al stood next to Liz and didn't realize that Max was moving farther behind them.

"But why a flood? Wha' does it mean?" asked Kate, trying to understand.

Suddenly it all made sense. The Maker had instructed Noah to build a boat miles from the sea. He had called pairs of animals from around the world to come to the ark. The gravity of what was happening hit Liz. She turned slowly to look at Al and Kate.

"Do you realize what this means? The Maker is going to destroy all life. He has saved Noah and his family . . . and us. Two of each kind of animal to preserve each species. The reason Noah built an ark was because it could float."

"Max, did ye hear that? Liz said it's goin' ta flood. Max? Max? Where are ye?" Kate said, turning around to look for Max. But he was gone. Max had bolted down the corridor. He was running from the thunderstorm, scared out of his wits.

294

Noah and his family stood on the upper level of the ark, gazing out the window at the scene below. They had built a platform on the upper deck to reach the windows where a roof hatch was located. The roof hatch led to a small observation deck outside.

As they stood inside, rain pounded the roof of the ark. The wind blew the rain in on them but they couldn't step away from the scene. They had never before seen a sight like this. Geysers were erupting, and the sky appeared to be melting with rain. It was terrifying and mesmerizing at the same time. They were witnessing the destruction of the earth.

Soon they heard screams coming from the panicked people in the village. Adah buried her face in Noah's chest. She couldn't bear hearing the people suffer. Noah just held her in his strong arms, saying, "Try not to listen. This will be hard to watch. Go to our living quarters, and take the girls with you."

Adah pulled back from Noah, nodding her head and wiping her eyes. The girls, likewise, couldn't bear to watch anymore. They stepped off the platform and headed for their rooms, covering their ears from the sounds that grew louder outside.

Some of the villagers were making their way up the road, fighting against the driving rain. A current of water was growing behind them. Noah, Ham, Japheth, and Shem watched as the people cried and fought against the storm to reach the ark.

Suddenly Shem saw him. Avi was running up the path, passing everyone in front of him. Shem's heart caught in his chest. He watched as Avi slipped and fell in the mud. Avi quickly got back up and made it to the base of the ark. From their vantage point forty-five feet high, they could not see straight down below them to the ground. Shem could no longer see Avi. Shem opened the roof hatch. He had to get outside and see his friend.

"Shem, stop!" Noah yelled as Shem opened the roof hatch and quickly stepped outside onto the observation deck.

Shem slammed the roof hatch behind him, yelling that he would be okay. The rain stung his skin like needles, and the wind blinded him. Shem held tight to the railing. He made his way to the edge and peered over at the ground below. His heart broke as he saw Avi banging on the door of the ark.

"SHEM! SHEM! YOU WERE RIGHT. I SHOULDN'T HAVE LAUGHED. PLEASE, LET ME IN! I BELIEVE NOW! I BELIEVE," Avi cried out as he banged on the door.

Shem closed his eyes as tears stung them worse than the rain. He couldn't save Avi. He had tried. Oh, how he had tried, but Avi would not believe him then. Now, it was too late. He couldn't bear to watch anymore and knew he needed to take cover inside. Soon Avi was joined by others banging on the door of the ark to get inside, pleading for help. Shem struggled to lift the roof hatch against the wind, but it was Japheth who lifted the hatch and helped his brother climb back inside.

Shem fell onto the wooden floor, dripping wet and holding his head, weeping for Avi. "He said he believes now! But it's too late. It's too late!" Shem got up and ran down the corridor away from the scene and away from the sounds of Avi and the other villagers clamoring to get inside.

"Let him go," Noah said as Japheth started to go after Shem.

The banging soon stopped and the voices were silenced as the people were swept away in the flood. Together the men watched the terrifying destruction of the village as it disappeared underwater. They felt sick with grief for the people, but they felt relief that they and their loved ones were safe and secure inside the ark.

Everything God had said would happen was taking place before their eyes. It had taken one hundred years, but it was happening. Exactly as God said it would.

CHAPTER 47

Max's Secret

Kate, Liz, Al, and the seagulls looked everywhere for Max. They didn't know where he could have gone, so they asked animals all along the way. No one had seen him. They decided to split up to cover more ground. Kate searched the upper deck with Crinan and Bethoo, while Liz took the middle and Al the lower deck. They found many nervous animals, but no Max.

Liz walked along the middle corridor, looking for Max while also studying the animals and their reaction to the flood. Some were hiding, some were huddling, some were eating, and a couple of them were actually sleeping.

Liz stopped to chat with Boomer the kangaroo, who was never at a loss for words. "I don't mean to knock them, but here we are in this rip-snorter of a storm, and those koalas are out like a light."

There resting comfortably on the eucalyptus trees that grew in their stall were the two koalas, sound asleep. "Fascinating, *mon ami!* I wonder if there is some substance in that plant to make them sleep."

"I don't know, but those two missed most of our trip here from down under. Sheila even carried them in her pouch for part of the way since they were asleep. It was a pretty spiffy way for them to travel!" Boomer continued, scratching his backside as he spoke with Liz, his loud voice echoing in the stall.

"*Merci*, Boomer. I shall see you later, no?" Liz said as she continued down the ark, knowing she needed to keep searching. She headed for the rain forest.

"Yeah, no worries. Ta-da," Boomer replied as Liz walked away. He turned to eat some grass, winking at Sheila, who was sitting down, obviously nervous from the storm. "Awe, chin up, love. This storm can't last forever. And I'm here to protect ya." Sheila smiled, glad that Boomer was there with her.

"Liz, there ye are. Now don't ye go disappearin' too. Kate and me can't find Max. She went with the gulls back to our stall, and I came to find ye, lass," said Al, jumping up to where Liz sat. She stopped in the corridor when she came upon the beaver stall.

Bogart had set up a workshop. There were piles of wood all over his stall. Bogart had met a beautiful female beaver, named Bev, on the way from Canada. She greeted Liz just as Liz jumped up on the railing for a better look. Al joined her on the rail.

"So where is Max the hero?" Bev asked, concerned.

"We aren't sure. He was with us when the storm began, and then all of a sudden he was gone," Liz replied, a wrinkle on her brow. She felt badly that her research distracted her from looking for Max. She needed to get back on track to find him.

Liz watched Bogart nervously select a chunk of wood, and with rapid speed, carve a figure with his front teeth as he stared at Al.

"What is he making?" Liz asked Bev.

"A little of everything. All this thundering noise outside the ark has got him worked up, eh?" Bev replied.

"I know what ye mean, lass. I'm jest about as terrified as a kitty can get," Al replied, holding his paws up over his ears.

Bogart nodded and handed the carved figure to Al. It was a figure of a fat cat, the spitting image of Al.

"What a handsome kitty," Al said with glee.

"*Mais oui*," Liz replied. "He is a busy beaver, no?"

Bev leaned in and whispered, "A little bit bipolar, too."

Just then the thunder crashed above them, causing the ark to vibrate again. The rain pelted the ark so loudly that the animals could only imagine what it was like outside. Suddenly they heard the wolves howl in response to the storm. Liz and Al looked at one another, fresh fear rising up in them. If the wolves were freely roaming the ark, and Max was missing, there could be trouble. It was well known that the wolves held a grudge against Max for leaving them behind on the shore of England. And from what Liz had observed, Max had some longstanding issue with wolves. Something had happened long ago that made Max dislike wolves, but he would not tell her what it was.

Liz wrinkled her brow, concerned. "The wolves could be out of their stall. This situation is growing serious. I think it would help if we enlisted more animals to help in our search for Max. Albert, let's find Rudy and Rosie to help."

299

"I know a pair of red howler monkeys who can swing quickly from the trees to look for him. I'll go see them and spread the word," Bev said. She turned and looked at Bogart, who was busy chewing another carved figure. "He won't even know I'm gone."

"*Merci*, Bev," Liz said. "I am grateful for your help."

"Okay, and don't worry about the wolves, eh? We'll find Max. He means a lot to the animals here," said Bev, smiling.

"*Merci, mon amie*," Liz said, smiling back as Bev turned to head in the other direction.

Liz and Al wandered down the ark, continuing their quest. The terrifying thunder clapped again. They hoped they would find Max soon.

The wolves panted heavily; the stench of their breath overtook the air with a foul odor. Restless, they jumped out of their stall when the thunderclaps seemed exceptionally close. They were looking for an outlet for their nervous energy and started walking down the corridor, their sensitive noses picking up the smell of fear radiating everywhere. That smell stimulated them and made them howl at the storm. The lightning flash could be seen through the windows above and lit up the corridor. They took off running, filled with the thrill of the hunt.

Shem's hands trembled as he lit the oil lamp in the storage room. He shivered from the cold that engulfed him. His clothes were wet, and he was soaked to the bone. But the coldness in his heart was far worse. His friend was drowning outside, and there was nothing he could do about it. Shem was drowning, too, in despair born by helplessness.

He knew he should be with his family right now. Nala was certainly frightened by all that was happening, and he should be there to comfort her. But Shem needed some time alone to grieve for Avi and to regain his composure. He couldn't comfort Nala, much less anyone else, in his emotional state. This storage room was a quiet place where he could wrestle with his emotions in private.

Shem pulled off his wet tunic and threw it on the floor, causing something to scuffle in the corner. He squinted as his eyes adjusted to the low light of the oil lamp. There panting in the corner was a little black dog. The tunic had landed on him, and he jumped away from it, clearly frightened.

"There, there. It's okay, little fella. I'm sorry I scared you. What are you doing in here?" Shem said as he went over to Max. He reached over to softly pet Max, who was shaking. "You, too? You're shivering like me. Come on, maybe we can warm each other."

Shem grabbed a blanket and placed it on the floor next to Max. He sat down, leaning his back on the wall, and patted the blanket. Max came over to sit next to Shem, his head down and ears pulled back, and his eyes full of fear. Shem gently patted Max's head, and Max slowly lay down, resting his head across Shem's knee. Shem put his arm over Max, his hand gently stroking the frightened dog.

The two sat there in silence for a long time. They listened to the rain outside pound and the wind roar. But here in this storage room there was an odd comfort with one another. This man and dog couldn't communicate all they were feeling, but they felt a mutual bond nonetheless. Perhaps the true source of the comfort came from the knowledge that they weren't alone.

"I lost my best friend today," Shem finally said, his lip trembling with emotion. "He was a good person. But he lost his way and wouldn't listen to me about God. I tried to help him, but I failed." Shem shook his head. "Listen to me, talking to a dog about this. I don't suppose you've ever lost your best friend, have you? How could you understand what I'm feeling?"

Max lifted his head and just looked at Shem, his soulful eyes trying to communicate that yes, he did indeed understand. He was feeling the same emotions right now about Gillamon. But on top of the grief, Max also felt fear. *Aye, I do know the grief ye feel. But do ye understand the fear I have from this storm? How could ye understand wha' I've been through?* Max thought to himself, wishing he could communicate with Shem.

Max lowered his head and gave a big sigh. Too bad humans couldn't communicate intelligently with animals. And humans didn't seem to be fearful of thunder and lightning. It was nice to have someone share in the grief, but he wished there was someone to share in his fear, also.

"Best friends can bring the worst pain when things go wrong between you. Sometimes I wonder if it was worth it, having friendships that went from joy to pain. Especially Avi. Oh, Avi," Shem continued to say aloud as he petted Max. "Maybe you could be my new best friend, little fella. I bet you'd never hurt me or reject me."

Max pondered all that Shem said. He never had a friend turn on him before, so he didn't really understand how Shem must feel.

301

He could only imagine how badly it would hurt. Max was glad to sit by and be a comfort to this sad human. And although Shem didn't understand that it was Max's first time to experience a thunderstorm without Gillamon, he eased the frightened dog just with his presence. Perhaps Max could be this man's best friend. And in turn, gain a new friend himself.

Shem and Max jumped when they heard the wolves howl. The sound grew closer. Max looked up at Shem, who rose to his feet saying, "Sounds like those wolves are out of their stalls. I better go check. I've been in here too long. Maybe we both better get back to our mates." Shem gathered his tunic and shook it out before slipping it back over his head. He squatted down by Max and patted his head. "But, do what you wish, little fella. If you feel safe in here right now, just stay." With that Shem left the storage room to go check on the wolves.

Max decided he should head back to Kate. He felt ashamed that he had left her alone during the flood. He shook his head, feeling like a coward. He left the storage room and headed down the corridor. He didn't trot. He slowly walked, wishing he had someone to talk to.

302

Max came to the wading pool on the south side of the waterfall. The waterfall had become the most popular spot on the ark. The pool had marsh grass with a warm tropical climate. But next door, on the north side of the waterfall, a winter wonderland had formed when the penguins and walruses moved in. It was complete with flat slabs of ice, frozen water slides, caves, and of course, snow. Normally the arctic animals were out having fun sliding on the ice or even having snowball fights. But everything was unusually still on the north and south sides of the waterfall at the moment. Max guessed that everyone was hiding from the storm.

Max had to regain his composure before he saw Kate and the others again. He plopped down next to the water and stared at its glassy surface. *Come on, laddie. Snap out of this.* Max thought to himself as he gazed into the still water.

The surface of the water was suddenly disturbed with movement. Max stood up, the fur on his back raised as he watched a ripple zigzagging in his direction. A low growl came in Max's throat. Not until the ripple came to the muddy bank did the cause of the rippled water become clear. It was Charlie the snake.

"Sorry to startle you, Max," Charlie said as Max backed up. "I don't think I told you that I'm a chameleon snake. I forget how I blend in with my surroundings, and sometimes I startle others."

Max let out a breath of relief. "Ye dun startled me, Charlie. I wondered wha' were makin' the water r-r-ripple then."

"Everyone is looking for you," said Charlie. "Where have you been?"

Max looked at the ground. "I've been hidin'."

"Hiding from what, Max?" Charlie asked. "The storm? Yes, this is the scariest one I've ever seen." The snake shivered as he considered the fierceness of the storm.

"Yer scared, too?" Max asked, looking up at Charlie. "I'm jest so ashamed. Everyone thinks I'm such a hero, an' there I were, hidin' in the storage room. Wha' kind of hero does that?" Max shook his head, standing up with this tail dropped behind.

"We all have fears, Max. I don't think there's an animal on board the ark who isn't scared right now. Even heroes have fears," Charlie replied, trying to lift Max's spirits.

"Gillamon were always with me when I got scared from storms. But me fear goes deeper than jest thunder an' lightnin'," Max explained. "Somethin' happened long ago when I were a puppy. It were the night Gillamon saved me."

"Go on, Max. Tell me what happened. It sounds like you need to talk," encouraged Charlie. Max sat back down and told Charlie all about how he ran from storms as a puppy, the night his mom disappeared, the night the wolves chased him, and how Gillamon saved him.

303

"It's kind of like me secret, Charlie. I've never told anyone this before. Gillamon were the only one who knew the truth. That's why I didn't want ta leave the Glen when the fire cloud came. I knew more storms would come, an' I wouldn't have Gillamon ta help me," Max said, feeling a release in his spirit from telling his secret.

"I see. I'm so sorry for what happened to you as a puppy, Max. It must be a hard burden to bear, knowing what happened to your mother. I don't blame you for not wanting to leave Gillamon and the Glen. Did he give you any advice as you left, on how to handle your fear?" asked Charlie, a look of concern in his eyes.

"Well, he told me ta turn ta the Maker for help. He also said that the Maker could use me fears for me good if I let Him," Max replied.

Charlie got a confused look on his face. "That's hard to do, I'm sure. The all-knowing One is the creator of everything, including this storm. He's causing the very thing that brings you fear, so I can understand how hard it must be to turn to Him at a time like this." The snake pulled himself further up onto the bank of the wading pool close to Max. "I don't understand what Gillamon said about Him using your fear for good. I must not be bright enough to understand, but I don't see how fear is ever a good thing," Charlie said, not really knowing how to encourage Max, but trying to just sympathize with his pain. "Why don't you come in the water, Max? It feels fine, and maybe it will soothe you."

"Aye, Gillamon said lots of things that were over me head an' take a lot of thinkin'. An' Charlie, along with the storms, there's another fear I have, as long as I'm tellin' ye me secret," Max said, wanting to confide in his new friend.

Charlie's head turned up, his brow wrinkled in question. "Oh? What's that, Max?"

"I kin't swim. I almost drowned the night the wolves chased me in the storm, an' I never learned ta swim. So water scares me ta death," Max said, relieved to get that off his chest. Somehow sharing his weakness to this new confidant helped lift the burden of carrying it silently.

"Oh, Max. But look how brave you were to overcome that fear. You figured out a way to cross the seas without swimming. And it was your idea that spread to help me and thousands of other animals to reach the ark," said Charlie excitedly, getting Max to lift his gaze as he listened.

"Maybe that's how me fears were used for good," Max observed. "Maybe that's wha' Gillamon meant."

"I think you're right, Max. I hope that makes you feel better. You see, you figured that out on your own. *You* figured it out. You're smarter than you think, my friend. So I'm sure you'll figure out a way to deal with the fear of storms on your own, too," Charlie said, slipping back into the water. "And I'm sure you can overcome your fear of swimming, too. Maybe I could teach you if you join me in the pool, but later. Now what do you say you get back to Kate and the others so they won't worry anymore about you?"

"Okay, Charlie, I will. An' ye won't tell anyone me secret, will ye?" Max said as he got up to leave the wading pool.

"Don't worry, my friend. Your secret is safe with me. But you might want to tell your friends. I think you'd find them accepting you just as you are," Charlie said, smiling at Max as he turned to walk down the corridor.

Max somehow felt a little better. He had two new friends who had helped him today—Shem and Charlie. Maybe he was smarter than he thought. The lightning lit up the sky overhead and the thunder crashed. Max ducked as he walked along the corridor. Then he raised his head. He'd find a way to overcome this fear of storms . . . and maybe even his fear of swimming. He had to. He couldn't run and hide every time this happened. Gillamon wasn't there anymore, and it was time he grew out of these fears. Yes, he would find a way to deal with his secret fear and be done with it once and for all.

CHAPTER 48

Forty Days and
Forty Nights

Shem, oh, love, are you okay?" Nala said as Shem joined everyone in the kitchen. She rushed over to give him a hug.

"Yes, yes, I'm alright. I'm sorry I bolted like that. I still can't believe what has happened. I sat in the storage room awhile to collect my thoughts and then had to put the wolves back in their stall," Shem replied, hugging Nala. "What smells so good?"

A warm fire burned brightly on the stonework stove where Adah cooked some vegetable stew. This atmosphere was totally opposite from that outside the ark. Inside there was safety, warmth, and the love and security of a close family. Outside there was cold, lonely destruction.

"You have a big heart, Shem. I know you tried to reach Avi," Adah said with a reassuring smile. "The stew will be ready shortly. Why don't you put on some dry things?" Adah added some spices to the pot and then tasted the stew with a wooden spoon.

"Thanks, mother," Shem said, smiling. He was grateful for his supportive family.

"You had to put the wolves back in their stalls?" Noah asked as he handed Shem a dry tunic.

"Yes, I was in the storage room when I heard them howling and moving up the corridor. I went to find them and they acted suspicious. They acted as if they wanted to attack something," Shem responded, taking off his still damp tunic and changing into the dry one.

"I don't trust those wolves," Ham added, chewing on a piece of flatbread.

Japheth nodded his head in agreement. "Yeah, they have an aggressive, mean nature about them."

"Well, many animals are aggressive," Noah said, "but they are just acting the way God made them. They operate on instinct. It's wise to be alert around the wolves, but don't think any less of them."

"Now that dog I really like, though. He was hiding in the storage room when I was in there. I think he was nervous about the storm," Shem added, picking up a piece of flatbread and sitting down next to Noah.

Noah smiled, "Yes, he is a friendly little animal. He always seems to be smiling. Just the opposite temperament of the wolves." Noah's face then turned solemn as the thunder again pounded and a fresh wave of rain poured down on the roof. It swept over them in sheets.

"How long do you think this rain will last, father?" asked Lillie, bringing a bowl of dates to the table.

Noah looked up at the ceiling. Being on the upper deck, the rain was loudest where they were. "Well, God told me that a flood would cover the entire earth, meaning the mountains will be underwater. I think we're in for a long period of rain for that to happen. So we just need to settle in for a while. Besides, we all

307

need to rest from what we've been through. And please everyone, be gentle with one another, as our emotions are heavy."

"Yes, and we need to help the animals as much as we can," said Adah, tapping the spoon on the side of the pot. "They are already nervous like the little dog. As long as this storm lasts they'll need our reassurance, so keep an eye out for those needing comfort."

"And keep an eye out for those wolves," said Ham.

"The laddie's back," Al exclaimed, seeing Max walking toward their stall.

"Thank goodness, Max. Where have ye been this time?" Kate asked, running up to greet her mate.

"I'm sorry, lass. I . . . I have somethin' ta tell ye—all of ye," Max said, clearing his throat.

"What is it, *mon ami*?" asked Liz as Max walked to the center of his friends gathered there. The seagulls and hummingbirds sat on the railing of the stall, waiting to hear what Max would say.

Max hung his head low before raising it back up, determination set on his face. "I have ta tell ye why I went missin' today. I know ye think I'm not afraid of anythin' but . . . I am."

Al gasped in disbelief. Liz raised an eyebrow. Crinan and Bethoo looked at one another in shock. Rudy and Rosie shrugged their tiny shoulders. And Kate smiled in understanding.

"I'm afraid of thunderstorms. The sound of the thunder has always made me r-r-run, ever since I were a pup," Max said. He wasn't ready to tell them the whole story, so he didn't go into the 'why' of his running. "So when the thunder started boomin' today, I jest r-r-ran. I hope ye aren't too disappointed in me."

"A logical explanation for your disappearance, *mon ami*. Thank you for sharing this information. But please, this is nothing to be ashamed of," Liz said encouragingly.

"Of course it isn't, me love!" Kate said, nudging Max. "I'm so proud of ye for tellin' us all. I'm jest relieved ta know wha' happened ta ye then."

"Aye, the lassie is right, mate. Takes a lot of courage ta admit yer fears," Crinan said, giving a solid nod of affirmation to Max.

"*Sí*, pride is useless, no? It keeps us from being, how do you say, 'real' with our *amigos*?" said Rudy, buzzing over to hover around Max's head, smiling.

"Ye can say that again! I'm not proud about anythin', bein' the big scaredy cat I am. Max, I'm kind o' glad to know ye aren't totally unafraid o' everythin'," said Al, coming over to give Max one of his big, smothering hugs. "Makes me feel a little closer with ye."

Max was surprised. The very thing he dreaded telling his friends actually made him feel relieved to tell. Kate and his friends here loved him. They weren't disappointed in him, but admired him for admitting his fear. Charlie had been right.

"Since Max is back, can we eat now? I'm starvin'," said Al, walking over to the berry bush.

"Now that we have Max back, we can focus on the events of the day, no? I estimate that in order for the ark to float, the length of time required for it to be lifted by water will be significant. I cannot be sure of the time, but I intend to keep track of daily rainfall to mark our stay aboard the ark."

Just then Racket the woodpecker flew into their stall. Racket started banging on the stall beam and everyone turned to see the crazy bird.

"Wha' in the name of Pete are ye doin'?" Max asked with a frumpy brow.

"Gotta work off my nerves with this storm. Just checking out your wood, eh?" explained Racket before giving the beam more rapid-fire bangs.

"Never mind him. He's a bloomin' woodpecker. He bangs his head on wood for the fun o' it," Al said to Max and the others. He then whispered, "Murray said he's a hoser."

"Wha's a hoser?" Kate asked, somewhat amused at the funny bird, and smiling with her usual peppy grin.

"It is a figure of speech Canadians use that means someone of lower status; it is not very complimentary," Liz said, frowning at Al.

"But Murray called him that, not me," Al protested, feeling bad about being caught name calling.

"Actually, the woodpecker is a fascinating creature, no? And there is a point to their head banging. They drill holes to make homes in trees, and they get food from within the bark. So they do what they were made to do, however strange it looks to us," Liz explained, studying Racket as he continued to bang away.

"Laddie, would ye please stop bangin' in our stall then? Don't ye have yer own stall?" Max asked the noisy bird.

"Sorry, eh? I just can't help myself. This ark is like paradise for a woodpecker. So much WOOD," Racket exclaimed, smiling.

Liz jumped up on a rock next to a beam where Racket had not yet banged. "I believe, Racket, that you could be of great assistance to us."

"How's that?" Racket asked.

"I need to keep a record of the number of days it rains, and the number of days we spend on the ark. Would you please use this beam to make a mark, *mon ami*?" Liz asked, patting the beam with her dainty paw.

Racket grinned. He was being asked to bang his head . . . for a purpose. "Be glad to, eh?" He proceeded to make the mark on the beam as the others watched.

"*Merci*, Racket. The first day of rain. Let's see how many marks Racket has to make before the rain ends," Liz said, giving all the animals pause to wonder.

The rain fell for two weeks. Racket daily banged his head against the wooden beam in Liz's stall to track the days of rainfall. As his noisy tick marks filled the beam, Liz tried to estimate when the ark would lift off the ground. Al got to where he could sleep through anything, including Racket. Some unusual spiders had made him a hammock out of their super strong webbing. Al tied it between two trees in their stall, and happily slept in peace.

Max coped as best he could with the continuing thunder, lightning, and rain. Most of the time he just hid next to the rock in their stall. A couple of times he took off running down the corridor, but that habit was getting easier to break. It helped knowing he didn't have to go hide in the storage room. He could hide from the storm right here with his loved ones, and that was the biggest help. Still, he was tired of all this. Every one of the animals were tired of the rain, also, and wondered if it would ever end.

One day during the third week of rain Al was walking back to his stall after visiting the rain forest to eat bananas with the monkeys. As he waddled down the corridor with his full belly, he fell flat on his face. A sudden movement knocked him off his feet and briefly shook everything aboard. The ark was moving.

Al looked at the moose, beavers, and black bears in front of the stall where he fell. "Did ye feel that?" Al said, apprehensive with the movement of the ark.

"Feels like the ark moved, eh?" said Bogart as he momentarily stopped chewing a piece of wood that he was carving.

"Whadda 'yat!" said Racket, flying in and knocking his head on the beam in the stall. "Did ya feel that?"

Al just looked at the woodpecker and wondered what would possess any creature to voluntarily bang his head into a solid beam of wood. He understood why he'd do it to help Liz track the days. But to just bang his head for no reason? *He must be daft*, Al thought to himself.

"Aye, but do ye feel anythin' in that banged up head o' yers after bangin' it," Al asked, staring at Racket, who moved over to another beam.

Murray laughed, "He even bangs my antlers 'cause they look like wood."

"Quiet, you two. Listen," Mel the bear said as they all paused and listened to the sound of the ark creaking. "Something is moving the ark."

311

Al stood there motionless with the Canucks as they tried to figure out the movement. Was the ark breaking? Was something hitting it? "Me wife will know. I'm goin' to ask Liz," Al said as he run-waddled down the corridor to their stall.

Racket flew after Al, curious to learn what was causing the movement. "Hey, wait up!"

Al and Racket reached their stall to find Liz absolutely thrilled. "*C'est magnifique!*" she exclaimed excitedly to Max. "Do you realize what this means, *mon ami*? The ark is now floating! This means that the water has covered enough of the earth to lift the ark."

"So will the rain end soon?" asked Kate.

"Hmmm. I do not believe so, no. The humans said that God would send a flood to cover the entire earth, which would include the mountains. In order for the tall mountains to be submerged, it will take much more rain. We were at lower elevations before we began to float," Liz explained, her mind working furiously as she thought out loud.

"So ye mean ta tell me we'll be above the mountains then?" asked Max, amazed at what Liz said.

"*Oui, mon ami.* And we can expect movement in the ark as we rise with the increasing water levels. So brace yourselves," Liz warned, looking over and smiling at Al, who was clinging to the stall railing. "Albert, I do not mean to brace yourself so very hard, but just know that when you feel movement, it is simply the ark hitting things like tree lines and mountains. You can let go."

Al sheepishly grinned and let go of the railing.

On the fortieth day, it finally happened. The rain stopped. The animals were so used to the loud sound of the rain that when it stopped, everyone noticed.

Max looked around and listened. "Do ye hear-r-r that?! The r-r-rain isn't r-r-rainin' then!"

Kate nudged Max, "Ye've done so well, bein' brave with the storms, Max. Ye made it. It's over."

A "hurray" started in their stall and quickly traveled throughout the entire ark. The animals were thrilled! The rain stopped! The lightning stopped crashing and the thunder ceased booming. The storm was over.

"Now what?" asked Al, nibbling on some berries as he lounged in his hammock. He let out a big burp.

"Well, if the entire earth is flooded, it seems to me that we will be aboard the ark until the water goes back down. This will take time, no?" Liz said as she walked over to a new, unmarked beam. "I will have Racket keep track."

CHAPTER 49

Liz Hatches an Idea

Father, have you noticed all the sea creatures gathered around the ark? I've never seen the likes of these before," said Shem as he and Noah stood looking out the windows at the blue waters surrounding them. The sun had returned, and danced like diamonds on the water.

Noah breathed in deeply, closing his eyes and enjoying the salt air, the sound of the sea birds, and the warmth of the sunshine. He was so grateful the rain was over. His family had grown weary of listening to it—it cast such gloom over the ark. But the sun brought light to their eyes and hearts.

Noah opened his eyes. "Yes, look at them all. These creatures were never intended to board the ark but God is meeting their needs within reach of this safe haven. Their underwater world has changed, too. Perhaps His provision extends from the ark to the surrounding sea."

"Look! Those fish are jumping out of the water. Are they flying?" Ham asked, coming up behind them.

Noah and Shem smiled as they, too, saw the flying fish. "God's creation is staggering," Noah said. "I thought we had seen most of

God's creation here aboard the ark, but I never considered so much life to be around us in the seas."

The pelicans were squawking with the web-footed sea birds above deck, which was quickly becoming covered with feathers and bird droppings. "I kind of wish God would send some rain to wash off the deck," said Ham.

"NO!" Shem and Noah said together in response.

"Hey, I was just kidding," Ham replied with his hands up in defensive posture.

"Come on, we've got animals to take care of today. They are very restless and tired of being confined. I don't know what all we can do, but the larger animals need to do some walking to stretch their legs. While one of us walks the animals, the other can clean the stall. Let's head to the lower deck. See you later, father," Shem said as he and Ham turned to leave.

"Japheth can clean—I'll help you walk," laughed Ham as they went down the ramp.

Noah stood looking out over the sea, wondering how long this was going to last. Forty days of rain had been a long test. But what if it were only the beginning? The water levels were still rising, as they observed the mountaintops shrink each day. Noah kept his journal up to date with daily entries so he could keep track of the days aboard the ark. He knew it would be important to tell the generations to come about this incredible miracle.

Max covered his ears as Racket banged away at the marking beam. Liz watched Racket work, grateful for his help. *If only all the creatures had something to do, like Racket. They are growing so very bored being locked up in their stalls. I wish I could come up with something to occupy them,* Liz thought to herself.

"Aye, I've got ta get out of her-r-re away fr-r-rom all this r-r-racket. I'm goin' ta str-r-retch me legs," Max said as he trotted out of the stall.

Liz smiled as she watched Max walk down the corridor. She sat and thought a while, tuning out Racket's racket. Suddenly, an idea came to her. It could be a solution to the boredom. And she couldn't wait to see if it would work.

"Adah, real eggs. How did you . . . ?" Lillie said excitedly as Adah grinned back with a wink, breaking another egg over a bowl.

"Your sweet husband has been collecting eggs from the hen each day, and keeping them cold in one of the cooler stalls. He brought me a basketful this morning as a surprise. We'll enjoy them for breakfast," Adah explained, reaching for the coarse salt.

"Oh, how delicious. What a wonderful man I have. Eggs," Lillie exclaimed, clasping her hands in eager anticipation of their breakfast. "Everyone is going to be happy about this."

"Go round up the family. We'll be ready to eat soon. Oh, and tell one of the men to get me a few bananas, please," Adah instructed. Lillie took off to go find the others. *Eggs,* she exclaimed to herself again as she hurried down the corridor.

316

Japheth walked along the corridor with the bull and cow behind him, still marveling at how the stalls had transformed aboard the ark. It never got old seeing the animals in their natural habitats.

Don Pedro was relieved to go for a walk and stretch his legs—especially to get out of the stall away from Henriette. She wasn't bossing him as much lately since the bull didn't need her coaching while locked up in the stall, but her constant chatter got annoying. Isabella walked slowly behind him, also enjoying the walk but mostly enjoying grazing the vines and flowers of the stalls she passed.

"Isabella, I wish I could take off running down this corridor. My legs are crying out to go for a run," Don Pedro snorted.

Isabella, not concerned about manners, spoke with her mouth full as she replied to her anxious mate, "*Sí,* I know you want to, but be thankful for the walk. Besides, if Henriette catches you trying to run, she'll have to start coaching you again."

"*Sí!* You're right. I'd rather have no running—and no Henriette. *Sí*, I'll try to be content like you," Don Pedro replied.

Liz walked up behind Don Pedro and Isabella, jumped up on a railing and then over on top of Isabella. "*Bonjour, mes amis.* How are you today?"

"*Buenos dias, señora.* We're enjoying getting out of our stall to walk. I'm glad the humans figured out we needed to move about," replied the bull.

"But Don Pedro wants to run—I warned him that Henriette would be on his case again if he tried," Isabella explained, still chewing.

"Ah *oui*, this is true," Liz said with a chuckle. "How is Henriette spending her time these days?"

"She and Maria the raven have become great friends, and they spend a lot of time together. Jacques accuses her of befriending the enemy since he's still at war with Ricco. But Henriette ignores his complaints," Don Pedro said with a snort.

Isabella flicked her tail to get the two flies away from her. "But like all of us she has *mucho* time on her hands. She lays a daily egg. The humans keep taking them, which is good. Otherwise, we'd have a huge mess in our stall with all those eggs piling up."

"*Oui*, exercise is important, no?" Liz said as she jumped off Isabella's back. "Enjoy the walk. I'm off to find Rudy and Rosie."

Liz went trotting happily down the corridor, passing Japheth and meowing a "*bonjour*" to him as she walked by.

Japheth smiled at the petite kitty who seemed to have command of the ark. She was able to go anywhere she wanted, unlike most of the other animals aboard. Just then he heard Lillie calling him, "Japheth, those wonderful eggs you gathered are ready for breakfast."

"Be right there, Lillie," Japheth replied. Then patting Don Pedro on the snout, he said, "Gotta go back in your stall, big guy. Breakfast is ready—eggs!"

317

Don Pedro snorted in protest as Japheth led him and Isabella back to their stall. Even now Henriette was able to disrupt his life. Her eggs were cutting short his walk.

The mist from the waterfall continually hung in the air as the water cascaded into the pond. It was cool and refreshing. Rudy and Rosie buzzed around the flowers that surrounded this tropical paradise, enjoying the sweet nectar as well as the company of new friends they had made on the ark. They were especially fond of their flamingo bird friends, Normando and Lea. They were so full of life and energy, while Toby and Tippin, the toucans, were never at a loss for words. Felix and Carmen, the macaws, kept the place alive with their loud mouths and colorful presence.

"*Bonjour,*" Liz called to the hummingbirds as she sat on the railing of the stall, closing her eyes to let the mist gently fall on her face. *C'est magnifique, this waterfall,* she thought to herself.

"*Hola, señora,*" Rudy said as he and Rosie buzzed over to land on a branch nearby. "What brings you to the rain forest today?"

Liz opened her eyes and smiled, studying the creatures filling this habitat. The birds, frogs, and reptiles were thriving in this environment. "I have been working on a plan to help with the boredom of the ark's inhabitants. I wish to talk with some of your friends, but I need your help to enlist them," Liz said, smiling at the tiny, colorful birds.

"Oh, what is the plan?" Rosie asked enthusiastically. "You always have the best ideas, *señora.*"

"Boredom is becoming a problem for the animals. Since we do not know how long we will be aboard the ark, we must take measures to keep ourselves physically active," Liz explained.

Rudy and Rosie looked at each other and shrugged their tiny shoulders. "What exactly do you have in mind?" Rudy asked.

"I understand that the flamingos from Trinidad are quite athletic, so they would be perfect to lead daily exercise, no?"

Liz replied, snapping out her paw to wipe away the mist on her face.

"That sounds *muy bueno*. And you mentioned us helping?" Rosie asked.

"*Oui*, I would like you and your feathered friends to help me spread the word about what we are going to do—an exercise schedule, if you will. There has to be order and a schedule for this to work. Would your bird friends be willing to help communicate with the animals? Crinan and Bethoo will help, too, of course," Liz said, eyeing the birds up in the trees surrounding the waterfall.

"*Sí!* Of course we will help. After all, birds of a feather do flock together, no?" Rosie replied, already excited about Liz's idea.

For the next hour Liz met with Normando and Lea to discuss daily exercise options for the animals. The flamingos were ecstatic and couldn't wait to get started. They determined that exercise would begin tomorrow morning, and would take place at one-hundred-foot intervals along the corridor so the animals could view the flamingo instructors from their stalls. The daily thirty-minute routine would begin with a warm-up, followed by aerobics, and a cool-down with deep breathing and stretching.

Liz was excited as she returned to her stall. Al lay there snoring in the hammock, his large belly full of food, drool streaming down his chin, and a goofy grin on his face. *I know the creature who will benefit from exercise the most,* she chuckled to herself.

319

CHAPTER 50

Flamingorobics and Falling Objects

L iz awoke, stretched out long and nudged Al with her head, "Wake up, dear Albert. It is time for exercise, no?"

Al replied with his eyes closed, "I can't wait." He rolled over in his hammock and snored. Liz tried to rock him awake by nudging him again and again with her head. Nothing. Liz finally gave a huge push and Al fell out of his hammock. He shook his head, yawned, and scratched his backside. "Okay, me love. I'm awake then."

"*Bonjour!* Everyone up! It's time to join the flamingos for exercise," Liz called as she left the stall and wandered down the corridor. Her happy voice trailed down the stalls, encouraging the other animals to join in.

Normando and Lea stood in the corridor, warming up and stretching their legs. Tippin the toucan, Rudy, and Rosie sat on the railing next to them.

"*Bonjour, mes amis.* I have looked forward to your class this morning. The birds talked it up throughout the ark last night, so I hope we get many animals to participate," Liz said looking around at the stalls as the animals began to stir.

"Okay, Ah be ready," Lea said to Normando. "Let's shake our bamboo coat and get going! Tippin, go tell dem monkeys it's time. And yuh hummingbirds go get dem songbirds."

"Monkeys? Songbirds?" Liz asked.

"We need dem monkeys to give us a beat for our exercises. Dey will beat on wood beams and energize dis place along with dey hoopin' and hollerin'," Normando explained.

"And dem songbirds can make de prettiest tune to go with de beat. Yuh'll see nah!" said Lea as Rudy and Rosie flew off to get a group of nightingales, warblers, and buntings.

Tippin flew down the corridor, calling for Rufus and Jovita and their monkey friends to join the flamingos. Tippin appeared to be cross-eyed, but none of the other animals brought attention to her problem. Evidently, her small black eyes were so drawn to her large yellow beak that they became crossed and locked after time. It didn't slow Tippin down; but it did cause her confusion from time to time when she flew into objects or mistook one creature for another. It didn't take long for the monkeys to make their way down the corridor. Rufus let out a big "OOH-WA-OOH-WA-OOH-WA-OOH-WA-OOOOOH!" that roused animals throughout the stalls.

Lazo the llama was none too pleased at the monkey's loud call. "Ah said it before, and Ah'll say it again. Dey is de most obnoxious tings Ah ever did hear!"

Estelle the llama was quick to remind Lazo that the monkeys were helping with Liz's anti-boredom campaign. "Yuh should be grateful fuh dey help. Lighten up, llama. Enjoy yuhself nah." She gave Lazo a grin that made the grumpy llama smile.

Rufus, Jovita, and a group of chimpanzees and orangutans started banging on anything they found—wood beams, railings, water jars, the floor. The songbirds landed on the railing next to them, listening to the rhythm before piping in with an upbeat melody.

The steady, rhythmic music got Lea to bounce her head to the beat. She and Normando stood in the center of the corridor as she called to the animals, "Goooooooooooood mornin' to allyuh. It's time fuh Flamingorobics. Everyone get up and let's start stretching. Come on nah, stretch with us—yuh can do it."

Normando and Lea moved in perfect unison, slowly stretching their wings up in the air one by one. "If yuh have a wing, an arm, or a leg, stretch it high to de sky! Duke, yuh just stretch dat trunk nah," Normando said when he saw Duke the elephant looking confused as he tried to lift his leg.

Duke lifted high his trunk, stretching it to reach the ceiling beam in his stall. His wife followed right along. "Hey, this actually feels good," the large elephant exclaimed with a grin.

"Nah roll yuh head around to get dat neck loose," Lea continued. The monkeys were having a ball beating their "drums," and they rolled their heads right along with their instructors. The birds sang at the top of their lungs and energy buzzed throughout the corridor.

Liz walked along the stalls, watching to see which animals were joining in. Murray and Myra the moose, Mel and Ethel the bears, and Bogart and Bev the beavers all moved together in the front of their stall. Rodney and Hazel the skunks stayed behind them, moving but careful not to "fire."

"Okay, nah we going to take it down de road! Pick dem legs up—right, left, right, left—yuh can do it! Good! Dat's de way," encouraged Lea as she moved her legs up and down like squashing the slimy mud in the pond.

As Duke lifted his heavy legs up and down, the ark moved slightly under his shifting weight. Liz laughed to herself, meanwhile calculating how much movement the two elephants could make on the ark. She figured no harm would come and decided not to worry with it.

Iggi and Zula the zebras were into the rhythm, moving their striped bodies back and forth in time with the beat. Jafaru and Sasha the lions marched in place, while Jafaru swished his tail in tempo. He liked the beat.

Upendo the giraffe told Chipo, "I don't think my neck will stretch any farther."

Hippos, rhinos, tigers, penguins, antelopes, rats, ducks, ostriches, hyenas—creatures of all kinds were enjoying this movement. Even the bugs were getting into it. The lightning bugs flashed their tails on and off with the music. Liz looked up and her smile grew widest when she saw the least likely creature there exercising.

Al shook his belly back and forth and put his front paws into the air. Max and Kate stood by Al, moving and twirling as they followed the flamingos. "Oh, Albert, it's wonderful to see you enjoying the exercise," Liz said as she joined Al and the others.

"Aye, I'm a bit surprised meself, lass. All that eatin' I keep doin' is catchin' up with me. I could stand to lose a few pounds. But ye still are the littlest lass—ye could stand to *gain* a few pounds," Al said, leaning over to peck Liz on the cheek.

Liz smiled and said, "Perhaps I could eat a little more. But for now I will, as they say in Trinidad, 'shake my bamboo coat' with my noble, famous warrior." Al smiled and held her paw as they moved into an aerobic dance.

Normando called out the next move, "Okay nah reach fuh dat fire cloud by getting up on yuh toes—or whatever yuh got."

"Another gr-r-rand idea, lass. Look at the ark. All the beasties are havin' a wonderful time. Looks like those koalas are the only ones asleep then. An' the wolves aren't joinin' in, good thing," Max said as he and Kate looked to see the wolves sitting still in the back of the "class," watching.

"Aye, even Henriette is into this," Kate exclaimed, wagging her tail. The animal friends looked over to see Henriette with her wings out to her sides, kicking her tiny drumstick legs up and back, closing her eyes as she got into the rhythm. Jacques was even enjoying himself.

The seagulls landed next to the group and Crinan started laughing his head off when he saw the fat hen doing Flamingorobics. "Now that's not a sight ye want ta see very often."

Liz wrinkled her brow. "Come now, Crinan, perhaps Henriette will lose a few pounds and not be so grumpy, no? Besides, get used to it. Looks like Flamingorobics is here to stay." Liz laughed inside. Henriette was indeed a funny sight to behold.

Shem, Japheth, and Ham were pulling fifty-pound sacks of grain from the storage room and stacking them to the side of the ledge that overlooked the floors below when they got distracted watching the animals. They looked at each other in amazement.

"Do you think . . . ? No, the animals couldn't be doing all this moving together, could they?" Ham asked.

Shem laughed at the monkeys. "It does look like they're doing something together. As long as a few small creatures are the only ones out of their stalls, there's nothing to worry about."

"But it seems rather organized if you ask me," Japheth remarked, curious as he watched the flamingos. "All the animals are mimicking the pink flamingos."

Noah walked up behind them. "Nature has a way of knowing what it needs. These creatures have been cooped up and know they need to move. So that's what they're doing. And they're having a marvelous time. Let them enjoy," he said, smiling as he turned to walk back to draw on his tablets. "I think we could learn a thing or two from them."

The brothers turned and followed their father, not realizing that they had left the grain sacks a little too close to the edge.

The wolves left the class as Flamingorobics came to a close. The animals were cooling down with slow stretches and the monkeys stopped their banging, leaving only the birds chirping soothing tunes for the animals. Lea and Normando led the animals in deep breaths with eyes closed.

"Okay nah, dat's it. Good job, everyone. We'll see yuh all tomorrow," Lea exclaimed as the animals applauded with agreement. It was a great first day of exercise. Yes, Liz's idea was a tremendous success.

Energized, Max thought he would go see Shem to see how he was doing. He tried to check in on this human from time to time, giving him comfort and just being a friend. He picked up his reed and was passing the wading pool when he saw the ripple on the water and paused. Charlie appeared.

"Did you enjoy your workout?" he asked.

Max dropped the reed at his feet. "Aye, 'twas a good stretch, it were. An' did ye join in then?"

Charlie smirked, "Not a whole lot for me to lift and stretch. So, are you going to join me in the water today?"

"I'm on me way up ta see Shem," Max replied, still uncertain about getting in the water.

"Only for a minute. It will feel good after your workout. Come on, Max. The water feels fine," Charlie insisted.

Max hesitated. "Maybe later, Charlie. It's really a kind offer." He picked up his reed and turned to go.

Suddenly a grain sack on the ledge above shifted and was falling over the side right toward Max. Charlie looked up with alarm and shouted, "MAX! GET OUT OF THE WAY!" as he shoved Max clear of the falling sack.

Max quickly moved out of the way and was narrowly missed, but the sack landed squarely on the end of Charlie's tail, causing him to scream out in pain.

"CHAR-R-R-LIE! Ar-r-re ye alr-r-right?" Max yelled as he pushed against the sack. It was too heavy and wouldn't budge. The animals nearby looked in their direction and saw the snake squirming furiously to get free.

Max looked for a larger animal to help. "Someone get Duke. Or Don Pedr-r-ro. I need some help gettin' this sack off his tail."

Some of the animals ran to get help while Max continued pushing against the heavy sack.

"AHHHH! Max, help me! Ahhh, it hurts. Help me, Max!" Charlie cried in anguish.

Max, feeling helpless, spun around in circles and put his shoulder to the sack again. He looked up but there was no Duke or Don Pedro. Then he saw his reed. "If ye kin stop a log ta cr-r-ross the river, ye kin lift a 50-pound gr-r-rain sack."

He picked up the reed and put the end under the grain sack. Miraculously, the sack became light as a feather. Max was able to lift the sack off Charlie's tail without effort. Duke and Don Pedro rushed up, along with the other animals, and they stood in amazement of the reed. They looked at the reed and then at Max. A secret was out. Max had been given special powers through the reed.

Adah and her three daughters-in-law looked over the rail at the commotion below, and saw the animals gathered around the fallen grain sack.

"Now what would we do if any of these animals should get hurt, or worse, die on our watch?" Nala said.

"I agree. We can't have any more accidents like this. I'll have Noah enclose this part under the rail," Adah answered.

"Okay, citizens, go back to your lives," Duke said as the group of animals dispersed, making their way back to their stalls. "Nothing more to see here."

Max stayed behind with Charlie as the snake eased carefully back into the water. He made his way to the arctic side of the waterfall so he could put the end of his swollen tail in the cold, icy water.

"I kin't thank ye enough, for savin' me," said Max with a pained look on his face to see his friend hurt.

Charlie grimaced from the shooting pain, "Right place, right time."

"I'll ever be grateful ta ye, Charlie. Ye saved me life," Max insisted.

Charlie smiled but then turned serious. "I just hope I'm there the next time they try."

Max cocked his head to the side. "Next time? Wha' ar-r-re ye talkin' aboot, Charlie?"

"I can't be sure, but I think I saw movement right before that sack came flying over the ledge. I think that sack was given a shove," Charlie explained.

"But who would do such a thing?" Max said, gulping at the thought of being a deliberate target.

"Look around, Max. Who is always sneaking around? Who is always watching? And who is it you said you don't trust?" Charlie asked, looking Max right in the eye.

Max's spine stiffened. His thoughts didn't need to drift very far. The wolves had it in for him—that much he knew. Charlie's train of logic made sense. A feeling of dread came over him. If the wolves were trying to harm him, they might try to hurt him any way they could. Perhaps by harming that which was most precious to him.

"I've got ta find Kate, Charlie. I need ta make sure she's okay. Thanks for yer help, lad. I owe ye for savin' me life. I'll ever be grateful," Max said humbly but urgently. "I'll meet up with ye later."

Charlie smiled, "I understand, Max. Go! Make sure Kate's okay. And it was an honor to save your life. I know you'd do the same for me."

Max nodded, picked up his reed, and took off running back down the corridor, leaving Charlie behind.

CHAPTER 51

Explanations
and Diversions

KATE! KATE! Where are ye?!" Max called out as he reached their stall. No one was home. Max's heart dropped, and then a deep, seething anger welled up inside him. He bolted from the stall and started heading for the wolves when he saw Kate, Liz, and Al coming down the corridor, laughing and talking about the morning. Kate looked up to see Max and ran toward him.

"There ye are, me love. We've been lookin' for ye," Kate rambled on before stopping to look at Max, who stared at her with silent gratitude. "Wha' is it, Max? Why are ye starin' at me like that then?"

Max dropped his reed and gave Kate a huge embrace. "I'm so glad ta see ye, lass. I thought somethin' had happened ta ye."

Kate embraced Max and looked with confusion to Liz, who walked up beside them.

"*Mon ami*, what has you so upset?" Liz asked.

Max let go of Kate and took a deep breath. Kate was okay. He could focus on the urgent matter at hand. "Someone tr-r-ried ta kill me with a fallin' gr-r-rain sack, but Charlie pushed me out of the way. We think it were the wolves," Max rambled on a mile a minute, his Scottish brogue growing thicker with every word. "Kate, I jest had ta see that they didn't tr-r-ry ta hur-r-rt ye, too."

Kate squeezed Max in alarm and relief, "Someone tried ta kill ye? No. I kin't believe it. I'm so glad Charlie were there. Oh, Max, are ye okay then?"

Liz held up her paw, "Calm down, please. One thing at a time. Max, I'm glad you are okay. Everyone, let's go back to the stall. There is a logical explanation for these things. Let's sit and calmly look for it, no?" Liz led the way and Max picked up his reed as he, Kate, and Al followed Liz back to their stall.

"Ye mean them beasties were out to kill ye?" Al said, awash in fresh fear.

"Aye, aye, it's got ta be them," Max said. "There were lots of animals around who saw everythin' happen."

"Let's not jump to conclusions," said Liz. "Did any of the animals actually see the wolves push the sack?"

Max sat there, a frown on his face. "Well . . . no."

"Always look for the logical explanation. It appears that the sacks were placed too close to the ledge. It would not take much for one to just slip over the side, no? So we cannot just assume the wolves were out to get you, *mon ami*," Liz said, trying to bring some sense into things. "I know how you and the wolves feel about one another, but do not let your emotions get to your head."

Max frowned. He indeed did not like the wolves, nor they him. It was easy to place blame given the situation. Charlie made more emotional sense, but Liz made more intellectual sense. Max was confused. "Aye, but the animals there gathered around saw me

329

r-r-reed do somethin' amazin' when it lifted the grain sack. I were pushin' an' pushin' but couldn't get the sack off Charlie's tail. But I took me r-r-reed an' put it under the sack an' it lifted it as light as the mornin' mist."

Liz sat there silently, her tail twitching. Max's reed defied explanation. It held some power that caused illogical things—impossible things—to happen. This, of course, didn't sit well with Liz. "Well, I am sure that this event has rattled the animals who witnessed it. I will need to observe the ark creatures to see if tension about the wolves has spread. And if so, a diversion will be necessary."

"A diversion?" Kate asked.

"*Oui.* Another activity to get their minds off the wolves," Liz said as she walked out of the stall.

Kate and Al looked at one another and then followed Liz. They wanted to see what activity she was thinking about this time. Max had had enough for the morning. He decided to get some rest and stay put.

Liz and Kate sat on the tropical side of the beach near the waterfall. Liz closely observed the animals gathered there. She watched their behavior and listened to their conversations. She did this frequently, always fascinated to observe what made creatures tick. Liz would even try to anticipate how they would react to certain situations or conversations.

There was some buzz about the events of the morning. Everyone had, of course, enjoyed the Flamingorobics. But the news had spread about Max the hero and his near miss with the falling grain sack. Speculation ran rampant. Was it the wolves? Or were these humans not all that they seemed? Could there be one among them who would try to harm them as the mean villagers had done? Was there a human stowaway? Was it an accident? Liz felt a restlessness stirring among the animals.

Liz's train of thought was interrupted when she heard Al snoring loudly. She shook her head at Kate. "*Mon amie,* this cat is impossible to wake. He sleeps through everything."

Kate looked at Liz and giggled. "We should have a wee bit of fun with him."

As if on cue, the iguanas that were nestled in a vine on the other side of Al picked two trumpet flowers and hopped down from the vine. They each took a flower and carefully slid it into each of Al's nostrils. Al continued to sleep, mouth wide open, trumpet flowers hanging out of his nose, which now gave a new trumpeting sound to his snore. The animals gathered around started howling with laughter. Liz and Kate had to shout above the snores and the ruckus.

"This is exactly my point, Kate. The animals are restless and this diversion with Al seems to help. We must find something to keep occupying their minds," Liz said as she looked around at the pairs of animals gathered there. "What about a dance?"

"Wha' aboot a talent show?" Kate replied.

Kate and Liz paused only a second as they read each other's minds. "WHAT ABOUT BOTH?!" they shouted.

331

CHAPTER 52

Talent Night

Several days later Al was out for his morning banana run when he came by Peter and Pearl the polar bears' stall. Bogart beaver was nearby noisily building something across the corridor by the waterfall.

"Would it surprise ye to know that Bogart is yer cousin?" Al asked the bears.

"Da, this vould be a surprise!" Pearl replied, watching Bogart. "Vat makes you believe such a thing?" Peter asked, not so sure about Al's information.

"His wife told me. Said he is two parts bear, he is," Al explained.

Liz happened to be walking by and overheard their conversation. "Albert, dear, if I may correct you, Bev said Bogart was bipolar." She continued walking on.

Al shrugged his shoulders and scratched his head. Isn't that what he just said?

Down by the waterfall, Liz took a seat next to Kate on the other side of the rock where animals lined up. Behind the rock hung a web banner that the spiders had made:

> ## TALENT SHOW AND DANCE
> ## TOMORROW NIGHT. SIGN-UP HERE

A pair of frogs hopped away from the rock as Charlie slithered up.

"Good mornin' ta ye, Charlie," Kate said with a grin. She was so indebted to Charlie for saving Max's life. Her tail wagged as she greeted him.

"Good morning, lovely ladies," Charlie replied.

"Charles, your tail is better, *n'est ce pas?*" Liz asked.

Charlie whipped his tail back and forth. "I'd say I'm back to my usual self. If I may, I'd like to sign up for the talent show."

"And what is the talent of a snake?" Liz asked, curious.

"A secret. You'll see what I can do tomorrow night. I'll need volunteers, though, to make this work," Charlie replied.

"Would ye like ta pick from the audience tomorrow night or would ye want us ta help ye find someone?" Kate asked, eager to help this kind snake. She looked to the next animals in line and smiled at the guinea pigs. The guinea pigs stared back.

"I'll pick from the audience. I usually have better participation when it's spontaneous," Charlie explained as he bowed with courtesy before he slithered away.

Tippin the toucan served as the "human watcher" to ensure that the humans were in bed for the night. She flew to the lower deck, accidentally hitting a beam next to where Liz sat. The toucan shook her beak to clear her head, smiled at Liz, and gave the word, "All's clear, Liz!"

"*Merci*, Tippin," Liz replied as she daintily walked to the center of the waterfall area and jumped onto a boulder. The murmur of animals fell to a hush as Liz assumed "center stage." All the animals had come for this big event, including the wolves, who sat in the back of the crowd.

"*Mes amis*, I am pleased to welcome you to our first animal talent night and dance aboard the ark! We have a *bonne nuit* planned for you, so let the show begin," Liz said as she nodded to William the frog, who hopped up on the rock where she stood.

"It is my delight to introduce our first performer, William the frog, who will recite poetry. Juliette the frog, and James and Celeste the crickets will provide musical accompaniment. Enjoy!" Liz exclaimed as she lifted her petite paw in a gesture of welcome. The animals applauded as she walked over to join Al, Max, and Kate.

A hum of music like the sound of strings slowly grew from the corridor as William the Frog took center stage. The crickets rubbed their legs together in harmony to create a crescendo of delightful music. William bowed low and long before standing upright and clasping his hands over his heart in thoughtful repose. He lifted high his head in dramatic form and began to recite poetry:

334

> *Water, water everywhere,*
> *And all the boards did shrink;*
> *Water, water everywhere,*
> *Nor any drop to drink.*
>
> *The many men, so beautiful!*
> *And they all dead did lie:*
> *And a thousand thousand slimy things*
> *lived on: and so did I.*
>
> *Day after day, day after day,*
> *We stuck, nor breath nor motion;*
> *As idle as a painted ship*
> *Upon a painted ocean.*

Juliette started singing, echoing the lines of his poetry while William stood with head bowed. The crickets continued their musical accompaniment, smiling with delight as the sound of the creatures filled the air with perfect harmony.

Meanwhile, Adah lay in bed, unable to sleep. She nudged Noah, who was fast asleep. "Noah, do you hear that?" She nudged him again.

Noah begrudgingly opened his eyes, listened, and rolled over. "Frogs and crickets, Adah. It's just the sounds of night," Noah replied, yawning and falling back to sleep.

Adah sighed and put a blanket over her head to drown out the sound—"Frogs and crickets."

After a short musical interlude, William continued:

He prayeth well, who loveth well
Both man and bird and beast.
He prayeth best, who loveth best
All things both great and small;
For the dear God who loveth us,
He made and loveth all.

335

William bowed low again to indicate his performance was complete. The animals all began to cheer quietly as they didn't want to wake the humans.

"Bravo! Bravo!" said the big, white albatross seabirds. "What a lovely poem!"

"*Magnifique!*" Liz exclaimed, clapping her dainty paws together. "It was wonderful poetry, don't you agree, Albert?"

Al sat there with a wrinkled brow. "Uh, I don't know too much about fancy words and such. Sure, but I'm glad ye enjoyed it, me little lass."

"I do say, that was quite exhilarating to recite prose to the ark inhabitants. I hope all enjoyed the performance. Thank you ever so much, Liz," William said, bowing slightly in humble appreciation.

"But *merci* to *you*, William. Aptly chosen words, no? Pardon while I introduce our next performer," Liz said, jumping up again on the boulder to take center stage.

Liz looked to see Don Pedro and Duke setting up a long, low rail in front of the waterfall and nodded to Charlie. "I see we are ready for our next act. Brace yourselves, *mes amis!* We are not really sure what it is, but we do know he'll need volunteers. Ladies and gentlemen, Charles the snake."

Max perked up, along with Al. "Aye, now *this* will be much more interestin' than that poetry. Charlie will steal the show," Max hoarsely whispered.

Charlie slithered up as the crowd applauded. "Good evening. Bogart, Racket, if you two will take your place."

The beaver and woodpecker took stage left next to a pile of wood. Charlie slithered back and forth as he looked out over the audience. He smiled at the guinea pigs. "I'm going to need a little help with this, so when I call your name, if you'll please come up and stand behind the rail." Charlie called a flamingo, a zebra, a black bear, a red howler monkey, a toucan, and Peter the polar bear.

"Peter, I know being out of your arctic stall will be a little hot for you but it will not be for long." Charlie continued, calling a peacock and a baboon. He whispered something to the baboon, who nodded, as all the animals took their places behind the rail.

Charlie slithered up the far left post and nodded to Bogart and Racket, who began a hip-hop percussion arrangement. He then started a slithering dance across the rail.

As Charlie crawled in front of the flamingo, he instantly turned pink! The crowd erupted with gasps of astonishment. Next he slithered in front of the zebra and turned striped. He disappeared in front of the black bear as he turned black and then stopped halfway in front of the red howler monkey to become half black, half red.

It was like magic. The animals cheered with delight, and could not believe what they were seeing. Charlie then went in front of the toucan's bill and became multicolored. In front of Peter, he turned transparent white. Then the snake moved in front of the open feathers of the peacock and the crowd ooohed and aaahed. How could he top this? they wondered.

"Awesome! That's truly amazing stuff," shouted Boomer, the kangaroo. "Sheila, did you see that?" Sheila clapped her small hands with delight, amazed at what she saw.

The fainting goat fainted, he was so startled at the sudden change. His legs were stuck up straight in the air as his wife rolled her eyes but cheered on the snake.

Bogart and Racket picked up the beat, and the animals got into the rhythm. Now Charlie sat still on the railing while the baboon danced a move in front of him. Charlie turned blue. The baboon spun around and Charlie turned brown. Blue. Brown. Blue. Brown. The crowd started going wild, shouting and laughing.

Noah snored loudly, much to Adah's dismay. She stared at the ceiling. "The sounds of night . . . ,"she sighed, yanking the covers over her head.

Liz once again took center stage, with Ricco and Jacques joining her on the railing below. Other animals joined Bogart and Racket, who were still playing percussion. The raccoons, squirrels, and possums each held instruments fashioned from sticks, rocks, and spider webs. Liz motioned for the crowd to calm down so they could hear her.

"*Merci*, Charles. Now you are in for a real treat, *mes amis!* Grab your partner and get ready to, how you say, 'dosey-do'."

The audience laughed as Liz tried to abandon her French accent.

"Ladies and gentlemen, I present to you—Jacques and Ricco," Liz said as she jumped down from the boulder.

The animals applauded wildly while the two birds nodded and bowed, waiting for the noise to die down to complete silence. Then, the two birds looked at one another and cleared their throats. The animal band waited for their cue as Ricco started the dueling bird song a capella:

"Caw-ca caw caw caw caw caw caw ca."

"Cock-a-doodle doodle doodle do," Jacques replied.

"Caw-ca caw caw caw caw caw caw ca."

"Cock-a-doodle doodle doodle do."

Then the dueling birds really took off, with the animal band picking up the beat. The animals hit the floor with their partners. Everyone was having a marvelous time dancing.

Liz stood to the side with Kate, growing concerned that the humans would surely wake to this noise. But there was little she could do now. Al came rushing up to them.

"How about a dance?" Al asked.

"Just a moment, Albert dear. I wish to make sure everyone is having a good time. Kate, why don't you dance with Al?" Liz replied, gazing out at the animal pairs filling the corridor.

"Are ye sure ye don't want ta dance with yer beau?" Kate asked.

"You two go on. Have fun, *mon amie*." Liz encouraged.

Al and Kate headed to the floor. Max walked up to Liz, smiling at all the dancing animals and chuckling at the scene of Al shaking his booty. He noticed that even the wolves were tapping their paws at the back of the corridor.

"Ye've done a bonnie good job, lass. I tip me tam ta ye," Max said, grinning wide.

Liz sat there, suddenly serious with a frown on her face. Her tail slowly moved back and forth. She didn't respond.

"'Tis a success, Liz. No need ta fr-r-ret then," Max encouraged, curious as to Liz's demeanor.

"Max, look around. It *is* a success. Everyone is dancing with their partner. With one exception . . . ," Liz said, gazing at one creature in particular.

Max followed Liz's gaze. He hadn't noticed it before, but everyone had a partner.

Except Charlie.

CHAPTER 53

Trouble Afoot

Adah was in a foul mood. She swung an empty bucket as she yelled for her sons, "HAM! SHEM! JAPHETH!"

Shem poked his head out of the storage room, and Ham came up behind him. Japheth was just coming up the stairs.

"Yes, mother?" Shem asked as he and Ham made their way to the kitchen.

Adah pointed to the mess in the corner. "Who overturned the buckets? And before you answer, I'd like to remind you that 'not me' wasn't one of the animals brought on board."

The sons looked at each other but didn't answer. Noah continued drawing on his tablet, keeping quiet.

"Well?" Adah asked impatiently.

Nala stopped preparing the meal and tried to help the situation. "I did see a rabbit up here earlier."

"So you're telling me it was the rabbit? The rabbit kicked the bucket?" Adah asked, her hands on her hips.

No one dared answer.

"Sleep is such an underrated thing," Noah mumbled under his breath.

"But of course she'll see me now," said Raja Peacock, perturbed that Al was trying to keep him from seeing Liz who was still sleeping. "I have a marvelous idea that I know she will want to implement right away."

Al sat firm, his big body fluffed out to block Raja from entering their stall. "I've told ye already, ye blue-green menace, Liz is asleep and I'm not goin' to wake her. So ye'll jest have to come back later." Al didn't know how to whisper, so he ended up waking Liz anyway as he shouted.

"What is it, Albert?" Liz asked sleepily, yawning and arching her back in a stretch.

Al frowned. "Now look what ye done," he said to the peacock. Then turning to Liz, "Sorry lass, this bird wants to speak with ye."

"It's alright, Albert. I can speak to Raja," she said as she walked over to the stall gate. "*Bonjour*, Raja, how may I help you?"

Raja fluffed out his colorful wings and preened his crown feathers before clearing his throat. "A-hem, good day, Liz. I have a wonderful idea that I wish to share with you. But first, may I commend you on the brilliant idea for daily exercise and the fabulous success of talent night?"

"*Merci*, Raja. What is your idea?" Liz asked, trying to suppress a yawn so as not to be rude to her guest.

"Well, given my flair for fashion and my eye for decor, I thought I could offer a fun-filled 'tour of stalls' to ark guests where they could see how the other side lives," Raja said nonchalantly.

Liz thought a moment. The idea had merit. Give animals the opportunity to visit other habitats and learn how their arkmates live. Yes, it had tremendous educational value for teaching animals about creatures from all over the world. "Hmmm, Raja, I believe you have come up with a *bon* idea. How do you propose doing this?"

Raja glared at Al in triumph and said, "I say we hold the tour of stalls when the humans are asleep, just like talent night. Obviously, the animals will need to leave their stalls to roam the ark. I will lead the tours, of course, but I must limit it to two nights per week and can take no more than thirty guests on a tour at a time. So of course, this will be rather exclusive due to obvious limitations."

Liz wrinkled her brow. "Well, we will have to see how this will work. You see, Raja, activities should be for all the ark inhabitants to enjoy, no? I do not know how limiting participation will work. But I am willing to try. What do you say we begin tomorrow night? I will get the bird messengers to pass the word today. Oh, but how do you make a list of who will go on the tour?"

"Oh, but by invitation only. That way we can keep the numbers manageable. I will give you a list for the messenger birds to make the invitations. I'm sure everyone invited will want to come! Now I must be off to plan the great event," Raja turned and flared his feathers in a grand display as he walked down the corridor.

341

Al gave a low growl, "Sure, and that is the cockiest peacock I've ever seen. He is one snobby bird. And so selfish."

"Oh, Albert, I understand your feelings. Raja is quite the show-off, but his idea does have merit. We will see how it goes, no?" Liz said, rubbing her head on Al's cheek. "Smile. Don't let Raja upset your day."

One corner of Al's mouth slowly turned upward, then the other. He wiggled his whiskers and chuckled as Liz directed his thoughts to lunch and more positive things to think about. Food always worked miracles for Al's mood.

"And as you can see from the draped vines in these lush trees, this stall is perfectly adapted for monkeys who enjoy swinging, hanging upside down, and getting the most from their up-in-the-air view," Raja said to the group of animals on his premier tour of stalls.

The monkeys sat in the trees, gazing back at the animals that stared at them, and wondered what they were doing. "Check this, hey? Raja's got a bunch of friends down there looking at us," said Keb the chimpanzee to his wife, Okapi.

Okapi was hanging upside down by her tail, peeling a banana. "*Is it?* Looks to me they like our stall. That annoying peacock is talking about our place. Shame, makes me feel funny to be looked at in our stall by them outsiders, hey?"

Lazo the llama looked at Tumo the rhino and rolled his eyes. "How did we ever get stuck doing dis ting? Humph! Tour of stalls! Ah'd rather be sleeping in mah bed dan see dis!"

Tumo yawned, showing his wide mouth under his long horn. "You said it, friend. Who cares if we see monkeys in a tree? I saw them back home. We best tell the other men on the ark not to go on this tour if their wives ask them about it."

"Fuh true! Ah be telling every male Ah see to just stay in bed! Ah just can't believe dis peacock likes it—it was all his idea!" Lazo replied. He and Tumo shared a snicker before their wives looked back and said, "Shush!" The ladies were enjoying the tour immensely.

"And we're walking, we're walking . . . ," Raja called from up ahead as he led the animals down the corridor to the next stop. All the females followed Raja at the front of the line while Lazo and Tumo lagged behind, talking about the downside of this tour with the males.

"How much longer will dis tour last?" Lazo complained.

"I kind o' like it," Al said. The group of male animals gave a quick snap of a look to Al. "What? I get to eat lots o' new things at each stop. Sure, ye got to admit the food samples are grand."

"Always thinking with your stomach," Iggi the zebra said, shaking his head.

Liz looked behind to see if Al was enjoying himself. He waved and smiled, but she noticed the other males seemed a little perturbed. Liz smiled back at Al and turned her attention once again to Raja, who was explaining the eucalyptus branches where the koalas slept.

"And the wonderful aroma in this stall is provided by eucalyptus. If you ever want to cover that zoo-like smell, eucalyptus is the plant to use. Even a few leaves will make your stall smell fresh," Raja said, breathing in deeply and encouraging the others to smell the fragrance.

"What's this, hey? You like this tour?" Tumo asked Al, who munched on a mango.

"Sure, why not? Free food, and I like gettin' 'cultured,' by learnin' so much," Al said, burping loudly.

"To each his own, friend. To each his own," Tumo said as they continued down the corridor.

Isabella was grazing the overhanging vines and flowers as the group went along when they came to a stall that had lush, green grass. The grass was far greener and thicker than in her stall, and the sheep chewed it while grinning at her. She was put out. "Liz, do you see this? Why do these sheep get better grass than Don Pedro and me?! Our grass is no where near as nice as *this* grass."

"Perhaps the grass just looks greener on the other side, no? Remember that you and Don Pedro are large animals with big hooves. It is logical to assume you trample on your grass much harder than these sheep, making it appear less green. I am sure the Maker provided what is perfect for you," Liz said, her tail swishing slowly back and forth.

Isabella was suddenly not content. "No, I'm sure of it. This grass is greener. What did these sheep do to deserve such nice grass?"

The cow drooled as she gazed at the grass. The sheep looked at one another and then the male baaahed, "Whaaat are you lookin' aaat? Go get your own graaass."

Isabella turned up her nose and walked on by, not answering the sheep. Liz's brow wrinkled as she felt emotional rumblings beginning to emerge with the animals. Isabella wasn't the only

343

animal who was discontent. This feeling was beginning to spread throughout the ark.

Noah turned over blankets and moved chairs around, looking frantically for his journal tablet. "I know I left it right here, Adah. Are you sure you didn't put it somewhere?" He was getting frustrated now.

"No, I didn't touch it. You must have put it down somewhere in the ark and forgot about it," Adah said as she went behind Noah, straightening the mess he was making. She was getting even more frustrated. Yesterday, the overturned buckets. Today, a man in search of a missing item. She shook her head as she considered which problem was the lesser of two evils.

"I never take it out of our room just so this won't happen," Noah insisted as he kept taking things off shelves looking for his tablet.

Adah folded another blanket and put it away. "I hope you find it, Noah, because if you keep looking for it, I'll never get my work done."

"It's gone, gone, I say," Upendo the giraffe said, nearly in tears.

"Now hold on, Upendo, it's got to be in here somewhere. Are you sure you didn't put it way up in the mimosa tree? Maybe Jafaru's messin' with you," replied Chipo, looking around the stall. The wooden giraffe that Bogart had carved for him was missing.

"I'm positive!"

"Well, it's bound to show up, hey? And if not, I'm sure Bogart can whittle you a new one," Chipo said, trying to soothe her husband.

"I bet some jealous animal took it because they didn't get one yet. Humph," Upendo sulked as he tore off a mimosa branch. But there was no Jafaru. Nor Al. Nor his wooden giraffe. Just mimosa branches.

Chipo looked throughout their stall, but the wooden giraffe was nowhere to be found. Where in the world could it have gone? And why would anybody want to take it? Chipo decided she'd better tell Liz about this.

"I'm tellin' ye lass, me r-r-reed were r-r-right here jest yester-r-rday," Max growled. He was in a huff, unable to find his reed anywhere. His nose was sniffing all around the stall. "If I get me paws on whoever-r-r took me r-r-reed, they'll wish they never-r-r boar-r-rded this ar-r-rk."

"Calm down, *mon ami*. I'm sure there is a logical explanation. Perhaps an animal borrowed it for some purpose," Liz explained, trying to make sense of things. She had heard reports of missing items all over the ark this morning. Tippin told her she even overheard Noah complaining about a missing tablet. Now this, and right in her own stall.

"Well, if ther-r-re is a logical explanation, some beastie has a lot of explainin' ta do. I'm goin' ta look for-r-r it. Tell Kate I'll be back later," Max said as he stormed out of the stall.

Kate was down visiting Isabella this morning when she heard the cow was upset from last night's tour of stalls.

"Liz, I think ye better come have a look here," Al called from the corridor, a banana in his hand. He had just returned from the rain forest for his morning banana run.

A line had formed outside Liz's stall, and it was all Al could do to keep the irritated animals back. His fur fluffed out as he told the animals to just hang on. At the front of the line was something he couldn't believe. The koalas were actually awake, and they were clearly upset. Their cute faces were scrunched up in a frown and their hands were on their hips as they asked to see Liz.

"*Ooh-la-la*, but what is this?" Liz asked, looking at the line of disgruntled animals.

"Looks like more trouble, lass. What do ye want to do then?" Al asked, keeping his eye on the animals.

345

"Hmmm, well, I need to talk with them to get to the bottom of this, no? Send them in, Albert." Liz agreed to see the animals one at a time to give everyone a fair turn to express their grievances.

After hearing from the koalas, the rats, the monkeys, the turtles, the peacocks, the raccoons, and Tippin, who flew in to represent the giraffes, Liz sat in her stall thinking. Al left her alone as she sat there, her tail slapping the ground slowly and methodically. Al stayed over by the berry bush, keeping his mouth full and shut from talking. Kate came back in the stall, and Al called her over.

"Shhh. Liz is thinkin', lass. She had a bunch o' beasties in here complainin' about missin' things, feelin' insulted at bein' stared at, upset at bein' uninvited to the tour o' stalls, the men irritated at the women makin' them go on the tours, and such like that," Al explained.

"Oh dear, it sounds like a bloomin' mess. Isabella is upset, too," Kate replied.

"Aye, and Max can't find his reed. He stormed out o' here like I never seen him before. He said to tell ye he'd be back," Al said, reaching for another berry cluster.

"Al, how kin ye eat at a time like this?" Kate asked, then placed her paw on Al's back in understanding. After all, this was Al she was talking to.

Kate and Al stayed quiet for a time until finally, Liz spoke.

"It is clear to me that something is happening to upset the ark inhabitants—both human and animal alike," Liz said, her brow still wrinkled.

"But wha' could be causin' all this trouble?" Kate asked, knowing Liz could get to the bottom of things.

"The question isn't necessarily what—but *who*. I will need to go take a look for myself. So far, Max's reed is missing, the koalas' eucalyptus branch is gone, Upendo's wooden giraffe and several other of Bogart's figurines are nowhere to be found, and Noah's tablet is not in his room," Liz sighed. "Also, my seed sack is gone.

In addition to the missing items, there is jealousy brewing, and insensitivity to others' feelings is growing. Some animals are accusing the raccoons of stealing the missing items, saying they look suspicious, like they're wearing a mask to hide their motives. I'm going to investigate," Liz said as she left the stall. There was much to get to the bottom of here.

Kate and Al wondered if they should join her. "I think we jest let her go on her own for now. Ye kin look for her later, Al," Kate suggested.

"Aye, that's what I'll do," Al said, jumping up in his hammock. If he couldn't do anything now, he might as well take a nap. He curled up with a full belly and fell fast asleep.

347

CHAPTER 54

The Mysterious
Wind Returns

Max grumbled to himself as he walked up and down the corridors. The animals knew he was upset, which in turn upset them. It didn't set well to have the ark's hero out of sorts. They were used to a happy hero.

"Have ye seen me r-r-reed then?" Max asked Duke, who was doing additional stretching exercises, even though he participated in Flamingorobics earlier that morning. The elephant just loved stretching.

"Sorry, Max, haven't seen it. Where did you last have it?" Duke asked, now lifting his back leg up while holding on to the stall railing with his trunk.

"It were in me stall yesterday, an' I didn't take it anywhere," Max answered, plopping down on the floor. "Duke, it makes me mad but also sad. That r-r-reed means a lot ta me. It's like havin' a piece of the Glen with me."

Duke shifted to his other back leg and stretched it out. "That's perfectly understandable, Max. You should be upset to lose something so special."

"But I didn't lose it!" Max replied, frustrated.

"Is everything okay here? What's wrong, Max?" said Charlie as he slithered up next to him.

"No, Charlie. Things are not okay. Me r-r-reed's gone missin'," Max explained, resting his head on his paws.

"And it's important to him," Duke added, now reaching out his front leg, remembering to breathe correctly, as the flamingos instructed.

"That's terrible. Who do you think took it?" Charlie asked.

"Why do you assume someone took it?" Duke asked.

Charlie laughed, "Well obviously the reed doesn't walk about on all fours like its owner."

"Aye! I agree—someone had ta take it. How else could it be missin' then?" Max said, perking up. "Do ye have any ideas, Charlie?"

"Well, it would have to be someone who either wanted the reed for themselves, or someone who just wanted to make you upset," Charlie answered.

349

Duke snorted from his trunk. "I think you two may be jumping to conclusions. I'll let you two talk, though. I'm going to lie down and do my side stretches now, if you'll excuse me."

"Sure, lad. Enjoy yer stretchin' then. Charlie, want ta help me look?" Max asked as he began trotting down the corridor.

Charlie slithered alongside Max, trying to keep up with him. "I'll be glad to, but wait up. You are a dog on a mission. But that's good. Like I always say, you've got to look out for yourself first so you can stay ahead."

Max turned his head to look at Charlie with a wrinkled brow. "That's not wha' Gillamon told me. He always said ta put others first, an' yerself last. That way, yer spreadin' kindness an' then ye get happy yerself."

"But how can you possibly put others first if you're miserable to begin with? No, I think you need to take care of yourself and make sure you're happy first, then you'll be able to help others. If you're happy, then you can spread the joy," Charlie reasoned.

Max thought about what Charlie said. "Hmmm, I'll have ta think aboot this one. I see wha' yer sayin' but I'm not sure. I guess it's jest different from how Gillamon explained it ta me."

"Well, I know you'll come to the right conclusion, smart as you are," Charlie replied. "Now let's find that reed."

Al woke from his nap, refreshed. Kate snoozed in the corner. Max and Liz were still gone. "Guess I'll go look for me kitty lass then and get an afternoon snack," Al said as he stretched and went toward the rain forest. He had heard that farther down the ark grew cocoa beans. *So much ark still left to discover, and so much time to go and see it,* he murmured to himself. He was one happy cat. The ark was so big that he hadn't yet seen all there was to see. Or to eat.

Al hummed as he strolled along the corridor when he looked up to notice he was in new territory. The trees here looked thicker and darker. The birds were flitting from tree to tree, enjoying the bounty of food in the branches. *This must be the place,* Al thought. He didn't see anyone at home in this stall and wasn't exactly sure who lived here.

"Anybody home? Halloo?" Al asked, but didn't see any movement except for the birds up above. "Oh well, guess I'll jest help meself." Al jumped up on the stall railing and then climbed up the branches. He could smell the cocoa; the delicious aroma made his mouth water. He followed his nose until he came across a huge cluster of the beans.

"Ah, come to me, me little gems," Al said as he reached over to grab a mouthful. As he pulled the branch back he was met with a loud "ROAR!" that startled him so badly he fell backward, landing on a thick branch below.

Shaking, and with a mouth full of cocoa beans, Al stuttered "Ja-jafaru, is that ye?"

All he could see were two huge golden eyes staring at him, and all he heard was heavy, panting breath. Al got scared. He closed his eyes and stayed still, hoping he would be invisible to whatever beast he had just awakened. Al heard the leaves rustling and the sound of heavy breathing come nearer until he felt the hot breath blowing in his face.

He dared to open one eye. Then he quickly opened the other. He couldn't believe what he saw. There in front of him was an enormous, sleek black cat, staring at him.

"LIZ! What happened to ye!? Yer-yer-yer HUGE! I know I told ye to put on a pound or two but don't ye think this is over-doin' it a wee bit? And how did ye do it so fast?" Al clumsily said, spitting cocoa beans everywhere.

The big black cat cocked his head to the side and said, *"Maafkan saya? Nama saya Java."*

Al sat there, now totally confused. Not only had Liz gotten huge, she was talking gibberish. "What are ye sayin', lass? What have they done to ye?"

The big black cat shook his head and then began to chuckle. The chuckle grew and grew and grew until he was laughing so hard his sharp, pointy teeth were all Al could see. "No, no, no!" the big black cat finally said in a deep, mysterious accent. "I'm not Liz. I'm Java."

Al blinked once, then twice while turning his head to look the big black cat up and down. "Are ye sure then? Ye look like me lass, only bigger. Ye sure don't sound like her, though."

"Allow me to introduce myself. I'm a black panther from Malaysia. My name is Java, and this is my tree. *Apa khabar?*"

Al felt really silly now. Here he had mistaken a giant sized look-a-like for his petite wife. If Crinan heard about this, he'd never hear the end of it. "Aye, ha-ha-ha," Al laughed nervously, "I were jest kiddin'. Ha-ha, I knew ye weren't Liz. Ha-ha-ha." He didn't sound convincing. Java chuckled.

"*Apa khabar?* What does that mean?" Al asked, sitting up and staring at Java, amazed at his striking resemblance to Liz.

"It means 'how are you?' or 'what's new?' in Malay," replied Java, swishing his big tail like Liz, only powerfully whacking the branches with great force.

"Aye, well, I'm relieved now. Sure, and it's great to meet ye, Java. I'm Al. Hope ye don't mind I were helpin' meself to some o' yer cocoa beans. I heard they were really good," Al said, hoping the big cat wouldn't be angry.

"*Kembali*—ah, you're welcome. Help yourself, Al. I was just telling my wife—" Java started to say when they suddenly heard a loud roar coming from outside the ark.

"What's that?" Al exclaimed as he and Java looked up to the windows. They couldn't see anything.

"Sounds like the wind has returned. I heard the wind roar like that when the Maker called us to follow the fire cloud," Java said. He and Al looked at each other. "I wonder what it means."

"I don't know, lad, but I know how to find out. I'm goin' to find me own black beauty, Liz. No offense, but I sure am glad she didn't get big like ye. She's always tellin' me that French cats never get fat, so I were worried. I'll see ye later, Java," Al said as he jumped down the branches to head back to their stall.

"*Jumpa lagi,*" Java called. "See you later!"

Liz was already working on one mystery. Now the mysterious wind had returned. It certainly went along with the mood. Liz climbed to the top level so she could see what was happening. The wind was powerfully blowing whitecaps on the water, as if the water were being driven back. According to Racket's timeline of marks, they had been aboard the ark for one hundred fifty days with nothing new since the waters had covered the face of the earth. Could a change be coming?

"Quite the wind a blowin', it is. Have ye found anythin' yet, dear?" Bethoo said as she landed on the railing next to where Liz sat, gazing out to sea.

Liz kept her gaze at the water, and slapped her tail on the railing. "*Bonjour*, Bethoo. No, I have found nothing. Evidence points to the wolves . . . ," Liz said before pausing with a sigh. She wrinkled her brow. "But things aren't always what they seem, *mon amie*."

"Okay, just to make sure we're hearing you correctly, you said you heard a pair of animals running and panting down the corridor sometime before dawn?" Charlie asked Peter.

"*Da!* They vere running and panting and I vondered vhat they were doing up and out of their stall so early," Peter replied.

"Did you get a good look at them? Could you tell what kind of animals they were?" Charlie continued.

"No, I could not make them out. But I did hear them drop something right outside our stall," Peter said.

"Wha' were it, lad?" Max jumped in, sliding on the icy floor. "Wha' did they drop then?"

Peter put his big paw up to his chin as he thought for a moment. "I vasn't sure then, but I think it vas something vooden. *Da*, something vooden by the vay it sounded vhen it fell. It vas vood dropping on vood."

Charlie looked at Max. "Wood, Max. It could be your reed." He then turned to Peter. "Did you see the object that fell?"

"No, the animals picked it up and ran off vith it," Peter replied. "Is this helpful?"

"Yes, yes! Thank you, Peter. You've been most helpful. We've gained some clues that will lead us to the thieves," Charlie said, bowing in gratitude to the polar bear.

"Vat are friends for, *da?* I'm glad to help. I vill let you know if I see anything else," Peter said, slapping the snake on the back and sending him crashing to the floor.

Max grimaced, "Aye, uh, thanks then, Peter. We'll see ye." Max helped Charlie up and they left the icy stall.

Charlie shook his head. "That polar bear doesn't know his own strength, but at least he gave us important information. If we just

353

keep questioning the animals along the corridor, I'm sure we'll find other witnesses who saw something."

"Aye, but I think I already know who it is," Max said, a frown on his face.

"Who, Max?" Charlie asked.

"The only two beasties who I kin think of who'd want somethin' that didn't belong ta them an' who would want ta upset me— the wolves," Max replied, picking up his trotting pace.

Charlie caught up with Max. "I think you're right, Max. It has to be the wolves who took your reed. Who else could it be? I know you want these guilty ones caught. You want justice. And they deserve your vengeance, too. It's understandable how you must feel."

Max wrinkled his brow. "Gillamon always told me it's okay ta be mad, an' ta want justice but never ta seek revenge. Always be the bigger animal, not stoopin' ta the bad beastie's level."

"But Max, you've been wronged. You deserve payback," Charlie insisted.

"Aye, maybe yer r-r-right, Charlie," Max said with a growl. "An' I'm goin' ta see aboot that payment r-r-right now!"

As Max turned to go find the wolves, he saw Al running toward him, followed close behind by a hundred panicked animals.

"FIRE! FIRE!" Al screamed as he ran up to Max.

"Fir-r-re?" Max asked, putting his paw out to stop Al.

"FIRE! In the storage room. Head for the deck!" Al screamed, his eyes wild with fear. He took off running, screaming all down the corridor.

Max turned to look back to the storage area, and a low growl rumbled in his throat. "It's them again. Now they're tr-r-ryin' ta kill us all."

Max took off running in the opposite direction of the thundering herd of animals fleeing the fire. He headed right for it.

CHAPTER 55

Trials by Fire

Adah and her daughters-in-law were doing their best to help the animals move to the outer deck. The animals were shoving and pushing in a panic. The women threw some of the smaller animals on the backs of the large ones. Birds were squawking and flying every which way. Animals were screeching and clawing. Feathers and fur were flying. It was utter chaos.

Noah and his sons were racing about with buckets, running between the storage room and the waterfall, trying to extinguish the flames that licked the doorframe. Smoke billowed upward, filling the upper tier of the ark and causing the animals and humans to cough and making it difficult to see, as their eyes filled with smoky tears.

Liz anxiously sat on a railing nearby as Max reached her. "MAX! The humans can't get this fire under control."

"Wha' should we do, lass?!" Max shouted.

"Hurry! Get Duke and Fareeda and lead them to the waterfall to fill up their trunks and get here as fast as you can," Liz said as she jumped off the railing.

As Max ran to get the elephants, Liz ran to get Don Pedro. She jumped on the rail and unlatched his gate. "Don Pedro, come with me. You must push water barrels to the supply room. There's no time to lose!"

The humans were coughing and staggering in the thick smoke. Noah was especially having a hard time. It seemed their efforts were not making a dent in the fire. The flames mocked their feeble efforts. Suddenly a huge spray of water rushed past them. "The elephants!" Shem exclaimed as he saw the two beasts shooting water out of their trunks. Max was at their side. "Look, father! The little dog has brought the elephants."

Don Pedro pushed a water barrel from an adjacent stall and Duke and Fareeda refilled their trunks. "And look. The bull has the right idea. Get more barrels!" Ham shouted as the brothers ran to the other stalls nearby and lined up water barrels for the elephants.

Liz stood next to Max as they hoped beyond hope that their plan would work. After ten minutes, the fire was brought under control as the humans worked with the animals to douse the flames. Everyone was exhausted. Duke and Fareeda were huffing and puffing from their hard work. Don Pedro's hide was sweating from pushing so many barrels. And the humans were exhausted. Noah sat on the floor and Max came up to make sure he was okay. Noah rubbed the little dog on the head, thanking him.

"Father, better come in here," Shem called, wiping his brow with the backside of his arm.

Noah looked up and pushed himself off the floor. He joined his sons in the storage room. They were kicking through the charred rubble. Shem reached down, pulling out an overturned oil lamp.

"Father, here's the culprit," Shem said, handing it to Noah.

Max and Liz stood at the entrance of the storage room, watching.

Japheth tossed some boards and oil-soaked clothes from a pile. Shem reached down and this time pulled out a palm-sized chunk of wood. Max recognized it as the figure Bogart had carved for

Chipo the giraffe. Shem picked up another figure, this one a burnt likeness of Al. Carvings of the rhinos, panthers, penguins, all charred but still recognizable. Max looked at Liz, whose brow was furrowed in thought.

Noah struggled to free something from the backside of the extinguished bonfire. Strings were intertwined with the wooden planks on the pile. Noah finally pulled a charred cornhusk sack loose. It was Liz's seed sack. Liz's heart leaped.

Once the sack was dislodged, something else protruded from the rubble. Uncharred. Intact. It was Max's reed.

"I recognize this. This is the dog's stick. Strange," Shem said, rubbing his head. "The fire didn't burn this at all." Shem handed the stick to Max, who gently took it into his mouth.

Max looked at Liz, eyes full of questions yet full of relief.

Ham suddenly spotted something. He pulled out some pieces of clay and stood to inspect them. "Father?"

Noah looked up. He, too, recognized the broken pieces.

"My tablet. The one I have been looking for." Noah scanned it quickly, then looked into his son's eyes. "This was the journal of our voyage aboard the ark." He looked down at the now ruined clay fragments in his hands.

"If I thought it were possible, father, I'd say this was intentional. If they were capable, I'd say one of the animals did this," said Shem, throwing a branch of charred eucalyptus on the pile.

Out of the corner of his eye, Max spotted movement in the corridor. The wolves were running past. A low growl rumbled in Max's throat. As he ran out into the corridor, Liz lifted her paw to stop him.

"Where are you going, Max?" Liz asked.

"I'm goin' ta confr-r-ront them wolf beasties once an' for all. Charlie an' me were talkin' aboot them jest before the fir-r-re broke out. Mor-r-re evidence, lass. They did this, I jest know it," Max angrily replied.

357

Liz looked at Max's reed, still amazed at the powers it held. Then she looked her friend square in the eye with a seriousness Max had never before seen in his feline friend. "The evidence is inconclusive," Liz said sternly, her tail slowly curling up and down.

Max frowned, then added, "But wha' aboot them tryin' ta kill me then?! I still think them beasties must have pushed the grain sack over the railin'."

Liz looked at Max. "I'm sorry you were almost hurt, *mon ami*, but there is no evidence to suggest that the grain sack was pushed. Things are not always what they seem."

Max frowned even more. *Gillamon used ta say that*, he thought to himself. He put that thought out of his mind and continued his argument against the wolves. "Well, the polar bears heard some pantin' beasties outside their stall. They dropped a wooden object that sounded an awful lot like a *r-r-reed*. Wha' aboot that?" Max was trying hard to make the connection between the wolves and all the strange activity.

358

"How many animals do you know on this ark who pant when they walk? It could have been Jafaru and Sasha out for a stroll, dropping any number of things," Liz argued.

Max was not at all pleased. "I know wha' I know. Them wolf beasties are tr-r-rouble. Always have been. Always will be."

Liz placed her paw on Max's shoulder. "Have you asked the Maker about this, Max? What does He tell you in your heart about the truth?"

Max looked to the ground, then up to meet Liz's face. He knew he hadn't talked to the Maker in a while. He had been too caught up with his popularity aboard the ark, and looking at things his own way. All he could say was, "Nothin'. The Maker's told me nothin'."

"You have been a good friend, Maximillian. And as my friend, I worry about you. And your friendship with Charles."

Max was taken aback. "Wha' are ye sayin', lass? He saved me life, Liz. He's done nothin' agin' me. I know ye have yer questions aboot the snake but he's been a good friend. An' I know that ye been a good friend ta me, too."

"Please, Max. Be careful," Liz said, concern for her friend written all over her face.

"I got ta have some answers, Liz," Max said as he got up and wandered down the corridor. He felt confused and wanted to be alone.

Liz called after him. "Be on your guard, Maximillian. Be on your guard."

CHAPTER 56

Not Always What
They Seem

L iz sifted through the charred rubble in the supply room after the humans left to return Duke, Fareeda, and Don Pedro to their stalls. Thankfully, the fire had been contained quickly. Not much was destroyed—just a few bags of grain, some wooden tools, and a few old blankets.

The humans thought an overturned oil lamp started the fire. Liz wondered if perhaps it was their carelessness that started the fire. She had to rule out deliberate intention as the cause.

The overturned oil lamp was lying on the floor. Upon closer inspection, this, indeed, looked like the source of the fire. The fire had followed a stream of oil from the lamp over to the grain sacks. But it appeared that oil was also sprinkled all around the room. If the lamp had simply fallen over, the oil from the lamp would have burned up. But the excess oil spilled out everywhere suggested that this fire was deliberate.

Liz's heart caught in her chest. There on the ground near the lamp were Noah's broken and burned tablets. A charred, unreadable mess, Noah's work was destroyed. His record of specific animals making their way onto the ark, and the daily details of their time aboard—gone. Liz felt sick. Who would want to do this? Who would want to wipe out any record of what Noah had written? It was as if someone wanted to erase history.

And if the fire had succeeded and burned the ark, to change history itself. This would require further pondering. Liz picked up her seed sack and left the storage room.

Max's mind raced with confusion. He came to the beautiful waterfall. All was quiet here. Most of the animals had gone to the upper deck to escape the fire. Max stopped next to the wading pool and stared into the calm water. Something strange began to happen. A form started taking shape on the surface. Max blinked. It was the face of Gillamon reflected in the water.

"Gillamon! How I wish ye were with me," Max cried.

"In many ways, I am," the Gillamon figure replied.

"I'm not doin' too good, me fr-r-riend. I'm tryin' hard ta live up ta me name, but I'm not feelin' too br-r-rave right now. Me dreams keep comin' an' I don't know who ta tr-r-rust," Max said, shaking his head.

"For years I have told you of the Maker. For years I have given you instruction," Gillamon reminded him.

Max remembered how his friend had guided him. "But Gillamon, yer not here an' the fire cloud's not here. I'm strugglin' with a lot of things an' I desperately need someone ta tell me wha' ta do!"

Suddenly the water started to churn and ripples covered Gillamon's face. Max struggled to hear what he was saying. He could only make out one word:

"... reed ..."

"The reed? Wha' aboot the r-r-reed?" Max desperately replied, willing the image to remain.

361

But Gillamon's image was gone. In its place was Charlie, whose swimming had disturbed the water.

"Max, hello. Terrible about the fire, isn't it? I'm just glad no one was hurt," Charlie said as he came up on the bank.

Just then, Ham started yelling from above decks. "Father, Shem, hurry! Come see!"

"I wonder wha's happened now. I best go have a look," Max said.

"Why don't you take a dip, first? Get that smoke off your fur?" Charlie suggested.

"I could do with some fresh air. Ye know, me home always had the mist an' the clouds. I've always liked me skies overcast, but today I find meself needin' the sun," Max said as he turned from the pool and headed for the stairs.

When he got outside Max squinted from the light dancing on the water. It was a sight to behold. Animals of all kinds were up on the outer deck, and the humans were celebrating. The fire had been successfully contained, and something new was happening outside that had everyone excited. The horses, gazelles, and fainting goats were running around. Rabbits and kangaroos were jumping and stretching their legs. The birds were flying free, landing on the railing here and there. And the wind was powerfully blowing, whipping Max's fur out of his eyes. Max spotted the wolves sitting over on the far side of the deck, gazing out to sea.

William the frog hopped over to the edge and looked in all directions. "Water, water, everywhere . . ."

The ark was indeed still surrounded by water, but whitecaps were covering the surface. Noah stood looking at the sea with his sons as they discussed what was happening with the wind.

"The waters are definitely receding, father," Shem pointed out. "Look how the wind is blowing it back almost in layers."

"The wind hasn't blown like this since the flood," Japheth added.

The sons looked to their father, who continued to study the sights and sounds around him. The wind blew over them in gusts, causing Noah's robe to flap in the wind. "Just as He caused the earth to be covered with water, God will cause the earth to be dry once more. It could be that this wind is the tool He will use to do just that. I want each of you to keep an eye on the horizon. As soon as you see any sign of land, let me know immediately. For now, we must wait."

"How long will it take for the waters to recede?" Ham asked. "I don't know if I can take much more of being adrift like this, especially now after the fire."

Noah smiled, his wrinkles following the pattern of grooves on his face as his beard blew in the wind. "Well, if our experience thus far is any indication, I wouldn't pack my bags just yet, son. Remember, it took a hundred years to build this ark. I don't think God is ever in a hurry like we are." Noah put his hand on Ham's shoulder. "You can do this, Ham. You are fully equipped to handle this part of the challenge. We all are. Just keep trusting and waiting. And God will certainly take care of us as he did with stopping the fire."

Ham and Japheth walked over to Shem, who was with the women to tell them about the wind. Noah stood at the railing of the bow of the ark, breathing in the salt air. A dark, stealthy shadow was weaving in and around the legs of the animals. Just as Noah turned to watch the animals on deck, the shadow lunged for his throat. Noah, caught totally off guard, jumped from fright and started toppling over the rail. Max was close by and saw what was happening. Fortunately, a spike protruding from the rail caught Noah's garment, preventing him from falling over and hitting the water forty-five feet below.

A low growl rumbled in Max's throat as he saw Noah in peril. He ran over and instinctively grabbed part of Noah's loose garment

363

in his teeth, and not a moment too soon. The fabric of Noah's robe that was caught on the nail began to rip. Max was the only thing keeping Noah and the water apart. Max tugged and tugged, leaning hard on his back legs and digging his nails into the base of the rail, but he couldn't pull the old man upright. He also couldn't call for help nor grab his reed that was stuck in his collar.

Noah finally yelled out to his sons, "HAM! SHEM! JAPHETH!"

Shem looked up, alarmed, and took off from the other side of the deck to reach his father. He was able to get a stronghold and pull Noah back to safety. By now the humans and the animals all saw what was happening. Once Noah was clear, they erupted in cheers and a flurry of activity. None of them noticed the shadow lunging at Max. And no one saw Max fall through the rails.

Max felt like he was in the middle of his dream as he fell, only this time he wasn't falling past a steep jagged cliff. He was falling past the slick wooden planks of the ark. On the top deck of the ark were the yellow eyes watching him fall to his death. Yet another difference from his dream sent Max's mind reeling. The yellow eyes didn't belong to the wolves. They belonged to Charlie.

Max hit the surface of the water hard, then shot down, down, down into the depths. It felt like an eternity, but Max's descent finally slowed so he could make his way to the surface. But he was far under water. The air escaped his lungs as bubbles traveled upward faster than he could move.

Charlie turned and called out to the animals, "Somebody help! Max has fallen overboard. Hurry!"

The animals rushed to the railing and looked over the edge, drawing the attention of Noah and his family. They, too, ran over to the edge.

"What are the animals looking at?" Adah asked.

All they saw were bubbles slowly appearing where evidently something had fallen into the water. Max's head suddenly bobbed up to the surface before going back under.

"It's the little dog," Shem said as he immediately took off his robe, ready to dive in to rescue Max.

Noah grabbed Shem's arm. "It's too far to jump. The distance could kill you."

Shem hesitated and looked around, trying to figure out what to do. He took off in search of something.

"Hang in there, Max. We're going to get you help," Charlie shouted when Max's head surfaced again.

Max doggie-paddled as best he could, but his fear kept dragging him under. He saw his reed floating nearby, and desperately tried to reach it. No use. He paddled and sank, paddled and sank.

Crinan and Bethoo came flying over Max, calling, "Max, grab our legs. We'll try to lift you."

Every time the seagulls tried to position themselves, Max slipped back into the water. His reed was only a couple of strokes away. If only he could reach it. He took one big stroke but slipped under the water. The onlookers kept willing Max to stay afloat, but the little dog didn't reappear.

365

Shem pushed his way through the crowd and hurriedly threw a rope ladder over the side. He tried to run down the ladder but his feet tangled in the flexible rope. He had to take slow, deliberate steps. Meanwhile, Max had not resurfaced as the seconds agonizingly ticked away.

"Come on, Max. Come on," the animals called.

"Come on, little one. Come on," Noah and family called to Max.

"COME. COME," spoke the Voice.

The water was still. Then . . . a bubble. Then another. And suddenly . . .

WHOOSH! The waters parted and Craddock the whale came shooting onto the surface with Max on his back. The humans and animals went wild.

Max was coughing up water and trying to catch his breath.

"Hello, old boy. Splendid to see you. I say, have you enjoyed the rains as much as I have?" Craddock asked.

"I hate . . . ." Max coughed and coughed, "water."

"Right. Well, the waters won't be here much longer. They are receding, you know," Craddock replied.

Crinan picked up the floating reed from the water and landed on Craddock's back. Bethoo joined him as she patted Max on the back with her wing to help him cough.

"Well done, Craddock," Crinan exclaimed.

"How did ye know Max were in trouble?" Bethoo asked.

"I heard a Voice call me, lass," Craddock calmly explained as he swam over to the side of the ark just as Shem reached the bottom of the ladder.

Shem scooped up Max in his arms and the animals and humans cheered. A warm, orange glow suddenly covered the water as Shem carried Max back up on deck. Everyone looked to the skies. The fire cloud hovered above them.

366

Noah gazed at the gigantic form of Craddock, who floated next to the ark, remembering the drawing in Adam's cave. "Whale," he muttered in wonder.

CHAPTER 57

The Mountain

Things were quiet for a while after that surge of trouble. Max recovered from his scary fall, and spent a lot of time being quiet. For a few weeks he didn't wish to see anyone. Wolves, Charlie, Shem, no one. He just wanted to be with Kate in their stall. Shem came by frequently to check on Max just to make sure he was okay. Noah and his family thought the little dog was nothing short of a hero, something of course the animals already knew full well.

Nothing went missing again and Liz cancelled the tour of stalls so as to not add to the upset feelings of the animals. Raja was not happy, but Liz knew it was the right decision. The male inhabitants were thrilled—no more tours. Talent night and Flamingorobics continued, of course, but there seemed to be a dwindling enthusiasm among the animals. Tensions remained, and a feeling of mistrust grew among the animals as the weeks passed.

Liz, Max, Kate, and Al continued to discuss the troubling events as the mysterious wind returned. The sudden fire followed by Noah's and Max's brush with death caused fresh speculation to grow. Max remained wary of the wolves, but as usual, the wolves kept to themselves and never spoke to the other creatures. Max kept his eyes always on the alert, just waiting for the wolves to do something wrong. Then he would have them where he wanted them. Charlie believed Max, and that made him feel better to know he had an ally. Liz didn't rule out the wolves as the source of trouble. She even said they were the most likely candidates but at this point, there just wasn't enough proof. She said they would have to wait for the truth to emerge.

One thing that wasn't quiet for two and a half months was the wind. It blew and howled and whipped through the rafters in the upper deck, frequently scattering feathers from the birds down to the lower levels. It never ceased, day or night. Still the water remained with no dry land in sight.

One day as Al walked along the lower corridor on his way to see Java, a mighty jolt hit the ark, sending Al flying into the moose's stall. Animals were screeching and yelling with fear. The elephants sounded their trumpet calls with their trunks as they crashed onto the floor, nearly squashing the mice that were in their stall. The mice went running into the horse stall, where Giorgio and Pauline reared up on back legs in fright. The fainting goat was so terrified he didn't recover immediately but stayed stuck with legs up in the air. Upendo cried out to Chipo, "Whiplash! I got whiplash!"

Chaos spread throughout the ark. The spider's web broke off from flying debris. "And I worked all morning on that design," said Takako, the Japanese jumping spider. Her husband Masami tried to console her. "*Gomen nasai*—I'm sorry. You can spin one even better later. For now, HIDE!"

"Crikey, that was a rip-snorter of a jolt. I wonder what that was all about," Boomer shouted above the chaos.

"I think we should pray! The world could be coming to an end!" Stewart the praying mantis exclaimed. He and Cookie were visiting the kangaroos that morning.

"Nah, that already happened, bloke. The end of the world came with the flood, remember?" Boomer exclaimed hopping over to the mantids.

"Could it be an aftershock then?" Cookie said, folding her hands in prayerful thought.

"Well, it's sure part of the package. Hey now, we'll give it a fair go and see what's going on. No worries." Boomer jumped out of his stall to see if he could see anything.

Many animals were hovering around the corridor, talking and trying to learn all they could from their neighbors. When Al opened his eyes from the traumatic bump, he found himself sitting in Rodney the skunk's lap. "Don't shoot! I couldn't help it—somethin' flew me across the corridor," Al screamed.

"Relax, Al. I'm not going to shoot you, eh? That was quite a jolt. I don't know what happened," Rodney replied as Al scrambled off his lap to stand up.

All the stalls were out of order. Buckets were knocked over, hay was scattered everywhere and animals were moaning as they slowly and fearfully got to their feet.

369

Al saw Crinan and Bethoo flying up above and yelled out to them, "Hey, Crinan, what happened?"

Crinan looked below and found the source of the call. "We're goin' ta check it out now, lad. Things are a bloomin' mess up here."

Al started walking back toward his stall, but then picked up his pace to a full run. It felt like the ark hit something. And if it hit something, who knew if it would stay afloat? Al panicked. He had to find Liz.

"Craddock, can you tell me what you see, *s'il vous plaît?*" Liz calmly asked out the porthole that Racket had drilled for her, trying to piece together what was happening.

"Permit me to take a look around and I'll report back," the whale replied as he disappeared beneath the surface.

Max held Kate in a secure embrace. She was quite shaken with the crash. "Wha' did he say, lass?" Max asked Liz.

Liz slowly curled her tail up and down on the rock as she peered out their porthole. She was studying the outside as best she could. "Craddock is assessing the situation beneath the water and will report back. I sent Crinan and Bethoo to give us an aerial report. We should know something soon."

Liz looked at Racket's marks on the beam. "It's been five months since the flood began. Hmmm . . ."

A spray of water misted Liz's face as Craddock surfaced near the porthole. "I do say, I believe you've made landfall, my dear. It appears that the ark is wedged onto a rock."

A jolt of energy shot through Liz. "*Merci*, Craddock! But that's no ordinary rock. It's got to be the top of a mountain! Tell me, what is the sea life doing?"

"Well, many of the sea creatures have been departing for weeks now as the waters have receded. If the ark has indeed landed on top of a mountain, I'm afraid I better join them to make my way back home," Craddock explained. "Is Max nearby? I wish to bid him farewell."

"But of course. I'll get Max. It has been enchanting to meet you, Craddock. I hope to see you again someday. *Au revoir*," Liz said as she motioned for Max to come over to her.

"It was utterly splendid to meet you, Liz. I was thrilled to be able to spend time around the ark throughout this time of waiting. If you return to France, I shall swim the channel over to see you. Farewell!" Craddock said as his warm eyes smiled back at Liz.

Max hopped up on the rock and poked his head out to see Craddock. "Craddock, I hate ta tell ye farewell then. It's been gr-r-rand ta see ye in these waters. An' I kin't thank ye enough for savin' me life."

"It was my duty, my privilege, old boy. Yes, and parting is indeed such sweet sorrow. I do hope you return to Scotland so I can see you and Kate again," Craddock said, now becoming quite emotional. "And Max, know that Gillamon would be terribly proud of all you have accomplished on this mission. You are a natural born hero, old chap."

Max lowered his head. He was indeed a hero, but lately, he didn't feel like much of one. It still stung his heart to think of Gillamon. Telling Craddock goodbye was like telling Scotland goodbye all over again, since he was such a part of Max's life back home. Yes, back home. Who knew what would await them there? The flood would have wiped out everything. Max was grateful that Gillamon had died before the flood. To think of his mentor caught up in the drowning waters made Max shudder. Yes, it was good that Gillamon had died when he did.

"Thanks, me friend. I hope I see ye back home. I'll keep an eye out for ye then," Max said to Craddock.

"RIGHT! Cheerio then. Do tell Kate and Al farewell. Ta-ta," Craddock bellowed as he blew one final spray of water before descending into the depths.

Max watched until he saw the swirl of water around Craddock disappear. *Goodbye, old friend,* he whispered to himself. He cleared the lump in his throat, then turned to Liz. "So wha' now, lassie?"

Crinan and Bethoo came flying into their stall, landing on the rock. "Guess wha'? Ye won't believe wha' s happened," Crinan said excitedly.

"We've landed on top of a mountain, no?" Liz said matter-of-factly.

Crinan looked deflated. He wanted to tell the good news. "How did ye know then?"

"Craddock gave us the word from beneath the sea. What can you tell us from the aerial view?" Liz asked, snapping out her paw to lick it clean from the salt water.

"Well, ye really kin't see much yet. There's still water everywhere. But I knew the ark must be stuck from the way it's restin' on somethin'," the seagull explained.

"This calls for a closer inspection. I need to go to the upper deck. Anyone care to join me?" Liz said as she jumped down to walk out of the stall.

Just then Al made his way to the stall and grabbed Liz by the shoulders. "LIZ! Somethin' terrible has happened. Everythin' has crashed over and the animals are upset and we might be sinkin' and—"

"Shhhh! Albert, there is nothing to fear. The ark has landed on a mountaintop. We are not sinking, dear. This is good news," Liz explained, wishing to calm Al's fears.

Al sat back and closed his eyes in relief. "Well that's the best news I ever heard. Ye mean we can get off now?"

"No, no, it will still be quite some time, I believe. You must be patient, Albert," Liz said with a smile and her dainty paw under Al's chin.

Liz led the others to the upper level. Even though there were some bumps and bruises from the landing, this was a great day. Everyone wanted to find out as much as they could about the exciting developments aboard the ark. They had landed. It wouldn't be too much longer that they would be aboard, or so they thought. Little did they know that they were on a mountain nearly 17,000 feet tall. Water wasn't going anywhere soon.

CHAPTER 58

The Big Send-Out

Adah winced and covered her ears as she listened to the rooster and the raven go at it, waking the ark. "Noah, one of the things I look forward to most when we get back on dry land is a quieter beginning to the day." Adah stretched and yawned, patting Noah on the back to see if he was getting up.

"Well, I think it might get quieter here soon, even before we get to dry land," Noah replied with a yawn. He rubbed his eyes to get them focused.

"What do you mean?" Adah asked, tying her sash around her waist.

Noah lit the oil lamp for Adah. "When we begin to see dry land, I'm going to do a test. I'll send out a bird to scout the area and test the water levels. I was thinking I might use the raven."

"Do you really think that day will come soon? It's been over two months since we made landfall. We knew it would take some time for the dry land to appear, but two months? Ham is beside himself, wanting to get off this ark," Adah said as she made their bed.

Noah chuckled. "I bet if Ham could fly, he'd be the first to volunteer to go scout out the land. He barely leaves the observation area. He keeps scanning the horizon for dry land, willing it to pop out from the water. I heard Mabir scolding him for falling asleep out there more than once."

"If we're so antsy to get off the ark, I can only imagine how the animals must feel cooped up in their stalls. Poor dears. They have to be reaching their limit, too," Adah said.

"Now left leg. And one, and two, and three, and four! Dat's right, yuh can do it! And five, and six, and seven, and eight! Come on nah, a few more! And nine, and ten, and back again!" shouted Lea the flamingo as she led the animals in morning exercise.

Despite their readiness to leave the ark, the animals couldn't deny that they were in excellent shape from the daily exercise routine. Liz's idea probably saved them from gaining a lot of weight and feeling physically bad over these past few months.

Al shook his belly and counted along with Lea. "And now shake dose tails if you have dem." He circled his fluffy tail around in circles to the beat of the monkeys and songbirds. He couldn't wait for breakfast. He always justified eating more at breakfast since he had just worked out. Unfortunately, he ate about as much as he worked off, so he remained pleasantly plump.

Suddenly the animals heard the humans yelling from the upper deck. It sounded like they were cheering. Al stopped in midshake and looked over at Liz, who sat listening intently to what the humans were saying. A big grin broke out on her face as she turned to Al. "It's finally happened." Liz trotted away quickly to the ramp leading to the upper level.

"What finally happened?" Al called behind her.

"Land! They've finally spotted land," Liz yelled back with enthusiasm.

At those words the animals erupted in a cheer that spread like wildfire through the stalls.

"And just where do you think you're going?" Henriette said, her feathers puffed up as Shem carried Ricco the raven away. She wasn't grumpy as much as she was concerned.

"Beats me, *señora*. Tell Maria to follow me—hurry!" Ricco squawked back.

Shem rubbed his thumb on Ricco's head and smiled. "It's okay fella, father's got an exciting mission for you. You get to be an explorer today."

Henriette went run-waddling down the corridor to get Maria, her wings spread wide as she went as fast as she could. "*Au secours.* Help! Maria! The human is taking Ricco away! *Vite!* Hurry!"

Maria turned quickly and took off flying down the corridor just as Henriette reached her. "*Gracias, amiga,*" she called out as she flew away.

Henriette was out of breath. "Humph! If only I could fly." The fat hen turned around and started run-waddling toward the ramp to reach the upper deck. It might take her a while but she had to see what was happening.

Noah gently took Ricco from Shem's hands and held the raven up to look him in the eye. "You have an important mission, my friend. The mountaintops are appearing. I need you to fly and look around to be my eyes for the condition of the earth."

"Father, really. This bird can't understand a word you're saying," Ham chuckled.

Liz caught Ricco's attention and smiled, rolling her eyes at the silly humans. How little they truly understood. "*Bon voyage, mon ami!* What an honor for you to be chosen by Noah for this important mission."

Noah smiled at the petite black cat that meowed and circled his legs as she looked up at the raven. "Perhaps they know more than we think, Ham." He chuckled and lifted Ricco above his head. "And now, fly and see what you can see." Noah released Ricco and the black bird took off in flight.

"Wait for me, Ricco. I'm coming, too," Maria exclaimed, flying out and joining her mate.

"Ah, *bonita* love, *sí,* let's go together!" Ricco said as the two ravens flew toward the far horizon.

Maria called back to Liz, "*Por favor,* tell Henriette *adios* and that I love her."

Noah observed that as the ravens flew in the distance, they kept landing from place to place on top of the water. But they weren't landing on pieces of earth. They were landing on floating debris. They continued on to the horizon.

Henriette was huffing and puffing by the time she reached the upper deck, placing her wing on the railing as she caught her breath. "*Madame* . . . what . . . is happening?"

Liz softly walked over to Henriette and placed her dainty paw on the hen's shoulder. She knew what a special friend Maria was to Henriette. "*Mon amie,* Noah has given Ricco an important mission to go see how far the waters have receded."

Henriette looked at Liz. "So where is Maria? Does she know?"

Liz smiled thoughtfully at her dear friend. "*Oui.* Maria has gone with Ricco. She did not want to be apart from him. You can understand this, no?"

"But will they be back?" Henriette asked, her eyes filling with tears in a rare show of emotion.

"I do not know, *mon amie.* It appears they keep landing and taking flight again. But they keep flying further away. Maria did ask me to tell you farewell. And to tell you she loves you," Liz softly replied.

Henriette cleared her throat and lifted her head to the horizon as she watched Maria fly off in the distance with Ricco. The humans were cheering and talking excitedly about what the raven might find, and the thoughts of soon being able to leave the ark. Liz felt sorry for Henriette. No, the humans had no idea about animals and birds and how they felt about things. Their laughter felt almost irreverent in light of what Henriette was feeling.

Liz decided to give Henriette some time alone to gather her emotions, giving the hen a squeeze on the wing before leaving the upper deck. The humans all followed and made their way back to their living quarters.

Henriette remained alone at the railing, barely able to see her friend now. Two black dots were visible in the distance. Henriette was not good with goodbyes, so was somewhat relieved things happened so quickly. She looked up and lifted her wing in a gesture of farewell, though Maria couldn't see her. *"Au revoir, mon amie. Merci, et au revoir."*

"I'm telling you I cleaned this mess up last night," Japheth said to Shem, furious about the overturned buckets of dirty water everywhere.

Tensions were already high, and everyone was on edge. The raven had not returned. Their initial hopes of getting off the ark rapidly dwindled.

"Maybe you *thought* you cleaned up this area—it's a big ark, you know," Shem said. "Don't try to get out of work, Japheth. Fair is fair and it's your turn to clean."

Japheth grabbed Shem by the arm. "I'm telling you, I CLEANED IT! I had all these buckets ready to be dumped overboard this morning. Maybe *somebody* came behind me and messed it up on purpose."

"Hey, don't look at me. I didn't do anything," Shem said, holding his hands up to defend his innocence.

Ham called from the upper deck, "You done down there yet, Japheth? Whoo-wee! It's extra ripe in here today."

Japheth looked at Shem, fuming, "I'm going to kill him. I worked until late last night and fell into bed exhausted, and I wake up to find this mess. I bet HE did this." Japheth took off running after Ham.

Liz sat with a concerned look on her face, slapping her tail up and down as she watched this argument heat up between the humans. "I don't like this," she murmured.

"Don't like what, *señora?*" Don Pedro asked. He was in a great mood. Henriette had been so quiet after Maria's departure that he didn't let anything get to him.

"The humans are arguing, and this could turn ugly," Liz worried.

Liz's gaze followed Japheth as he reached the upper deck where Ham stood, laughing at his brother. Japheth grabbed Ham by the collar and accused him of making the mess that he would have to clean all over again.

"YOU did this! I'm not going to clean it up, either. You're going to be the one to do it," Japheth yelled.

"I had nothing to do with this. I didn't do anything. Get your hands off me," Ham yelled back, pushing Japheth away.

Japheth fell back onto a pile of hay and hurriedly scrambled back onto his feet, lunging at Ham. The two brothers started having an out-and-out fist fight. Shem saw it, too, and ran to break it up.

Ham and Japheth exchanged blow after blow, each knocking the other against the upper railing, which towered forty feet above the lower corridor. Liz shuddered as she saw part of the railing begin to give way. If one of the humans fell, they could be killed.

"This isn't good. We must intervene," Liz said as she jumped up on the stall railing and opened the latch to the gate. "Don Pedro, look at me. I give you full permission to run down the corridor."

Don Pedro couldn't believe his ears. "What, *señora?* You actually want me to run?"

"*Oui, mon ami!* Run like the wind. Now GO!" Liz said as she slapped the big bull on the backside to get him to take off.

Don Pedro snorted and scraped his hoof before bolting out of the stall. He ran like he hadn't run in months, flying down the corridor. He was exhilarated with the speed and had no intention of stopping.

"*Madame!* How could you let the silly *boeuf* do this?" Henriette exclaimed, not believing her eyes.

"Patience, patience, Henriette. There is a method to my madness. I had to create a diversion to get the humans to stop fighting. Someone is going to get seriously injured or worse if they don't stop," Liz shouted as she ran out of the stall toward Duke.

"Duke! Quickly! Sound your trumpet blast to get the attention of the humans," Liz directed.

Duke lifted his trunk high in the air and let loose a loud blast that shook the ark. Shem, startled with the sound, looked down and then noticed the bull running like mad down the corridor.

"Stop it, you two. You can beat each other up later. The bull is out and some damage is going to be done if we don't stop him NOW," Shem yelled as he pulled the two fighting brothers apart. "COME ON, FOLLOW ME!"

Ham wiped the blood from his mouth and Japheth held his eye as they grudgingly agreed and followed Shem back down the ramp.

"It's working! *C'est bon,*" Liz exclaimed as the humans ran past her to chase after Don Pedro.

"Why do I ever doubt you, *Madame?*" Henriette said.

"*Merci*, Henriette. I'm sure Don Pedro will need your help once again to calm down after this experience," Liz said, smiling.

Henriette smiled and straightened up. She had purpose again. Her mind would be distracted from missing Maria now. She had a bull to get under control. "*Mais oui!* I will have that silly *boeuf* back to good behavior in no time!"

Liz smiled. This experience turned out to serve a dual purpose. Save the humans and help Henriette out of her sadness. She gave a silent "*Merci*" to the Maker for the wisdom to know what to do and turned to Henriette. "I'm sure you will, *mon amie*. I'm sure you will."

Noah was understandably upset. He paced back and forth across the room, glaring at his two sons. Ham and Japheth were a mess. Blood covered the front of their tunics. Ham's lip was fat and Japheth's eye was black and swollen shut. Mabir and Lillie gave their husbands pieces of ice that they'd chipped off the polar bear stall, frowning as they saw how ridiculous the brothers looked.

"I don't want to hear anymore about it. I don't care who started it—both of you are responsible for how you handled it. Grown men like you fighting—it's ridiculous. You're over one hundred years old, for goodness' sake," Noah ranted. "Plus, while you were fighting, the bull got loose and knocked over more of the dirty water buckets as he ran down the corridor. It took all four of us to get him under control and back in his stall. Now there's even more mess to clean up."

Ham and Japheth looked to the ground. They may have been over a hundred, but they were still acting like boys, and now their father was scolding them. They felt like ten-year-olds.

"I'm sorry, father. I started it. I'll own to that. I don't know who messed up my hard work, but I shouldn't have gone after Ham the way I did," Japheth said.

Noah pointed to Ham. "Don't apologize just to me—apologize to your brother."

Japheth looked at Ham with his one good eye and swallowed his pride. "I'm sorry, Ham. I was out of line, even if you were acting the way you were. I should have held my temper."

Ham looked at Noah, who glared at him with a "better-apologize-back-to-your-brother" look in his eye. "Apology acthepted. And I'm thorry I methed with you and egged you on like that."

Japheth couldn't withhold his laughter. Ham's lip was so swollen that he spoke with a lisp. "What'th tho funny?" Ham said, starting to chuckle himself at the sight of Japheth's puffed-up bruised eye.

"I think you both gave each other equal reminders of this argument," Noah said, happy for the comic relief for his sons. "We need some peace around here."

Shem entered the kitchen area, carrying a dove. "Here he is, father."

"Oh, good. Thank you, Shem. Listen up everyone. The raven has not returned, and I assume he will not be coming back. So now I'm going to send out this dove to search the land. I have a feeling we will see him again," Noah explained as he looked the dove in the eye. "You look like a peaceful fellow. Japheth and Ham, as I send this dove off, I want you two to pledge to keep the peace from here on out. Agreed?"

Japheth and Ham nodded and got up to follow their father to the observation deck. Noah held up the dove. "Okay, my little friend. Today you symbolize peace between us. From this day on, we will not allow our tempers to get out of control, but will maintain peace in the ark. As you fly away, take our frustrations with you, and return with hope. Go in peace."

The dove flew off to the horizon as Noah and his sons watched. This time it would be different. Noah just had a feeling. Little did Noah know, the dove's name was *Shalom,* meaning "peace."

381

CHAPTER 59

Surprises

COCK-A-DOODLE DOO!

COCK-A-DOODLE DOO!

COCK-A-DOODLE DOOOOOOOOOOOOOOOOO-
OOOOOOOOOOOO!

Jacques was in rare form today. "Ah, life is good, no?" he said
as he strutted by Henriette, Don Pedro, and Isabella.

Isabella let loose a PFFFTTT, and swished her tail to disperse
the smell. "What's up with him?"

"Ignore him. He's just so pleased with himself that he alone is
the ark waker now," Henriette said while holding her nose.

"And why should I not be pleased? Things are as they should be,
no? Finally, I am the only voice that everyone hears. My beautiful
call fills the ark with wonderful sound now that that garbage-eater
raven is gone. Humph!" Jacques said as he strutted the other way.

"I think you need an attitude adjustment, *señor*," Don Pedro added. A broad grin came over the bull's face. Then he looked at Henriette. "Don't you think you should work on your husband, *señora*?"

"*Oui*, you are right, my bright *étudiant*. He does need an attitude adjustment, and his lesson will begin NOW!" said Henriette as she puffed up and waddled over to Jacques.

Don Pedro beamed. He wasn't her target. For now anyway.

"He's coming back, father," Ham called. Noah hurriedly got up from the table where he was writing and went to the observation deck. He had started drawing on a new clay tablet since his first one was destroyed in the fire. He lost much of the detail he had previously captured, but at least he would capture the general events of the ark and the flood.

Shalom the dove was returning to the ark. Noah held out his hand for the dove to land. "You look exhausted, my little friend," Noah said as he gently stroked the dove's soft head. The dove closed his eyes for a moment, breathing heavily.

"Shem, take the dove back to his nest. We will give him a week to rest before we send him out again. It will also give the water more time to go down," Noah said as he carefully placed Shalom in Shem's hands.

"What does this tell you, father?" asked Lillie, who had joined Japheth when she heard the exciting news about the dove's return. Max and Liz had joined the humans up on deck. They wanted to hear every word.

Noah knew his family would not want to hear this, but he had to tell them the reality of the situation. "When I sent out the raven, it flew over the water and landed on floating debris. It did this because ravens are dirty birds, eating garbage or dead animals. The raven kept going, not requiring earth to make landfall. The dove, however, is a clean bird and will not land on floating debris.

The fact that this dove came back tells me that the waters have not yet receded far enough. We will need to wait longer."

"Oh no," Ham said as he stomped off. "I can't believe this. How much longer are we supposed to wait?" his voice trailed off.

Although Ham said it out loud, he voiced the thoughts of everyone aboard the ark. Adah watched her family, concerned with how weary they were. They needed a boost. They needed something to lift their spirits. She pulled Lillie aside and whispered in her ear, "Lillie, go get Nala and Mabir. I have an idea. Meet me in the lower deck supply room."

Lillie smiled and squeezed Adah's arm before turning to go get the other girls. Liz overheard Adah and wondered what she meant. "I'm going to follow the female humans, Max. Noah's wife is planning something and I want to know what it is. Then I'm going to go question Shalom the dove to learn about what he saw. But let's not spread this negative news about more waiting to the other animals, *oui?*"

"Aye, I'll keep it mum. We don't need any more bad news spread then," Max said, as he and Liz walked along the upper corridor.

Adah was pulling spices off the shelves when Liz quietly jumped up on a crate. Adah smiled and went over to rub Liz under the chin. Liz closed her eyes in delight. Ah, the humans did know how to give an animal a good rub.

"Hello, little friend. Did you come to see me? Oh, but you just love being scratched under the chin, don't you? That's all you care about, yes?" Adah said as Lillie brought Mabir and Nala into the supply room. "Good, you're all here."

"What's going on, Mother?" Nala asked, picking up a bunch of herbs to smell, her eyes closing with the delightful fragrance.

"I have an idea to help lift our spirits, but you must keep this a secret from Noah," Adah said excitedly.

The ladies looked at each other and giggled. "Okay, what is it?" Lillie asked.

"Noah is getting ready to turn 601 years old, and I want us to plan a surprise birthday party for him. We'll have a big feast, and I've saved some of my best spices to make one of my special cakes. It will take days for each stage of the cake so we best get started now," Adah explained.

Mabir clasped her hands together with glee. "How wonderful, mother. He will be so happy."

"And doing this will help everyone feel better. We've got a couple of weeks to plan it, so let's get your husbands in on this, too—especially Ham. He's having a rough time waiting. This party will give us all something to look forward to that will keep us busy," Adah said, handing the spices to the young ladies.

"The men can help us decorate and keep father occupied elsewhere while we get ready," Nala suggested.

"Exactly. Now, let's talk about our menu for the feast, and what we'll need to do," Adah said. Liz smiled and jumped off the crate. The humans had a great idea here. It would be helpful for them to plan the surprise birthday party for Noah. And Liz had the perfect idea for a gift.

385

"Father, he's coming back," Ham shouted from the observation deck. Noah, hoping this time would be different, came running up to greet the returning dove that he had sent out early that morning.

Noah, Ham, Shem, and Japheth all strained against the evening sun to look at the dove in the distance. "It looks like he's got something in his beak, father," Shem said. "I can't quite make it out, though."

Noah held out his hand to shield his eyes from the setting sun. A big smile grew on his face. Ham and the others watched their father, wondering what he saw. "What do you think it is?" Japheth finally asked.

"It's a branch of some kind," Noah said as he turned his hand level to receive the dove. Shalom lighted gently in Noah's hand.

"An olive branch!"

Liz made it to the observation deck just as the men started shouting and cheering. She looked over at Shalom, who caught her eye and gave a wink. Liz nodded in reply, a big smile on her face.

"This means the water has finally receded enough for plants to grow. Praise God! How blessed I am to get this sign of vegetation growing on the land. The dove could have stayed on the land, but he returned with this olive branch," Noah exclaimed. He was dancing around the deck, laughing and celebrating.

Ham, Japheth, and Shem were also caught up in the excitement over the good news. "This means we'll be leaving soon," Ham shouted. "It has to mean that! Right?"

Noah, out of breath, gave Shalom to Shem, and wiped his brow. "Well, Ham, we are definitely close to leaving, at least closer than we were, but we'll need to do another test with the dove. Be excited, yes, but remember that the water has to be gone from underneath us as well as throughout the land for the animals to be able to depart the ark."

Ham's smile faded from his face. "I'll try to be excited. This is good news, after all. But it also still means one thing—WAIT!"

"Come on, let's go tell the women the good news. I'll put the dove in its nest," Shem said as the men slapped each other on the back for joy.

Liz followed Shem down the corridor and jumped up to Shalom's nest when the human was gone. "Well done, *mon ami*. You have made Noah and his sons very happy."

"Thanks, Liz. But it was your idea for me to get the olive branch for Noah's birthday. He did seem happy, didn't he?" Shalom said with a yawn.

"*Mon ami*, you must be tired, no? But tell me quickly, what did you see this time?" Liz asked.

"Oh, Liz, it was the most beautiful sight I've ever seen after being cooped up in this ark for so long. Lush, green trees and shrubs are growing. The receding water is carving beautiful

386

canyons with rivers, and wildflowers are growing along the banks. But this is only in a small area at a higher elevation. There is still much water left to go down," Shalom explained.

"*Magnifique!* How I wish I could see what you have seen! *Merci* for the report. And *merci* for the olive branch. *Oui*, it is the perfect present for Noah. Next time he sends you out, you must take your mate with you. Now rest. You need your strength," Liz said with a tender touch of her dainty paw on the dove's wing.

"Yes, I need to sleep," the dove said, his eyes heavy with sleep.

Liz grew excited with anticipation. She went back to her stall and looked at Racket's marks. It had been 285 days since the flood began. How much longer could it possibly be, she wondered, before they could leave the ark? Only time would tell.

"Happy birthday, dear No-ah! Happy birthday to you!" the family sang as they clapped and shouted.

Noah's eyes were alive with surprise and delight. His family had kept him completely in the dark about this celebration. He wondered about all their secretive scurrying about and hushed voices. He thought maybe they were talking about how the dove had not returned since Noah sent it out last week for the third time, and were wondering what it could mean. Now it all made sense. Noah loved surprises.

Adah set a beautiful table with fine linens and a full feast. The centerpiece was her special cake with none other than the olive branch stuck in the center. The olive branch was the best present Noah could have received, Adah thought. How good God was to Noah. Her heart was full of joy. Her idea had worked out beautifully.

PART FIVE

THE TRUTH AND
THE PROMISE

CHAPTER 60

Dry Land

Noah was full from the feast and the cake, but he wanted to climb to the upper deck. His surprise birthday party had given him such joy. But he really had been celebrating for a week, ever since the dove returned with the olive branch. When he sent the dove out again and it didn't return, Noah knew their time of departure from the ark must be near. He hoped that the early birthday present a week ago could be surpassed by an even greater gift today. He decided to open the roof and step outside.

Noah walked up the few steps to the outside, and put his feet on the outer deck. He closed his eyes as he felt the breeze softly blowing on his face. He turned completely around as he viewed the horizon that encircled him. He studied the distant landscape and was overjoyed. The earth was almost dry.

"Thank you, God!" Noah exclaimed. "Hurry everyone, come up and look."

Ham, of course, was the first one to scurry up the steps, followed by the others. The eight surviving humans on earth stood and looked out to see a whole new world emerging from the depths of the water. New growth sprouted from the ground, and the land was nearly dry.

Max noticed the humans had opened the roof and stepped outside. He had to go check this out. Max hopped up the steps and poked his head out. Shem noticed Max and smiled, walking over to him. "Hey, little guy, come on out. The land is almost dry," Shem said as he patted Max on the head. "But stay clear of the railing."

Max wagged his tail at Shem and hopped outside onto the deck. He carefully peered through the railing. It was true! The land was almost dry. Max shouted with joy, "'TIS A GR-R-RAND DAY!"

Shem laughed at the little dog who barked and wagged his tail. "Look, father, the little dog seems to know this is good news, too!"

Noah went over to where Max stood perched on the railing and smiled. "Yes, my little friend, today is a day to celebrate. The Lord has been faithful to keep us safe, and He is making the way out for us as this new world recovers from the flood." He petted Max on the back as he gazed out over the horizon. "You animals will have a wonderful new world to call home."

"Noah, when do you think we can actually set foot on the land and leave the ark?" Adah asked.

"I can't say just yet. Although the land is drying, it is not completely dry. But I know it will not be as long as it has been. Just hang on a little while longer. Be patient. Our deliverance will soon come," Noah said.

The family started singing and celebrating. The couples danced on the deck, shouting for joy that this day had finally come when they could see with their eyes the Lord's handiwork preparing the earth for their return. Ham didn't even complain about having to wait longer. He just needed hope that they weren't stuck on the ark forever. If there was one thing he had learned through this long ordeal, it was patience.

Max smiled as he watched the humans celebrate. His heart lifted, and he couldn't wait to tell the others. He jumped down the stairs and made his way down the corridor. As he reached the waterfall, Charlie called him over.

"What's going on up there? I thought I heard happy voices above decks," Charlie remarked. He saw Max hesitate coming near the pool and chuckled. "Don't worry, Max, I'm not going to ask you to come in for a swim anymore after your terrifying fall over the side of the ark. I'm just glad I was there to call for help."

Max had been confused with the events of "the fall" as it came to be known around the ark. At first he thought Charlie had lunged at him, but then he had realized he must have been mistaken. Charlie called for help to save him. Charlie had twice saved Max's life. Even though Liz had said to question Charlie about these incidents, Max was afraid to ask. He was most afraid of the answers he might get to his questions about Charlie's mate and Charlie's actions. He just decided to ignore his fear and enjoy his friendship with Charlie. Yes, Charlie was his friend, that much he had to believe.

"Aye, I don't want to be near any more water. An' speakin' of that, there's good news, Charlie. The water has dried up. We'll be gettin' off the ark r-r-real soon," Max said excitedly.

Charlie looked at Max with a look of seriousness. "The day we've all waited for."

"Aye, well, gotta go tell Kate, Al, an' of course, Liz. That brainy kitty will be waitin' for this good news then," Max said as he turned to trot down the corridor.

"We need answers. And I am sure we'll find those answers at the end of the hall," Liz was saying to Kate, Al, and the seagulls, who had stopped by.

"Sure, and ye won't catch me goin' doon there," said Al as he swung in his hammock.

"I'm afraid, also, Albert," Liz said. "Crinan, do you think you could nonchalantly fly over Charlie's stall?"

"It's hard to be nonchalant when he's at the end of the hall, lass," Crinan replied.

Just then Max entered the stall. "Guess what? The land is dr-r-ry. Looks like we'll be off the ark r-r-real soon."

Kate rushed over to Max. "Oh, Max, I'm so happy! I kin't wait ta get off this ark, an' away from all the dangers here. I jest want ta be with ye on dry land again."

"Aye, bonnie lass. It'll come soon, real soon," Max replied as he nudged Kate in a fond embrace.

Liz sat staring at Max. She needed to have a private discussion with him, but not here. She didn't want to alarm Kate and the others. She would wait and then arrange to meet Max outside their stall. He needed to hear some things . . . some hard things.

CHAPTER 61

The Truth

A few days later Liz asked Max to follow her to the supply room where the fire had broken out two months earlier. Tensions had been riding high over the past few weeks as the animals remembered the fire and the fall, and as they waited for the land to dry out completely.

Moments after Max and Liz arrived, Racket flew into the supply room, banging his head faster than they had ever seen him bang. They knew something must be up to cause Racket such excitement.

"What is it, Racket?" asked Liz.

"Something big is happening. I just heard Noah tell his family that the land is completely dry. He feels like it might be time to get everyone off the ark, but he's waiting for a word from the Maker. He's up there praying right now," said Racket excitedly. He flew off to tell the others, banging on the beams as he went down the corridor.

"We better check this out, Max. I have a bad feeling that I cannot put my paw on," said Liz.

"Why, Liz, could it be that ye aren't usin' yer head for once, but yer heart then?" asked Max, playing with his reed.

"Don't make such a fuss over what I do or don't do, Max. I'll use whatever I think is best to make the right decision," said Liz, feeling vulnerable that Max had seen her beginning to have a faith greater than her intellect.

"Tell me why ye have a bad feelin'. This is gr-r-rand news. We get ta leave the ark after so long. Wha' could be goin' wrong then?" asked Max.

"I've been watching all the troubles between the animals and the humans on board. It's been steadily increasing over these past months, especially since the fire. I have been slowly concluding that the ones causing the trouble were the wolves as the most likely explanation. Over the months we have had comments from witnesses who thought they heard or had seen the wolves," explained Liz.

"Aye, it's good ta see ye finally see things me way. So wha' are ye thinkin' then, lass?" asked Max.

"I do not believe I'm saying this. It is not what I'm *thinking*, Max. It is what I'm *feeling*. Someone has tried stirring up trouble with each step closer to us leaving the ark. Why? What could be the problem with leaving the ark after being cooped up for a year in this floating habitat? Who in their right mind would want to keep that from happening? As I thought about how this problem got started in the first place—the sin of the humans that the Maker could no longer take, I had to consider who would have gotten satisfaction from the downfall of the humans. Who? And who would want to prevent the humans from reentering the world to start the human race over again?" asked Liz.

"Aye, who indeed? It has ta be those wolves. They been troublin' me an' the rest of the creatures since before we were even on the ark. An' they don't even like humans. Ye said yerself they are the ones causin' all the trouble," said Max.

"This is what I do not know, Max. Nothing makes sense. Although the wolves appear to be the ones causing the trouble, what motive could they possibly have to stop the humans? I've gone through every possible explanation in my head, and I cannot make it logically come together. I feel there's something I've been missing all along," said Liz with a wrinkled brow.

Liz hesitated. What she was about to tell Max would most certainly upset him. It could damage their friendship. But she didn't see another way around it. She had to speak what she felt to be the truth. Too much was at stake here.

"Max, you need to listen to what I'm about to tell you, *mon ami*," said Liz.

"Aye, lass. I'm listenin'. Ye know I always respect wha' ye have ta say. Ye give everythin' such a thorough thinkin' that ye know wha' yer talkin' aboot," said Max with an encouraging smile.

Liz smiled back weakly. She took a deep breath and spoke.

"Max, do you remember sharing with me the story that Gillamon told you about the humans and the Maker in the Garden?" asked Liz.

"Aye, lass. Gillamon told me the story of how they betrayed the Maker. The Evil One in the Garden tricked them. Wha' aboot it then?" asked Max.

Liz looked at Max, knowing this wasn't going to be easy for him to hear.

"I, too, have heard that story. It was passed down from my ancestors. My family kept the story alive so we would never forget. It was important to our family that we stay smart and aware of the world around us. It was important that we understood about the Evil One, and the trouble he could bring," Liz explained before pausing to gather her wits about her.

"Max, there is something you do not know about that story that I do. Gillamon did not give you the identity of the Evil One, did he?" asked Liz.

397

"No, he didn't. I'm sure he knew, but no, he didn't tell me who the Evil One were. I'm sure he had his reasons for not tellin' me," answered Max, an anxious feeling growing inside of him now.

"I know who the Evil One was in the Garden, Max. And I think he has come to the ark to destroy the remaining humans," said Liz, feeling her heart beating harder.

"Who is it, lass?" asked Max with a growl.

"You will not want to hear this, *mon ami*. You have always told me and the other creatures to trust you. I am asking you to trust me now," said Liz.

Max stood erect, with tail up and fur raised, clearly on the defensive. "Who do ye mean, Liz?" he growled sternly.

Liz gulped, not wanting to reveal who the one was that she knew would pierce Max's heart. But she had to make a choice. She knew she had to be bold and risk this friendship that was so precious to her.

398

"In the Garden, the Evil One was . . . a snake. Max, I think he has returned. And I believe it is Charlie," said Liz, looking Max square in the eye.

Max bristled with anger. "How dar-r-re ye!! HOW DAR-R-RE YE! Charlie has been one of me good fr-r-r-iends on this journey. He helped me when ther-r-re were pr-r-r-oblems . . . not hurt me! He even saved me life—twice! How kin ye even think such a thing?! Are ye completely daft, kitty," said Max with a rumbling growl that sent shivers up Liz's spine and crushed her spirit.

"Max, listen to me! I know this goes against every logical bone in your body and mine, but you have to consider what I'm telling you. It was a snake in the Garden who caused the evil to enter the world and begin to destroy the human race before it had really even begun. He did it by *deceiving* them, Max. He made them prideful, thinking they could do things themselves without the Maker's help. Don't you see? The enemy we're looking for isn't the obvious! He's the one who's the least obvious—the one who is subtle and cunning.

"Max, Charlie has always given you words you wanted to hear, even when you wondered if they were right. I've seen you struggle with the things he has told you. You have chosen to believe what you've wanted to believe, not necessarily what was right. When was the last time you asked the Maker about these problems, Max? More and more you've turned to Charlie, not the Maker. And it was he who started all the hero worship of you on the ark. What does this tell you?" Liz pleaded.

Liz jumped up on a crate to be eye level with Max and continued.

"Listen to me, *mon ami*. I have struggled trying to figure out the truth in this situation. And what the Maker has revealed to me is that truth cannot always be explained by the logical. You have been telling me this since we met. Faith is not about logic. It is about believing what you cannot see. When I was looking for who was causing the trouble, it led me to answers that made a certain amount of sense. Yet, it stopped short of the truth that is burning to get out, and is breaking my heart as it tries. Max, I think there are three snakes on board."

Max's anger was bubbling at the surface. He didn't want to hear any more of what Liz had to say. The shock was too great. He couldn't face the possibility that what she was saying was true.

"Max, search your heart. Talk to the Maker. I finally understand it, now. The Maker is the One with the answers—not logic, not my intellect, not others. He alone! And if Charlie is the Evil One, he is going to try and hurt the humans. You must listen to me. Something here is very wrong, and I am afraid it is about to take place," said a very emotional Liz.

"The only thing I see wrong is ye accusin' me fr-r-riend. An' I talk ta the Maker still . . . sometimes," said Max as he picked up his reed and headed for the door.

"Max, wait!" Liz called.

Max hesitated with his back turned to Liz.

"Did Charlie ever tell you his full name?" asked Liz.

"No, he never offered it, an' I didn't ask," growled Max.

"I asked him because I needed to know. His full name is Novel Charlatan. It means *original impostor*," explained Liz.

Max furrowed his brow. He couldn't accept this. It hurt too much. He didn't respond to Liz but took off running down the corridor, leaving her standing there alone.

"It takes a true friend to tell you the truth, even when it hurts," Liz hoarsely whispered to herself.

Liz felt helpless. Here she finally practiced her faith and what did it get her? Rejection from her dear friend. Still, she knew in her heart she had done the right thing. She would have to trust the Maker with this pain. And with what she needed to do next.

She had been telling Max to face his fears, but now it was she who needed to do so. Liz straightened up her tail and proceeded confidently down the corridor. She paused when she reached the edge of the beavers' stall. She had never been past this point before.

Liz moved slowly, stealthily, bravely looking in the stalls to her right and left as she passed. They were now empty. The animals were making their way off the ark and had vacated these stalls.

As she neared the end of the hall, it grew cool and dark. She looked into the wolves' stall to see the cave covered with overgrowth, but no creature was there. She listened and waited. Nothing. It was then she gazed into the stall at the end of the corridor. It was Charlie's stall.

Liz grimaced. She started walking toward the stall, and turned her nose to the foul odor coming from inside. It was dark and dank. It appeared to Liz that there once was green vegetation but now there were only dry bushes, dead tree limbs, and decaying vines overhead. There were large rocks scattered about and in one corner, a pile of rubble.

Liz cautiously approached the pile, her eyes gradually making out the things stacked there. It was a pile of the wooden objects

Bogart the beaver had carved for his friends. And near the top of the pile was the very first one he'd made: the burnt carving of Al.

Suddenly a sound caused Liz to startle and look behind her. Hidden behind a large rock was something she couldn't quite make out. It was moving and making sounds. She took tiny, cautious steps toward the sound.

Upon closer inspection, Liz saw that it was two snakes tied around each other in a tight ball. They were tied to a stick that was firmly planted in the ground. Their mouths were muffled by the way their bodies were tied. It was hard to tell where one snake left off and the other began.

"How long have you been this way?" Liz asked as she started loosening them. The snakes' eyes were full of fear and they slithered off into the darkness, not answering Liz.

Liz's feeling had been right. There were three snakes on board. Above decks there was a thundering of running animals. Liz's heart caught in her chest. The animals were leaving the ark. There was no time to waste. She had to get to Charlatan before he struck. She would make her way to the humans, but then do what? She was but a small cat. How was she supposed to do anything to make a difference? Her heart ached as she thought of Max. He was the brave one who could protect the humans, but he didn't believe her.

"It is just you and me, *Monsieur*," Liz whispered to the Maker. "*S'il vous plaît,* show me what to do."

As she left the stall, the snake slithered from behind a rock, making its way down the corridor directly behind Liz.

CHAPTER 62

The Choice

The scene before Max was astounding. Thousands of animals were exiting the ark on the top of this majestic mountain peak. Noah's family was herding the creatures slowly off the ark, trying to maintain some semblance of order. The animals seemed disoriented, as if not quite knowing what to do or where to go. After all, this wasn't their original home territory. They didn't know where the ark had drifted to in the world. All they knew was that they were on an elevated slope with far-reaching horizons.

Which way to go? Max shared this feeling emotionally. He had just walked out on a tough conversation with his dear friend. How could he have done that to Liz? She wasn't trying to be mean, she was trying to speak the truth in love. And Max didn't want to hear the truth. Confusion reigned in Max's heart as it reigned in the hillside below.

The giraffes were gingerly making their way out the front door of the ark, ducking to miss hitting their heads on the lintel. Max heard Chipo telling Upendo, "Don't look down, don't look down." Poor giraffe. Afraid of heights. Something deeper struck Max.

Don't look down. Is that what he had been doing these last few weeks? When was the last time he had looked up to the Maker? Max felt ashamed. Liz was right. He had looked to Charlie for direction, not the Maker. Would the Maker even listen to him now? He had to try. He had nowhere else to turn.

Max made his way to a solitary spot on the outer deck and raised his eyes to the skies. There was no fire cloud in the sky. Yet he knew the Maker was there.

"Um, it's me—Max. I know it's been a while since I talked ta ye. I need ta ask yer forgiveness. I been so caught up in things here on the ark an' tryin' ta be the hero that I didn't ask ye aboot things. Liz were right. I asked Charlie aboot things. He made me feel important, an' like I could do everythin' on me own. I didn't start out this way when I left the Glen. Gillamon told me ta go ta ye for guidance, an' I did for the long while. But then I lost me way. I took me focus off ye, an' put it on meself. That were wrong. I'm sorry. I know Gillamon would not be proud of me. I know ye aren't. An' that hurts me heart," sighed Max as he prayed with more heartfelt anguish than he had ever known.

Even though his heart was breaking, he began to fully realize how he had been behaving. There was a sweet release in his spirit as he laid everything out for the Maker. He didn't feel rejection from the Maker . . . he felt acceptance and forgiveness.

Max suddenly remembered something Gillamon had told him long ago.

"Max, remember that things aren't always as they appear. Sometimes you have to dig deep to find the truth beneath the surface."

"I were too hard on Liz. The things I said ta her. Aye, wha' a mean-spirited lad I were. I may not agree with wha' she's feelin' but I have ta at least listen. She were diggin' deep for the truth while I been lookin' at everythin' on the surface," said Max, getting angry now at himself.

"Wha' if she's right?" Max thought out loud.

403

He remembered what Craddock had told him about the wolves. He had returned to England to bring them across the channel because of the feeling in his heart that it was the right thing to do. Ah, when was the last time Max felt that tug on his heart by the Maker? Max hadn't allowed himself to feel it in recent weeks. He shook his head sadly.

The wolves had been called by the Maker to the ark. If they were the ones causing the trouble, it wouldn't make sense that the Maker had put them there, especially if they were going to attempt harming the humans. Things were truly not what they seemed.

A feeling of dread came over Max. Suddenly he, too, had a bad feeling about what could be happening below. If there were any shred of truth to what Liz had told him, then something bad was about to happen. Oh, how could he put himself in the place where he was not doing his duty? He had always been the protector of creatures. What if he missed the mark now? Max had to find Liz so they could together figure out what to do. He frantically scanned the sea of animals, looking for her.

Al and Kate were making their way through the crowded line of animals. Neither of them was very tall, so they hitched a ride on the polar bears, Peter and Pearl.

"How could we have gotten separated from Max an' Liz?" Kate asked Al, feeling frustrated. "I kin't stand ta not be able ta find someone like this!"

"There, there, lass. We'll find them. Jest keep yer chin up and yer eyes out and they're bound to turn up," said Al reassuringly.

"Vould you like me to get on my hind legs so you can get a better view?" Peter asked Al.

"What a wonderful idea, lad. I'll hold on tight," answered Al.

Peter raised up high on his muscular back legs, towering above the other creatures. Al moved up to sit on Peter's head as he scanned the crowd for any sign of Max or Liz. The other animals in line behind got impatient.

"Hey, down in front! We're dying to get off this boat! Keep it moving!" called Raja Peacock.

"Hold yer feathers! I'm lookin' for Max and Liz," answered Al with a frown. "Well, I don't see them yet. Ye can get doon now, Peter. We'll try again in a bit," Al instructed.

"Da. This is okay," said Peter.

Suddenly Kate thought about Crinan and Bethoo. Of course. Just as the gulls had found Craddock, they could help find Max and Liz.

"Pearl, I need ye ta do yer famous polar bear growl an' call for Crinan an' Bethoo. Ye got the only voice I kin think of that they'll hear over this noisy crowd of creatures," said Kate.

"Okay, Kate. Al, you might vant to close your ears for a minute," said Pearl.

Al put his paws over his ears as Pearl let out a rumbling polar bear growl that made the fainting goats fall over and the caterpillars roll up into balls at the loud sound.

"PEARL CALLING CRINAN AND BETHOO! PEARL CALLING CRINAN AND BETHOO! COME HERE, AT VONCE!" shouted Pearl.

"Good goin', Pearl. That will get those gulls here. They'll be our eyes ta find our mates then," said Kate.

Al looked at Peter and commented, "Sure, and I don't know how ye put up with such a loud wife."

Peter shrugged his shoulders and replied, "Her voice is like music to my ears. She vas belloving like that the first time I laid eyes on her and it vas love at first sound."

Liz scooted around the larger animals towering above her. She was so petite that she could squeeze through the narrow openings. She jumped up on animals occasionally, begging their pardon. Tumo

405

the rhinoceros even gave her a bit of a ride as he trotted down the corridor, causing the wooden planks to bend and creak under his weight. But soon he was caught in the bottleneck of animals backed up in their hurry to leave the ark.

"Sorry, Liz, this is as far as we go for the moment," said Tumo.

"*Merci*, Tumo. By the way, have you seen Albert?" asked Liz.

"Not since breakfast. Al was in the jungle sharing a bunch of bananas with the monkeys," replied the rhino.

"*Merci*. If you see him, tell him I'm looking for him, *s'il vous plaît*," said Liz as she jumped down and ran through the legs of her transporter, careful not to let him step on her tail.

Liz could see daylight streaming in the open door up ahead. Soon she could get outside and assess the situation.

Crinan and Bethoo were sitting on an outcropping of rocks when they heard Pearl bellow for them. They had been watching in amazement the exodus of pairs of every kind of creature that inhabited the earth. They never knew so many different kinds of "love birds" existed.

"Dear, I believe that were Pearl callin'," said Bethoo.

"Aye, me love, an' I know where she is callin' from. Let's go," answered Crinan.

The two birds flew over the sea of colorful creatures, sometimes swooping down to bid hello to their friends before reaching Peter and Pearl, who were slowly making their way down the exit ramp from the ark.

"Halloo, Kate! Al! Ye bellowed, Pearl?" said Crinan.

"Halloo, ye two," Kate answered. "We kin't find Max an' Liz. We got separated this mornin' before Noah called all the creatures ta leave the ark, an' the crowd is too big. Kin ye fly around an' see if ye kin spot them then?" asked Kate.

"Aye, lass. It won't be easy. We never seen so many creatures before! There are thousands an' thousands of them. 'Tis a crazy scene an' will be hard but we'll do our best. Peter an' Pearl, carry Kate an' Al ta that cluster of rocks an' stay put there so we kin find ye again. Off we go!" said Crinan as he and Bethoo went flying up in the air.

Every square inch of ground was moving, with every color and texture imaginable, packed tightly together. Fur, scales, hides, and feathers blended to form a spectacular sight. The two gulls flew up high for a better view. They could see the ark perched solidly on top of the mountain peak. Back behind the ark was a steep cliff that descended into an abyss.

"I hope no creatures go down that side of the mountain, dear. They'd be in for a terrible fall," exclaimed Bethoo.

"Yer right, me love. But the humans are helpin' the animals know which way ta go. It looks like all is well," answered Crinan.

They continued surveying the ground but didn't see a trace of Max or Liz. This would take some time.

407

Max remained on the outer deck. He scanned the sea of creatures below, looking for Liz. He noticed an outcropping of rocks about 100 yards from the base of the ark. Ham and his wife Mabir were helping the farm animals gather together. Isabella, Don Pedro, Giorgio, Pauline, Jacques, and Henriette looked as if they were holding a meeting. Henriette, of course, was running the meeting, pecking at Jacques. Then he spotted the wolves.

"Wha' are they up ta?" growled Max to himself. They were running against the flow of animals, heading straight for the humans, whose backs were turned.

It was then he spotted Liz. She was further down the mountain slope. She appeared to have jumped up on a rock ledge, obviously to get a better view. Max's heart caught in his throat. Charlie was slithering toward her from behind.

What was he to do? Something was wrong with both scenes. The wolves were making their way to the humans, their back fur raised, clearly signaling trouble. But what was Charlie doing, sneaking up behind Liz? Why would he be going in her direction? Max was torn—which way was he to go? Who was he supposed to guard? The feeling of dread intensified as he considered either option. If he went in the direction of the wolves to help the humans, he couldn't make it over to Liz. If he went in the direction of Liz, what would happen to the humans?

Whom did he believe? He was torn. He didn't want to choose either. It appeared that both choices offered a sacrifice.

"Oh, help me! I don't know which way ta go! Please give me a revelation, an' show me wha' ta do, Maker!" cried Max in anguish.

The Maker spoke to him,

"TRUST WHAT GOES DEEP."

Goes deep?! WHA' goes DEEP? thought Max frantically.

He had just been thinking about trust and about truth. Gilla-mon said to dig deep for truth. Craddock was always searching for the next right thing in truth and he goes deep—deep in the water! Craddock believed in the Maker's calling of the wolves. He believed in them enough to help them. And Liz. Liz had been dig-ging deep for the truth. It hurt her deeply to tell Max the truth, and that truth had pierced Max's heart deep within.

Max knew where he had to turn. He hurried down the ark to the exit ramp, accidentally dropping his reed as he headed off run-ning toward Liz.

CHAPTER 63

The Original Impostor

Kate and Al sat on top of Peter and Pearl watching the parade of animals. Still no sign of Max and Liz. Kate was beginning to get nervous.

"Wha' if we kin't find them? Wha' will we do, Al? I kin't live without me Max. He's everythin' ta me," said Kate, trembling.

"Oh, Kate, I know how ye feel. Don't let yer emotions run away with ye, lass. Max and Liz would not leave without us, ye can be sure o' that! Jest be patient. Either Crinan and Bethoo will find them, or Max and Liz will find us," replied Al, trying desperately to ease Kate's concern.

"Aye, I'll try. I jest feel so lost without Max. An' I know it's not like him ta not be near me. I feel somethin' has happened," Kate said as she scanned the skies for Crinan and Bethoo.

Liz sat looking over the crowded landscape before her. Surely never before had any creature seen all of creation gathered in one place like this, she thought. It was magnificent. She found herself counting the pairs, trying to calculate the total number of animals that had been aboard the ark.

Stop this. This is not the time for calculating. Stay focused, she said to herself.

Charlatan eased his way up onto the back of the ledge where Liz sat, her back to him as she looked out over the crowd. His forked tongue tasted the air as he slithered closer to Liz. He tasted fear.

Good, he thought. *Fear will make her freeze.*

Liz suddenly turned to see Charlatan right behind her. She hissed as her fur stood up on end, doubling her size.

"There, there, kitty, kitty, kitty," said Charlatan, a wicked grin forming on his face. "You don't frighten me. In fact, I think you're the scaredy cat now."

Liz's heart was pounding in her chest. "What do you want?"

"Oh, I want to keep the truth buried until I can do what I came here for. I want you to be silenced," replied Charlatan as he slithered closer to Liz.

"Why? What is it that you don't want me saying, Charlatan, or should I say, EVIL ONE?" asked Liz, trying her best to appear calm. "You were in the Garden."

"Ah yes, *Lizette Brilliante*. Oh, you are so very smart, aren't you? Always figuring things out," Charlatan said as he slithered slowly to his right. "Correct. You brought me here, Lizette. I came in your seed sack," Charlatan hissed, taking great pleasure in terrifying this cat.

"Not my garden. *The* Garden," Liz said, frowning as she came to understand how this third snake came to be aboard the ark. "*Mais oui.* It took me a while to figure out your ruse. My intellect was no match for your deception. The Maker made it clear to me who you really are," said Liz, feeling emboldened.

At the sound of the name of 'the Maker,' the snake shuddered. He shook it off and began to raise up off the rock, revealing large curves around his face as he towered over Liz. He looked totally different from before. His scales even turned from a soft gray to a deep black. He was a king cobra! He was massive and drew closer to Liz, his menacing eyes boring into her now.

410

"Don't ever say that name again. *I'm* the clever one! *I'm* the one who's going to win! *I'm* the one who's going to beat the M—" Charlatan stopped before he spoke the Name. He gathered his composure and calmed down before he continued.

"You've presented me quite a challenge on this journey, you know. You stayed one step ahead of me many times. Yes, I was the one who took the objects to stir up turmoil and mistrust in the ark. I was the one who made the grain sack fall near Max so I could 'save him.' Ah, yes, good times. Max really trusted me after that little trick," the snake said, smiling as he remembered all he had done aboard the ark.

Liz's chest heaved up and down. Her heart raced and her breaths came faster with each revelation confessed by the snake, who drew closer to her. He was enjoying this, telling her all he did. He was bragging about it. He was full of himself—full of pride. She grew angry, yet it all made sense now. All the strange happenings in the ark were a result of Charlatan's influence. Liz felt a sense of resolve as she realized her instincts had been right.

411

Liz wanted to do the accusing. "It was you who set the fire. It was you who tipped the buckets and got the humans fighting. It was you who tried to kill Noah and Max. It was you who destroyed Noah's record of this journey. You made us believe the wolves were behind all this."

Charlatan moved closer and smirked. "So tell me, smart one. Am I here to tip buckets? Am I here to pass blame?"

Liz raised her back as the snake moved closer.

"I'm here to finish what I started in the Garden. I did nothing more than show what man is made of. It was so easy. Tell them what they want to hear. Twist the truth just enough to tempt them. 'You will not die. Eat the fruit.'" Charlatan wickedly chuckled.

"Or how about this half-truth, 'The one who made you does not appreciate your offerings. Your brother is at fault. Kill your brother.' Easy. Just tell them what they want to hear. Then sit back and watch. It only took ten generations for them to self-destruct. Only ten generations! I knew He would get angry and regret having made them. I knew He would destroy what He had created," Charlatan hissed with delight.

"He did not destroy them all," Liz said defiantly.

"Correct, oh smart one. I have a job to finish," said Charlatan threateningly. Liz felt the evil pouring out of this beast inching closer to her.

The snake moved in as Liz became immobilized by fear on the rock. He reared back his head and struck.

Crinan and Bethoo drifted on wind currents as they noticed a commotion on the rock ledge below. It was Liz! They were glad to see her, but wait—something was wrong. The large snake was slithering away and Liz lay there on the rock. The two gulls landed next to her.

"Wha's happened, Liz? Are ye alright?" asked Crinan as Bethoo looked over her small form.

Liz struggled to breathe. "You've got to stop him. Tell Max to get to them."

"Oh, Crinan, she's been bitten by the snake! She's delirious. Hurry, get Al! I'll stay with her. Now go!" said Bethoo to Crinan.

Crinan took off in flight, flapping his wings as hard as he could. He had to get to Al. He felt helpless and overwhelmed. How was this happening? Even if he reached Al, there was a sea of creatures on the ground to cross in order to reach Liz. It looked hopeless.

Bethoo sat next to Liz, putting her head down to hear the erratic heartbeat of this gentle, loving creature. Liz was violently shaking.

Bethoo felt tears burning her eyes as she whispered, "Oh please, Maker, help Liz! An' help Crinan ta reach Al before it's too late."

Max was almost to the rock ledge where he'd seen Liz. His side hurt from running so hard after being confined to the ark for a year. And he had never run faster in his life. He saw Crinan flying above him, and wondered where Bethoo might be. How had things become so chaotic? No one was where they were supposed to be. Especially him. Here he was, running to help Liz, but his heart was in anguish of not knowing if the humans were in harm's way from the wolves. Not to mention that he had left Kate and Al alone. Where were they in all this?

Max saw a trail leading up behind the rock and ran around the back. He was too close to actually see Liz or Charlatan up above him now. He bounded up the slope and reached the top of the rock, already growling at Charlatan, "Stay away from me fr-r-riend!"

But Charlatan was no longer there. Bethoo leaned over Liz, eyes brimming as she turned to look at Max. Max ran over to Liz's side. She was shivering and struggling to breathe.

He was too late. Charlatan had struck his dear friend.

"Max!" cried Bethoo. "It was the snake!"

With that, Liz's eyes opened and she looked at Max, who was now leaning over her, his heart breaking.

"Max," Liz said weakly. "You've got . . . to—" her voice trailed off.

"Oh, Liz, I'm so sorry. This is all me fault. I didn't believe ye, an' I turned me back on ye. Ye were r-r-right, ye were r-r-right. I wish it were me layin' here . . . I should have been the one. I were supposed ta protect ye, an' I failed," Max cried out in anguish.

Liz gathered all the remaining strength that she had so she could speak to Max.

"All forgiven, *mon ami*. You are still . . . and ever will be . . . my dear friend. You are here now . . . that's all I need to see . . . to know. Now go . . . he's headed to the humans. No time. Go," said Liz with a barely audible voice.

Liz closed her eyes and took one deep gasp of air. Then, nothing.

She was gone. Max laid his head on her small body and wept bitterly.

413

CHAPTER 64

The Next Target

The animals had been exiting the ark for hours now. Shem waved up to Japheth to see if they were nearing the end of the long line of creatures. The three decks, which extended 450 feet, held tons of animals. Shem remembered the days when the animals had boarded the ark. That had taken forever. At least the exodus was going faster.

The animals were backlogged down below at ground level. Ham and Mabir were sorting out the farm animals and the birds, but they had to figure out a way to get the other animals down the mountain. The animals just didn't want to leave the area.

Japheth signaled to Shem that the exit line was almost complete. Shem was glad. If he and his family felt so free, he could only imagine how these creatures must feel after being in those stalls for a year. Shem scanned the scene below, looking at the vast number of animals that had journeyed with his family on the ark. How had this even been possible? Only the one true God could have pulled this off. He shook his head in wonder and joy, thanking God for the hundredth time for their safe delivery to dry land.

Shem told Noah that he was going to walk down the mountain and try to herd the animals forward. He shouted to Ham and Mabir where he was going. Shem's wife Nala was with them, and she waved and smiled as he blew her a kiss. He had not seen her because she was crouched down behind a group of animals. It appeared she was tending to a wolf. Maybe the animal was injured in the mad rush off the ark.

Ham and Mabir waved to Shem as they continued to work with the animals they had charge of. Shem noticed the small reed lying on the ground by the exit ramp of the ark. He picked it up and twirled it in the air as he began walking through the animals, prodding them gently along.

Crinan reached Al and Kate, and immediately Kate knew something was wrong.

"Crinan, where is Bethoo? Somethin' is wrong, I kin feel it. Where is Max?" asked Kate.

Crinan's head hung low as he landed in front of them.

Al jumped off Peter and asked the gull, "Where's me Liz?"

Crinan looked up and into Al's eyes and said, "There's been a tragedy. Al, Liz has been wounded. Bethoo is with her now." He turned to Kate. "No sign of Max, lass." And to Peter and Pearl, "Carry Al an' Kate on yer backs as fast as ye kin. Follow me. There's no time ta lose!"

Al looked at Kate, despair filling their eyes as they jumped on the backs of the polar bears, who took off bounding through the crowd of animals. Al felt his world falling apart. Never had he been so afraid. Kate felt sick to her stomach. *Liz was wounded? Where was Max when this happened? Where is he now?* She dreaded the answers to her questions.

Peter and Pearl looked at each other, saying nothing, but saying everything with their eyes of concern. Crinan led the way, uncertain as to what they would find when they reached Liz and Bethoo.

Max was shaking. He had failed. Liz was dead, and it was his fault. He was overcome with grief but something made him lift his gaze. His mind was writhing in anguish and confusion. He looked to see Bethoo sobbing as she, too, grieved for Liz. Anger burned inside Max. He had allowed himself to be deceived by the Evil One. This same one Gillamon had warned him about. How could he have been so blind? Now he knew how deceptive evil really was. It was masked with niceties and half-truths. It was a fraud. It was an impostor. It was Charlatan.

"I've got ta stop him before he strikes again!" Max yelled as he jumped up and turned to Bethoo. "Stay with her until I kin bring Al back," said Max.

His heart sank anew as he realized that the loss of Liz would devastate Al. And when Al found out it was Max's fault, the pain would be doubled.

Max ignored the trail behind the rock, taking a bold jump off the front of the rock, picking up the scent of the snake.

"This time, he won't deceive me. On me life he won't," growled Max to himself as he bolted across the area below.

Shem was enjoying the walk among the animals. They seemed to enjoy walking with him, also. Shem was kind and had been good to them. The animals knew how hard Shem had worked to keep them fed and their stalls clean. His work never ceased, yet he didn't allow his fatigue to keep him from caring for them.

They commented to each other as Shem walked by. "Look, dere's dat human dat brought us de fresh hay," remarked Lazo the llama. "Ace, he kept our stall clean and dry," answered Boomer the kangaroo.

But all that Shem heard were snorts and funny whinnies. He grinned and thought to himself, *Oh, if only animals could talk.*

The animals parted for Shem as he walked behind them, saying, "Move along now. That's it, come right along. There's nothing to fear here. You're on dry land now. God has seen fit to provide for you. Don't be afraid to go down the mountain."

Shem looked back behind him at the exodus of animals following along. He wondered if Adam had felt the same sense of awe that *he* now felt about God's vast creation.

Charlatan hissed as he moved along the ground, angry at the curse God had given him long ago—that very day in the Garden. Snakes would have to slither on their bellies for the rest of existence because of the betrayal of humans. It not only was degrading, but it made him slow.

"Just wait until Your precious humans are no more," Charlatan hissed under his breath.

The animals ahead were fearful of the sound they heard, and moved out of the way.

"Oh, how nice. I'll start with him. He's the main one I wanted to kill anyway. His seed will never be able to crush *my* head," said Charlatan.

He made his way toward his next victim. Shem was only 100 yards away. This would be all too easy.

417

CHAPTER 65

The Sacrifice

Max was shouting as he ran through the crowd, "Move out of the way! NOW!" The animals gladly obliged. After all, it was Max, the bravest hero on the ark—the protector, the fierce guardian, the provider of the way across the sea. Yes, Max was coming. They passed the word to get out of his way.

Max couldn't think too hard about the horrific things that had happened. If he did, he most certainly would fail at his one chance to do the most important thing he had ever been called to do. Max felt ashamed. How could he possibly be used for something important now after he had failed, with such disastrous results?

The noise all around Max seemed to fade away as he heard the words of his old friend, Gillamon, echo strongly in his mind, *You have been chosen, Max. I believe you are being called because of your character. The Voice knows you are brave. The Voice knows you are trustworthy, and that your heart is good. The Voice has something important for you to do.*

Could it be that the Maker would still use him? He had used Max to help get the animals to the ark. Max had thought that was the most important thing. Was there something even more important? Did the Maker still think he was brave, trustworthy, and good? Max held on to the gentle voice of Gillamon still ringing in his mind, hoping beyond all hope that indeed, the Maker could use such a failure as himself to accomplish something good.

Crinan looked below to see if Peter and Pearl were still keeping up. They were almost to the rock where he had left Liz and Bethoo. The polar bears were blazing through the ground below, Kate and Al holding firmly onto their faithful carriers. Crinan circled above to let them know they were close. He directed them to the trail leading up behind the rock. Peter and Pearl ran up the trail.

Al didn't wait to reach the top before jumping off Peter and running over to Liz. Kate and Bethoo shared a look of pain while Al put his arms around Liz, wailing and crying with the realization that his love was gone.

Charlatan slowed his pace. It wouldn't be long now, and he didn't want to alarm Shem. He wanted to savor the anticipation of the man's death.

Max felt an urgency to pick up his already hurried pace. He pushed his small body to the limits of his speed and kept his eye on the horizon. At least his enemy was low to the ground. He would have no trouble seeing him. The scent of the snake grew stronger. Max was closing in.

Charlatan lifted his body off the ground, rising up to striking position. His head grew as he arched his back and hissed. Shem turned around to see the snake swaying back and forth, poised and ready to strike.

Max came running and jumped on Charlatan, bringing him to the ground with a thud. Shem and all the animals were startled and moved back.

Charlatan shook his head and raised himself back up in defiance to Max. He hissed and gave an evil smile, "Why Max, my dear friend. How ever are you? I'm so pleased to see you."

"Save it, ye impostor-r-r! I know who ye ar-r-re. Ye deceived me all this time an' I fell for it. I were a fool, but I know better-r-r now! Yer not goin' ta hur-r-rt anyone else here," growled Max.

The animals were in shock at what they were hearing, and moved back even further as they murmured to themselves. Shem stood there watching this small dog barking at the very large snake that had been ready to strike.

"Hurt anyone? Oh, yes, Liz. I take it you've seen her. Poor you. She had to go, you know. She knew too much. And she was right about me. Obviously, she got through to you after all. Otherwise, you'd be back up with your other hero-worshipping friends, leading the celebration of coming off the ark. Max, the great hero whom all the animals admire. And I could be taking care of business here. As it is, though, now you're in the way. What should I do about you, Max?" hissed Charlatan.

Max was awash in a sea of fear. No fear of water or thunder could compare to the fear of facing pure evil. This evil was indeed the mightiest beast he had ever faced. He struggled to keep his composure but he was visibly shaking.

"What? Don't tell me you're *afraid*, Maxxxxx. How could that be? Why, you're Maximillian Braveheart the Brucccccce. Oh, I guess after neglecting to sssave your feline friend, there's not much brave left about you, issssss there?" accused Charlatan. The snake began to hiss a deep laugh, tearing Max to emotional shreds.

"Go ahead and tremble in fear of me. Watch there ssssilently as I finish what I came to do! I'm not about to let these eight humans ssssstart this human race all over again. And this one, Shh-hhem, I especially despise. The prophecy was wrong to say that One would come from Adam who would crush my head! Ha! Watch and cower in fear, little dog, as I destroy the sssseed of the One by killing this sssson of Adam."

Charlatan was foaming at the mouth as he maniacally ranted. But his raving didn't make Max more afraid. The mere mention of Liz's death by this cruel killer brought Max back to his defensive posture. And the threat of wiping out the humans put Max back on his feet. He now understood what the Maker had called him to do. This was the important thing. All the wisdom of Gillamon and the strength of the Maker came pouring into Max's being.

"Ther-r-re's more br-r-rave in me than ye could ever hope ta have, ye r-r-repulsive beast! The Maker is the One who makes me br-r-rave! An' only a cowar-r-rd hides behind a mask!" taunted Max back at Charlatan as he growled and dove toward the snake.

Max grabbed him by the tail and tossed him into the air. The snake went flying but landed unhurt and turned quickly to strike back at Max.

Shem continued to watch this spectacle, wondering if he should intervene or not. He held his ground, gripping the reed tightly in his hand.

As the snake hit the ground, Max grabbed its back with his strong jaws, shaking it back and forth. He dealt the snake a devastating bite, but the sheer size of the snake was too much for Max to handle alone. He wasn't prepared when the snake's head came swinging around, mouth open wide and fangs out. The snake pierced Max's back leg and filled him with toxic venom. Max felt the agonizing pain and released the snake from his jaws as he fell to the ground.

The animals were gasping and yelling to Max, "Get up, get up!"

It was no use. Max had sustained a deadly blow. He lay writhing in pain and looked up to see Shem holding his reed. His reed. That was it.

Max used his remaining strength and yelled to Shem, "Use the reed! Strike the snake. Do it now."

Shem watched this little dog frantically barking at him. Was this animal trying to communicate? He had clearly been fighting with the snake. No, not just fighting, this dog was protecting him. This dog had put his life on the line for him. And the snake had struck this brave little dog in return.

Shem felt the sturdy reed in his hand and held it up. The snake was up off the ground, towering over the little dog with a stiff neck and hissing tongue. Shem raised his arm holding the reed and came down hard, striking the snake in the back of the head.

Charlatan had been so busy gloating over the demise of Max that he didn't see the blow coming. He went crashing to the ground. Shem brought the reed up again for another blow to his head. Blood came out of the snake's eye, and he began to hiss even louder.

Shem screamed at the snake, "How dare you harm this dog! You're repulsive and wicked! I will crush you for what you've done to my small friend."

Charlatan gathered up his defensive posture as best he could, knowing he was weakening from the blows to his head. He could only see out of one eye.

"You will never defeat me," Charlatan hissed as Shem brought one more blow across his head, sending him flying across the ground.

Shem walked over and placed his heel on the head of the snake, who was twitching, dust clinging to the blood that covered him. He took Max's reed and lifted up the wriggling body of this wicked beast, causing Charlatan to scream as the power of the reed burned into his evil skin. Shem looked out across the mountains and walked over to the edge of the cliff face. He hurled the snake into the air off the side of the mountain.

The animals heard the snake screaming as he plummeted into the abyss. "You'll never defeat me. I'll . . . never ssstop," the snake's voice trailed off.

Shem ran to Max. The little dog lay there shivering, gasping for breath. Shem picked him up in his arms and held him close to his chest, rocking Max back and forth. "Oh, you brave, wonderful creature. You gave your life to save mine."

The animals hung their heads as they watched the scene before them. Max was indeed the bravest heart of them all.

A shadow flew overhead, and behind the animals was a commotion. Kate was making her way through the crowd as Crinan came in to land next to Shem and Max. Shem recognized the little white dog he had seen with Max. Oh, these were the only two dogs aboard. Now only one would remain.

Kate ran up to Max, crying out his name as tears streamed down her face. Shem gently lay Max down on the ground so Kate could reach him.

"NO! Max, no! Not ye! Not me Max!" Kate nuzzled her face into Max's chest.

Max opened his eyes, struggling to see Kate as he spoke with broken words.

"Aye . . . me bonnie lass. I saved him. I did it for the Maker . . . ta save the humans from . . . the Evil One."

423

Kate kissed Max on his long nose. "I kin't go on without ye!"

"Ye kin . . . do it, lass. I love ye . . . always," struggled Max as his eyes closed. His breathing was getting almost impossible now.

Max's body shook as the venom overtook him. Suddenly his eyes opened wide.

"Kate, I see him. I see Gillamon. He's callin' me. I have ta get . . . ta him," stuttered Max as his eyes closed and he heaved a heavy breath.

Silently then, Max was *gone*.

This was more than Kate could bear. She fell over Max, melting into his lifeless body, weeping and groaning. Tears rolled down Shem's face as he realized the sacrifice that had been made for him. There could be no greater love. Shem gently held the two small dogs in his strong arms as the other animals gathered in close around them, weeping.

CHAPTER 66

The Promise

N ever had any of the creatures known such sadness, and on today of all days. Questions rippled through their minds. They had endured forty days and forty nights of rain. The flood had kept them cooped up inside the ark for a year. All that was now behind them. Hadn't they struggled enough? Wasn't this supposed to be the day of deliverance? Today was to be a glorious, happy day. But now this day turned horribly tragic. Couldn't the Maker have prevented this?

The ground began to vibrate. Shem and the animals looked up to see Duke the elephant walking toward them. In his trunk he gently carried Liz. Al, Crinan, and Bethoo were riding on top of Duke's back, followed by the polar bears. The gulls were trying unsuccessfully to comfort Al. When they reached Shem, Al looked down to see Max lying still in Shem's arms, Kate weeping next to him.

"No! No! No! This can't be happening," yelled Al as he slid down Duke's side and rushed over to her.

"Al! We've lost them! We've lost them both," Kate cried into Al's fur.

"Oh, Kate, me heart is broken. I see no way I can go on with-out them. The pain is too great. Now I wish I'd never left Ireland!" cried Al, his grief speaking.

Shem stood up and walked over to Duke. *Not the sweet black cat, also!* he thought.

Shem lifted Liz from Duke's trunk and held her close to his chest. Her petite, lifeless form filled him with more sadness.

"Oh, God, both these creatures are lost! And on this happy day of new beginnings! How could anything be good in this new world if it starts like this, with the death of such innocent ones?" Shem cried out.

Shem looked at the big orange cat and the little white dog. Their mates were dead and they were grieving, or so it seemed. The other animals gathered there also appeared to be distressed, for no one moved or made a sound. Shem had to tell his family what had happened.

Carrying Liz, Shem walked over to where Max lay.

"I'm sorry, little one. May I?" he asked Kate, not knowing whether she understood him or not, as he softly gathered Max into his arms next to Liz.

Kate and Al moved aside. Shem stood up, holding the two fallen creatures, and began walking back to the ark. Duke lifted Kate and Al onto his back with his sturdy trunk. He and all the animals followed respectfully behind.

Noah and Japheth stood at the entrance ramp of the ark, surveying the animal passengers they had carried for so long. They marveled at what God had done through them.

"People said I was crazy for building this ark. They used to walk by and mock me. And son, I know how hard it was for you and your brothers. For a hundred years we built this ark. It seemed such a long time to see a purpose behind it. So much ridicule and uncertainty to endure," said Noah, shaking his head sadly, as he remembered those he tried to convince of God's coming judgment.

"Now I see. I understand why God instructed me as He did. Our family is safe. And all of God's creation is safe. Safe to start God's world all over again," said Noah as he smiled and gently patted Japheth on the back.

"Yes, father. You were wise to heed God's call. Although it appeared to be foolish and totally impossible, you obeyed. And your obedience saved our lives. And theirs," said Japheth, pointing out over the thousands of animals.

Noah's face was kind and full of wrinkles. His long white hair and beard blew in the breeze as he spoke. A pair of hummingbirds buzzed around his head as if to say, "Goodbye," and he grinned and playfully reached out to touch them.

"God is faithful. He does what He says. His word is true, His wisdom unmatched, and His power unbeatable. There is no other God. And I am humbled that He would choose me to accomplish such a thing. We will offer Him praise and thanksgiving," said Noah.

Ham was down below, preparing the altar as Noah had instructed. A sweet fragrance drifted up to heaven.

Suddenly Ham called to Noah and Japheth, "Hurry! Father, Brother! Come quickly!"

Noah and Japheth saw Shem walking back up toward the ark, surrounded by a sea of animals following along. The elephant walked slowly behind, carrying animals on his back.

"What is this?" Noah asked out loud as he began walking down the exit ramp of the ark.

Rudy and Rosie shrugged their tiny shoulders and frowned as they flew along with Noah and Japheth.

Japheth walked close behind Noah. "Shem is carrying two creatures, Father."

Nala and the other wives ran over to Shem to see what had happened. They put their hands to their mouths as they spoke to

Shem, clearly disturbed by what they heard. All eyes turned to Noah as he approached the group.

"Father, the snake. It came up behind me and was getting ready to strike when the little dog came running up and fiercely fought with it. He was brave and put up a hard fight, but the snake killed him. I struck the snake with a reed and threw it off the side of the mountain. And the little black cat. I didn't see what happened, but she, too, is dead from a snake bite," Shem spilled out.

Noah walked over and placed his weathered hands on the two small creatures in Shem's arms. He closed his eyes as sadness poured into his being.

"Will this evil never cease? Oh, God of Adam, have You brought us so far, only to have us destroyed again? On this voyage not one creature was lost. And now upon our landing, death strikes as soon as we tread the earth?" cried Noah as he looked up into heaven.

The humans gathered around Shem, a feeling of despair and vulnerability engulfing them. The ark had been a safe haven from death and destruction. They were saved from the horror of the flood and the death that swept away all the humans and creation on earth. They were preserved to start this world over again, weren't they? But death had struck them upon landing.

They had escaped evil for a time. But evil was not washed away and drowned with the flood. It was very much alive.

A rumble of thunder permeated the heavens. All creatures great and small looked skyward. Two white puffy clouds quickly emerged, and fire burst from the center, burning brilliantly and lighting the sky with majesty.

"The fire cloud," whispered Bethoo.

She looked at Kate, who echoed her remark with a nod. Kate was weak with grief. She felt as if she would die from heartache.

Noah studied the fire cloud and realized it was the presence of God hovering above them. His family gathered in close around

427

him, gazing in awe at the power coming from the cloud, feeling overwhelmed by God's holiness. They all knelt in reverence.

Not a creature moved. Not a human spoke. They looked and they waited. There was a rumble of thunder. And out of the thunder came the Voice of God.

"NOAH, MY TRUSTED SERVANT, YOU HAVE DONE WELL. YOU FOLLOWED MY CALL AND DID AS I INSTRUCTED. YOU OBEYED ME WHEN OTHERS TURNED AWAY. BECAUSE OF YOUR OBEDIENCE, I HAVE SAVED YOU AND YOUR FAMILY."

Kate looked up, her heart beating fast as she heard the Voice of the Maker. She turned to Bethoo, somehow energized by the Voice.

"Bethoo, we were right. The Maker is in the fire cloud."

"Aye, dearie. We were right. It's the Maker Himself," Bethoo replied.

Noah bowed his head in humility as God continued.

428

"BECAUSE OF YOUR OBEDIENCE AND THE OBEDIENCE OF THE CREATURES I CALLED TO COME TO ME, THEIR LIVES ALSO HAVE BEEN SPARED. THESE PAIRS OF CREATURES WILL GO FORWARD AND REPOPULATE MY WORLD WITH EVEN GREATER NUMBERS THAN BEFORE."

Shem looked at Max and Liz and then over to Kate and Al, who would never know the joy of puppies and kittens. His heart was saddened to think these wonderful creatures would no longer roam the earth as God intended.

As if hearing Shem's thoughts, God turned His attention to Max and Liz.

"DON'T GRIEVE THESE TWO. THINGS AREN'T ALWAYS WHAT THEY SEEM."

Al and Kate looked at each other, wondering what the Maker meant, their hearts pounding in their ears. God continued:

"JUST AS I CALLED YOU, NOAH, TO COMPLETE A SPECIFIC MISSION, SO, TOO, I CALLED THESE TWO CREATURES. A SMALL BLACK DOG AND A PETITE BLACK CAT. UNLIKELY CHOICES TO COMPLETE SOMETHING GREAT FOR ME.

THEY WERE GIVEN CHALLENGES TOO GREAT FOR THEM TO DO ALONE—JUST AS WITH YOU. I GAVE THEM WISDOM, COURAGE, AND ANSWERS TO THEIR MANY QUESTIONS AS THEY OBEDIENTLY HEEDED MY CALL. I PROVIDED THEM WITH ENCOURAGERS TO KEEP THEM GOING WHEN THEY WANTED TO GIVE UP. AND I GAVE THEM MATES TO PROVIDE LOVE AND COMPANIONSHIP DEEP IN THEIR HEARTS."

Kate and Al felt warmth pour into their broken hearts as they heard God speak of them:

"THESE TWO CREATURES FAITHFULLY FOLLOWED ME. NOT PERFECTLY, OF COURSE, BUT NONE OF MY CREATION IS PERFECT SINCE THE FALL IN THE GARDEN. BUT DESPITE THEIR MISTAKES, THESE TWO CREATURES ACCOMPLISHED THE MISSION I GAVE THEM. THEY GAVE ALL THEY HAD— THEMSELVES—FOR ME."

Kate and Al sat speechless, overwhelmed with the gravity of what the Maker had done through Max and Liz. Their mates were called by Him to do something important, and the Maker acknowledged their sacrifice and their job well done:

429

"YES, EVIL IS STILL HERE ON EARTH AND DEATH WILL COME TO ALL CREA- TURES AS A RESULT. BUT I REMAIN IN CONTROL OF THIS WORLD, EVEN WHEN IT APPEARS OTHERWISE. THESE TWO CREATURES WERE SENT TO PROTECT THE HUMANS FROM THE EVIL ONE. I KNEW HE WOULD ATTEMPT TO STRIKE THEM AS HE ONCE DID IN THE GARDEN. NOTHING CATCHES ME BY SURPRISE. I KNOW THE THINGS THAT WILL HAPPEN, GOOD AND BAD, LONG BEFORE THEY EVER DO. SOMETIMES IT APPEARS THAT EVIL HAS WON. BUT NEVER BE FOOLED BY APPEARANCES. REMEMBER THAT I AM THE ONE IN CONTROL. IS ANYTHING TOO HARD FOR ME?"

Noah looked up at the heavens and answered in his heart, *No, my Lord. Nothing!*

"BECAUSE OF THEIR BRAVERY, THEIR OBEDIENCE, AND THEIR WILLINGNESS TO DO MY WILL DESPITE THE COST, I NOW RETURN TO THESE TWO CREATURES IN ABUNDANCE WHAT WAS LOST TO THEM. SHEM, LAY THE REED ON THEM."

Shem jumped as his name echoed through the mountains. Heat radiated throughout his body as a light shot down his arm and through the reed. It was a force of energy greater than his being. He could not hold on to Max and Liz. He gently laid them on the ground, placing the reed on top of them.

"MAX ... LIZ ... BREATHE ONCE MORE."

Kate and Al were standing close, hearts aching with the hope of life again for their beloved mates. Crinan, Bethoo, Rudy, Rosie, and all the other creatures leaned in close to see what was happening.

Max's feet began to twitch as they always did when he dreamed. His chest expanded as he took a deep breath. A smile grew on his face and he slowly opened his eyes to see thousands of other eyes staring back at him.

"Wha' in the name of Pete are ye lookin' at? Kin ye give me some r-r-room," said a very lively Max.

Liz, too, rolled over and stood up, arching her back before stretching out long and yawning. "*Mais oui*, what is all this fuss?"

"HURRAY!" exclaimed all the human and animal voices in one chorus! Max and Liz were alive. The Maker brought them back to life. It was a miracle!

"God of heaven be praised!" exclaimed Noah, along with his family.

Kate and Al rushed over to Max and Liz, embracing them with love and giving gratitude to the Maker.

Kate licked Max's face. "Oh, me love, ye were gone. Gone! But now yer here, alive with me."

"Aye, me bonnie lass. I'm never-r-r leavin' ye again," said Max.

"Liz! Oh, me pretty Liz! I can't believe me eyes! Me precious beauty is alive," said Al as he wrapped his paws around Liz's small frame, enveloping her in his big orange fur.

"*Oui! Je t'aime*, Albert," replied Liz, purring as she rubbed her head on Al's chin.

The celebration was quickly quieted as God spoke again from the fire cloud.

"NOAH, IT IS OBVIOUS TO ME THAT AS YOU HUMANS BEGIN TO POP-ULATE THIS EARTH ONCE MORE YOU WILL NEED HELP. I NOW GIVE YOU THE GIFT OF PETS. THESE ARE TO BE GUARDIANS AT YOUR SIDE AS YOU GO THROUGH LIFE. WITH TIME, DOGS AND CATS WILL BECOME PART OF YOUR FAMILIES. THEY WILL BRING COMFORT AND CARE, AND THEY WILL BRING MY LOVE INTO YOUR HOMES. TREAT THEM WELL. THEY ARE A GIFT FROM ME."

Shem looked at Max, grinning as Max caught his glance and seemed to smile back. God continued:

"AND NOW BE VIGILANT. KNOW THAT EVIL IS STILL HERE, AND EVIL WILL BE ON THE ATTACK AGAIN AND AGAIN. IT WILL NEVER CEASE . . . UNTIL I PUT AN END TO IT ONCE AND FOR ALL. YOU HAVE WITNESSED THIS DAY A RES-URRECTION. I TELL YOU A GREATER RESURRECTION IS COMING STILL. FOR NOW, I GIVE YOU A PROMISE. MAY YOU KNOW THAT NEVER AGAIN WILL I DESTROY THE EARTH WITH A FLOOD. THIS IS MY PROMISE. AS A REMINDER, I GIVE YOU A SIGN THAT WILL FOREVER SEAL THIS PROMISE I HAVE MADE TO YOU AND ALL OF CREATION. I GIVE YOU . . . THE RAINBOW."

431

All eyes were turned to the heavens as the fire cloud began swirling in the sky. It was spectacular. The fire shot out in a burst of color that spilled across the sky. An arch of the full spectrum of color—red, orange, yellow, green, blue, and purple stripes—spread from one horizon to the other. It was beautiful, majestic, and illuminating.

The eight humans danced and sang to the awesome wonder of God's promise. The creatures joined in, using the noises God had given them to offer praise to the Maker.

"Oh, beautiful heaven. God is the One, the One true God! May You ever be praised by Your creation! You alone are God! You alone are good! The world will know of Your greatness because of what You have done!"

While the celebration roared with life, all heard a gentle rumble of thunder—except for Max and Liz. They didn't hear thunder. They heard the Maker's Voice.

"Max and Liz, this is for you alone to hear."

Max and Liz kept their gaze upward to the rainbow like everyone else, but they were listening to the Maker.

"Max and Liz, because of your sacrifice and your supreme bravery and intelligence, I have now made you immortal. You will be My special envoys for missions in pivotal points in human time. You will never die, but will go through time on earth until a new heaven and a new earth are made. You've proved yourselves worthy and up to the challenge. Your mates also have proved themselves worthy and so I give to them life eternal as well. Do you accept this assignment?"

The two friends looked at each other, locking tails to shake in agreement. They and their mates were partners for life . . . forever.

"Aye, Maker. Count us in then," said Max.

"*Oui, Monsieur*, we are at Your service. What are we to do next?" asked Liz.

"For now, be fruitful and multiply. Enjoy starting your families. There's a world out there to populate with dogs and cats. Teach your offspring to take care of humans. Teach them how to pick up on human emotions. Teach them how to know when humans are hurting. Teach them to play with humans and to protect them. Enjoy life. When it's time, I'll let you know."

"How?" asked Liz.

"I'll send a messenger. One that you, Max, already know quite well," replied God.

"Gillamon!" exclaimed Max.

"Aye, laddie," chuckled God. "Gillamon, it is."

With that, the Voice was silent once more.

Max and Liz were beaming, happy that the Maker had given them so much. Life eternal and life forever as dear friends. Life with the Maker would ever be a grand adventure.

"So, Max, do you believe me now?" teased Liz.

"Aye, lass, ye be the smart one, 'tis true. But I be the br-r-rave one. Ye make the plans, an' I'll listen ta ye an' carry them out like a good laddie!" replied Max.

"*Oui, mon ami.* But remember the Maker is the One with the revelations, plans, and the courage. He just gives to us all that we need," said Liz.

"Aye, I'll not be forgettin' it either. We make a gr-r-rand team, lass. Where do ye suppose we'll go next?" asked Max.

"Oh, the Maker will tell us. But for now, I just want to settle down with Albert and have a family of smart, beautiful kittens," answered Liz.

"Aye, 'Be fruitful an' multiply' is our mission now. Me an' Kate will love havin' puppies. I already know wha' I'm namin' the first boy," said Max.

"Gillamon, no?" said Liz.

"R-r-right, lass," replied Max with his big, wide grin.

"Ah, Max. I'm glad I learned to have faith by being friends with you. I look forward to the next—how you say—gur-rand adventure?" asked Liz.

"Oooh, little lass! Hopefully ye'll have time ta work on yer "r-r-r's" before it comes," teased Max.

Kate and Al walked over to Max and Liz, who were still gazing skyward.

"Isn't the rainbow amazin', Max?" declared Kate.

"Aye, lass, amazin' indeed," he replied, putting his arm around Kate.

433

"Ye didn't seem to be afraid o' that thunder jest now," said Al, handing Liz her seed sack.

"Thunder?" replied Max.

"*OUI*. Thunder—that all the creatures heard just now, Max," said Liz with a wink.

"Oh, aye . . . thunder. Maybe I'm cur-r-red," replied Max, picking up his reed.

Max and Liz grinned.

Max and Kate, Al and Liz joined the sea of creatures now headed down the mountain. No longer was there anything to keep them here. All the creatures now moved with excitement, ready to journey to the ends of the earth.

And begin again.

Epilogue

As the animals departed, God gave further instructions to Noah. Then He left the humans to begin their lives anew.

Noah, Ham, Shem, and Japheth walked back to the ark to get the supplies they needed for the night. Earlier when the animals were leaving the mountain, Noah had seen two snakes slithering away.

"Shem, you said you threw that snake over the edge of the mountain?" asked Noah.

"Yes, father. I threw it off the steep cliff. It is long gone from here," replied Shem.

"Well, what do you know? There were three snakes on board," said Noah pensively.

The gravity of what this meant hit him as he realized who the third snake must have been. Now Noah realized what had happened with his journal, and who would have wanted to destroy it with fire. And who would have willed to destroy all of them with fire. Noah shook his head in gratitude to the Maker who had protected them from the presence of evil.

Ham ran up ahead and looked inside the ark. He yelled back, "Father, something has happened!"

"What now?" said Noah, already numb from the glory of all that had taken place this day.

"The ark—it's like it was before when we built it. No more natural habitats. No desert. No arctic. No rain forest. No waterfall. Just wood," said Ham.

Noah grinned as he realized the continual movement of God in every detail. God chooses to create and to take away. It is His alone to decide.

"Father, do you think anyone will ever believe a story of a great flood and a boat that can carry thousands of animals?" Shem asked.

"Time will well, son. Time will tell," Noah replied.

436

Mabir and Nala were with the farm animals when Shem brought the food supplies for their campsite.

"What were you doing with the wolves when I was leading the animals down the mountain?" asked Shem.

"The female wolf was having a difficult time and we helped her," replied Nala.

"What was wrong?" asked Shem.

"She was in labor. The pups were turned so she couldn't deliver without help. The wolves came to us, Shem. I helped her deliver seven precious young ones. Look, they're back here behind this rock," explained Nala excitedly.

Shem walked back and saw the seven small, wriggling baby wolves whose eyes were still closed. The mother wolf was licking them clean and looked up as he approached.

"Easy, girl," said Shem.

The father wolf lay next to her, but did not stand up, indicating he wasn't threatened. Shem walked over for a closer look. Three girls and four boy pups.

"I think I'd like to keep one," Shem said to Nala.

"Why?" she asked.

"Oh, to be a watch dog and a companion as we start our family," he replied.

Nala smiled, thinking of the new hope of having children and starting a family. "Which one?"

"That boy pup there—the one with the dark fur. He looks like the runt of the litter. I think I'll name him . . . Max," he replied.

437

Worldwide Animalia: A Guide to the Animals, Their Countries, and Their Languages

There were countless animals on the ark that aren't mentioned in the book. The ark had far more room to hold them than do the pages herein. If your favorite animal is missing, imagine what they would have done on talent night or during Flamingorobics. What about their stalls? Have fun picturing their natural habitat aboard the ark. Just remember—your favorite animal was on Noah's Ark.

Here is a guide to the animals featured in this book, and some of their sayings or "lingo."

Africa   Chimpanzee (Keb & Okapi)
Giraffe (Upendo & Chipo)
Gorilla (Katungi & Mashaka)
Lion (Jafaru & Sasha)

Ostrich (Kirabo & Juji)
Rhinoceros (Tumo & Kamili)
Zebra (Iggi & Zula)

African Lingo

Check	*To look or see*
Chuck	*To leave or go*
Graze	*To eat*
Hey	*Used for emphasis. "Let's eat, hey?"*
Howzit	*How is it?*
Isit?	*Really?*
Just now	*Soon, eventually, never—funny phrase*
Moffie	*Wimpy*
Oke	*Guy, chap*
Shame	*Figure of speech for something good or bad—funny word*
Tune	*To tell, talk, provoke*

440

America   Raccoon (Patrick & Sallie)
Fainting Goat

Antarctica   Emperor Penguin
Leopard Seal

Arabia   Camel
Scorpion

Argentina   Hummingbird (Rudy & Rosie—see Spain for Spanish lingo)

Australia   Bearded Dragon (Itchy & Spike)
Kangaroo (Boomer & Sheila)

Crocodile (Sydney & Alice)
Duck-Billed Platypus (Mort & Quilpie)
Koala

New Zealand Praying Mantis (Stewart & Cookie)

Australian/New Zealand Lingo

Ace!	*Excellent, very good*
Aussie	*Australian*
Back of Bourke	*A very long way away*
Beaut	*Great, fantastic*
Bush	*The hinterland, the outback, anywhere that isn't in town*
Come a guster	*Make a bad mistake*
Down under	*Australia and New Zealand*
Fair go	*A chance*
G'day	*Hello*
Heaps	*A lot*
Hooroo	*Goodbye*
Mate	*Buddy, friend*
No worries!	*Expression of forgiveness or reassurance*
Reckon	*You bet! Absolutely*
Rip snorter	*Great, fantastic*
Rock up	*To turn up, arrive*
Shark biscuit	*Somebody new to surfing*
Sheila	*A woman*
Spiffy	*Great, excellent*
Squizz	*Look, take a look at this*
Stoked	*Very pleased*
Walkabout	*A walk in the outback with no set time limit*

Borneo Chameleon Snake (Charlie/Charlatan)

441

Canada	Beaver (Bogart & Bev)
	Black Bear (Mel & Ethel)
	Moose (Murray & Myra)
	Mosquito (Tito & Blanche)
	Skunk (Rodney & Hazel)
	Woodpecker (Racket)

Canadian Lingo

Canuck	*A Canadian*
Cooked it	*Something done wrong*
Eh?	*A nice way of saying 'huh?'*
Gorby	*Tourist*
Hoser	*Stereotypical Canadian male, lower- to middle-class*
Whadda 'Yat?	*How are you doing?*

China	Giant panda bear
	Siberian tiger
	White duck

England/	Bat
Wales	Bumblebee
	Cricket (James & Celeste)
	Frog (William & Juliette)
	Right Whale (Craddock)
	Dolphin (Alex)

France	Cat (Liz)
	Hen/Rooster (Henriette & Jacques)

French Lingo

Attendez un moment	*Wait a moment*
Bien sûr	*Of course*
Boeuf	*Beef*

Bon appétit	*Good appetite/eat well*
Bonjour	*Good day/hello*
Bonne chance	*Good luck*
Bonne nuit	*Good night*
C'est assez	*That's enough*
C'est impossible!	*It is impossible*
C'est magnifique/	*It is great/good*
C'est bon	
C'est ridicule!	*Nonsense*
Chien	*Dog*
Comprenez vous?	*Do you understand?*
Enchanté	*Delighted to meet you*
Et	*And*
Je comprends	*I understand*
Je m'appelle	*My name is*
Je ne sais pas	*I don't know*
Je ne comprends pas	*I don't understand*
Je regrette	*I regret*
Je t'aime	*I love you*
Le chat est fou!	*The cat is crazy!*
Mademoiselle/	*Miss/Mrs.*
Madame	
Mais oui	*But yes*
Merci beaucoup	*Thank you very much*
Mon ami/amie/	*My friend (m.)/(f.) my friends*
Mes amis	
Monsieur	*Mister*
N'est ce pas	*Isn't that so?*
Non	*No*
Oooh la la!	*Oh my!*
Quel dommage	*What a pity*
Pardon	*Excuse me*
S'il vous plait	*Please*
Sortez!	*Get out!*

443

Très malheureux	*Very unhappy*
Très bien	*Very well*
Voila!	*There you have it*

Galapagos Islands	Galapagos Tortoise Iguana

Greenland	Reindeer

India	Antelope (Vijay & Varada)
	Elephant (Duke & Fareeda)
	Peacock (Raja & Opal)
	Water Buffalo (Jag & Ballari)

Indian Lingo

Yatra	*Journey or pilgrimage*

Ireland	Cat (Al)

Irish Lingo

Aboot	*About*
Aye	*Yes*
Bonnie	*Pretty*
Daft	*Crazy*
Doon	*Down*
Jest	*Just*
Me	*My*
O'	*Of*
Sure	*Figure of speech emphasizing certainty, usually starting a sentence*
Ye/Yer	*You/Your*

Italy	Horse (Giorgio & Pauline)

Italian Lingo

Buon giorno	*Good morning*
Capisci?	*You understand?*
Grazie	*Thank you*
Mi dispiace	*I am sorry*
Non importa	*It doesn't matter*
Prego	*Don't mention it, it's a pleasure*
Signore/ Signora	*Mr./Mrs.*
Scusate	*Excuse me*
Si	*Yes*
Spicciati	*Hurry*

Japan

Jumping Spider (Masami & Takako)
Rat
Flying Squirrel

Japanese Lingo

Domo arigato	*Thank you very much*
Gomen nasai	*I'm sorry*
Konnichiwa	*Good afternoon (day)*

Malaysia

Black Panther (Java)

Malaysian Lingo

Apa Kabar?	*How are you?*
Jumpa lagi	*See you later*
Kembali	*You're welcome*
Maafkan saya	*Excuse me/I'm sorry*
Nama saya	*My name is . . .*

Mexico

Raven (Ricco & Maria—see Spain for Spanish lingo)

Russia   Arctic Fox (Yuri & Dessa)
Polar Bear (Peter & Pearl)
Snowy Owl (Ivan & Natasha)

Russian Lingo

Da	*Yes*
Ne boysa	*Do not be afraid*
Privyet	*Hi*
Tebye zharko?	*Are you hot?*
Tochna	*Exactly!*

Scotland   Dog (Max is a Scottish Terrier. Kate is a West
Highland Terrier.)
Seagull (Crinan & Bethoo)
Mountain Goat (Gillamon—originally from
Switzerland)

Scottish Lingo

Aboot	*About*
An'	*And*
Aye	*Yes*
Bonnie	*Pretty*
Bumbees	*Bumblebees*
Daft	*Crazy*
Jest	*Just*
Kin	*Can*
Me	*My*
Wha'	*What*
Ta	*To*
Ye/Yer	*You/Your*

Spain   Bull/Cow (Don Pedro & Isabella)